S0-DFI-718

HERE I AM, STANDING AT THE LIGHT . . .

and not a damned thing is happening, Terris thought.

He took a step closer and then another. The vibration increased, a humming along his bones. His senses swam with it. A milky veil dropped across his eyes, misting the brightness of the sky and the contours of the caldera walls.

The pulling which he'd felt for the whole trip now returned, magnified a thousandfold. Whatever this Light thing was, it recognized him for its own. His feet stumbled forward of their own accord.

"Terris!"

Kardith's voice called out to him, tinny and distant. From the corner of his vision, he saw her face like a faded shadow, the ghostly shimmer of her long-knife. He thought she was racing toward him, yet she seemed to be hardly moving, a figure trapped in frosted glass. She was close enough to touch. He reached for her, even as his body was jerked forward.

Then, with a blast of eye-searing flame, the two of them burst into the center of the Light. . . .

Be sure to read both of these acclaimed
DAW Science Fiction Novels by

DEBORAH WHEELER

NORTHLIGHT
JAYDIUM

NORTHLIGHT

DEBORAH WHEELER

DAW BOOKS, INC.
DONALD A. WOLLHEIM, FOUNDER
375 Hudson Street, New York, NY 10014

ELIZABETH R. WOLLHEIM
SHEILA E. GILBERT
PUBLISHERS

Copyright © 1995 by Deborah Wheeler.

All Rights Reserved.

Cover art by Jean-Francois Podevin.

DAW Book Collectors No. 975.

All characters and events in this book are fictitious.
Any resemblance to persons living or dead is strictly coincidental.

If you purchase this book without a cover you should be aware that
this book may have been stolen property and reported as "unsold
and destroyed" to the publisher. In such case neither the author nor
the publisher has received any payment for this "stripped book."

First Printing, February 1995
1   2   3   4   5   6   7   8   9

DAW TRADEMARK REGISTERED
U.S. PAT. OFF. AND FOREIGN COUNTRIES
—MARCA REGISTRADA
HECHO EN U.S.A.

PRINTED IN THE U.S.A.

For my children

ACKNOWLEDGMENTS

Warmest thanks go to Bonnie Stockman, who rekindled my love of horses, to James Brunet for his insights into the politics of Laureal City, to Sheila Gilbert, my editor at DAW, for encouraging my first attempts at telling this story and being patient while they gestated into maturity.

But most of all, this book owes a special debt to Kung Fu San Soo Grandmaster Jimmy H. Woo, who taught me how to fight and when not to. "You can take my life, but not my confidence."

CHAPTER 1
Kardith of the Rangers

Scaling the final hill was like climbing into a sea of ice. Up and up we went, one shivering, dogged step after another, woman and mare. My fingers had gone numb, laced in her mane, and I could no longer tell whether she pulled me along, or if it was the other way round. I envied her, with no thought but to keep going.

As we neared the crest, I squinted up at the sky, as white and airless as if some vengeful god had sucked it dry. I reminded myself there were no gods here in Laurea, vengeful or otherwise.

The mare plodded on, head lowered, one ear cocked toward me and the other flopping, snapping at a suckerfly without breaking stride. Her neck and shoulders were so wet they looked black, the dapples hidden under flecks of foam. Suddenly her head shot up, ears pricked. She snorted and lunged forward, nearly yanking my arm off.

The next moment, I stood on the crest of the hill, sweating and shivering at the same time. As far as I could see stretched green and yellow patches of wheat, barley, and hybrid oats, all outlined by orange bug-weed. A farmhouse flanked a silo, pond, and vegetable plot. The mare nickered, scenting the ripe grain.

On the horizon, a line of trees marked the river. Serenity, it was called, typical dumbshit Laurean name. The trees looked blue from up here and I could almost see the smaller tributary snaking in from the northwest. Where it dumped into the Serenity, colder than winter snot, the trees bunched as if they'd scrambled up on each other. Buildings hid among them, glass and rock as pale as weathered bone.

Laureal City. Back on Kratera Ridge, I thought I'd never see it again. Now I remembered the streets, so smooth and flat, the rows of trees in flower and fruit at the same time. The courtyards with their fountains and gardens, set between angular geodesics or inside tall, square houses where a dozen families might live together.

I remembered standing in the Starhall with the other Ranger candidates. Pateros hearing my oath, just as Guardians have heard Ranger oaths for hundreds of years. The light in his green-gold eyes and the grainy softness of his voice as he talked about beginnings and moving beyond the past. But it didn't sound like the usual Laurean wishcrap. It seemed to me the demon god of chance had finally turned my way and smiled.

I remembered too much.

The gray mare shook her head and stamped one hind hoof. The metal shoe clicked against a stone buried under the trail dust. By now I'd stopped sweating, but I was still shaking and my hands hurt. I opened my fingers and pulled free of her mane. My right hip twinged as I mounted up and swung my leg over the rolled sleepsack and saddlebags. I let my body sway with the mare's easy gait and my lower back popped and felt looser.

The gray mare tucked her hindquarters like a cat and started down the hill, reaching and sliding in the loose dirt. She was Borderbred, from the wild hills between Archipelago and the Inland Sea, the best horse I ever owned. I spent a year's pay to buy her rough-broke, then started to gentle her all over again. The first thing I did was take that Mother-damned bit out of her mouth. . . .

Listen to me, nattering on to hide how scared I am.

Me, Kardith of the Rangers. Scared.

I don't scare easy. The Rangers still talk about "Kardith's Leap" as if I were some kind of hero. Six or seven years back, three of us got jumped by a pack of hothead norther kids out for their manhood blood or shit like that. That was before the northers came looting and burning clear past Brassaford until General Montborne's army stopped them. There was Derron, just made captain, and me, and a blustery man named Westifer who didn't make it back from Brassaford alive.

I unhorsed one norther kid, vaulted on his pony's back and wheeled around, trying to spot the breaker. Not the leader—the breaker. The heart of them. Not the big one screaming orders. Take him out and some other damned fool would jump up and do the same. But kill the breaker and all you've got left is a bunch of solo heroes.

There he was—a skinny kid, not got his growth yet, the only sane one of the bunch. Edging toward Westifer, who was down on his knees in the freezing mud. I booted the pony into a gallop, drew my long-knife and stood up on the saddle pad.

Westifer was about half a second from explaining his sins to the father-god. I leaped for all I was worth. Landed splat on top of the norther kid. He twisted out from under me, grabbing for a leverage. I shoved my knee hard into his balls. His grip went slack for just an instant, long enough for me to whip the knife around. He let go just as I nicked his face, high on his cheekbone, a nasty cut that would leave a scar. Then the yellow-haired kid galloped by and scooped him up and they all bolted out of there.

"Wolf-bitch," Derron said to me back at camp, "isn't there *anything* you're scared of?"

Not what gave him nightmares, that was sure. Norther steel, a quick death or a long bloody one, it was all the same to me. The twisted places on the Ridge you couldn't quite see but only feel on the back of your neck, the nameless things that came snaking into your dreams. He was right, they didn't scare me.

Going back empty-handed without doing what I'd come to do, that scared me.

It was past dark when I reached the city and I'd mostly shoved my ghosts back into their graves. I let the gray mare pick her own pace and browse in the grainfields along the way. I couldn't take her into the city, and besides it was too late to do anything more today and I was tired, bone tired.

The trail broke into part-cobbled roads, warehouses, stock pens of smelly brush-sheep. Blue Star Stables had a big dirt yard, raked clean and smelling of sweet alfalfa. A barn on one side and a house on the other, solar lanterns hanging above the door. I caught the familiar sounds of stamping and hay-crunching.

I swung down and dropped the reins and the mare stood as if I'd tied her. I rapped on the house door. For a long time I heard nothing, just the soft *pat-pat-pat* of moth wings against the lantern glass and the animals settling down in the barn. The mare sighed and tipped one hind hoof. The shadows made her flanks look hollow.

Heels clicked on a bare wood floor and the door opened. A big-handed man, clean, no smell of drink on him.

"You got room?"

"Sorry, I'm full up." He stepped down into the yard. He was no fighter, that was sure, but there was something about the way he moved through the darkness. . . . He held the shadows close, as if he belonged to them instead of to the open yard. This man had secrets, I thought, or maybe it was my own I was seeing in him.

"You know how it goes," he said. "Noon today I was empty except for the rental stock and a few head for sale. Then suddenly everybody's either coming or going. You could rub your mare down, feed her, and tie her in the yard here with a blanket, but if she were mine, I'd get her a decent box indoors. It'll be cold tonight."

The mare butted her head against my hip, rubbing the places where the dried sweat itched. I liked it that the stableman hadn't tried to touch her. He wanted to. He knew horses and his eyes were hungry on her.

"Where else?"

"Cheap or good?" he asked, looking right at me for the first time. His eyes flickered over my Ranger's vest, half-hidden under my cloak, and the long-knife strapped to my thigh. "Never mind. God help anyone who tries to cheat *you.*"

"Which god?"

"Any one you like. They're none of mine, I'm Laurea-bred."

Who would I pray to, anyway? The father-god, whose secret name is death for any woman to pronounce? Mother-of-us-all? I'd sworn by her, though she never answered me. The demon god of chance—ay! There was one worth praying to . . . if I were the praying kind.

The stableman scratched the stubble on his chin. "All the big places are likely just as full, but if you don't mind the feathers, Ryder's got a stall or two extra. He runs a barnfowl yard. The feathers go to the bedding factory and the meat for sausages. The yard gets pretty bloody then, but it should be all right now. The priest comes the first of the month to give the blessing and Ryder cleans up good afterward."

It wasn't the death-stink I minded so much as the priests with their light and harmony shit. I'd seen the thrills they got from all that blood. They could sprinkle it on the ground and mumble their prayers to make it holy, but what difference did that make? They were all the same, priests everywhere.

I rubbed the mare down slowly, stroke after stroke, leaning my weight into the leather-backed brush. Trail dust and sweat crystals billowed into the air and clung to my face, my hands, and clothes. The mare was slow to settle. She smelled the old blood out in the yard and every few moments she lifted her nose from the hayrack, jaw slack, ears pricked. Then she sighed, rubbed her whiskery nose across my shoulder, and chewed again. She finished the best of the hay, knocked over the empty grain bucket, and began to doze. I put away the brushes and closed up the barn.

The holding coops were on the far side of the yard, but still I found little piles of feathers everywhere—between the wood slats of the box stall, in the corners of the tack room. Bits of fluff too light for any broom. You can never get rid of them or hold on to them. Breathe on them and they're gone.

Out in the yard, the air had a bitter edge. I drew my wool cloak around me and pulled the saddlebags across my shoulders.

A cobbled street led toward the lights at the center of the city, and there I found the inn the stableman had recommended, two rambling stories of weather-stained board siding, warm and well lit. I stepped over the threshold, from wooden steps to unglazed tile. The entryway led down a step and under an arch to the common room. The arch bore the usual carvings—flowers, birds, mythical insects with broad, bright wings, here painted in blue and yellow. A hum of voices reached me, along with the smell of ale and bread and maybe bean stew. I hated beans, but my mouth watered anyway.

In the common room, someone chanted a bardic to the beat of a drum. I never could understand them, long-winded things stuffed with fancy words. *How Gaea Slew Teknos. How Man Stole Sorrow from the Ahtoms. The Triumph of the Cosmick Pod.*

Opposite the common room sat a clerk's desk and a staircase. As usual, sleeping rooms were upstairs and tub rooms along the corridor behind the office. Laureans were as crazy for baths as they were for bardics. You couldn't find a house here without solar pipes across the roof. I remembered the first time I sank up to my ears in the hot springs near Darmaforge. All that water—Mother-of-us-all, so *much* water—and just to get me clean. Aviyya used to tease me about it.

The warmth of the common room seeped through my cloak. Standing in the entryway, I wondered if I could stay awake long enough to both eat and bathe. I started toward the clerk's desk and then stopped, caught by a ripple of music.

The bardic chanter, another man, and a woman in the bright woolens which Laureans favored, sat on a raised platform holding lap harps and a small drum. They settled into a melody, the drum marking the beat and the men's voices weaving in and out of the woman's clear soprano. First a courting tune, followed by a jig-dance

that had me and everyone else clapping and stamping
our feet.

Then an old, old song:

> *"Harth now dons her robe of glee*
> *Flow'rs and trees embrace her.*
> *We go forth in harmony,*
> *Children of one Mother.*
> *For as we this glory see,*
> *All the sacred season,*
> *Reason learns the heart's decree*
> *And hearts are led by reason."*

Led by reason. I shivered suddenly. The lighted room
seemed dim and far away. The saddlebags slipped from
my shoulders to lie in a heavy lump on my feet.

Led by reason. Maybe here in Laureal City. But out
on Kratera Ridge there was no University to be the safeguard of all learning, no Guardian, no Senate. Only a
handful of us Rangers between these rich fields and the
hungry north.

Led by reason. Not me, and not here.

The performers packed up their instruments and left
the dais for a drink with their friends. I headed for the
clerk's office. A hollow-eyed man looked half asleep behind the desk. How could he serve me? he asked.

"A room and a meal, meat if you've got it."

"No, magistra, we keep to the old ways here."

"Beans then, and plenty of bread, but none of that
yak-piss you call ale. What's the charge for a bath?"

"No charge, magistra, it comes with the room."

Ah, yes, I sighed, *this is Laureal City.*

I left nothing in my room except a pile of dirty clothes.
Bags, boots, and knives all came with me. The big
wooden tub was set halfway into the tiled floor, with a
shallow step outside and an inside ledge for sitting. It
would probably hold four or five people, if they were
friendly. Hand painted tiles in flowery designs decorated
the floor and wood-paneled walls. I hung the pink cotton
robe the inn supplied on a wooden peg.

Despite the illusion of safety, I double-checked the bar and hinges of the door. There were no windows, only a pair of narrow ventilation grilles that ran the length of opposing walls, and they were only about six inches high. I kept my long-knife right where I could reach it.

The steaming water smelled herbal and astringent. I sighed and lowered myself inch by inch. The heat turned my skin red, except for the whitened knife scars. Straight and clean-edged—hands, arms, shoulders, chest, thighs. One fool's cut low on my ribs. Behind my back, where I couldn't see them, knotted ridges twisted like thread-worms, strips of skin that had neither feeling nor memory.

I should add that to my list of things that scare me. Remembering.

Remembering Aviyya's fingers, light and quick. Her indrawn breath. We weren't lovers yet, when we took leave together at Darmaforge. I didn't know why I let her talk me into the steaming rock pools in the hills above the public bathhouse. I told myself afterward it was curiosity. I told myself it was the dark, only one moon, and all those stars. The truth was, we'd been in three skirmishes that week and something in the still being alive, the hours and moments of fighting back to back with her, had left me half crazy and hungry in ways I couldn't name. And there was something in Avi—a wildness, a secretness, a loneliness, Mother only knows. But it was hard to look right at her. I turned away, fumbling for the lantern, and she touched me.

"Ahhh, Kardith. . . ."

I fled into the shadows. I couldn't face her, couldn't show her my back again. Her eyes—the color of rain, the color of steel—they were wide and dark. It was my own soul I saw in her eyes. Her throat moved, jerking up and down. No words, only that whisper, as weightless and persistent as a feather.

"You forget I'm not Laurean," I said slowly, searching for words. "On the steppe, to the east, we call ourselves the Tribes."

I don't remember what else I told her—learning knife-forms with my stepfather, wrestling and laughing in the alkali dust with my half brothers, the water-plague that took them all. All except me. The endless, formless days lost in a fog of ghostweed and endurance while that old ghamel the priests whored me off to dreamed himself into permanent oblivion. And the son whose father I must never name—no! I didn't tell her that. I don't remember what else I couldn't say, the years and deeds I had no words for, only that it didn't matter.

Mother-of-us-all, take away those memories. How she cried for me, me who never cries.

I must think only of what I have come to do, of the man I must find.

I lay in the tub, the back of my head resting on the wooden rim, staring up at the grille on the far wall. Biting my lip. Gripping the hilt of my long-knife until my fingers cramped. Hearing my blood race through my ears.

Out, I had to get out of the water. It was the heat making me think crazy.

I wouldn't get out. Not until my mind was clear of everything but my purpose here. Tonight I would sharpen my knives to steady my nerve. Tomorrow I would find him, Pateros, the Guardian of Laurea. Then, *then*, it would be safe to remember.

CHAPTER 2

I wore the long-knife in its thigh sheath, and the leather vest with the Ranger insignia. In one of the vest pockets I carried the folded single-edged knife I used for eating, skinning small game, camp work. A careful search would find two more knives, one in my boot top and the other in a forearm sheath. Maybe, if the searcher knew what he was doing, the one in the hollow belt buckle. Maybe not.

After a breakfast of fruit and ripened cheese, and an easy round of exercises—with the buckle knife to remind my hands of the heft and reach of a short, flat blade—I felt fit and awake. My shirt was clean, the worst of the trail dust scrubbed from my boots.

The saddlebags stayed in my room, along with the cloak. The packet of papers from Captain Derron—accounts, reports, Mother knows what—I weighed it in my hand as I stepped into the morning sunshine and headed for the central square. Such a little thing, but enough to make my presence here official. All I had to do to follow orders was hand it to General Montborne.

But it was Montborne who gave the command—no searching past our patrol limits, no forays into norther territory, no retaliation for raids. It was Montborne who set the penalty for insubordination at the loss of a hand. It was Montborne who drove me here.

*　　*　　*

So many flowers grew in Laureal City that the women wore them fresh in their hair. Everywhere I looked, I saw gardens, strips of blossoming herbs, borders around fountains and benches, pots crowded together on window ledges. Courtyards with vine-covered arches. Trees and more trees.

The market stands were piled high with fruit and vegetables, grains and dried beans, cheese and yogurt, a dozen kinds of freshly-baked bread, fish from the rivers. People milled around, buying and selling, calling out their wares, pressing against each other, all going in different directions. They moved out of the way when they spotted my Ranger's vest. A countrywoman with a tanned face said, "Free samples to you, magistra," and handed me a plum from her cart. I bit into it and the tart juice squirted over my tongue.

Past the market lay the merchant district, row after row of shops selling everything from spices and cloth to ceramics to books and musical instruments, even children's toys. I paused to admire a display window of metals, wonderfully crafted knives set with semiprecious stones, belt buckles, bits and spurs, medician's tools I didn't recognize. All with their little square approval certificates from the gaea-priests.

The plaza paving stones were light gray and so closely placed that not even a weed pushed through the hairline cracks. The plaza reminded me of the steppe, vast and flat and white with the bitter dust that nothing escaped.

Terrible things happened in places like this. Lives were taken and then given back again.

I'd been inside the Starhall before, seen its ancient heart, the chamber lined in faded tapestries and wood carved with symbols no one knew anymore. Here Pateros took my hands in his, according to ancient custom, and here I repeated the oath after him. Each word I said burned through me, over and over, until I was sure nothing remained of who I once was.

I was wrong about that, but for all those years when I was a Ranger first and only, I had no idea how wrong I was.

The Senate Building faced the Starhall across the

plaza as if they were born enemies. It was big—three stories—and flat-sided except for the balconies and columns along the front, all of pink glittery stone. The Senate met in the Great Hall and important people had offices inside. No one lived there.

The military wing stretched from the Senate Building along the north edge of the plaza, two stories with a thin band of carved letters between them. I couldn't read them the first time I was here; Avi told me later what they said.

"It is better to plant a single seed than conquer a world."

And if Montborne believed that, then I was a flame-addled twitterbat.

Inside the wide wooden doors was a foyer of sorts, a desk with an alert-looking officer. When I was last in Laureal City, the Rangers answered directly to the Guardian. Now, since the raids—the Brassa War they called it—Montborne commanded. I'd never been inside this building before and the people here didn't know me.

To his credit, Captain Derron had prepared me well—what I was to do, the passes, and how to use them.

"Promise me, Kardith," he'd said. It was the night before I left and we were sitting together in his office at the fort, drinking the last of his excellent barley-ale. It was cold, as nights are on the Ridge. "Promise me you won't go off on any expeditions of your own and I'll believe you."

I clamped my mouth shut. Anything I said, I said as a Ranger. "I'll go right to Laureal City."

"And give the papers to Montborne."

"Yes."

"There may be a reply or orders to bring back. If not, take a few days, rest, enjoy the city. Cool off." He paused. "Let go."

"Let go? Avi saved my life at Brassaford! Shit, she saved *yours* a dozen times over. She could be hurt out there, dying, taken by the northers, I don't know! How can you tell me to *let go?*"

"Don't fool yourself, Kardith," he said. "Since when

do northers take prisoners? I've lost one of my best people out there. And *one is enough.*"

I downed the rest of my cup. If I tried to answer, I might say anything, do anything.

"If you do go messing around out there," he went on, "if you disobey Montborne's orders, then I must enforce them."

Only if you catch me first.

What was the use? With my right hand or without it, I'd no longer be a Ranger.

But here I was, having come straight to Laureal City, just like Derron said and at a pace fit to kill my good gray mare, repeating to the officer that I'd deliver the packet to General Montborne and no one else.

"The general's in meeting with Pateros and the Inner Council," he said, as if everybody knew that. "You want to wait here—" a bench against the painted stone wall that made my rump ache just looking at it, "—or outside? Maybe catch a sight of them as they come out?"

A thrill for a know-nothing country girl, but I'm no girl, you with your fancy uniform and your little batsticker knife. Out on the Ridge it's you who'd be a sniveling worm in less than a week.

All those tough words to cover how scared I was. Mother-of-us-all, did I imagine this would be easy? I knew I'd have to face Montborne to finish my official mission here. I knew I'd have to somehow get to Pateros. But I hadn't counted on having anything to do with the Inner Council, even in passing.

The Inner Council. And *she* would be there, Esmelda of Laurea, who would have been powerful enough just speaking for the University. I'd heard of her, even on the Ridge. Who hadn't? Twenty years ago, the story goes, a plague swept through Laureal City—pestis fever, they called it. Nasty stuff, all fever and flux and oozing boils. They said the Guardian was near dead of it and half the Senate, too, looting and wildfires from the solar foundries, people leaving to spread the plague to the countryside. They said Esmelda made a speech right there in the plaza and while she was talking, the rains came and put the fires out. They said she went everywhere, night after night, keeping people's hopes alive until the medicians found a cure. They said no one died whom she'd touched.

I'd never in my life met a woman like that, or a man either. But Pateros lived and the City was still here.

Esmelda of Laurea. Aviyya's mother.

Avi told me about her as we lay together under the stars, camped in the Brassa Hills or on Ridge patrol. Everything seemed sharper then, maybe more real, I don't know, but different, that was sure—all the things inside of us that we could never say aloud. I came to understand that Esmelda had given her own life to the University and Laurea and expected her daughter to do the same. She kept pounding it in until Avi couldn't tell who she was, so full of rage and hate she had no place there, until Avi finally left and carved out a new life in the Rangers. That part I understood very well.

From the top of the steps, I saw a knot of people filing out of the Starhall. First some kids—pages, they were called—running off on their errands. Then Pateros. I recognized his loose easy stride, even without the ashy-silver hair. Tall and gaunt in his long green robe. Stooped over a little, talking to a man in a red and bronze uniform, who held himself like his spine was all one solid piece, a couple of military aides playing shadow—that had to be Montborne. Half a dozen older men and women with their own assistants. A gaea-priest in flowing rainbow silks who shuffled along as if his eyeballs were permanently rolled up in his shaved skull.

They moved on to the plaza. The two City Guards, who'd been waiting at the entrance, strutted along either side, their hands on their batons. Montborne went off with one of his officers and a green-robed woman, gesturing as he talked.

Whatever Montborne was up to, she wasn't having any of it, her arms clamped around her chest. A man still three parts boy, yet too old for a page, trailed behind her.

The people who'd been waiting gathered around Pateros, their voices like the cries of rock-doves. They surrounded him, touching his sleeve and shaking his hand, each one in turn. Then they backed off, lingering. The few still scattered across the plaza began to hurry, to reach Pateros before he was gone. One of them caught my eye, like a raptor-bat in a coop of barnfowl. There was no outward reason he was different, maybe his dark blue clothes, overly somber by Laurean standards. I saw nothing in his hands.

Suddenly a man in the crowd started yelling and waving his hands. The City Guards rushed between him and Pateros. The gaea-priest waded in, arms lifted, probably chanting something like, "Let me help you to attain cosmic attunement, my child." The man skittered away, still shouting.

The man in blue kept coming, faster now. He was on an angle, slicing right for Pateros. He disappeared into the crowd, working his way inward. But I felt him in my blood, not anything of who he was as a man, but what he was in this place, which was all that mattered. The breaker's breaker, that's what he was.

No one else took any notice of him. The Guards were still busy calming the yelling man.

I started yelling, too, some dumbshit nonsense like *Stop him!* or *Watch out!*—and then I was pounding across the pavement, running on fire instead of breath. My riding boots slapped and clattered on the stones. No one heard me above the shouting, milling crowd.

What's wrong with them? Why can't they see?

A little space opened in the crowd and I spotted him again, the man in blue—standing right next to Pateros.

I needed only a few more moments, but I was still halfway across the plaza. I tried to scream again. The air whizzed by me. I couldn't get a lungful.

Pateros paused, bending his head toward the blue man as if listening intently. The blue man sidled closer and his right shoulder hunched forward. Montborne and his aides were already moving, the City Guards elbowing back through the crowd.

I was too damned late and too damned far. There would be no Kardith's Leap this time.

The blue man twisted, a quick spiraling thrust, and

Pateros's long green robe rippled and jerked. Pateros fell slowly at first, as if he weighed nothing. Then he crumbled against Montborne, pulling him to the pavement.

Someone screamed, high and light like a wounded pig. The blue man burst free of the crowd. I swerved toward him. His teeth made a jagged line. Dark sweat stained his shirt. He spotted me and started to run. A woman from the crowd grabbed him hard around the hips. He pulled free, but a heavy-shouldered man in a military uniform was right on him and I caught the glint of a drawn knife.

Pateros lay sprawled on his back, cradled in Montborne's arms. I pushed my way through the onlookers and knelt by his side, still hoping wild and stupid hopes. It was a hurried thrust, a dagger I'd guess, and on the right side, away from the heart. It could have missed a fatal target. It could have. Liver or guts, yes, he'd bleed inside but this was Laurea, Mother damn it, *Laurea!* There were medicians and a hospital here, and there wasn't a person here, me included, who wouldn't empty their veins to have him live.

There's not enough blood, I thought dazedly.

I caught a glimpse of the dagger—it *was* a dagger, with a hilt of bone carved norther style. It sat in the center of a spreading red stain like the heart of an aging, blowsy flower.

Why didn't I start running a moment sooner? Why didn't anyone else see?

The other Inner Council woman shoved me aside and bent over Pateros. Pale red hair parted along a line of sunburn, but I couldn't see her face. Her movements were quick and deft. She breathed into Pateros's mouth, and his chest rose and fell as if he were still alive. Then she shifted to pumping on the breastbone next to the heart's great chambers. Montborne took over the breathing. People whispered and held on to each other, as if they could hold on to Pateros, too. The gaea-priest raised his hands, chanting more dumbshit.

He's gone, he's gone. I felt this place without him, this vast and terrible place.

The red-haired woman kept pounding as if the pattern hadn't changed.

"How can that help now?" I whispered.

"It'll keep him alive until they get the unit from the hospital." The voice was young and shaken, the eyes rainwater-gray. Black hair spiked out in all directions. The kid trailing the old woman who said *No* to Montborne.

Not just any old woman, either.

I got to my feet slowly, the military aides still pulling people off the man in blue. Someone said, "He's dead— his throat's cut." He should have been captured alive, and what for? Would knowing whatever crazy thing drove him to it bring Pateros back? Or give me someone else I could ask for help finding Avi? Or make Montborne take back his damned orders?

Mother-of-us-all, here I am, thinking only about my own pain! Is that why you never answer me? Is that why you kept me from acting until it was too late?

But I was praying to the wrong god. It was the demon god of chance, the god without a soul, who owned me now.

CHAPTER 3

The plaza filled with people who'd heard the commotion or happened to wander through on other business. Some of them stayed, caught like moths at a candle. A few of them darted away to spread word all over the city. Over and over I heard the same cries of *No!* and *Why?*, the same throttled silences.

The two City Guards and the military aides moved us, the original crowd, off to the side. Whether we were witnesses or suspects, they themselves weren't sure. A uniform never made anybody think straighter and there were too many people in authority here. Besides Montborne and the gaea-priest, there were the members of the Inner Circle, each used to giving orders and not about to be herded around with a bunch of civilians.

More Guards and military people came running full scramble. Montborne turned Pateros over to an older officer and got to his feet. In a few moments, he had them all sorted out, some off to summon more help, some keeping us away from the newcomers and everyone away from the two bodies. The crowd settled a little.

Around me, people held on to each other, a few sobbing out loud, a few as pissed as if they'd been accused of the killing themselves. Some of them chanted along with the gaea-priest, trying to pray life back into Pateros.

The hospital team arrived in one of those solar-powered carts you see only in cities. They fussed over Pateros and hauled him away, not saying anything definite, as if they couldn't tell death without their machines.

What's wrong with these people! Don't they know how much worse it is to hope?

My body was aching to hit or scream or run. I couldn't stop thinking of the day Westifer died. When we made it back to camp in the hills above Brassaford, after a day and a half of fighting straight through, I thought I was too tired to move. But every time I sat down, I felt just like I did here in the plaza. What I did then was to take the camp hand ax and start chopping the biggest tree I could find. Swearing all the time to keep from crying, me who never cries, because here in Laurea, everyone makes holy-holy over their thousands of trees and out on the steppe there are no trees. And there was no Westifer, not now, not ever again, no matter what those damned priests said. Fire or blood or cold or thirst, it gets you in the end and then it's all for nothing.

For nothing!

I screamed it out until my throat was raw. My hands blistered and my shoulders went to fire and my back and legs cramped so I could hardly stand. I kept thinking I couldn't go on, and as long as that was all I was thinking, I did.

Captain Derron came out and yelled so loud I finally heard him. "You wolf-bitch! The rest of the squadron's dead-tired. They need rest even if you don't. Who do you think you're helping by cutting down half the forest? You think *Westifer* cares what you do now?"

I stopped and stared at him, gulping night air so cold it turned my lungs to ice.

It wasn't Westifer who made me act like that, and I knew it. I didn't even *like* the man, but we'd shared each other's ale, stitched up each other's cuts, saved each other's lives. Someone else would take his place and we'd go right on putting our skins between Laurea and the north. Nothing changed because one man died.

I couldn't understand why I felt this way.

"Sometimes I think I know you and then something happens and I realize how strange you are. I can't understand you."

It was Aviyya in my memory now, whispering by the fading campfire when everyone else was asleep. I didn't remember where or when, only the bitter-cold night and the stars edged with blue.

I made myself lie still to hear what must come next. My heart beat once, twice, ripples spreading outward, stopping at my skin. I told myself, *I am a Ranger. This is my life, my place when I have no other. If Westifer dies, if Avi turns away from me, what does it matter?*

Avi went on, her voice soft as a feather. "Maybe that's why I love you, because *understanding* has so little to do with it. Understanding is what my mother's so good at. You—you are for me, just for me."

After that, I was still a Ranger, but no longer only.

Now, standing in the plaza in Laureal City, I held myself absolutely still, as hard a training as any knife-form. I tried to spot the man who'd drawn the City Guards off by shouting, but I couldn't find him. No surprise. I could be looking right at him and not know his face. He could have slipped away after Pateros was stabbed. Nobody was watching him, that's sure. Running wouldn't prove he had anything to do with the man in blue. In his place I'd have run, too.

Finally the City Guards Chief arrived, a short, dark-skinned woman in her middle years. The scrapper type. If she were a man, I'd say she had to be twice as tough and twice as stupid to make up for a few inches in height. She stepped aside with Montborne and when they came back, she was the one who gave the orders.

Mother-of-us-all, they'll be hours questioning us. Days. What did I see, why am I here, why didn't I wait for Montborne at his office? What am I doing in Laureal City? Why did I start yelling and running? How did I know what was going to happen? Why didn't I warn someone sooner? What am I doing in Laureal City?

A young Guard walked up to me. It hadn't sunk in for him. He was still at the stage when doing something helped. "Come with me, Ranger. General Montborne wants to see you when we've finished."

I followed him across the plaza and down a short, wide street to the Guards Headquarters. It was going to hit real soon, like twister on the steppe, when these people felt in their bones what they'd lost.

I've never been a judge of buildings, but the City Guards Headquarters was anything but a joy to look at, a lump of lichen-gray stone so ugly I couldn't believe anyone built it that way on purpose. Up the shallow steps, through a foyer, I handed over my long-knife, boot-knife, and the folding knife from my vest pocket. That was all. I wasn't fool enough to go into this place unarmed.

We went down a corridor and into a large room. Bookshelves, mostly empty, and in the center, a table of gray wood, polished very shiny. I sat down and the young Guard asked if I wanted anything to drink— herbal tisane, water, juice?

Rotgut, more like.

I settled for water. After all, there was a time in my life when it was more precious than steel.

He watched me sip it, dying to find out what happened out there in the plaza, what *really* happened. Mother knows what he'd heard and how much of that was truth, but it wasn't his job to ask, only to wait.

To hell with him.

I didn't have too long to wait, just halfway through the second water glass. We moved to another room with recording machinery and an officer taking hand notes. The City Guards Chief shook my hand and told me her name, Orelia. That was something anyone in Laureal City would know and now I did, too. Other than that courtesy, I wouldn't have picked her as a drinking partner. She was drowning like the rest of us, pretending harder, holding to her work as if no part of her died with Pateros. Maybe it hadn't.

I showed her the passes and packet from Captain Derron. "Stationed on Kratera Ridge," she repeated. "Years in service?"

"Seven. And yes, I fought at Brassaford."

She didn't blink when I said the man in blue was trouble, I didn't know how. After all, I was a Ranger, and from the Ridge. She couldn't decide if I had powers beyond the lot of ordinary humans or was just a lunatic to be humored and posted back to the wilderness as soon as possible. The officers took it all down, and where I was staying.

We went through the questions again, and a third time. Orelia liked to look tough but all I had to give her was a Ranger's hunch.

A tap on the door. The nearest officer cracked it open and took the slip of paper passed through. Orelia opened it. Her eyes flickered but her face didn't change.

"From Chief Medician Cherida. Pateros has been taken off resuscitation. This is now a . . . an assassination investigation."

Montborne's aide, a junior officer, offered me more to drink. It was now past noon and I wasn't one to grumble about missing a meal or three, but I was tired of water, tired of answering questions, tired of staring at uniforms and most of all, tired of sitting still.

The room, at least, was an improvement over Orelia's. It was on the second story and windows ran along one side like a greenhouse, bright and warm. They looked west, over roofs of blue and gray ceramic tile and tree-tops rippling in the breeze. A big desk, barkwood I thought, sat at one end of the room and a patch-stone fireplace with a real fire at the other. The aide offered me a padded armchair.

The door opened and a heavy-shouldered, slab-faced man wearing a senior officer's uniform stepped in and gave me a look that said I'd be dead if I so much as twitched the wrong way. From the way he moved as he stood aside for Montborne to enter, quick yet powerful, his fingertips just grazing the hilt of his knife, I thought he could do it, too. The aide disappeared and came back a few moments later with a portable table heaped with covered platters. The bodyguard closed the door behind him and stood where he could see the entire room. I decided to keep my hands in plain sight.

I got to my feet, holding out Derron's packet. Montborne waved it aside, saying he'd read it later. He sat down and proceeded to lift the dish lids one by one.

"I assume you've had your fill of beans." He pushed a platter toward me.

My mouth watered and my muscles melted like candle wax. It was sliced lamb, rare and steaming hot, swimming in its own bloody juices.

Montborne uncovered a basket of bread and a dish of sweetroots washed in butter, indicating I should take what I liked. He loaded up his own plate. "Wine or barley-ale?"

"Water."

Weakly, I reached for a fork. The meat was rich and tender. I was still working my way through the roots and more meat when Montborne put his plate on the tray and leaned back.

I'd thought he was handsome when I saw him on the plaza, and before that at Brassaford where he turned the northers. No, not handsome, *arresting*. Hair like bronzewood, lying close against his head. Skin so clear and fine it was hard to believe he was ever in the field. Eyes brown like the steppe sky before a twister. He smelled of soap and leather.

He looked back at me. "All right, let's see that packet."

I handed it to him, watching while he slit through the seal, unfolded the papers, read them. His eyes moved in jerks across the pages. Once or twice he glanced up at me.

"You know what's in here?"

I shook my head. Between the fireplace and the sun pouring through the windows, it was too hot in here.

Montborne folded the papers along their crease lines. "You fought at Brassaford, didn't you?"

"Yes, sir, but I didn't think you'd remember me."

"I confess, not personally. But each of you Rangers were worth ten of my own men. It was a hard time we had of it."

"Yes, sir."

The muscles of his jaw rippled under the smooth, fine skin. "We could have followed on their heels, razed their villages, and put them back a hundred years. We could have bought a hundred years of peace for Laurea with a single stroke. But Pateros thought it better to let them scuttle back to their holes."

I looked down. We none of us understood why Pateros held us back, though many were grateful just to be coming home with their skins still in one piece.

Montborne touched the folded papers. "One of my Rangers has disappeared. This captain, Derron, he wants permission for an extended search. An extended search which would leave areas of the vital Ridge border unpatrolled. Tell me, what would you do in my place?"

I didn't know what he wanted, certainly not my advice, and it was dangerous to keep secrets from this man. "It's not for me to decide. I gave my oath to Pateros."

"No." He sat up, very straight. I felt the fire in him, the twister behind those dusty brown eyes. "You gave your oath to *Laurea.*"

I thought, *If only Pateros were sitting here instead of Montborne.* Pateros took my oath, but he also gave me one in return, the same one he gave Aviyya. And, policy or no, he would have found a way to honor it.

Then I thought of Pateros lying on the gray pavement, with the red blossom unfurling on his green robe. I thought of its heart, the hilt of carved bone.

A shiver built deep in my muscles. In a moment I would be shaking. A little while ago, when everyone else was acting like a headless barnfowl, then I could still think straight. I knew what had happened, what I'd lost.

Now I didn't know any more. Aviyya, Pateros, the Rangers, the steppe—what was gone? What was left?

Montborne watched me like a snake, his brown eyes unblinking, his skin white as milk, and suddenly I remembered that Pateros died in his arms.

He was testing me, testing *his Ranger,* the same way I'd test one of my own knives before a battle. He was a soldier, this man who'd stopped the northers at Brassaford. Avi—one single woman Ranger—was nothing to him. He cared only for his own oath to Laurea, and whether his tools would serve him or shatter in the heat. In his place, I'd toss away any weapon I had doubts about. My life might depend on it.

Without Pateros, all Laurea might depend on Montborne's choice.

"I would keep my oath," I said slowly. "I would do
whatever I have to, to protect Laurea." My words,
forced through my tight throat, burned like a twister
worse than any I'd lived through on the steppe. They
scoured me to the bone.

He leaned back and his eyes darkened, the pupils
huge. "Then be my witness, my Ranger," he said in a
half whisper. "Tell me all the things that happened out
there today which an ordinary person wouldn't see."

And, Mother help me, I did tell him. I kept the secret
of why I'd really come to Laureal City, but that was all
I kept. Every detail of the killing, every moment, every
heartbeat, every flicker of my Ranger's intuition, over
and over again until he'd wrung me dry.

When it was over, I sat looking down at my hands,
the old scars, the calluses, the trail dirt that not even the
long bath last night could soak off. I thought they might
never have held a baby to my breast, never have touched
a flower, never have wiped away a tear. I thought they
were good only for killing.

There was no help for me here, or anywhere. Avi was
lost. I had come to Laureal City on my captain's orders.

I was a Ranger, first again and only.

CHAPTER 4:

Terricel sen'Laurea

Earlier that morning, as Kardith made her way through the market square toward General Montborne's headquarters, with no premonition yet of the events which would shake her life, a group of dignitaries assembled on the steps of the Starhall. Each succeeding Guardian of Laurea had left his mark on the ancient structure, his own personal translation of its role—as shrine, museum, personal residence, governmental center. Over the centuries it had evolved into a patchwork of architectural styles, modern solar-collecting lenses set between antique ceramic roof tiles, the crumbling friezes of one era bordering the gables and columns of another.

Pateros had drawn his advisers from a spectrum of institutions, from the University which was the heart of Laurean culture and technology, to the military, judiciary, and priesthood. This bright morning, Esmelda of Laurea, the University representative to the Inner Council, stood a little apart from the others. She was a short woman, so muffled in the traditional green silk robe that from a distance she seemed no more than an overdressed doll. The slanting light made her cropped hair gleam like unpolished steel and brought out the filigree of lines on her face. On her left hand, she wore a signet ring of age-patinaed gold, incised with a dotted double circle. As she waited, she rubbed the ring and twisted it around her finger, tracing the design, around and around in an unending circle.

At Esmelda's side stood her son and adjutant, Terricel sen'Laurea. The "sen" in his place-name denoted his status as a University senior. Although he appeared slightly built, his bones were big enough for an athlete's—a swimmer or a gymnast—but they were covered by soft flesh instead of muscle. His skin was as pale as any scholar's, his hands uncallused except for his right index finger. Below colorless eyes, his lips pressed together, whitening the skin around his mouth still further. Despite the chill of the morning, a bead of sweat trickled down the back of his neck, yet he gave no sign he'd felt it. Instead, he kept his eyes fixed on the Starhall, as if by will alone he could wrest some secret from it.

Pateros, brimming with confidence and energy in the prime of his life, arrived. He greeted each of his advisers with a touch and a friendly word. He stopped for a moment to ask Terricel about the progress of his master's thesis proposal.

"Doing well," Terricel answered. "My presentation's scheduled for next week."

"History, still? Following in your mother's footsteps?"

"Not exactly, sir. Same field, but different subject. I'm trying something no one's done before."

Pateros patted Terricel's shoulder before going inside. "You'll do us proud, I'm sure of it."

Terricel squared his shoulders, took a deep breath, and followed his mother and the other Councillors through the heavy bronzewood doors, past the contemporary-styled offices and the display cases containing the personal journals of Guardians from past dynasties. Above them swept the ancient spectators' balcony, where even now visitors stood and wondered at the bygone times when the entire Senate could gather in the hexagonal room below. Since the great Senate Building had been completed, it was used primarily for the administration of traditional oaths to judges and Rangers, as well as meetings of the Guardian's Inner Council.

Although Terricel was prepared for it, the brilliant light of the central chamber set him squinting. He re-

membered the discussion when, only a few years ago,
Pateros had installed the banks of batteries and intensi-
fying lenses in the roof. The traditionalists on the Council felt that a dimmer illumination would have been more
flattering to the ancient walls, for the warped paneling
was only partially covered by the tapestries hung by Pateros's grandfather. Terricel liked the sense of age in the
room, as well as the time-battered mosaic floors which
depicted the All-Mother planting a seedling.

Old tales spoke of a treasure buried deep beneath
those floors, beneath the Starhall's very foundations, and
Terricel had studied them all in his history classes. Some
said it was all that remained of the starship which carried
humankind to Harth more than a thousand years ago.
Others said space travel was impossible, an offense to
decently controlled science, and it was something else
entirely, a device to travel through time perhaps, or
across dimensions. Yet others claimed, completely illogi-
cally, that it was an altar to some blood-craving norther
god, or else the sort of god the northers would pray to
if they had any gods at all.

Yet Terricel knew that more lay beneath the Starhall
than legend. One day, he promised himself for the hun-
dredth time, one day he'd find out what it was, this thing
that only he could sense, find it and beat it back out of
his nightmares.

Over the years the Starhall had shifted in Terricel's
imagination from an implacable enemy to a tool against
which he honed his will. He'd learned to sit absolutely
still through the long meetings, not a muscle quivering.
Learned to keep his breathing slow and deep, his hands
steady, his eyes unflinching as he followed the debate.
It became a matter of pride that he let nothing show of
what he truly felt.

Pateros entered the central chamber first, followed by
the Inner Council and their various assistants. Green silk
robes rustled as they took their places around the oval
table. Last to enter was the gaca-priest. The tree and
sunburst charms on his breast clinked gently with each
step. Above his lined face, cheeks sunk almost to the

bone, his head was smoothly shaved. His eyes bore a slightly glazed expression, as if he hadn't quite emerged from his morning meditations. Carefully he set the ritual silver bowl and planter on the table. The bowl was filled with water. He dipped his fingers into the water and touched his lips, then dipped again and sprinkled the drops over the miniature tree.

> *"In the name of all oneness,*
> *Which we pledge to preserve*
> *In thought and deed.*
> *May the cycle of life*
> *Bless these proceedings."*

He placed the tree in the center of the table and passed the bowl to Pateros.

Pateros dipped into the water with his tapering, big-knuckled fingers. With his silvery-gold hair and strong-boned features, he had not aged visibly since Terricel was a boy. Like most Laurean men, he used a beard suppressant which kept his face smooth for months at a time. He wore a single ring, a river-opal set in silver. The gemstone, wet, shone as if it had been set afire. As he stooped to reach the planter, his hair fell forward across his eyes. He brushed it back absently as he handed the bowl to Esmelda, who stood in her usual place at his right side. When his eyes met Terricel's, they crinkled in a fleeting smile.

When the bowl had passed around the circle, the gaea-priest received it again and indicated the dedication had been properly performed. With sighs and scrapings of chair legs, the members of the Council sat down in their padded armchairs. The aides and adjutants, Terricel included, settled into their seats behind their principals.

"It's good to see you again, Markus. I trust your retreat was restful," said Pateros, nodding to the gaea-priest. His hazel eyes flickered across the table. "Hobart, what's happening with the Cathyne tariff debate?"

The Senate presidio drew in his breath, his shoulders hunching under the brocaded yoke of his robe. His rank medallion, an ornate disk of copper and gold, glittered in the bright light. Terricel had heard rumors that he was scheming to get his daughter married to Pateros, who did not yet have an heir, a situation which had recently become a cause for some uneasiness.

Terricel bent over his notepad, transcribing the discussion for Esmelda's records. His pen skimmed the paper in line after line of his precise cursive script, each letter sloping at exactly the same angle as its neighbor, each descender brief and unflourished. The rhythmic movement helped steady him, pushing back the enveloping presence of the Starhall from his consciousness.

Hobart made a small, almost apologetic gesture. "It's hard to say at this point. The Traders' Guild wants one thing, the city fathers another. And of course Redding and the other river towns have got their interests at stake, too. If the traders win too many concessions here, they'll start aiming for other ports."

"What you're saying," Pateros observed dryly, "is that the problem's bogged down in the usual endless debate and whatever gets decided—if anything—will be some hopelessly inept compromise."

He leaned forward and tapped the table in front of him. "I've had enough of every port city skimming whatever it can. No wonder our traders won't go farther north than Brassaford—their profits are eaten up tenfold by the time they get back to Cathyne!"

With reduced tariffs, Terricel thought, *they'll search out new markets, new sources of goods.* He sat up straighter, his attention sharpening. This was not going to be an ordinary meeting, not if Pateros was talking about shifting the fundamental balance of power in Laurea.

Esmelda leaned forward, her eyes flashing. "You're talking about establishing trade with the north, aren't you?"

"You always were a half step ahead of me, Esme," Pateros answered.

Not just the balance of power in Laurea—maybe all of Harth!

General Montborne shook his head. "I wouldn't advise it. Not with the kind of hostilities smoldering there."

"These aren't civilized people," said Karlen, the Senior Court judge. "They don't think the way we do. Any overture we make, official or not, they'll interpret as weakness and attack again."

"The northers aren't going to disappear, no matter how many times we beat them back," Pateros said somberly. "Not so long as we have what they want. We have to create an alternative to fighting for it."

Esmelda rubbed her ring, frowning. Terricel noticed the characteristic gesture and felt her thoughts racing ahead of Pateros's words. "The norther culture is marginal at best," she said in a deceptively mild voice. "The pressures of accumulating furs or elkskins or whatever they have that we might want could easily lead to overharvesting or disrupt wildlife migration patterns. Not to mention the effects of putting a string of trading posts up there. We'll have to be careful."

"I don't see what any of this has to do with coddling the traders," said Andre, the elderly representative of Laureal City. "Squeezing the port cities won't make the northers any less dangerous. If anything, it'll weaken our own economy. We *need* those tariffs."

"I don't intend to cut you off," Pateros replied. "What I want is an incentive for our traders to take the risk of opening up the north. I intend to levy a single tariff—a fair one—for goods shipped anywhere along the great rivers."

The Senate won't like that, Terricel thought. Hobart, across the table, frowned and shook his head.

"I know cities will be unhappy and you," Pateros nodded to Montborne, "are justifiably wary about the defense aspects. That's why I've brought it up privately here. I need you to chew it over, tell me all the reasons it won't work. And then help me find the way it *will* work."

Montborne traced a design in the wood grain of the table, his usually smooth forehead creasing. "Are we talking about military escorts for traders, increased border patrols, what?"

"It's your business to tell me what we'll need," said Pateros. "Even with our Rangers, we're no better than a sieve up there."

"If I had more men, or weapons ..." Montborne leaned back in his chair, a cryptic expression twisting his mouth, "But we've been all through that, haven't we?"

"We have," replied the gaea-priest, "and you have had your answer—the Law *forbids* it. Would you have us go the way of the Ahtom and rain destruction on all Harth?"

"What would *you* do, lie down and let the northers run right over us when a simple invention could make the difference?" snapped Montborne.

Terricel's spine stiffened minutely as he caught the shift in tension. Montborne was making no effort to disguise his anger at Markus, but there was something else there, too, something hidden. Terricel glanced at Pateros and noticed his flash of awareness.

Markus had jumped to his feet, gesturing wildly. "There are no *simple* inventions, there is only the blindness which leads the *simpleminded* to extinction! The Ecologs tell us so, which is why this priesthood exists in the first place and why we have the ultimate decision over any new technology. It is our divine responsibility to ensure that no *simple* invention destroys our entire world!"

"And it's *mine* to make sure we're around to debate the issue!"

Pateros silenced both of them with a single raised finger. Terricel heard the quiet power of his voice and marked how smoothly the Council came under his command. "If we let our own fear of the northers force us into a military state," Pateros said, "then we will be living under their yoke just as surely as if they' had burned the Starhall to the ground."

The gaea-priest lowered himself into his chair, his face still flushed. Montborne looked away, as if accepting the rebuke.

Pateros signaled the end of the discussion by charging the Councillors once again with finding the innovative solutions that would make his plan succeed. This time there were no objections. The rest of the meeting was filled with ordinary business, yet a sense of unresolved tension hung behind every word.

* * *

Terricel stepped into the flat light of the plaza, sand-wiched between his mother and one of Montborne's aides. The morning breeze turned the beaded sweat on his face slick and cold. He took a deep breath. The knots in his shoulders eased as the burning-ice pain in his belly faded. The pavement beneath his boots felt comfortingly solid.

Voices reached his ears. "Why else could I speak so frankly to you?" Pateros was saying to Montborne. "I'm as sure of your devotion to Laurea as I am of my own, on some days even surer...." Esmelda murmured to Cherida, the head medician, something about changing a theater date, and Hobart tried to get Pateros to accept a dinner invitation.

One of the other adjutants said a few friendly words, and Terricel nodded back. They'd been friends as junior students, having both lost fathers during the epidemic, when they were still babies.

Pateros finished declining Hobart's attempts to induce him to play honored guest with his daughter as hostess. The Guardian moved away into the little crowd which had gathered, as one always did whenever he appeared in public. Esmelda once remarked to Terricel that this hadn't always been the case, only in the last five years, since the Brassa War. Whenever she herself was recognized by visitors from outside the city, it was all, "*The* Esmelda, still alive?" Now she angled away from the crowd, as sour-faced as if some poor fool had tried, once again, to kiss her hand.

Montborne matched his stride to Esmelda's, the officer who served as his bodyguard only a pace behind. "We didn't have time to discuss the youth situation, but—"

"There's no point in wasting our breath," Esmelda folded her arms across her chest. "We don't need another military division, whether you call it the Youth Corps or the Brainless Battalion. What's wrong with this country is *not* the inability to follow orders."

"I agree absolutely," Montborne said smoothly. "That's why I need your counsel. During your time as

Senate presidio, you led Laurea in a bold, new direction—"

"I led Laurea in the only direction possible for her
survival."

Terricel, trailing behind them and only half-listening,
arched his back and took another deep breath. He
glanced across the plaza, toward the University complex
hidden beyond the Senate Building. With any luck, he'd
be able to slip away before lunch and get in a solid
afternoon's work on his dissertation proposal. He still
had a few references to check and his written summary
to polish. All he needed now was a little more time.

And yet, Terricel thought as he turned his face to the
gentle breeze, it would be a shame to waste such a day
indoors. The sun was high enough to burn off the night's
chill, the sky clear and blue. Somewhere along the western coast, waves thundered against jagged rocks. He
could see them in his mind, could almost taste the salty
foam and feel the shards of deep-sea shells beneath his
bare toes. If he sent his imagination soaring in the other
direction, out toward the eastern steppe, he could hear
the alkali winds wailing around the nomads' felt and
wicker jorts. Ghameli, their pack-saddles safely stowed,
lowered themselves to the bare rock and prepared to
wait out the storm. Within the shelters, he breathed the
dense, pungent smoke of sandalwood and ghostweed.
Deep inside of him, something which had been hard and
twisted, like a plant struggling in the darkness, now
began to open, reaching hungry tendrils to the sun.

Terricel's gaze lingered for a moment on the steps of
the military building. A Ranger stood there, but whether
man or woman, he couldn't tell. All he recognized was
the pocketed leather vest, the emblem bright on one
shoulder. His heart beat faster. But no, the Ranger's
hair wasn't black like his sister's, it was dark red, like
bloody copper.

In the center of the crowd, a heavyset man in laborer's
overalls began shouting something about the Cathyne
tariffs. The two City Guards elbowed their way toward
him, placing themselves between him and Pateros. "This
is no place for petitions," said one. "Take it to your

Senator!" The other drew out his baton, ready to seize the man in a pain-control leverage.

"The man has a grievance, even if this is not the proper time for it," Pateros said gently. "I won't have him hauled off like a common criminal for speaking his rights."

The Ranger was no longer standing on the steps, but yelling something unintelligible, sprinting toward the crowd. Terricel's stomach, which had almost regained its equilibrium, twisted suddenly.

What the hell is going on?

The shouting man sounded more belligerent than ever. Around him, the crowd muttered and surged. The Ranger was nearer now, and Terricel could see it was a woman. Her face contorted with effort, her legs pumped fast and hard. Behind him, his mother and the general were still talking, now on some more neutral subject.

"Esme—" Terricel began.

But it was Montborne who spun around first. His eyes followed where Terricel pointed, flickered over the Ranger, the crowd, Pateros. The next moment, he darted toward Pateros, shouting to his aides. His bodyguard whipped out his knife and rushed after him.

The milling bodies parted in front of Terricel for an instant and he saw a man, all in blue and lean as a norther wolf, standing beside Pateros. Pateros nodded to him and stooped over a little, as if to listen better. Terricel could almost see the familiar expression of concern on Pateros's face, the light in his green-gold eyes, his ready smile.

The next few moments came to Terricel in fragments—a swirl of green silk . . . the man in blue sprinting away . . .

Pateros falling back into Montborne's arms . . . someone screaming.

Terricel's legs, after having somehow gotten him to Pateros's side, folded suddenly under him. The gritty pavement burned his knees. At first all he could see was the blood on Pateros's green robes and the hazel eyes open so wide that they seemed to take in all the sky at once. They were all green now, the gold drained from them. Cherida bent over Pateros, beginning resuscitation. Her hair was coiled off the back of her neck and the muscles stood out like twin ropes of steel.

"What good will that do now?" came a whisper at Terricel's side, a woman's voice.

The Ranger knelt beside him, breathing hard, her lips drawn back from slightly uneven teeth. Ragged chestnut curls framed her face. For a moment her eyes, pale translucent amber, held his. He'd never seen human eyes that color before.

He wanted to grab her and ask how she'd known what was going to happen. She *must* have known, the way she came charging across the plaza.

The Ranger spiraled to her feet, taut and graceful and looking fit enough to fight off half of Laurea. A moment later, more City Guards arrived and herded all the bystanders to one side. People muttered as they crowded together, a few sobbing, others praying aloud with the gaea-priest.

Terricel broke into a cold sweat. His hands started shaking. Someone shoved an elbow into his side and he gasped in a lungful of cheap floral scent, sweat, and stale garlic.

He stepped back, almost stumbling over Esmelda's feet. Somehow, in the horror and confusion, he'd lost sight of her, yet there she was, right behind him. Steady, unwavering, and always in the center of things.

He'd rarely seen her so inhumanly still. She might have been stone except for the movement of her breathing. Her eyes, dry as a lizard's, focused inward, on something no one else could see. He wondered if she were remembering other times—the Brassa War, perhaps, or the epidemic when she'd taken over as Senate presidio, her husband dead and she alone with two young children, one of them, himself, a mere baby.

Esmelda grasped Terricel's shoulder with one hand. He opened his mouth, but his throat had gone dry, his voice paralyzed. No words came. Her fingers, thin and hard, dug into his flesh.

"Right now, we're all in shock," she said. "It's a natural reaction and will pass, that and the grieving. We have work to do, meanwhile, so get your brains uncorked. Orelia will hold these people for questioning, but she'll release us as soon as she can." She put a slight emphasis on *us*.

"Work?" Terricel stared at her. For all that he'd been twenty years her junior, Pateros had been her friend as well as her political ally.

"We must begin setting up the electoral college immediately," she said.

He frowned as he searched his memory for the details of succession which he'd studied only because they were part of a compulsory civics course. He couldn't remember how a nondynastic Guardian was elected, except that the process was complicated. The Senate, however, could appoint an emergency *pro tem*.

The Senate, he thought grimly, *couldn't appoint a dishwasher without written instructions.*

Esmelda released Terricel's arm. "There are forces at work here that even I can't see," she said, then went on in a tight, bleak voice. "But I suspect that today's horrible business is only the beginning."

CHAPTER 5

Terricel held himself very still under the covers, hardly daring to breathe, lest the movement catapult him into full waking. The slats of sunlight which penetrated the shutters hadn't reached his eyelids yet. He still had a little more time. On most mornings, he clambered out of bed as soon as he woke, no matter where the sun was on his pillow. But today he lingered, waiting for that half-magical moment from his childhood, when time assumed a strangely liquid substance and its ripples could carry him in any direction he wished.

The Ranger woman yesterday had stirred up memories of the night his sister left for good. He'd lain in this very bed, a boy of nine, in this same almost-dreaming state, staring up at the walls which were not yet the dark, depressing blue they were today, but eggshell color, like all the rest, his mother's choice. He'd always wondered why she'd let him choose his own color.

He'd waited for the house to grow quiet after the visitors left, the ones from faraway places with exotic names, the ones he must never, never interrupt.

Ripple—here was the moment he crept downstairs when, instead of the usual night hush and the quiet patter of the rain, he heard Aviyya and Esmelda screaming at each other.

Ripple—here he crouched in his favorite hiding place at the base of the banister, listening.

"What does it take to make you *see?*" Aviyya's back was to him and raindrops quivered from the ends of her tangled black hair. "Maybe you just stepped into your own mother's place without a fight. Maybe that's exactly what you wanted all along. But I'm not you! I can't live with your secrets! I've got to have *my own* life!"

A heartbeat pause and then, from the shadows of the living room, his mother's voice: "We none of us have *our own* lives."

"I've sworn your gods-forsaken oath and I'll keep it, damn you!" Avi rushed on. "You talk about family pride and honor and the balance of all Harth—don't you think I care about those things, too? But that's all—"

"Keep your voice down!" Esmelda's voice came like the slither of a hunting snake. "The boy might hear."

Ripple—here he lay awake in his room, listening to the rain thrashing on the roof. The storm had worsened, thunder crashing in the distance. The air smelled of wet grass and lightning. Minutes passed, hours maybe. His door opened slowly and the bed creaked as Aviyya sat down beside him. She was fully dressed, an oiled-wool cloak over one arm.

"This is good-bye, baby brother. I'm going to miss you, but I can't let her do this to me."

"What if something happens to you?"

She laughed, then smothered the sound with one hand. "I hope something *does* happen to me. Otherwise it would be a waste, running away. I intend to have lots and lots of things happen to me. Wild things, wonderful things. Like we used to play, only real."

Despite Aviyya being seven years older, she'd been an excellent playfellow. She never fussed about her clothes and she never ran out of pretend adventures. Together they'd turned the living room into a norther tundra swept by bitter winds and bloodthirsty raiders, turned the glass-walled solarium with its masses of potted greenery into a forest south of the great Inland Sea. The staircase had become a terraced eastern steppe, and the polished banister the perfect stake to which to tie the victim for the nomads' mystical rites.

"Take me with you!"

She rumpled his hair and sighed. "Oh, baby brother, if only I could."

Years later Terricel discovered that Aviyya had joined the Rangers. Esmelda had always known, as she knew so many other things that happened all over Harth, not just in Laurea, and she'd never told him. Pateros had received her oath, but Terricel never blamed him for keeping her secret safe, as he had so many others.

Ripple—and here was that other woman now, knife strapped to her leg and looking crazy enough to try anything. Terricel wondered if he met Aviyya today, would she be like that, too? Would he even recognize her?

He thought of all the stories she'd told him about their father—so many and so vivid that surely she must have made some of them up. But he'd never questioned her. He'd needed to believe in them as much as she did— how their father had taken her to his weaving studio, taught her to tie knots, use a camp knife, catch dragonspiders, how he'd danced with her and sung her songs from his childhood.

Sometimes Terricel could hear those songs echoing through his own dreams. Once, when he was four or five, he'd heard Esmelda singing a country ballad as she arranged the flowers Annelys had brought in from the garden. But as soon as she realized he was crouched behind the banister, listening, she broke off. Without a word, she'd taken him into her arms and held him, rocking him gently.

Finally the ripples died down, their substance bleached away by the morning light. There was no denying he was awake and it was today instead of yesterday, and he'd seen Pateros, the Guardian of Laurea, Gatekeeper of the South and a dozen other archaic titles, knifed down in the open plaza and lying bloodstained at his feet.

Terricel rummaged in the pile of clothing on the floor of his closet and extracted a shirt and trousers that looked reasonably clean. In the washing alcove adjacent to his bedroom, he bent over the sink and splashed cold water on his face. He wet his hair and ran his fingers through it, not that it would make any difference to the way the cowlick swirled out from the back of his head. These ordinary tasks, usually performed without thought, now felt unnatural, as if one part of him understood that life went on, but some other part could not.

Downstairs, the house lay quiet, undisturbed. Although there was no sign of Annelys, the house steward, Terricel caught the aroma of her special breakfast bread. She was probably tending to the opal-eyed house snakes, rounding up the mated pair. They were turned loose each night to forage for rats and cockroaches. Their dark world of hunter and prey remained untouched by yesterday's events.

Esmelda's everyday cloak of gray wool still hung on its peg by the front door. Terricel took an apple from the bowl on the table and made his way down the corridor.

He cracked open the door. Inside, directly beneath Esmelda's bedroom, lay the cave of a room that served as her home office. Behind the overflowing bookshelves lay walls which were once a soft peach color, the sole relics of the time before she'd painted everything eggshell white. Years of candle smoke had darkened them.

Candles, beeswax candles, as costly as steel—the corners of the room reeked of them, even though Esmelda rarely actually burned them anymore. The smell always made Terricel uneasy, as if some inarticulate longing within him, roused by memory, stirred fitfully in its sleep.

Esmelda, on the other hand, drew the smoky darkness of the room around her like a protective cloak. She sat at the desk, its blotter-covered surface piled with history books, notes, and a tray of bread and ripened cheese. Ashes smoldered in the ceramic crucible she sometimes used to burn letters. She'd turned her chair toward the uncurtained windows and when Terricel entered, she was gazing over the garden, pen raised in mid-stroke.

"Orelia says the dagger was norther." She put the pen down and jabbed one finger at a sheet of yellow message paper.

"Norther ..." Terricel repeated. Saying the word aloud brought a shock of its own. He remembered Esmelda's words from the day before, *". . . only the beginning . . ."*

But no, she hadn't said the dagger was norther, she'd said *Orelia* said it was. He tilted his head, one eyebrow lifted questioningly.

She got to her feet. "Let's have a look at it."

Terricel took a slice of bread, smeared it with the soft cheese, and followed his mother down the corridor. She lifted her cloak from its peg and settled it around her shoulders. The heavy woolen folds enveloped her, leaving her shrunken, frail.

For a moment Terricel's vision shifted. He saw her as he'd so often imagined her—for he'd only been an infant at the time—standing on a dais in the plaza where she gave her famous speech. Her shoulders were thin and angular under her cloak of purple mourning, her eyes half-feverish as she studied the anxious faces below. She seemed more desolate and yet more resolute than he'd ever seen her. Rain slicked her black hair to her skull, as if leading the city through the epidemic had pared her to the core.

Give us hope, they cried to her in his vision. *Give us strength.*

"It will be our measure as a nation how we conduct ourselves in the days to come. It is not enough to merely survive." He wasn't sure if he'd ever heard her speak those words or only imagined what she'd said.

"We must remember who we are."

He blinked and saw her again, one image overlaid on the next, past, present, and future blurring together. Again she stood on a dais, again bareheaded, but now in sunshine so clear and bright it turned her hair to silver-white. She wore green, with the Guardian's medallion around her neck. The people cheered as she raised her hands.

It was all nonsense, all childish yearnings, these pictures he painted in his mind.

Then he saw himself, standing at her side, still raw with the realization that he would be Guardian after her. He felt no sense of triumph or pleasure. Instead, the distant flowering trees pressed in on him like perfumed walls, closer and closer until he could no longer breathe.

Orelia's office would have been put to better use as a conference room. It was too big for any sense of intimacy, with its empty bookshelves and massive table of cheap grayish wood, polished to a high gloss. There were no outside windows, only a double panel of solar-battery lights along the ceiling. When Esmelda and Terricel arrived, the City Guards Chief sat in an armchair at the far end, facing Montborne and Cherida. Standing along the wall behind Montborne was the grim-faced officer who went everywhere with him. Terricel had never heard the man's name; the story was that Montborne had saved his life at Brassaford.

"Esme. Come in, sit down," Orelia said. Her eyes slid past Terricel. "Can I offer you anything? Tisane, juice?"

"Thank you, no." Esmelda shook her head, a movement that sent the muscles in her neck jumping like plucked strings. Montborne nodded to her as she pulled up a chair and sat down.

Terricel slid into the next seat, wondering what Montborne was doing here. He'd always thought Orelia was jealous of the general's popularity. And Cherida . . . he'd known her since he was a child. She was one of Esmelda's few personal friends, they'd been students together at the University, she'd known his father. Terricel had never seen her so shaken as now. She looked as if she'd gone a week without sleep, wearing the same pale green medician's smock. Tendrils of her hair had pulled free from her usually tight braids, encircling her head with a fuzzy red halo. The skin around her mouth was waxy pale.

Terricel forced the air smoothly and slowly through his lungs, keeping his belly muscles unknotted as he'd learned to do in his years at the Starhall. Calmness pulsed through him. His eyes flickered to his mother's face and he saw himself mirrored there for an instant. He'd never told her what he felt in the Starhall, never asked if she'd felt the same.

Blinking, Terricel realized he'd missed a beat of the conversation.

". . . does have a bearing on the autopsy," Orelia was saying.

"He *didn't* die of the stab wound." Cherida's mouth hardly moved as she spoke, her lips as wooden as a ventriloquist's. "I'm still looking for the cause of death. But *nobody* outside my lab knows that."

Terricel's jaw dropped a fraction before he controlled his reaction. At his side, Esmelda sat very still.

"I don't understand," Montborne said. His fingertips traced the pattern of the wood, curving and looping in a hypnotic spiral. "I was there—I caught him as he fell. My hands were covered with his blood. I saw it happen—the dagger went right in."

"But it missed all the vital organs. No major arteries were severed. The liver capsule wasn't perforated, so there was no internal hemorrhage, just some local bleeding that any intern could have controlled. Infection would have been our chief concern, and we could easily have prevented that. He *shouldn't* have died from that wound."

"What, then?" Montborne demanded, his voice gone sharp. "Are you saying he died of some incredibly coincidental heart attack? At his age?"

Cherida held up her hands, fingers rigid. Terricel saw that she'd bitten several nails down to the quick. "I don't know. Not yet. I'm still investigating."

"It was the dagger, all right," Orelia said. "Hold on, I'll show you."

She got up and opened the side door. An older man wearing the black uniform of the City Guards entered the room, carrying a bundle wrapped in thick, densely woven canvas. The officer behind Montborne moved forward, tense and alert.

Terricel stared at the Guard's face, at the same time fascinated and repulsed. One eye socket was little more than a pleated mass of scars, which ran diagonally upward, slashing through the eyebrow so that it was divided by a shiny gap, and then downward through the substance of the cheek in a deeply puckered chasm. The socket itself was hollow, the flesh pulled back and twisted into a knot.

Terricel had never seen a deformity like that before. In his junior level courses, he knew a student who'd had a leg amputated because of bone cancer, but the wooden prosthesis was always covered by his clothing.

Why doesn't he do something about that eye—get a glass one or have the scars fixed? He could at least cover it. . . .

Wearing gloves of supple black leather, the weapons specialist lay the bundle in the center of the table and slowly unwrapped it.

"Ah!" Cherida cried, and Montborne leaned forward, his indrawn breath a hiss.

In the center of the cloth lay a dagger. Like most weapons, it used a minimal amount of metal. The guards, handle, and reinforcing strips were carved bone. The pointed tip and ribs running the blade's length were pig-steel of the type originally made in Laurea and then reworked in the cruder norther smithies. The northers were said to be expert at assassinations and sneak attacks on enemy camps, slipping their narrow blades beneath a victim's ribs in a quick, silent thrust to the heart.

Terricel's mouth went dry. For a terrible moment, the rest of the room faded. Nothing mattered, nothing existed except the dagger. *This thing killed Pateros.*

Orelia's weapons expert smoothed the folds of the canvas, carefully avoiding direct contact with the blade. The man's face was grim with concentration. Suddenly Terricel was ashamed of his own lack of compassion.

He must have fought the northers, perhaps at Brassaford. He lost an eye to keep us safe.

"Superficially," the man said, "this appears to be an ordinary norther weapon, adorned here and there," he indicated the hilt and guards, again avoiding any direct contact with them, "with their distinctive motifs. However, close examination of the base of the hilt has revealed something new in their arsenal. If you will observe the pin hidden there, undetectable to casual inspection . . ."

He pressed the pin and a sliver of ornamented metal

slid aside to reveal a tiny cup lined with a gummy residue. His mouth drew downward at the corners, except where the scar twisted his upper lip.

"We have also discovered, by virtue of magnified examination, a minute tube leading from the reservoir to an opening in the tip of the dagger."

"Poison," Cherida said, nodding. She gestured toward it, and Terricel saw that her hand trembled. "A device for administering a poison so deadly that only a small amount is needed. It must be brought down to the tip by capillary motion, like the fang system of a venomous snake.

"I want a sample of that residue sent to my labs right away," she said. "If there are traces of it in Pateros's tissues, I'll find them, even if I have to thin-section his entire central nervous system. My guess, by the speed of its action, is we're looking for a neurotoxin."

"I'll see that it's done," said Orelia.

The weapons specialist rewrapped the dagger and carried it from the room. Orelia watched the door latch behind him, then turned back to the others. "You can see why I brought you here."

"I knew it would come to this," Montborne said grimly. "Those gaea-priests have kept our hands tied year after year, while the northers are free to develop *that!*" He gestured at the empty table where the dagger had lain. "Who knows what else they've got by now? *They* don't have anybody yammering away at them about not 'disrupting the ecosystem'!"

Orelia laced her fingers together and touched her forehead to them. When she looked up, her face was gray. "If they can make something like this, if they can infiltrate an assassin this deep into Laurea, they're capable of anything. This means they're getting ready for something big. . . . We're looking at another Brassaford, aren't we?"

Terricel thought about the dagger. If Cherida were right, the thing was deadly even in the hands of an amateur. He pictured the convoluted figures on its bone handle and the pig-steel blade.

Pig-steel. . . . Something went *click!* in his mind.

He cleared his throat. Orelia looked at him, a little startled. "The northers can't even make their own steel. How could they come up with something like this?"

"That's just it," Orelia explained. "This dagger means they've now developed that capability. We're no longer dealing with the assassination of a single man. Even Pateros, may Harth grant him grace, can be replaced."

"No, it still doesn't make sense," Terricel said. "If they had a weapon like this and they could sneak it into the city, why would they pick Pateros? We'd only replace him with someone else, and he was a lot less belligerent toward them than another Guardian might be. Why not go for General Montborne here and really knock out our defenses?" He glanced at the general, who was listening, eyes narrowed slightly. "I don't mean any ill wishes toward you, sir, it's just that I can't understand the logic of it. . . ."

"Pateros and Montborne were root and branch of the same living tree," Cherida said slowly, her bloodshot eyes fixed on the general. "Like the old proverb about power and wisdom. The boy's right, Montborne, you *would* be their logical target."

Montborne brushed aside her warning as if his personal safety were a threat he had long since laid to rest. "I'm afraid you give the northers too much credit, lad," he said to Terricel. "That's the kind of logic a civilized person would use. These savages seize whatever they can, whenever they can get it. They mean to demoralize us, to take away our will to fight."

Terricel knew when he was being politely dismissed. Clearly, Montborne had his own unshakable vision of the northers. And who had more experience fighting them than the Hero of Brassaford?

"You see how touchy the political implications are." Orelia looked over at Esmelda. "We don't want to do anything which could be . . . which could cause panic, destroy public confidence, that sort of thing."

"I understand what you're getting at," Esmelda said evenly. "These are difficult times, to be sure. We must move cautiously. We'll have enough of a mess on our hands just straightening out the line of succession. If only

Pateros had left us an heir. But the worst thing we can do now is to lay a norther scare on top of it before we have hard proof."

Orelia raised one eyebrow as if to say, *You think it could be otherwise?*

"Initial appearances are often misleading," Esmelda went on. "Someone with your experience knows better than anyone how the truth can turn out to be something quite different."

"I suppose there might be other possibilities. . . ."

"The fact is," Esmelda said, "we have a single assassin, a dagger of apparent norther design—and *nothing else.*"

"Who else could be responsible?" Cherida sounded genuinely puzzled.

"There's no way we can keep the dagger a secret," Montborne said. "Besides, the people are going to draw their own conclusions. They aren't stupid, they all know what the northers can do. If we're too cautious in what we tell them, they'll think we're lying or covering up something worse."

"I agree with you on that. Most people will indeed think whatever they want to," Esmelda said, ignoring his oblique barb. "If they want to see a norther conspiracy, then the truth won't stop them." She jabbed one index finger at the cheap gray wood in front of her. "Maybe the northers are responsible. But maybe they're not. Maybe somebody would like us to *believe* they are."

For a long moment, no one said anything. Then one of Orelia's junior officers brought the residue specimen for Cherida.

"Who else would want Pateros dead?" Cherida asked again.

"To begin with, the Archipelago chieftains, the Cathyne merchant cartel, a madman," Esmelda said. "Even a leader who's loved has enemies."

CHAPTER 6

Outside the City Guards Headquarters, people went about their business unsmiling, voices subdued. The overcast sky hung above their heads like a dingy pearl. False-peach trees stood like sentinels along the street, their scentless blossoms stirred only by the lace-winged pollen flies. Terricel shivered, remembering the smothering perfumed walls of his vision.

"I've got meetings all morning," Esmelda said in the voice that meant her thoughts were three steps ahead of her words and she resented having to pause long enough to catch up. "I want you in the Archives, finding out how all the past electoral colleges were constituted, the problems they ran up against, how they ruled on them. Look for precedents on how the separation of powers was handled. Anything which was a *de facto* regency. Whether the candidates were drawn from the Inner Council or collateral branches of the current dynasty. Any instance when a candidacy, even a *pro tem*, was rejected on the basis of conflict of interest with the military chain of command."

Terricel ran his fingers thoughtfully over his jaw. "Wouldn't Karlen be the one to consult about that?"

"Karlen's expertise is in present-day law. Besides, he has his hands full. You'll have four, maybe five hundred years of records to search."

Terricel had done enough of that type of research to

know what was involved, the intense concentration, the meticulous attention to detail. He slowed his steps, mentally juggling the hours he would need for his proposal presentation, as well as his other academic commitments.

"I'll have to work around my schedule for the next week—"

"Cancel the schedule!" Esmelda said. "If this were trivial, something to be done whenever time permitted, then I wouldn't need you. I could just as well have one of my Senate pages do it. Not everyone has the training to know where to look and even more important, to understand the implications of what he finds."

She paused and turned back to him, her shoulders hunching slightly. "Terr, I need someone I can trust for this."

Terricel clamped down any further protest. "I'll take care of it. It's just this week that's the problem, anyway, and Wittnower can get someone else to handle my tutoring. Do you want a daily report, or only when I've found something important?"

"I knew you wouldn't fail me." She touched his hand and he was surprised, as he always was, by how warm her skin was. He always expected her to be cold, like a house snake.

"Things may get hectic for both of us," she continued in her usual brisk tone. "If I don't see you at dinner, leave your notes on the library desk. Every day, even if you have nothing for me."

Terricel found Wittnower, his History mentor, in the sunlit lounge that served the faculty and master's candidates of the Humanities school. Terricel hadn't been on campus since the assassination, and he found the atmosphere here still and dense, difficult to breathe in, as if the entire University had been placed under a bell jar. They sat together in a pair of oversoft armchairs wedged in a corner. Terricel refused the usual honeyed tisane, but his mentor drank cup after cup.

"This comes as no surprise, given recent events and your mother's position," Wittnower said. The oblique light gleamed on his pale scalp, giving it a sheen like marble. "Don't worry about the tutoring schedule. I'll shift that around and cancel the proposal presentation as well."

"No!" Terricel's voice rose above the hush of the room. "No," he repeated more quietly, "I intend to keep that." On his way to the University, he'd figured it all out. Once he'd gotten the approval, he didn't have to start on the project right away. He could put it aside until things settled down. Like the Starhall itself, it would still be there to come back to.

Wittnower's eyes, bright beneath shaggy brows, fixed on Terricel's. "I said before and I'll say again, you're asking for trouble. If you take my advice, you'll use this break to reconsider, find something else that you're interested in. Something that has a decent chance of approval. There are plenty of other worthwhile topics you can choose from. Your term paper on the norther raids during Worrell's time, for instance."

"We went through all that last year," Terricel said. "I don't want to rehash what's already been studied half to death. I want to do something new, something important. And you didn't say it couldn't be done. You said that with a tight enough argument, the committee couldn't find a reason to say no. You said you'd support my decision."

"That I did, and I'll stand by it. But it's a fool's chase, and we both know it." Wittnower leaned forward, gesturing with one hand. "If it were anything else, the committee would make allowances. After all, these are hardly normal times. But this—why does it have to be this topic?"

"Because it's what I need to—want to do. Because I want my dissertation to make a difference."

Terricel trusted his mentor enough to tell him that he intended to dig beneath the Starhall and bring to light the thing which lay there, solve the old debate, put the legends to rest. But he didn't trust Wittnower enough to tell him why.

Now, for a fleeting moment, he remembered that night, so many years ago, when he'd snuck into the Starhall alone. He'd been eleven, Aviyya had been gone two years, and his mother had started bringing him to meetings of the Inner Council, amid greetings of, *"So you're Esmelda's son, are you? We expect great things of you, lad!"*

At the time, he couldn't understand why he felt so dizzy inside the hall and yet well again as soon as he left, but it hadn't taken him long to see that no one else would admit to having the same reaction.

The Councillors teased him about being sick enough to throw up whenever he passed the great bronzewood doors. "He's such a sensitive, impressionable youngster," they said, laughing. "The excitement is too much for him." They did not add, although he could feel them thinking it, *Not to mention having to live up to being Esmelda's son.*

"There's no need to be ashamed of a little human weakness, lad," they said. "You'll get used to it in time, ha ha!"

Pateros had taken the boy Terricel aside and laid a hand on his shoulder. "Sometimes these things aren't meant personally. You have to use a different perspective, take the whole picture into consideration. They may be trying to use you to get at your mother, but you're stronger than that."

Terricel had lifted his chin and blinked the unshed, furious tears from his eyes. "They think I'm a crybaby."

"The same sort of thing happened to me when I was your age," Pateros went on in that casual tone that made Terricel feel so grown up. "People were always comparing me to my father or talking about what kind of Guardian I would make when I grew up. I survived, and I can see that you have the courage to do it, too. But remember that no matter what they say, all those important people, you have to follow your own dreams and make your own choices. Don't let them or anyone else do that for you."

Terricel had never forgotten what Pateros had said, never given up fighting the thing beneath the Starhall. All he lacked was a convincing reason to get the permission for the excavations.

How could Wittnower, or anyone else from the University, living as they did in Esmelda's shadow, understand?

A deep ache pulsed through Terricel's chest, as if something had torn inside him. *Pateros,* he thought numbly, *would have understood.*

"Have it your own way, then," Wittnower said, shaking his head, perhaps misinterpreting Terricel's silence for continued obstinacy. "I've warned you, but I won't stop you. But there's a limit on what I can do to rescue you from your own decisions."

After leaving Wittnower, Terricel went to gather his supplies from the suite of study cubicles he shared with the other History candidates. The friends who greeted him seemed distant and preoccupied as they went about their own business. Seeing him with notebook and pens, they probably thought he was doing the same. Then, suitably armed, he passed through the Library and into the velvet quiet of the Archives. The reference assistant on duty assigned him a carrel and issued him an access permit to the closed stacks and historical materials.

The light in the back rooms had a curious pastel quality, a sense of suspension, as if the same dust motes had hung in the air for centuries and never drifted to rest. Time slipped by, hours and then days. Terricel sketched out a chronology and methodically worked his way backward, looking for periods of political upheaval when the succession of the Guardianship might be subject to debate.

There wasn't much of interest until the Jeravian dynasty, three hundred years ago. In school, Terricel had studied the era, but from a different perspective. The flurry of norther raids had been used as a warning to maintain continual vigilance. But now, as Terricel worked his way through the actual records, words and deeds leaped off the pages to vivid life. He could almost hear the speeches, the bitter accusations and counteraccusations, hear the clash and smell the dust and blood of battle, look over the shoulders of people scheming for power, struggling amongst themselves as well as with the northers.

One Jeravian, nephew to the suddenly-deceased incumbent, had stepped in during the emergency and later become Guardian. The legal maneuvering was complicated, stemming from his having previously acted as *de facto* Guardian during his predecessor's illness and therefore he wasn't considered *pro tem* the second time. He appeared to have been confirmed by the leadership of the gaea-priesthood, without the convocation of an electoral college. A precedent from several hundred years earlier was cited. Terricel had never heard of such a procedure. He decided this was a lead worth following up.

At first, the senior archivist refused to allow Terricel access to the most ancient documents. Normally, the archivist insisted, these areas were off-limits to even senior scholars, their contents too fragile for ordinary research. They were not available for *casual browsing*. In the end, it took a written request from Esmelda to get an exemption to this policy.

The next morning, wearing a mask and cloth gloves, Terricel entered the temperature-controlled chamber. Journals and logbooks, each wrapped in specially-treated paper, sat in individual cubbies on the ranges of shelves. Terricel took them down, one by one, and began examining them. Some had been reprinted or copied over from earlier works, but many others were original, on parchment or elkhide vellum.

As Terricel went on, deeper into the past, the language became archaic and convoluted, the handwritten cursive more difficult to decipher. He felt as if he were entering a secret, vanished world. Whenever he saw a mention of the Starhall, he read more carefully. These records came from a time when the entire Senate, not just the Inner Council, met in the Starhall's central chamber. The people of those days must have seen the Starhall in a different light, held different beliefs about its origin. Perhaps they knew things which had since been forgotten or relegated to folklore. Perhaps someone then had even tried to find the hidden starship, or whatever lay beneath the Starhall.

A twinge of resentment curled through Terricel as he

realized that he would normally never have access to these records. He wouldn't have even known they existed. He set aside the notebook filled with political notations, and began a new one.

Late in the afternoon, he came across a section at the back of the archival chamber, a set of leather-bound volumes, very old even by the standards of the other materials. Terricel found that by working slowly and consulting his dictionaries, he could decipher much of the script. They appeared to be the diaries of some important official, although whether a Guardian or a gaea-priest wasn't clear. The writer or writers often referred to the priesthood and the Guardianship as if they were the same thing.

"The Guardian, though he be of the priesthood and sealed to its mysteries, must yet speak to and for the people. He must be Protector as well as Gatekeeper. Therefore, as the power of knowledge and the light of dedication passes through the Three in the fullness of time, the Guardian may arise from any One, according to his merits and the requirement of the day . . ."

Protector as well as Gatekeeper? Gatekeeper? Was this an indication that the Starhall object, assuming there was one, was indeed some kind of physical gate? Or was it merely a metaphorical allusion to the gateway of knowledge?

Terricel read on, hungry for more details, but very little of the rest was understandable. It seemed to be in code, marked by a familiar symbol: the dotted double circle. Perhaps Esmelda knew what it meant. He'd ask her when he turned in the rest of his findings.

Terricel copied down the most intriguing excerpts from the coded logs. As he did so, he noticed the archivist hovering just inside the door and wondered how long he'd been there. Terricel stood up and stretched, his spine crackling. He stripped off the mask and gloves and handed them to the archivist.

Notebooks in hand, he made his way back to the open stacks, where once more he immersed himself in more recent history. This time he didn't resent the work. At first, he'd thought that doing this research for Esmelda would take time away from his thesis proposal. He never imagined he might find such tantalizing clues, clues that might well lead to an even more fabulous discovery. All he needed now was the time to delve deeper.

CHAPTER 7

"Terricel? Terricel sen' Laurea?" called a soft female voice from behind his left shoulder. He looked up from the volume he'd been combing, line by line. As his thoughts struggled free from the intricacies of Senatorial debate over the status of an illegitimate minor heir, he felt amazed that anyone had known where to find him here.

The voice which had shattered his concentration belonged to a young woman dressed in a red and bronze uniform. No, he corrected himself as he took a closer look at what lay below the piles of brassy curls, she was still more girl than woman, fourteen or fifteen at most, despite the curves under her fitted tunic.

"Terricel?"

"I don't know you, do I?" he said, thinking he might have seen her in the junior classes. He didn't think he'd tutored her. Surely he would have remembered that impossibly bright hair.

"I've been instructed to bring you with me."

"I'm busy," he said, irritated by her officious tone. "As you can see. What's it about?"

"I can't *tell* you, I'm supposed to *bring* you."

Terricel relented. This must have something to do with Esmelda, some message to be passed on personally to her, too sensitive or urgent to be entrusted to the mail.

"What's the uniform?" he inquired as he gathered up

his notes and placed the volume he'd been using on the reshelving cart.

"We're called the Pateros Brigade. In honor of him."

Terricel frowned. On the day of the assassination, he'd overheard snatches of a conversation between Esmelda and Montborne—a paramilitary unit for young people, to keep them off the streets or something like that. He remembered Esmelda hadn't thought much of the idea. It was right before that man in the crowd had started shouting—the man Orelia's people still hadn't found— and that was right before. . . .

. . . Pateros's face, the mouth fallen open, the hazel eyes wide and blank . . . red blood soaking the green robes and spilling on to the pavement. . . .

He winced at the brightness as they stepped on to the shallow steps outside the Library. His temples throbbed. An invisible clamp settled around his skull and tightened with each pulse beat. It had probably been building for hours, but he hadn't noticed until now.

"General Montborne, he *believes* in us," the girl said. "He's willing to give us a chance. Not like my *parents,* they think my friends are nothing but trouble, right? They think all we care about are *parties.* But Laurea means as much to *us* as to *them.* More, because *we're* Laurea's *future.*"

Terricel smiled at her highly expressive speech.

"The *problem,*" she went on without missing a beat, "is there isn't anything to *do* except go to *school!*"

Some people run away and join the Rangers. "School's not such a bad idea," he said.

"That's all very well for *you* to say!"

"What does that mean?" he snapped.

"Well, you must *like* all those old books, right? or you wouldn't be spending your time *here.* But there're those of us who'd rather get out and *live* life instead of *study* about it."

"Is that what this Pateros Brigade is for—'living life' instead of studying?" It was a mean-spirited thing to say, but he couldn't help it.

The girl didn't seem to take offense. She grinned at him, and he noticed for the first time that her spectacular hairstyle was a wig. The grin told him he probably *had* seen her at the University.

"We don't have that much to do *yet*—meetings, you know, and getting our uniforms made, a few special errands like this, and, of course signing people up. Nothing compared to what we *will* be doing once General Montborne is Guardian. Then he'll *really*—"

"Montborne?" Terricel blinked. "Montborne, *Guardian?*" He shouldn't be surprised—the general was an obvious choice if you totally disregarded the problem of bypassing the traditional balances and concentrating so much power in one person—but he recoiled from the girl's shiny-eyed fervor. Yet if he protested there were other worthy candidates, that the whole process deserved careful consideration and not jumping with the first likely prospect, she'd likely tell him he was too old and too set to know what was really going on. Just as he dismissed Markus, the gaea-priest on the Inner Council, and many of the older Senators.

The Brigade girl led him north, along streets lined with budding cerise trees. The family-owned residences here enclosed courtyards with landscaped gardens, fountains and hedges of false jasmine and lace-from-heaven. Montborne's building was in the traditional Laurean style, an elongated "U" with a long courtyard in the center. A pair of armed, uniformed soldiers stood at the gated entrance. Security precautions made sense for someone like Montborne, but Terricel wondered how the neighbors liked having to walk by the guards every time they went in or out. In these last few days, they'd probably welcomed them.

The girl spoke to one of the guards and they were allowed to pass. They stopped at the door at the far end, the short leg of the "U". Here the girl turned Terricel over to a fresh-faced aide in a military uniform, who ushered him past a formal entry area, down a short corridor reeking of floor wax, and into a narrow, window-lined room, bright and warm from the sunlight trapped behind the glass panes.

The walls were plain, unadorned except for a single

pennon which was so faded that its original color was
difficult to determine. Montborne's senior officer stood
as usual inside the door. Montborne himself sat in one
of the comfortable-looking armchairs which had been
drawn up around a small table at the near end. Hobart,
the Senate presidio, occupied another, smoking an antique pipe. A strange, nose-tickling odor emanated from
it, possibly hothouse tobacco. Terricel couldn't be sure,
as the only thing any of his friends had ever tried smoking was ghostweed.

"It's good to see you again, lad, very good. I appreciate your coming so promptly." Montborne got up and
shook Terricel's hand warmly, covering it with both of
his. They sat down just as the aide came back with a
tray of mugs, a steaming carafe, and a pot of rose-honey.

Terricel sniffed his drink cautiously. The caramel-col-
ored liquid had a sharp tangy aroma. He blew across the
steaming surface, took a sip and found it pleasantly
astringent.

"It's boramy, from the northern islands of Archipelago," said Montborne. "A mild stimulant. The islanders
claim it sharpens the thought processes. When I was a
junior officer, I served along the western border states—
they weren't annexed then, that would be ancient history
to you young people. Anyway, I developed a taste for
the stuff. Here it costs almost as much as surgical steel,
so I save it for my special guests."

Terricel flushed. To give himself something to do, he
took another swallow of the boramy tisane. His head-
ache faded.

"Have you ever been to Archipelago?" Montborne
asked conversationally.

"No, but I'd like to. Someday."

"The University, while justly deserving of our reverence, is but a microcosm." Montborne gestured expan-
sively with his empty hand. "While you're struggling
through it, it seems like the whole world, but in reality
it's only a tiny particle. Out there," he indicated the
southern-facing windows, "*there* is the real Laurea, and
it's bigger than you can possibly imagine. Full of riches
and adventure, fascinating places, beautiful women. Not

all of them," with a confidential wink, "fellow students. There are thousands of people who never earn the right to call themselves 'sen.' It's time to start thinking beyond the walls of your august University."

What is this, a recruiting speech for your Pateros Brigade? "I'm a senior student," he said, a little stiffly. "I can't go trotting over half of Laurea, not until I've completed my studies."

"Listen to me, Terricel," said Hobart. Until now, he'd been sitting back, listening to the conversation and chewing meditatively on his pipe stem. "General Montborne didn't ask you here to make polite conversation about your academic career." He pointed one elegantly manicured finger northward. "The world out there is real, and it's filled with real dangers. We're on the brink of war, you know that, a war in which too many boys like you will never come home. A war which could see the University razed to the ground and its libraries used for kindling. What good will your master's degree be to you then?"

Terricel's immediate response was the traditional platitude that without the University to preserve and foster learning, they'd be little better than the northers anyway. He stifled it, for he sensed undercurrents to this conversation whose meaning he couldn't guess.

"This is no Solstice romp we're talking about." Hobart apparently took Terricel's silence for disagreement. "What faces us now is total annihilation at the hands of the norther savages. They have already struck at the very heart of our nation. They won't stop until we're ashes under their feet."

He leaned forward, resting his elbows upon his knees. "Terricel, you're a bright and perceptive young man, well trained in statesmanship by your mother. In your heart, you know what's at stake."

What is he getting at?

"I know this isn't a game."

"I have dedicated my entire life to Laurea's defense," Montborne said. "In some other time, some peaceful time, I would be content with patrolling the borders and an occasional parade drill on holidays. I'd gladly leave the running of the country to those trained for the job. But we both know the Senate has drifted along from one generation to the next until it can act in an emergency exactly as well as a headless barnfowl can."

Still unsure as to the direction of the conversation, Terricel tried a probe. "Perhaps what's behind Laurea's troubles is the lack of a single central ruler. There are some who say *you* should be Guardian."

Montborne waved the idea aside. "Me, *pro tem*? That might give us a bit more efficiency before the action breaks, but the position's time-limited. It would be asking for catastrophe if, at some crucial point, I had to turn over command to some civilian who knew nothing about national defense. It could cost us the war."

Montborne had deliberately misinterpreted his question. Why?

"War is inevitable, then?"

"It's my business to know such things," Montborne said. "The only question is on whose timing it will be, ours or theirs? I prefer not to stake the future of my country upon the whims of savages."

Terricel ran one hand through his hair, his thoughts racing. The confusion he allowed to show on his face was genuine. "Why are you telling *me* all this? You should be talking to my mother, not me."

"You are the wave of the future, lad, you and others like you." Montborne smiled, a flash of brilliance across his chiseled features. "It's time we stopped looking to the past to safeguard our land. Don't misunderstand me, I have nothing but the highest respect for your mother. She's served Laurea long and well. But let's face it, she's an old woman. Her stamina's not what it used to be. Even her ideas are worn out. Good enough, perhaps, for drifting along in peacetime, but now . . ."

Terricel stared at him, imagining what Esmelda would say to that.

"She's not stupid, your mother—she knows she can't go on forever. So she's been grooming you as her successor, taking you to all the Senate meetings, all the private conferences. Surely that can't come as a surprise to you."

"Yes, my mother has trained me as her adjutant. But I believe the University should be free to choose its own representative when it comes time to—for her to retire."

"Our boyhood plans must change when we become men," said Montborne gently. "It's Laurea that needs you now."

As he made an ungraceful exit, Terricel realized that Montborne fully intended him to tell Esmelda what had happened.

CHAPTER 8

The next morning, the day of Terricel's thesis proposal, he breakfasted with Esmelda in the solarium. The glass-topped table was piled with papers and reports, mugs of stimulant tisane, dishes of fruit and cold smoked fish. One of the opal-eyed house snakes had gotten in and was silently coiling its way between the potted palms.

Brow furrowed, Esmelda studied Terricel's transcription of the coded logs. "I've seen something like this before, but I can't read it. You're right about the insignia being the same. The ring is very old. It came to me from my mother and to her from her father. Among other things, she told me it was a copy of an even older design."

"What does it mean?"

Esmelda's face, which had softened minutely along with her voice, snapped closed. She shoved aside the page of transcribed code and picked up the next notebook.

The ring might have something to do with the old Guardians and this Gate or Gatekeeper, whatever it was. "What other things did your mother tell you?" Terricel persisted.

"It's a family heirloom, nothing more!" Her voice resonated with warning and her eyes sparked black fire.

An heirloom which should have gone to Avi, you mean. He wouldn't give up. "Then why is it the same symbol as in the logs? Why won't you tell me what it means? What's really going on here?"

"I don't know!" For the first time, Esmelda sounded more frustrated than adamant. The next instant, her voice was back under tight control. "I don't know why the dotted circles appear both on my ring and in those documents. That knowledge must have been lost generations ago. We may never find out. Our priority now is to the living, to the orderly succession of Laurea, not some detail of ancient history."

Terricel blinked, half in astonishment. Esmelda had hidden many things from him over the years, but he did not think she was hiding anything now. She truly didn't know, and that ignorance clearly rankled her.

He watched her face as she bent over the notebook, her lips slightly pursed as she read along. Was the link as trivial as she pretended, a *tidbit* only? Or was it a vital clue now lost, forever beyond her reach? Did her anger cover a deeper, human fallibility?

"Something else happened yesterday," Terricel said, drawing himself back to the present. "Montborne called me in for a private chat." He went on to describe the interview with the general.

"Of course Montborne's maneuvering behind the scenes," she said, making check marks across Terricel's notes on the Jeravian succession. "He hasn't gotten where he is by waiting for an engraved invitation. He's a man who takes full advantage of whatever circumstances he's given, as we all were grateful for at Brassaford. You're surprised he approached you?"

She took a mouthful of plum compote and swallowed it without chewing. "I'm not. He wants to know if you, as my adjutant and heir, are susceptible to his influence, like that girl in his—what was it, Pateros Brigade?"

My adjutant, she said, *and heir.* But only, he thought tightly, because Avi was long gone. Avi again. Why should he be thinking so much of her now?

Terricel noticed the time on the wall clock and pushed his chair away. "I've got to get going."

"Whatever it is, it can wait." Esmelda picked up the pad with his notes on legal challenges during the dynastic transfer to Worrell II. "We've got several days' worth of work to go through and I have a meeting in an hour."

"We can do it later today," he said. "My thesis presentation also starts in an hour. I want to go over my written summary once more, make sure all the details are ready."

She looked up. "I thought you canceled that."

"No, just the tutoring sessions." He didn't like the mild tone of her voice. His shoulders rose slightly, the muscles along his neck tensing. His words came out more belligerently than he intended. "I've done everything you asked. It's not so much to take this one morning for my own work, is it?"

"This," she jabbed the nearest stack of papers with one blunt finger, "*this* is your work. There is nothing— not even a finished thesis and certainly not an unapproved proposal—which could possibly be important enough to interrupt it."

"Corrode the work, then!"

"Don't you use language like that with me, young man!"

Terricel had half-risen from his chair. At her words, he sat back down, as if he'd been cut behind the knees. His hands curled into fists and as quickly opened again. He remembered Aviyya screaming, *"I'm not you! I've got to have my own life!"*

"Don't turn this into a confrontation," he said, his jaw muscles suddenly so tight he chopped off each word. "I'm not saying I don't care what happens to Laurea, for gods' sakes. I'm not saying I'm going to quit. I just want the chance to follow through with my own work. Why else did you encourage me to go on at the University?"

"Yes, your University training is valuable!" Esmelda shot back without missing a beat. "But what do you think it's *for*? Churning out one irrelevant monograph after another? Do you think that's what I would prepare any child of mine to do?"

"The way you prepared me?" he flared. His stomach clenched around a knot of fire. Words rushed unchecked from his mouth. "Or the way you prepared Avi?"

The next moment, Esmelda was on her feet, eyes blazing. "That's utterly unforgivable! Your sister knew what was at stake—"

"And was that why she left? Was it?" It was a cruel thing to say, and the next instant he wished he could call back his words.

For a fractional moment, Esmelda's face froze into an unrecognizable mask. Then she said, in that almost inhumanly calm voice of hers, "I think enough time and energy have been expended on this subject. We have too much work to do to waste any on pointless squabbling." With regal dignity, she lowered herself to her chair. "We will pretend this conversation never happened."

Terricel's heart pounded, his muscles wound so tight he felt the smallest touch would make him burst open. He pushed himself to his feet, the chair legs scraping on the tile floor. He moved away from the table, brushing against a delicate potted fern. It took all his control not to strike out at it.

The house snake had completely disappeared, waiting for the humans to leave and its natural prey to emerge. There was no sign of its mate.

Not trusting himself to speak, Terricel turned and left the room.

All the way to the University, Terricel struggled with his roiling emotions. By the time he arrived, he was able to talk in a normal tone of voice, although his hands still had a distressing tendency to shake. He told himself that once he got started, he'd calm down and concentrate.

To make matters worse, his presentation had been scheduled for a second-floor seminar room which he particularly disliked. It was too white and too big, too reminiscent of his mother's house. He supposed Wittnower had requested it to make him feel at home. But at home he didn't have to pass by the rows of formal portraits of University Deans and Senators, past and present, which lined the walls of the main building, larger than life in their carved and gilded frames.

Esmelda hated her portrait, although Terricel was

never sure if that was from personal modesty or good taste. It depicted her with one hand clutching a weighty tome and the other pointing to the horizon, where the city she had saved still burned.

Terricel once asked her how she lived with the constant reminder of what Laurea owed her. She'd shrugged and said, "By understanding it means nothing."

Normally he passed the portrait without any particular notice, but this morning the painted eyes seemed to be following him, measuring him. He paused in the middle of the corridor and glared up at it.

"This is mine," he muttered under his breath. "Mine. And you can't stop me."

The committee was assembled and waiting for him, even the old Sociology master who was notoriously ten minutes late to everything. As he took his place at the head of the conference table, Terricel decided this was a good sign, although his stomach churned uneasily. He was glad he hadn't eaten much breakfast.

He glanced around the room, seeing only the politely blank faces, each invisibly stamped with the authority of a different field within the School of Humanities—three Histories, one Sociology, one Art, fortunately from Written rather than Visual or Music, and, of course, Wittnower, who was History but who, as his mentor, couldn't vote. Because his field wasn't in Natural or Applied Science, he didn't need a gaea-priest present to sanction the proceedings.

The Department page brought in a tray with mint tisanes and scones for everyone, and the committee members munched and sipped. Terricel cleared his throat, tried to look poised, and opened with a discussion of the importance of Humanities, specifically History. He implied that no educated Laurean could be ignorant of his past, that a thorough understanding of what had gone before was necessary, not just for a scholarly life, but for a good life.

He thought he was doing well. The faces remained blank, but the eyes softened and from time to time he caught a faint, almost drowsy nodding. Perhaps the committee found solace in the timeless academic ritual, a reassurance that even in these days of uncertainty, the pillars of the University—students, masters, examinations, theses—still held firm.

Gathering confidence from his early success, Terricel raised his voice. "Laurea is Harth's oldest settlement, yet there's no concrete evidence we evolved here—for that matter, why do we have the *concept* of evolution?"

Well, perhaps that was a bit much. Sociology and Written Art coughed and shifted in their chairs. It was only a small departure from the orthodox, not a fatal misstep.

Before he could say anything more, Ancient History, who had appeared half-asleep, sat bolt upright and demanded his references for the effect of an exogenous origin of humankind on the cultures of Harth. Terricel pulled out his prepared list of fourteen published papers.

"You can't count Alladora's work," Sociology interrupted. "Her treatment of the desert nomad myths demonstrates scandalously poor methodology."

"Yes, you can," Comparative History snapped. "Her conclusions are absolutely correct, and her insights into the repeated motifs of occult wisdom from sources as diverse as the Archipelago epic chants and—"

Terricel couldn't afford to have his proposal taken over by an ongoing departmental feud. He remembered stories of other presentations, when committee members had so diverted the discussion that the candidate was failed for an incomplete proposal.

"If we didn't arise here," he began again in a loud voice, "then where did we come from? The few studies which address the issue of our origins have been essentially negative—studies of what *isn't* there. But there's one source of information they haven't examined."

Terricel placed his hands on the table and leaned forward for emphasis. He was sweating hard, but at least he'd stopped shaking. "And that's our oldest artifact, the Starhall itself. What it will tell us is that we didn't come here from someplace halfway across the night sky, we came from a place very much like Harth—"

Ancient History leaned forward with an expression of

predatory interest. "Describe the mathematics of this dimensional relationship."

Don't let the question throw you! Terricel stumbled through a superficial explanation. He knew to expect irrelevant questions, even misleading ones. They were testing his poise as well as his knowledge.

It came back to him now, that night so long ago, when he'd dared to creep into the Starhall alone. As he made his way past the public areas, he swore silently that he wasn't crazy, he wasn't a coward, and he would show them all, his mother and the Councillors and everyone.

Darkened passageways gaped at him and shadows turned ordinary objects into eerie shapes, but still he continued. The weight of hundreds of years, all the layers of wall and ornament, bracing and expansion, seemed to bear down on him. His breath rasped in his throat, loud enough to wake a sleeping guard, but no alarm came.

Deeper and deeper he'd gone, moving with childish stealth down one flight of stairs and then another. More than once he'd thought of turning back, and each time he'd stood against the wall, knees trembling, gulping air, fighting back the growing vertigo, until he was able to force himself on. At last he came to a landing, deep underground, dimly lit, the air gauzy with dust and cobwebs, and then he could go no farther. He told himself there was nothing more to find, but even then he did not believe it.

There was something hidden under the Starhall, he felt it then, as he did now, in every nerve and fiber of his body. He had thought to face it as a child, whatever it was, face it and conquer it. But when he stumbled home, retching and sweat-soaked, the feeling had not vanished. The following morning, when he accompanied his mother to the Starhall, the sensation of prickling unease had been replaced by sudden, whirling nausea and bone-deep shivers.

Terricel pulled himself back to the present. Through the partly-opened windows came the muted sounds from the courtyard below. Someone shouting. Boot heels clattering on the paved walkways. His head spun for a mo-

ment with the overwhelming normality of it all—
students rushing to classes, masters examining candidates. But things were not normal: Pateros had been cut
down right before everyone's eyes and Laurea would
never be the same again.

"Are we to understand," Sociology asked slowly,
"that you propose *excavating* the *Starhall*—physically
dismantling the oldest and most *revered* structure in all
of Laurea—not to mention the *risk* of *disrupting* vital
government functions—now, at a time of national *crisis*—all this, on the basis of a highly questionable
theory?"

"Yes, there's a certain amount of ... of disassembly
that must be done," Terricel stammered. "Removing the
wooden paneling, maybe, and some of the plaster."

Even as he spoke, he knew it was the wrong thing to
say. He shouldn't be debating how much damage might
be done to the Starhall, he should be—he couldn't think
what he should be doing. He glanced at Wittnower, hoping for some sign, but met with only a bland, impassive stare.

"We won't know how deep the artifact is," he went
on, praying he sounded more clearheaded than he felt.
"Not until we actually dig. I want to get beyond the
foundations and there's already been some—I'd work at
night and there wouldn't be any disruption—maybe a
little inconvenience, but it's not as if—"

"And you have the Senate's permission for this?"
asked Modern History.

"Well, no. I didn't want to apply until I had an ap-
proved topic."

"And have you consulted a gaea-priest as to the ecological correctness of this action?"

"I didn't think—"

"You mean you kept your scheme a *secret?*" Classical
History demanded. "Why was that?"

"More to the point, is there any historical precedent
to your proposed excavation?" Sociology asked.

Stammering, Terricel tried to address their questions.
Facts and arguments seemed to slip through his grasp,
his thoughts disintegrating into gibberish. His voice

stumbled on and on, but every point he thought of, no matter how rational it seemed, only made things sound worse.

Afterward, he couldn't even remember what he'd said.

They let him leave the room while they debated his fate. He leaned against the smooth white-plastered wall and shut his eyes. He couldn't hear anything through the door.

A few junior students wandered by. Terricel recognized them from the beginning courses he tutored. One of his friends from History, a tall redhead named Ralle, paused, looked at the door with a pained but sympathetic expression, clapped Terricel on one shoulder, and continued on his way without a word.

He shifted from one foot to the other, debating if he should just leave. He'd learned to master his body during those long years at the Starhall. If only he could control his emotions as well.

Finally, the door opened. Wittnower stood there, one hand on the latch, his expression unreadable. His eyes seemed blank, tired.

The committee began filing out, heads up, eyes level. They glanced briefly at Terricel, as if they were passing him in a hallway on the way to yet another lecture. Acknowledging his existence, nothing more.

"Come in, sit down," said Wittnower.

Terricel's hands were wet and cold. He kept them under the table.

Wittnower lowered himself into the nearest seat, turned it so they were almost facing, and ran his fingers through the meager fringe of his hair. Terricel stared at his hands, the age-mottled skin draped loosely over the veins and tendons except where the arthritic knuckles pulled it taut and shiny. There was an ink-flecked callus on the inside of the right index finger. Terricel thought his own hands would look like that in another fifty years.

"I never cease to wonder at the eternal optimism of the young."

"It was that bad?"

The old man sighed. "What are we going to do with you?"

"If I fail, I fail like everyone else."

"Have I said the proposal was a failure?" The wooden joints creaked as Wittnower straightened in his chair. "It was delivered with far more passion than precision, but so are many others, and, I might add, for the good. Would we want masters' projects no one cared about? I warned you when you first suggested this subject, and a few days ago I reminded you again, but no, you insisted on a topic which relies on evidence you cannot possibly obtain."

"That's not true!" Terricel burst out. "You said it would be difficult, not impossible. Besides, the evidence is all there, under the Starhall." *And in the Archives, if I ever get back to them.*

"Suppose the priests gave their blessing and the Senate agreed to allow the excavation—and after all that, you found nothing but a pile of rusty framing—"

"But there *is* something! There must be—I know there is—"

"What if, by some perverse and wildly improbable mischance, you prove to be mistaken? Have you considered what would happen then? I assure you that the committee has."

Terricel brushed the question aside. Besides, it was none of Wittnower's polluted business what he felt in the Starhall. "Worst case scenario, then. I'd prove it *wasn't* a starship. We *didn't* come from another planet. It's worth the degree to eliminate that hypothesis."

"All it would cost *you* is the difference between a brilliant thesis and a mediocre one."

"So what's your point? That it would cost someone else more if I'm wrong?"

If I were anyone else, anyone else at all, they'd let me try. It would be my own responsibility if I was wrong. But I'm Esme's son. . . .

He could fight Wittnower, he could fight the committee. He could even fight Esme herself. But how could he fight what she meant to Laurea?

Terricel's shoulders sagged. Even if the department

gave its approval, the Senate would never agree. He must have been smoking ghostweed to think they might. "I guess I'm out of History."

Wittnower waved one hand in negation. "We're not such bullies, and you're not such a bad student. We're giving you a 'no show.' "

Terricel blinked, then digested the words. 'No show'— just as if he hadn't come. As if the morning had never happened.

If this were another time, he could begin again. Begin where Wittnower told him to, with a topic of guaranteed success. In another semester or two, when things had settled down in Laurea, he'd pretend he'd never seen those ancient logbooks. He'd slog his way through the standard literature searches and put together a coherent presentation. He'd come before the committee again. It would be a scene out of memory, with the mint tisanes and scones, the imperceptibly nodding heads. This time they would shake his hand as they filed past, shake his hand and smile.

Another time. . . . But there would never be another time.

Everywhere he turned, Esmelda was there. Looking down at him from the University walls. Lurking in the minds of the masters. Not merely Esmelda the University Senator, but Esmelda of Laurea, Esmelda who had saved Laurea. He'd been a fool to think an academic career, or anything else, would give him any sort of life of his own.

CHAPTER 9

Only a few days ago, the suite Terricel shared with the other History candidates had been as familiar as his own bedroom walls. Now, as he drifted to his desk, he stared at the partition walls as if he'd never seen them before. As usual, the rooms hummed with activity—study groups, junior students being tutored, somebody calling for coffee or asking everyone to be just a *little* quieter, please, *some* people were trying to work.

He sat down in his chair and stared at the clutter on his desk, the piles of references and outlines. The mess looked only vaguely familiar and yet, although he'd never noticed it before, reminiscent of Esmelda's ubiquitous piles. The sheet of notes he'd made on the mathematics of interdimensional space was incomprehensible, the handwriting a stranger's.

Nearby, a handful of students raised their voices, carried away in debate.

"You've got it all wrong! Solstice means changing of the 'seasons,' " said one student, a dark-eyed girl. "It's clearly an allegorical construct to explain the passages in a human lifetime."

"The ancients weren't that sophisticated," said one of the boys. "Sol was their god, who was born each year at the Solstice and then sacrificed at Midwinter. Otherwise there's no difference between the two festivals. And cer-

tainly no esoteric significance. It's all just an excuse to
get drunk and party in the streets."

Terricel remembered having almost exactly the same
conversation with his own friends. He could predict the
argument phrase for phrase, point and counterpoint.
Any moment now, one of them would start talking about
reverence for the natural harmony and the preservation
of the environment.

"You don't have to posit the existence of a god to
recognize the importance of preserving your ecological
balances," the second boy said, right on cue. It was practically a direct quote from the junior-level bioethics
course.

The conversation veered into the traditional rituals
and how they ought to be eliminated, since their pur-
poses had clearly been long since fulfilled. Terricel had
heard enough.

Slowly, as if his body were no longer his to command,
he began taking down the pictures from the partition
walls. His favorite was a sketch done by Gaylinn sen'-
Raimuth, the art student with whom he'd been lovers
earlier that year. It was a seascape in colored charcoal.
He felt a distant tug, as if someone else named Terricel
sen'Laurea had once yearned to see such a wild, wind-
swept shore. The drawing was too good to throw away,
so he rolled it up and tied it with a bit of string he found
in the top drawer.

He placed it on the desktop and began making neat
piles of the books—some to keep, some to return to the
library. Everything else he tossed into the recycle basket.

Gaylinn's studio in the Arts Complex of the University was empty. The student in the adjacent studio, a
mousy-haired woman who looked like she hadn't had a
decent meal in a month, murmured that she never knew
where Gaylinn was, she wasn't any friend of *hers*. If
Terricel just walked in, it wasn't any business of *hers*.

The room smelled of paint solvent, and dayflowers.
Terricel closed the door behind him and sat down on
the stool in front of the oversized drafting table. He
remembered how, when he first started work on his proposal topic, they'd spread out the Starhall maps and

planned where to dig in the basements. Gaylinn had
teased him about being a mole at heart, and then they'd
laughed and made love on the big sofa. The lumps of
red and orange glass which she'd used to pin down the
maps now served as paperweights for pencil and charcoal sketches and portrait studies. She'd done a series of
one of her friends from Raimuth, a woman engineering
student who'd left the University suddenly last term.
Gaylinn had been quite upset about it at the time.

In the corner by the window stood a covered easel. It
bore a large stretched canvas, much bigger than Gaylinn
usually used. He walked over to it and lifted the muslin drape.

It was a study in oils, almost finished, the head and
torso of a young man, nude, lying on his back with his
face turned away from the viewer. The perspective, su-
perbly rendered, accentuated the lines of the jaw and
cheekbones, the sensuous curve of the collarbone, the
arch of the thin, slat-ribbed chest sloping down to the
velvet abdomen. The model's unkempt black hair fanned
out over the rumpled sheets. Sunlight filtered in from a
point above his head, deepening to blues and grays.

Terricel stepped back a pace to get a better look. The
skin tones were so lifelike that he almost expected to
see a pulse beating in the exposed neck. But lower down,
in the shadows, the flesh by degrees turned pale, as
smooth and perfect as marble. At the transition point,
right over the heart, there was just the hint of green, as if
a plant nearby had cast a reflection from its shiny leaves.

It was a master work, even he could see that. No student could have charged the canvas with such vitality
and such pathos. She had only to submit it to her committee and she'd receive her degree.

Terricel jerked the muslin cover over the canvas. He
paced back to the stool, sat down, and covered his face
with his hands.

She must have lain awake, watching him after they'd
made love, memorizing each line of his body. The way
his hair flopped away from the cowlick in back, the con-
tour of his shoulders, the faint shadows between the

muscles of his belly. He had slept on, unaware, even as the figure on the canvas did.

Terricel covered his eyes with his hands. He seemed to have grown a second skin beneath his own, like a layer of rotten bile. If only he could run, scream, sweat it out of his pores. If only he were a norther or one of those eastern nomads and had a god—any god—to cry out to.

The door latch clicked open and Terricel heard the rustle of full skirts and smelled the faint, sweet aroma of dayflowers. He opened his eyes. His vision swam as his retinas readjusted to the room's brightness.

Gaylinn, her dark brown curls tied back with an orange scarf, set down a basket of fruit on the sofa. "Terr? What are you doing here?"

She laid one hand on his shoulder. Her fingers felt warm and soft, yet the underlying muscles were hard. Once she would have taken him into her arms and held him, her body as round and strong as her artist's hands.

He jerked away from her touch. "I brought your seascape back."

"You took it down. . . ." Her eyes searched his. *Why? What's happened?*

"I gave my proposal today." *In case you'd forgotten.*

"And it didn't go well?"

"Not go well? Not go— What a joke!" He began to pace. A strange, hot energy boiled up in him, making him careless of his words. "My committee—those acidic bastards—they're so scared of Esme, all they could think of was what would happen if I dug up the Starhall, not whether I found anything or not. They don't give a contaminated damn for the truth. They're nothing but a pack of bootlickers."

He whirled around to face her, gesturing wildly. "The worst part is they didn't even have the guts to fail me. Just gave me a 'no show' to save their forking asses with my mother. And for about half a second I was actually *grateful* to have a second chance—I must have been an idiot to think I could have an academic career! I might as well follow in Esme's footsteps and have done with it."

Gaylinn nodded, chewing her lower lip. "I'm sorry you had a hard time. But do you think you're the only one to fool yourself? The only one to make stupid choices of what to do with your life? People have all sorts of dumbshit reasons—trying to please their parents, or wanting to kick their teeth in, or some half-assed compromise like yours."

"That's easy for *you* to say," Terricel grumbled, sounding very like the Pateros Brigade girl.

"Oh!" She waved one hand as if brushing away a cloud of pollen-flies. "This was pure batshit luck. I started out in my father's print shop back home in Raimuth, all set to take over the business with my big brother. But he started me doing illustration and saw how fired up I got. He even took my side when Father said *No* to University art training."

Terricel thought, *If Avi hadn't left, if she'd stayed, would she have fought for me, too?*

"The first painting I do as a master will be for him," Gaylinn said. "Maybe a portrait of his kids."

Portrait. Terricel's eyes went to the easel in the corner. "That's good," he said. "It's very good. A master's piece."

Gaylinn walked over, lifted the muslin cover and studied the canvas underneath, tilting her head and chewing on the inside of one cheek. "I haven't been able to work on it all week. That's why I covered the thing—it's an emotional piece, you see, and I couldn't face ... Now, coming back to it ... Yes, it *is* good."

It's me, isn't it? Why did you paint me like that—what did you see in me?

"I think it's good enough—" his voice came as if in a dream, detached from the anguish the painting evoked in him, "—to get your degree."

"That's not how it works in Art." She shook her head and lowered the muslin. "You do a solo show, a whole collection. I've got a gallery date for after Solstice, and that means working my ass off until then. This'll be in it." She picked up the seascape and unrolled it. "Maybe this, too. I'd forgotten how much I liked it."

"But you *are* almost finished—"

"Why, are you jealous?"

"What, me?" He forced a laugh. "And you'll go home then." Back to Raimuth as she always said she would, to be close to her large, affectionate family. She'd paint, maybe teach, marry, and have a houseful of laughing children.

"Yes," she said seriously. "I'd thought of staying here—the department's offered me a position—but now ... now I can't. I can't stay in a place where things like this happen."

"It could just as well have been Raimuth."

"But it wasn't, was it?" she retorted, tight-lipped. "It was *here* and I'll never be able to walk across the plaza without *remembering* ...

"Look," she said in a softer tone. "Anything's better than standing around arguing might-have-beens. Why don't we get out of here, maybe get roaring drunk for old times' sake? Someplace low and toxic, what do you say?"

"Low and toxic," he grinned at her. "Downright acidic. That's the best idea I've heard all day."

CHAPTER 10

THE ELK PISS SALOON.

The sign was a slab of unidentifiable wood, carved and painted with the figure of a quadruped with wildly improbable antlers. Time and weather had stripped away the color and most of the contours, leaving only a tracery of the original picture. The letters had been repainted, and only after staring at them for a moment did Terricel realize the original name was The Elk Pass Saloon.

The saloon occupied the ground floor corner of what was once a dockside warehouse. Above it, behind the shingled walls with their peeling green paint, lay the storage lofts and workshops of a furniture repair business.

Terricel pushed past the swinging doors and into the big, ill-lit room. A curved bar extended like a wooden tongue into the center and to either side, tables dotted the sawdust-covered floor. Shadowy doorways punctuated the far wall, bracketing a battery-lit tank where brightly-colored river jellyfish hovered and pulsated in the turbid water. At this hour, well past dinner but early yet, the place was still half empty. The barkeep, bald and jug-eared, looked up from wiping glasses and narrowed his eyes suspiciously when he saw Terricel.

Gaylinn walked up to the bar and slapped one palm on its pitted surface. "You old fart, what are you staring at? Are you working tonight, or volunteering for a blow-dart target?"

"Are you drinking tonight," he said out of one side of his mouth, "or just standing there, calling honest working folk names?"

"Only those who deserve it," she shot back.

They chose a table to the side and sat in cane-backed chairs which had undergone more than one reincarnation in the repair shop upstairs and were about due for another. The barkeep brought them pint mugs of frothy ale and plates of something steaming and unrecognizable.

The food turned out to be badly prepared salt-trout and potatoes, but it was hot and Terricel was surprisingly hungry. He found it was possible to disguise the off-flavors with generous amounts of ale.

Gaylinn sipped her ale and pushed her food around her plate with her fork. "Don't say you never imagined me in a place like this. It's where I go when I'm homesick."

"This—?" Terricel gestured toward the bar. The room was beginning to fill up with tradesmen, a scattering of ramblers off-shift at the docks, men and women with hard faces and drab-colored clothing. The smells of saw-dust and the jellyfish tank mingled with the sour tones of sweating, dubiously clean bodies. "You get homesick for *this?*"

"It's a lot closer to home—my real home—than the University is."

A chunk of greasy fish remained on his plate, but Ter-ricel's throat closed up and he couldn't eat any more. He threw his fork down with a clatter and shoved his plate away. His nerves itched. Gaylinn kept reminding him of the distance between them. He thought of how their closeness had ended, one misunderstanding after another. So different from the sunny afternoon when a fresh-faced art student had sauntered up and smiled at him. "Everyone says how stuck up you are," she'd said, "you being Esmelda's son and all that. You never say hello, as if you think you're too good for everyone else.

But I bet they're wrong. I bet I'd like you if I got to know you."

A girl in a rumpled smock came on duty as the barkeep's helper and went from table to table, refilling mugs. Terricel thought she looked vaguely familiar, but he couldn't place her. As she turned back to the bar, Gaylinn caught her arm and spoke a few soft words. The girl froze, head lowered. The girl's eyes flashed, the pupils dilated unnaturally against the glare of the fish tank.

"It's none of your business what I do! Who appointed *you* my Guardian?"

Terricel caught a whiff of the girl's breath and recognized the pungent reek of ghostweed. Trembling, she jerked out of Gaylinn's grasp, whirled and bolted for the inner doors.

"Wait here," Gaylinn said over her shoulder as she started after the girl.

"I'm coming with you." Terricel scrambled to his feet, almost overturning his chair.

She turned, hands on her hips. "I *said* I'll handle it."

Terricel caught her arm. "Look—"

"Damn it, Terr! Just stay out of this!"

Terricel remembered how stubborn she could be, how set on having her own way. He clenched his teeth together and didn't let go.

"You don't understand! I've got to get her out of here and she won't listen to me if you're there," Gaylinn said. "And yes, it's because you're Esme's son."

"Corrode it, Linni, I never expected *you*—"

"I don't have time to stand here and argue with you about it." She pulled away with such a look on her face that Terricel opened his fingers and let her go.

"I'm sorry tonight turned out this way," she added in a softer tone. "It isn't your fault, it's just that Silla needs me and you don't. I can't turn my back on her, not even for you. I'm not sure what you need, but it isn't me."

Chest heaving, Terricel watched Gaylinn disappear into the shadowy recesses of the saloon. He'd seen the girl somewhere before—then he remembered the portrait series in Gaylinn's studio. Her name was Silana or Silvena or something like that. She'd been developing a new communications system that nobody thought she'd ever sneak past the gaea-priests, but then she'd lost her stipend through some administrative foul-up and by the time it was straightened out, she'd left. Back to Raimuth, he'd assumed.

Gaylinn had been furious at him when he said it was just bad luck. "Look at what happened to Markill's uncle and his inventions," she'd said. "His sister's farm burned down and he ended up tending pigs. A master's in Applied Science, and he's *tending pigs!*"

"What are you hinting at?" Terricel had said. "There's some sort of conspiracy behind all this?"

"You of all people should realize that!"

" 'Me of all people'? What the hell does that mean?" he'd yelled, and that had been the start of one of their more explosive arguments. He wished—he didn't know what he wished—just that things didn't have to be the way they were.

He took a step backward, toward the bar, and bumped into a heavyset man in stained rambler's coveralls.

"Watch where you're going, mamma's boy." The stranger shoved Terricel in the chest with his knuckles, hard enough to sting. The ale-flush over the man's features mirrored the heat which instantly rose to Terricel's.

Something caustic and quicksilver surged through Terricel's veins instead of blood. "Watch who you're pushing!"

"I'll push anyone I crotting well like, any time I crotting well like, and there's nothing you or your bat-sucking mama can do to stop me."

Without any idea of what he was doing, Terricel swung at the man with all his might. His fist collided with the man's out-thrust jaw. A jarring shock shot up Terricel's arm and along his spine. The air turned bright in his lungs. His entire body recoiled from the impact. His knuckles went numb and then stung ferociously. He stared at his hand, momentarily astonished that he'd actually hit someone with it.

Suddenly a fist the size of his foot rushed straight at Terricel's nose, with the power of a heavy-muscled arm and shoulder behind it. Terricel caught a glimpse of

bared teeth and widened, bloodshot eyes before his re-
flexes took over and he ducked.

The stranger's fist clipped Terricel just above one ear.
He scrambled for balance, arms flailing. His feet caught
on something and he tripped. His hip slammed into the
edge of a table. Shouting pounded through his skull as a
distorted roar. Rough hands grabbed his shoulders from
behind, hauled him to his feet, and shoved him forward.

Weaving and bobbing, the rambler brought his fists up
in front of his face. His eyes glinted like polished metal
in the light from the fish tank. Although Terricel tried
to swerve, the next punch, a quick jab, caught him on
the cheekbone. His vision swam for an instant and his
eyes watered, but he felt no pain. He screamed and
lunged.

Faster than Terricel could blink, the rambler's foot
lashed out. The tip of the heavy leather boot caught
Terricel smack in the angle of his rib cage. His body
jackknifed over and the air burst from his lungs. For an
awful moment, he saw only the slow, sickening whirl of
the room.

The next instant, the rambler's fist smashed into Terricel's nose. His head exploded and the world burst into
black and red thunder. Pain lanced through his body.
His legs crumbled under him, but unseen hands dragged
him to his feet once more. Laughter pounded in his ears.
The rambler yelled something, Terricel couldn't tell
what.

More blows landed on Terricel's ribs and stomach. He
staggered sideways, blood spurting from his nose and
into his mouth.

"Hey, Jekk, give the kid a chance!" someone shouted.

The rambler straightened up, strutting and grinning.
"I'll give him a chance, all right! A chance to go home
in a medician's cart!"

As the rambler turned to glance at his audience, Terricel hurled himself at him. Terricel didn't think, he just
reacted to the instant the rambler's attention shifted. He
crashed into the rambler, knocking him off balance. The
rambler bellowed as he grabbed Terricel around the rib
cage with both arms. Terricel struck out with one fist

and then the other, not caring what he hit as long as he
hit something. His blows slipped off the hard-muscled
back, even as the rambler's arms tightened around his
chest.

A band of fire burst along Terricel's diaphragm and
his vision grayed around the edges. He struggled for
breath, but all that came was a strangled croak. All the
same, he kept on swinging and trying to kick. Suddenly
he felt the rambler's greasy hair under one hand. He
knotted his fingers in it and yanked hard. The man's
shoulders and torso jerked around, twisting sideways and
down. The crushing pressure lifted from Terricel's ribs.
He jumped back in surprise. Air flooded his burning
lungs. The next thing he knew, the rambler was lying at
his feet, splat on the sawdust floor.

Grunting curses, the rambler clambered to his feet.
Some distant part of Terricel's mind urged him to get
out of there now, before anything worse happened. Yet
he couldn't force himself to move. He could only stand
and stare, gulping air through his open mouth. Every
nerve danced and tingled. His skin turned to fire. He
wanted, more than anything else, for that corrosive bastard to get up so he could smash his face into bloody
splinters.

"Why, you little—" The rambler was on his feet now,
his face distorted and flushed. A knife appeared in his
hand, the light from the fish tank glinting off the deadly-
looking blade. He held it as if he meant to use it.

A burly figure stepped deftly between Terricel and the
rambler. Through a red blur, Terricel caught only the
shape of the man's shoulders and faded work shirt.

"Back off, Jekk, can't you see he's only a kid?"

"Ozone-frigging crot-sucker, he's gonna pay—"

"For what? For getting in a few lucky punches?
C'mon, that happens to all of us." The man in the work
shirt sidled forward, holding out one hand, open and
palm up. "Put the knife away and let's have another
round."

Terricel wasn't entirely sure what happened next, except that the rambler charged at him, the man in the
work shirt swiveled slightly, the rambler's knife went

straight past, made a tight arc and then ended up in the other man's hand. The rambler himself sprawled once more on the floor, this time facedown. A rumble of appreciative laughter rippled through the audience. The man in the work shirt turned and Terricel got a look at his face, homely, intent. Then the man grabbed the rambler by the back of his coveralls, heaved him to his feet, and shoved him bodily toward the front door.

Terricel watched them go. His heart pounded and his muscles ached. For an instant he thought of going after them. He sweated with wanting to hit something, *anything.* Then the silvery heat drained from his nerves as he realized what might have happened to him if the man in the work shirt hadn't stepped in. Shivering, he lowered himself into the nearest empty chair. The man in the work shirt came back a moment later, without either the rambler or his knife. Grinning, he clapped Terricel on one shoulder.

"How about that drink, kid?"

"Uhhh ..." Terricel's upper lip was wet with blood. He brushed his nose with the back of one hand and immediately thought better of it. The slightest pressure caused instant and excruciating pain. "Thanks, I really appreciate your helping me, but you don't need to buy me a drink."

"Harth's sweet tits, I was thinking of the reverse!" The man threw his head back and laughed. The sleeves of his dust-streaked shirt were rolled up, showing a line where the brown of his hands and muscular forearms gave way to incongruously milky skin. A tangy odor clung to him, a composite of animal sweat, manure, and sweet hay.

Somehow Terricel got to his feet, followed the man to the bar and slapped some money on the counter. "Barkeep, another round for my friend and me."

The man smiled as the barkeep set a full mug in front of him. He looked younger under the weatherworn wrinkles. Terricel thought with a start, *That could be me in ten or fifteen years.*

"Hold still." The man took out a clean-looking handkerchief, dunked it in the ale, and wiped it across his

nose, despite Terricel's moans. "Good, it's stopped
bleeding. You look almost human now. You'll have
some pretty souvenirs tomorrow to take home to
Mama."

Terricel lifted his fingertips to his nose and groaned.

"Your health." The man tilted his head back and took
a big swig. "Harth's health." Another big swig. "What
else? You're buying, you get to say."

"Hell, why not my mother's health?" *These days, she
needs all the help she can get.* Terricel gulped until his
breath ran out. He ordered another round.

"I had a mother once," the man said.

Not like mine, I bet. "Where was that?"

"Eh, you don't want to hear a bad luck story like
mine. Some of it might rub off on you. You tell me
yours."

"My mother? Toast her, then forget her, that's the
best."

"I'll drink to that." And they did. Shortly thereafter,
they adjourned to a table with a pitcher of ale.

"What's your name, friend?"

"Terricel."

"I'm Etch." He tilted his head toward the table of
onlookers, now absorbed in a dice game. "They thought
you were one of those University students."

"Me, too."

Etch grunted and returned to his ale in companionable
silence. Eventually, Terricel got him talking about himself. Like his father and grandfather before him, Etch
had raised horses on the high, rocky plains northeast of
the Inland Sea. Not as good for horses, he said, as the
Borderlands to the west, but good enough. Every season
the free-ranging horses were penned, wormed, rough-
broken, and turned loose again except for his working
stock and those he'd picked to train for sale. He didn't
earn much, but the work satisfied him.

Etch embellished the virtues and foibles of his favorite
horses—the stallion who got drunk on fermented wind-
fall apples, the runted gelding who could open any gate
devised by man, the mares who dropped twin foals year
after year.

"I had a mare once who could jump clear over a man's head and not mess a single hair," Etch said nostalgically. "She loved winter melon rinds, though they made her drool something awful. This man come buying stock to sell east, wanted her, wouldn't hear no. For his daughter, he said, as if I'd believe that. Probably for some eastern nomad to barbecue. I didn't want to lose the sale on the rest of them, not at the prices he was willing to pay, so I said fine, and when he came to collect 'em I'd loaded her up on the fattest, juiciest rinds I could find. She had green foam all over her muzzle and down her chest. She saw him, thought he had more, came running over, hightail. He changed his mind about her quicker than you could sneeze."

From there, Etch's story turned tragic. His wife and infant son had developed huge, lumpy tumors which distended their abdomens until they could neither eat nor breathe. When the local medician could offer nothing more, Etch mortgaged his horse farm and brought them to Laureal City, to the hospital. The boy died soon afterward, but the woman lingered on, as one treatment after another was tried. By the time she slipped away, the farm was forfeited. Etch was too proud to go back and hire on at someone else's ranch. He managed a stable on the northeast edge of the city, selling and renting horses to overland travelers. the place belonged to a city man who, according to Etch, *thought* he knew something about horses and ended up ruining them whenever he overrode Etch's advice, which was often.

"The work keeps me too busy to think most times." Etch glanced south, past the dingy walls. "I still have family back there—a sister and her kids. they run brush-sheep and she does a little weaving. Maybe someday I'll go back. It's only times like this, or Midwinter and Solstice, that I remember too much." He raised his mug to Terricel. "Here's to forgetting."

Terricel drank to forgetting.

Pound-pound-pound . . .

Someone kept clobbering Terricel over the head with sickening regularity. The bones of his skull had softened into exquisitely sensitive membranes, flexing and rippling with each blow. *Pound-pound-pound* ... Why didn't whoever it was just take an ax to his cranium and get it over with?

He opened his eyes. It was dark, and his teeth were coated with moss. Something bright wavered in front of his face and a wave of dizziness filled the interval between the beats of pain. His stomach gurgled and threatened to turn itself inside out. His nose throbbed. He touched it gingerly and wondered how something so small could generate so much pain.

"Awake, are we?" said a vaguely familiar, not unfriendly voice.

Terricel closed his eyes and rolled on his back. He was lying on something solid and much too hard. "It's the middle of the night," he groaned. Every part of his body seemed to be either bruised or stiff or both.

"Only an hour until dawn." Fingers dug into his shoulder, shaking him. "Here now, sit up and get this into you. You've got a walloping hangover or I'm a hoptoad's uncle."

Terricel forced himself up on one elbow, holding his head with the other hand. He groaned and took the glass thrust in his face. The drink, thick and hot, tasted of citron and cayenne. It burned all the way down, but his eyes opened wider.

"Etch, how could you do this to me?"

A chuckle from beyond the wavering light of a cheap solar lantern. "Maybe you'd rather I left you in a heap at the Elk's doorstep? A pretty boy like you, with money still in your pockets?"

"I guess I—"

"I didn't haul Jekk off you just to let those scum-bats have their turn. And I really needed another drink last night, but the barkeep doesn't give credit. I figured we were even and I dragged you home with me. Right now I've got to get some horses fed, but I fixed you my special concoction first. My uncle used to swear it'd cure anything from hangnail to scorbutics. He gave it to his horses, too."

"You dosed me with *horse tonic?*"

"It's probably too good for the likes of you, but what can I say? I got a kind heart." Etch slapped him on the back and stood up. Squinting against the lantern light, Terricel could barely make out his wavering form. "You can camp out here as long as you like, just clean up if you puke. It's not that I'm a trusting soul, but there's nothing worth stealing or I'd've pawned it last night. I don't expect you to believe me, but I'm not much for regular drinking."

Terricel tried to stand, sat back with a *plomp!* and buried his face in his hands. When he looked up again, Etch was gone. His head hurt, although less than before, and he didn't know where he was. Somehow he had to make his way home, wash and change, and drag himself to the Senate for the meeting this morning—among other business were the final plans for Pateros's funeral. As for the pain in his head and the roiling in his stomach, he deserved them as reminders of his own folly, if nothing else.

Holding his head with both hands, he got slowly to his feet. Windows ran along the wall in back of him, letting in a faint pink light. He could distinguish the outlines of furniture, the shadows of doors, two open, one closed.

A few steps into the center of the room and the slime in his mouth turned acrid. His stomach erupted into outright rebellion. He rushed for the nearest open door, praying he wouldn't end up in the kitchen. He did, and bent over the sink, heaving until nothing more came up. He ducked his head under the faucet and ran the water full cold over the back of his neck until he started shivering.

The other door led to a wide cobblestoned yard, filled with yellow dawn-light. Across the yard sat a huge barn with a bright blue star painted on it. Half a dozen men milled around with twice as many horses, some of them saddled and the others laden with packs.

One of the saddled horses, a black and white spotted animal that looked all legs to Terricel, stood up on its hind legs, whinnying. The man holding its reins waved his arms and cursed.

"No, not like that!" Etch appeared from behind two of the pack animals and took the reins of the spotted horse. He sidled up beside it, stroking its nose and speaking soothingly. Without turning to look at the other man, he said, "Get on, get on."

Terricel sat down on the wooden steps and watched Etch organize the chaotic assortment of men and animals into an orderly procession. They filed out of the yard, heading northwest.

"What a collection of fumble-footed twitterbats," Etch said. Shaking his head, he ambled over to Terricel. "The boss set this lot up. Another of his moneymaking schemes. If it was up to me, they'd be walking."

"Where are they headed?"

"The farming country past Oak Glen." Etch sat down beside Terricel. "They just might make it if they realize their horses have more basic common sense than they do. If I had half that much sense, I'd find some excuse to get out of here, too. What about you? You're looking better than the last time I saw you."

"I don't know if you saved my life with that horse tonic of yours or if I'm living to regret it," Terricel said. "I appreciate your taking me in, but truthfully, I don't know where I am."

"The Blue Star Stables, such as it is. Where do you need to get to on this fine morning?"

"Back to The Elk Pass will be good enough."

Etch narrowed his eyes. "So there's secrets behind that young face, are there? You keep them, friend, I've more than enough sad tales to last my own lifetime."

CHAPTER 11
Kardith of the Rangers

People hurried past me, some pulling their hoods forward over their faces, others bowing their bare heads to the rain. A few paused to open their umbrellas, bright round spots against the gray and purple.

The rain captured me as it always did, even on the Ridge. When I was fighting, I never felt it—the only way to stay alive was to not even know it was there. But there was never a time when I could just walk on, as if water from the sky were a thing that happened every day.

I'd seen rain before. It rained on the steppe—sudden, dark-moon downpours that burst into flash floods. This Laurean rain fell gently, pearling my hair and cloak. I lifted my face to it and tasted the pure soft water.

The taste carried memories of how I'd first come to Laurea ...

... running through the canyons that bordered the steppe, mile after mile of wind-eaten sandstone, with nothing but a knife and an old ghamel pack slung over one shoulder, stuffed with a stolen blanket and a few scraps of dried meat that didn't last long ...

... running until my legs could no longer hold me, never daring to look back, my breasts aching and finally drying up. Trapping small game when I was lucky and not too scared to stay in one place, once or twice beating off bandits ...

. . . sleeping huddled under rock ledges while the ice-tipped winds howled through the canyons. Drinking myself sick at each new stream to ease the cramping in my belly . . .

. . . running, hiding, running. And then, one day toward sundown, the sky half black with clouds, I came upon a little green valley with a stone hut and a trickle of wood smoke curling upward. Brush-sheep bleated from their pens and a dog barked. I could steal a sheep, but I wasn't sure I had the strength to carry it away. And if the owner caught me, I'd have to fight again.

Fight? I could hardly stand. I hadn't eaten in three days and the cuts on my back had broken open again and gotten infected.

Just then the door swung open and someone in a long sheepskin coat came out and stood there, staring at me.

I started down the slope, hands outstretched. My feet slipped from under me and I fell, the breath knocked out of me, fell and tumbled hard down the rocky slope. I lay there, too exhausted to care what happened next.

Beyond the hills, thunder rumbled. Moisture touched my face, cool as a blessing, trickling between my fever-parched lips. Smells arose around me—sweet grass, pungent herbs, the metallic stink of lightning.

I knew then that I was dead and the Mother had gathered me to her. She bent over me, her face shadowed in the dying light.

But it was a human face above mine, eyes buried in a mass of wrinkles, feathery gray hair braided loosely down her back. Gently she lifted me in her strong shepherd's arms.

I whispered, "Where . . . am I?"

"Laurea," she said. "You're safe in Laurea."

It seemed that half the city had gathered here in the plaza, rain or no. People moved out of the way when they saw my Ranger's vest. I moved through the crowd, uneasy from the closeness of so many strangers. My fingers kept touching my knives—long-knife, forearm knife, belt buckle.

A canopied platform had been set up for the people

too important to get wet, with more canvas stretched over a rectangular patch of earth. Some of the pale gray paving stones had been pried up and the plot lined with buckets of flowers. They'd bury Pateros where he fell and plant a tree on the place. It stood ready in its wooden pot, a well-shaped bronzewood that might live a hundred years or more. Longer than any of us would, that was sure.

On the Ridge, we burned our dead whenever we could, but on the steppe we had no extra wood. We placed the bodies of our Tribe up on great cairns of stone—funeral mounts, we called them—and offered them up to the father-god or Mother-of-us-all or whatever god bothered to answer our prayers. Actually, it was the bloodbats that came for them in the night, swooping down to suck out the last precious drops of moisture. In the morning there would be only scraps of paper-dry skin and scattered bones.

I wiped the rain from my eyes.

Damn.

When I came to Laureal City that first time, I never thought of the past. This was my new life, my whole life. I had no other. Now, wherever I turned, I saw the steppe all over again, pulling me deeper into things better left buried.

But not for long. This morning I'd been given a packet of orders for Captain Derron. Tomorrow I would be gone from this city, back to the Ridge where danger was something I could kill. For today, I had time for Pateros's funeral and that was all.

An old man stepped forward on the platform and lifted his hands for silence. The crowd settled down and, between the umbrellas in front of me, I caught glimpses of the people sitting up there out of the rain. A mass of gray Senate robes and the green of the Inner Council, the purple hoods draped over their shoulders.

Some trick of machinery magnified the old man's voice and sent it booming over the plaza. I listened for a few minutes but heard only words. The unbroken cycle of life, the great man living on in our noblest dreams, the strength of his legacy. Nothing but Laurean wishcrap. The old man gave way to another and their words rushed by me like so many dead leaves. I would turn my back on them if I could, but I was here to honor Pateros.

Now the gaea-priests with their bald heads and multi-colored robes came snaking along the cordoned-off pathways, singing and playing their flutes and drums. Their voices were like songbats in flight, one moment soaring together, the next moment breaking rank to weave and dart in amongst the others. They penetrated the crowd as if it were a labyrinth.

The people around me joined in the refrain, a simple melody, words that made no sense even as my lips silently shaped them:

> *"Ashes to ashes,*
> *Roots to roots,*
> *Let the circle be unbroken,*
> *O Life, we're one with Thee."*

Like I said, Laurean wishcrap.

The priests passed me, followed by six people carrying a railed pallet on their shoulders. They walked slowly, as if wading through honey. Montborne, his head bare in the rain, his face proud and stern like a hero's, his uniform a torch of color. Esmelda . . .

My throat clenched at the sight of her, strong as a tree in her flowing green robe, like a Laurean image of the Mother. If Montborne's face was a marble mask, hers was a mirror. Her eyes seemed to see everything and nothing. People murmured as she passed.

On the pallet lay a coffin wrapped in green silk, tied with ribbons of a dozen colors. As it went by, people threw flowers which slid off the silk to leave a trail of petals.

And tears. Around me, men and women began crying, some silently, others in strange, animal-sounding sobs. I could feel the calling in my bones—*Now is the time to weep.* But it had no power over me. My breath came easy behind my breasts, my heartbeat slow and regular. I stood here in honor, not in mourning.

You won't even mourn for Aviyya? a voice sifted through my mind.

I have not offered her up to the bloodbats. Not yet.

Then it came to me that there was nothing left to me but the promises I'd made. The one I spoke out loud, to Pateros and Laurea. The one I made silently, in my heart.

Once I ran away to save my own life. Now what will I do to save hers?

At the plot of earth, they set down Pateros's silk-wrapped coffin. Each pallet-bearer took a shovelful of damp soil and deposited it on the tarp the priests laid out. Soon the shovel passed to the Senators and other dignitaries, come down from their platform.

And now to the crowd. How the priests managed it with so many, I don't know, but there was something for each one of us to do, digging, lowering the coffin, burying it, planting the tree. By the time it was my turn, dirt covered the green silk. The man before me stood weeping for a moment, hands clasped in front of his body, and then moved on. I picked up a handful of flower petals, trampled and fragrant, and tossed them into the grave.

Words echoed in my head: *"Father-god, receive him well."*

Ay, what was the use of it? Dead was dead. There was neither father-god nor Mother, only darkness and the leering demon, laughing at us all.

I lifted my face to the sweet Laurean rain. *Laugh away, bastard god! It's not over yet.*

The gaea-priests climbed back on the platform for another round of wandering melodies and predictable dumbshit lyrics, composed a couple of centuries ago by someone with no sense of music. Now it was too late to do anything about it, the stuff was traditional. It went on too long, as everything official in Laurea did.

The shocky silence in the crowd seeped away. People around me first whispered to their neighbors and then spoke outright. A few of them shouldered their way toward the vendors, hawking food and drink on the edges of the plaza.

A vendor rolled his cooking cart by, crying out apples and sausages. He had plenty of takers. Me, too, although I should have known better. The sausages were soy, but steaming and spicy, wrapped in crispy fry-bread. I licked the juices from my fingers and continued making my way toward the platform. I didn't like crowds but I had nothing better to do except wait. Even with the City Guards pushing people aside, it was still too packed to push my way in. Eventually they would thin out and I'd be able to get through. Whether Esmelda would hear me was another matter.

We were a long time together on the Ridge before Avi told me who her mother was. "The only thing I ever wanted from her was my freedom," she said. "And I had to take it, like a thief."

Such pride, Avi had. "I'd never ask her for anything, not even if my life depended on it."

Once I ran away to save my own life. I had no pride left now, not even the pride of cowardice, to beg this formidable old woman for her daughter's life.

How did I know Avi was still alive? How did I know Esmelda could help? I only knew what I would have to live with if I didn't try.

I must have some pride left, after all.

An undertone in the crowd caught my ear. Not their words, something else ... I couldn't hear the pattern, couldn't feel what was going on, and that made me twitchy. Earlier I thought it was just the closeness of so many strangers with no fighting room, but now something prowled the plaza like a shadow panther. I'd seen them hunt gazelle on the steppe, crouching and rippling like gusts of sand, closer and closer, then suddenly the gazelle was dead and carried half a mile away before it realized what had happened.

The twitches must have been left over from that day with Pateros. I didn't trust this place, this vast and terrible place. Anything could happen here.

Damn.

Uniforms clustered thickly around the platform, City

Guards black and military bronze-and-red. Some looked too young to be soldiers, their faces too grim and too quick to show anger. They had none of the look of hard training. One kid in uniform shoved another in civilian clothing.

"I told you to stand back!"

"Who gave you the right?" the other kid snapped back, his fists up and ready. His body said, *Come on, try me.*

The nearest City Guard stepped between them. "Both of you, out of here."

I stood beside him and together we watched the boys edge back into the crowd. I kept my hands in plain sight, resting on my belt. The guard was a good ten years older than me, a little soft around the edges and pumped up with working the crowd, but not above a friendly nod for a Ranger. I nodded back and jerked my head in the direction the kid in the uniform had disappeared.

"What's that? Nursery recruits?"

"No, the new Pateros Brigade." By his voice, he didn't think much of it.

The rain let up now, umbrellas folded up, hoods shoved back. I heard a rumble in the crowd over toward the Starhall, like the shadow panther's snarl. The Guard frowned, though he wouldn't leave his post.

I couldn't see anything from here. "What's in the wind?"

He frowned harder. "Hard to say. There was some action by the western ferry last night, a bunch of those Brigade kids and some ramblers. Kids'd heard they might be norther spies and jumped them. Ramblers, they're pretty tough. You bash them, they bash you back."

"Standoff."

He grunted. "Bashed heads all round."

"Northers wouldn't hire Laurean ramblers for *any* reason," I pointed out.

"That's what I would've said, too. I get along fine with anyone who stays on his own side of the border." His eyes narrowed. "But now I think we trusted them too much." He didn't have to tell me who he meant by *them.*

I glanced toward the platform. "Any chance of getting me through?"

"Not a chance. What do you want?"

"To see Esmelda."

He laughed. "*Double* not a chance."

I waved, half-salute, and wove back into the crowd. Maybe if I got close enough, Montborne would clear me through the Guards. But then ... How could I tell Esmelda about Avi with *him* there?

I came to a standstill, sweating and muttering curses. Quick short breaths, trying to calm down enough to think—

It happened suddenly, practically under my nose. Shouts and scuffling. Guards jumping up and pushing people aside. "What's happening? What? Where?"

"Traitor!"

"They've caught a traitor!"

"Sold us out to the northers!"

The next instant everyone was screaming and running, nobody knew where—eyes wide, elbows and fists and folded umbrellas everywhere. The air stank of panic.

"Help! Help!"

"Out of here! I've got to get—"

"Get him!"

"Traitor? Where?"

"TRAY—TOR!"

Then there were no more words, only deafening noise. Bodies slammed into me, I twisted away, staggered, and somehow kept my feet. There was no direction to this thing, no focus I could see. Nothing to draw a knife against.

I heard a high-pitched scream, like a hamstrung brush-sheep, and remembered stories of them stampeding, trampling each other to bloody shreds. For the first time, I felt the clear danger in the crowd.

I pushed my way past the Guards and on to the platform, just as if I were sent there to help. From even this little height, I saw them, east of the platform—the knot of struggling bodies, maybe a few people fallen, Guards and Pateros kids striking out with their batons, others with bare fists. Everyone else was trying to get out of the plaza.

I glanced back. The Senators and Inner Council people looked frightened, the gaea-priests calling for calm. Montborne had gone off to one side, giving orders to his officers.

He gestured to the dignitaries. "My people will escort you back to the Starhall."

"My place is here—" began the head priest.

"It's too dangerous, Markus," Montborne said. "The crowd down there is unpredictable and dangerous. My men and Orelia's are trained to handle situations like this."

"But—"

"Just *go*." He shoved the priest down the steps at the back of the platform and into the arms of two uniformed men. The Senators filed down, glancing around them anxiously. Montborne spotted me and motioned me over.

I took the arm of the nearest, a woman in Inner Council green. The same red-haired woman who tried to save Pateros. Her face looked chalky, her eyes wide. I helped her down the steps.

A hand, fingers thin but sinewy, touched my arm. I looked down into Esmelda's gray eyes. I saw a strange expression in them, a hardness like granite, yes, but also a questioning, as if she almost recognized me. Me, or the Ranger's vest?

Her chin moved imperceptibly toward the mob below. "My son's down there." Her voice was grim and low.

The boy with rainwater eyes and Avi's black hair . . .

Then she would owe me, this formidable old woman, then she would *have* to listen to me. I nodded, got her down the steps and blended back into the throng.

This time I saw the crowd for what it was, an enemy with no real weapons and no brains to speak of, only the weight and number of its bodies. Only its flash-flood shifts in mood and direction.

I'd learned a trick on the Ridge, how to focus my will as if it were a physical thing. I saw an invisible spearpoint, my body at its base, one hand stretched in front

of me with the outside edge like a knife chop. I moved
rapidly through the milling people. They drew apart for
me. A stick swung at me at head-height, not a Guard's
baton but a thick length of wood. I slipped past and it
didn't even touch me.

A knot of bodies lay at my feet, curled up and screaming, a few lying flat, others bending over them crying,
calling for help in voices that couldn't be heard above
the racket. More men and women on their feet, pushing
their way toward the nearest street.

A boy, a boy with rainwater eyes ...

He wasn't down, not in this bunch. Quickly I searched
the others before they surged away. The crowd, the
many-headed enemy, shifted direction. It seethed toward
the center of the plaza like the sky before a twister.
Like tinder waiting for a spark, it hovered on the edge
of panic.

Behind me, up against the base of the platform, I
heard new screams and curses. I ignored them. Over by
the grave site, I saw another struggle and some instinct
drew me toward it. Once or twice some headblind fool
barreled into me. I bruised a few ribs and twisted a few
shoulders keeping free.

A man in rambler's coveralls, who reminded me a
little of Westifer at his worst, had squared off with a
red-faced boy in a Brigade uniform. People scrambled
out of their way, leaving a little open space. Swinging a
homemade baton, the kid screamed that the man was a
spy and a traitor. A fighting madness ran all through
him that no words could cool.

The rambler roared like a cornered bull elk and
bunched his shoulders. A knife slipped down the back
of his sleeve. The hilt smacked into his cupped palm,
the blade along his forearm so the kid couldn't see it.

I shoved through the tight-packed throng just as the
rambler, his back to me, drew back for a killing sweep.
The kid was wide open, throat and belly, no sense of
what was coming, all blind devil-dare, with his friends
darting forward and shouting him on.

I sprinted for the rambler and kick-stomped the back
of one knee. It broke his stance long enough for me to

land a knife-hand chop to the nerves in his forearm. His fingers jerked open. I slid my hand down his wrist and twisted the knife away. The next moment, the three Brigade kids rushed him.

Then I was fighting for my own skin, the rambler's buddy after me with a long curved knife, a sword, really. The rambler's knife was badly balanced, but I had no time to change it for one of mine. I spun and landed a side kick in one kid's solar plexus. Mother, he had a knife, too, and no sense of how to use it. But in these close quarters—

The rambler somehow got another knife and held it horizontal, backhand grip, blade level with my throat. Crazy in his eyes.

I pivoted and raised my knife for a down-stab, moving slowly so he would see it, would react and be drawn away from my real target—the man with the curved sword. I twisted and lunged sideways, past his reach as I reversed my stroke. Curved-sword saw it too late and jumped back. My knife tip ripped open the side of his thigh. A heartbeat later, I reversed again, same arc, other blade edge, slashing for his hamstrings. He jumped away again, blood drenching his coverall leg, and stumbled up against the edge of the crowd. A young woman in full skirts screamed as he landed on top of her. Two Brigade kids, knives raised, dove for him.

"Behind you!" someone shouted.

My body moved before I could think. I swerved to one side and pivoted around, one hand up in guard, the other holding the knife low by my leg. I sank slowly, gathering strength from the earth. My thighs tingled, ready to explode.

It was the rambler again, one shoulder cut open, coverall sleeve in strips. His eyes met mine, reading me. Breathing hard, his chest heaving. He was no fool and he'd seen blood before. He'd seen death. But he'd never seen me. Never seen the steppe knife-forms, honed by Brassaford and all those years on the Ridge.

The tip of his knife wavered. His eyes darkened, searching for a way to back out. There was a brief, sudden quieting of the crowd.

I forced myself to think. Not feel, not act—*think.* Pateros or Montborne or even Derron back on the Ridge would have found something to say—*"I'm not your enemy"* or *"Let's all back off"*—and then this whole damned showdown would be over.

The moment passed before I could wet my lips. Screams and cries rang out behind me. The rambler's eyes went wide and white. The knife disappeared back into his coveralls. Cursing, he pushed past me. I turned just as he hauled a Brigade kid off the tangle of bodies.

On the ground, Curved-sword rolled to his side, moaning. A wound bubbled from his upper thigh, up near his groin. The rambler knelt above him. His hands dripped with the bright, copper-stinking blood.

I dropped the knife and shoved him aside. Grabbed a scarf from a shock-eyed woman clambering to her feet. Wadded it over the spurting blood and leaned on it with all my weight.

Someone shrieked for the medicians. The scarf was already slippery under my hands. A sickening quiet settled over the crowd. People watched me with drawn, horrified faces.

Mother, let it be a nick and not cut through. I saw a man once cut like this and live, but it was a small artery in his shoulder. *The medicians couldn't save Pateros— what can they do for this poor fool?*

Just beyond Curved-sword's outstretched arm, I noticed a black-haired boy on his knees, cradling a young woman in his arms. Dark brown curls spilled out beneath her orange kerchief. Her face was white except for wine-dark lips and the ashy smudges beneath her closed eyes. There was blood everywhere, but I couldn't tell whose.

The boy looked up with eyes of rainwater and steel, so like Avi's and yet not like. Except for a faded bruise on one cheekbone, he looked soft and pale, as if he'd never faced anything harder than how to open a book. Even so, the light in those eyes was as hungry as any I'd ever seen.

"Your mother sent me," I said.

He couldn't hear my voice above the crowd, but he

understood me well enough. His face, locked in ice one moment, turned fluidly expressive the next but so tangled I couldn't read it. I could only imagine what Avi would have said in the same situation.

Now the City Guardsmen came pelting through. I got to my feet and smelled the shift in the crowd—the drawing back. Someone said, "Medician's station this way." People helped the injured to their feet and Guards cleared them a path. They carried the bleeding man, keeping pressure on the cut.

The boy—Esmelda's son, Avi's brother—tried to pick up the girl. He had no idea how to lift her. I could have slung her across my shoulders like a dead gazelle, but something held me back.

A medician, an older man, bent over her, shook his head, covered her face with another woman's fringed shawl. The boy stood up. He watched as two women from the crowd lifted the girl and carried her off, then turned, scanning the platform. His mouth twisted, his eyes dry as the steppe, and again I couldn't read him.

I jerked my head toward the Starhall. His eyes narrowed—good, he'd understood. He took a quick breath, gathering himself, and walked away from me.

CHAPTER 12

Esmelda's house, a homely, squarish lump of stone, paled in the glow from the solar lights along the walkway. It seemed to me to have pulled itself upright, as if it didn't want to get too close to its neighbors, shivering in a cold no one else could feel. It was an extravagance, even I could see that, two stories for just a single family—if you counted these three a family. Esmelda. The boy with eyes the color of Avi's. And someone else I hadn't seen clearly, only as a blurred backlit shadow against the half-drawn curtains.

The sky had gone lightless hours ago as I watched the house from the shelter of a tree on the opposite side of the street. The leaves hung thick and low, bitter-clean after this morning's rain. The smooth bark invited me to lean against it. In Laureal City, even the trees presented temptation.

For all my hours of waiting, I still didn't know what I was going to say. Everything I'd rehearsed was no dumbshit good. But the time for waiting had passed.

A few strides brought me to the walkway. The door was smooth wood, with no fancy carvings. Beside it hung a ceramic bell shaped like a hang-me-down flower, with a wooden stick to tap it. The sound was full and mellow. A moment later I heard footsteps inside.

A woman opened the door, small and tight-faced beneath a coil of white hair. Eyes with hidden light, we'd say on the steppe. Her gaze flew to the empty sheath on my thigh, for I'd left the long-knife with the gray mare's gear. I needed a different sort of weapon tonight.

"Yes?"

"I'm here to see Esmelda."

She blocked the opening with her body. "No."

"I know she's here." *Lie to me, mouse, and I'll break your neck.*

"She sees no *strangers.*" She slurred the word so it sounded like *Rangers.*

The woman pulled back a fraction to close the door. I slammed one shoulder into it and the next instant I was inside. On one side of the narrow entry sat a table littered with papers. On the other, a staircase with a carved banister and a corridor leading beyond it. Two doorways, everything low-lit except for the right-hand room.

Before I could head for it, she darted in front of me again, grabbing my arm. She had courage, this little Laurean mouse.

A woman's voice from the light room: "Lys?"

She faltered and I jerked away, an easy disengage that sent her staggering. The next moment I was through the doorway.

The room was bright after the dim light of the entry. White walls with woven hangings in sand-blown color, soft upholstered furniture. A low table with more papers and books, candles adding to the glow from the panels of solar lights. A carpet with a graceful, muted design. A room, I thought, for people who didn't get dirty.

Esmelda sat bolt upright in one of the chairs. The boy on the sofa jumped to his feet. His eyes had the look of someone too shocked to cry yet and I thought of the dead girl in the orange scarf. She must have meant something to him. Behind me, the mouse-woman said, "I tried to stop her—"

"It's all right," Esmelda said quietly.

Suddenly the room went still, except for my breathing, rasping as if I'd run all the way here from Pateros's grave. My head filled with the honey-sweet smell of the burning wax.

Esmelda waited, her eyes never leaving mine, metal gray that no candlelight could ever warm. Behind her, the boy as tense as a coiled viper. The mouse-woman disappeared back into the shadows.

"So, Kardith of the Rangers," Esmelda said. "Kardith of *no place* but the Rangers."

A hard one, this old woman.

The boy's eyes flickered—to me, back to her again. Wondering how she knew my name. So did I.

"Have you come to collect a reward?" Her voice was dry as a whip. She meant, for looking after the boy this morning.

I shrugged. The boy was a faceless, voiceless nothing. Like the young Guardsman who couldn't find the courage to ask how Pateros died. To hell with both of them. I wasn't here to play nursemaid.

But I didn't expect how hard this would be. For a moment, I couldn't make my tongue move. Something rose up inside me like freezing mud, choking me, drowning me. When I forced the words out, they sounded barely human.

"For Avi—I've come for Avi."

She watched me, still unmoving.

Not going to make it easy for me, are you, you old she-dragon? If it were just me, I'd walk out of here now.

"Avi," I repeated. "Your daughter."

For a moment I thought she would say, *"I have no daughter."* Avi told me that Esmelda cared more for power than her own family, that she sucked people dry like a bloodbat. "Not me," Avi'd said. "I've got my own life."

My own life. Mother-of-us-all!

"Esme?" The boy broke the overlong silence.

"When my daughter left my house, she made it clear she no longer wanted anything to do with me. No obligations either way. Those were her very words. Has she changed her mind?" A hint of scorn for such weakness of will. Or maybe triumph, that Avi would be so desperate to come crawling back, she had to send a messenger to plead for a truce first.

"Never!" I stammered, sweating, all the words I'd rehearsed outside forgotten. "But she's gone. I mean— she's disappeared. Out on the Ridge. Two weeks gone and no sign. She could be hurt, dying, killed by northers."

One eyebrow lifted. *And you expect me to do something about it?*

"I went looking on my night shifts until the captain— he put me on double to stop me. I couldn't get far enough from the fort between shifts and I knew I'd be caught if I missed a go. It's not as if none of us cares. We all— Avi's one of us. She fished one man out of a norther ambush—took a spearpoint meant for someone else." *And me, never mind about me.* "A dock in pay or a week's fort duty, that's easy for someone who'd risked her neck for you. We wouldn't stop looking until— But there's orders, new orders."

"Orders?" Again that whipcrack voice. Her eyes glittered as they went hard and narrow.

"From Montborne. Six months ago. Pull back the patrol lines. No wandering, no 'unauthorized expeditions,' no exploring, no provoking—no searching."

She stared at me as if I were a gutless sandbat.

"If it were just a pack of Mother-damned rules, do you think I'd be standing here now? I'd be out there searching and to hell with them. But the new penalty for insubordination, it's—*handing!*"

Now the room turned cold and still and dark, despite the candles and the solar lights. The old woman sat like a shadow panther watching a gazelle. But I was no gazelle.

"Handing?" the boy asked, flat voiced.

"The loss of a hand—usually the right," she said. "It's said to be a norther custom."

What was the old dragon thinking now, sitting there not even breathing? The boy watched her, too, and in his face I glimpsed something dark and nameless. Reckless, unformed. But hard, hard like steel.

"Aviyya left my house to make her own life," Esmelda said. Her words were slow and final as the Laurean river bells, tolling through the night-long fogs.

The bells that Avi always said sounded like the souls of drowned men.

Cold trickled through me. I had no answers for her, no pleas, no honey-tongued persuasion. For a moment I cursed myself for not having the right words, as if there were some magic in them to unlock her heart. But it was impossible. Even if he were still alive, not even Pateros could have moved her.

"I know you and Avi didn't ... agree," I stumbled on, cursing myself doubly for my weakness. "But she's your own, your child. That's got to count for something!"

Avi told me again and again that her mother's heart was harder than any stone, but in the end there must have been a link between them. I remembered my stepfather singing to me and my brothers through the howling, sand-swept nights. I remembered how he defied the Tribal ban and taught me knife-forms, saying I was his daughter as much as if he'd truly fathered me and he meant to give me the means to protect myself. I remembered the first time I held my son in my arms and such a feeling came on me, the tie between us that neither water-plague nor raiders could ever break. Surely Esmelda must remember something of that.

She shook her head. "Give it up, Ranger."

"At least tell me why!"

"I can take no action. None."

"What if it were me, lost out there?" the boy asked in a low, tight voice. "What then?"

"My answer must be the same." She turned to face him, a feral movement quick as a striking snake. There was something in the way she held herself, some hidden passion. "'There are some things which go beyond personal loyalties, beyond even love."

"What things?"

A tightening of her lips as she weighed what she should say, what she *could* say. Ay Mother, so much going on here I could only guess at!

"What things?" he repeated, his voice breaking. "More of your damned secrets, like the ring? I asked

you once what was really going on here? Are you saying the fate of all Harth is balanced against my sister's life?"

Quick, he was. From her expression, he'd hit too close to something he shouldn't know. She placed one hand on his and for the first time I noticed the ring she wore, heavy gold, the deeply incised design of two concentric circles around a single point. Nothing of the desperate tension in the boy's body lessened.

"Avi made her choice," Esmelda said. "She knew the risks. She didn't want my help."

He leaped to his feet, her hand thrust aside as if it might bite him. Me, I wondered just what sort of viper's nest I'd stumbled into.

To hell with them and their secrets!

Waiting wouldn't get me any help for Avi, only deeper into this quick-mire. I turned and headed for the door. Behind me I heard the boy's voice, muted. There would be no screaming fights like Avi told me about, not for him. I didn't think Esmelda would tell him why, either, only to keep his mouth shut and his nose where it belonged. Hell, Avi was his sister, what else should he do? But he'd lived his whole life in the shadow of this old bloodbat; he was probably halfway to being just like her.

Outside the door, the mouse-woman waited, her little hands knotted into fists. She shot me a look of pure hate.

"I didn't lay a finger on your precious magistra." I pushed past her, through the still-darkened entryway. She slipped around me and had the front door open before I could reach it.

The night swallowed me up.

I cut across the streets through the stench of crushed flowers, my running feet as sure as if they had eyes of their own. The night surrounded me, filling me with a broken darkness, a madness almost. It would pass, I knew, this dawn or the next. Or the next. Until then, I would do whatever I had to do to survive, just as I always had.

The next moment, it seemed, I was standing in the plaza in front of a newly planted tree. The place was not yet deserted, even at this hour, with late mourners still drifting by. Before my eyes, the Starhall blazed as if on fire. Everything looked pale and sickish in its light, like things grown too long underground.

It came to me that whatever was broken inside me happened not this night, nor even this week, but a long time ago. On a night lit with torches instead of candle-lanterns or these Mother-damned solar lights. The wind blew in fitful gusts up on the funeral mount. I still heard it in my dreams.

I still felt the blood streaming down my back to lure the bloodbats down to me.

Mother, why must I still remember? I've run, I've killed, I've frozen in that damned Kratera mud. And still it comes back to me, that night!

There was no answer. There never was. Or maybe the demon god of chance knew and kept it to throw in my face before I died.

Now I knelt on the smooth Laurean stone, jamming my knuckles into my eyes as if to gouge out the visions there. For the first time, I noticed the smell of the new-turned earth. The slender trunk, the leaves glimmering in the unsteady light of the candle-lanterns set about the shrine.

One by one I opened my fingers, each joint a slower heartbeat, a steadier breath. I held my hands out in front of me and they did not tremble.

I was not alone. I froze, searching for the shadow behind me. A man, I thought, from the feel of him. I slid a knife hilt into my palm, body-warmed and solid. I could spin around, be on my feet and the blade halfway through his guts before he knew I'd even moved. Blood smelled better than flowers or grave dirt.

I wouldn't do it. This was Laureal City, after all, not the Ridge. Not the steppe. Pateros promised me it would be different here.

Is it? Is it ever different anywhere?

Slowly I rose, slowly turned. The boy's face shimmered in front of me like a polished skull. No more rainwater eyes, but pits of darkness.

Movement at the edge of the plaza. More mourners,

still too far to hear more than their murmured voices. The skull-faced boy followed me into the night.

"Look," he said when I paused. For an instant I heard steel in his voice and then it was gone. "You need— *Avi* needs help." One shoulder jerked back toward the big, empty house. "I don't know what the hell is going on or why—but I'll find a way to get it for you."

"Wishcrap." Even the mouse-woman would be more use than this pale, city-soft boy.

"I'm her brother, damn it!" His body tensed as if he'd like to grab me and shake me. He didn't—the first sign of sense he'd shown yet. "There's got to be— I'll find something. I swear I will!"

"Forget it, cub. I'm leaving at dawn."

But his curses, shouted into the night, brought me a strange and unexpected comfort.

CHAPTER 13
Terricel of Laureal City

A solar lantern brightened the usually dim entryway. The rest of Esmelda's huge house lay dark and silent, except for the faint, almost secretive creaking as it surrendered its warmth to the night. Just inside the door, beside the table piled with notebooks and correspondence, a travel pack sat on the floor. It was made of soft, oiled leather, with buckled outer pockets and felt-padded shoulder straps. Alongside lay a woolen cloak, neatly folded, and Terricel's best pair of boots.

Leaving the front door to swing closed behind him, Terricel knelt in amazement beside the pack and clothing. When he'd stormed out of the house, he had no idea he'd have any need for travel gear. But someone else had known: Lys, who'd tried in her own way to be the mother Esmelda never was.

At first he couldn't believe that Esmelda refused to take action, even for her own daughter. He'd pleaded with her, "How could you turn the Ranger away? Couldn't you at least say you'd think about it?"

"Why give her false hope?"

"It's because of Montborne, isn't it?" he cried with a strange, savage desperation. "You're afraid that whatever you do, he'll find out."

Age lines deepened in Esmelda's face, foreshadowing her death mask. "I can't afford to give him a single ..."

She paused, as if searching for the right word. "... a single weapon to use against me."

"I don't understand. Montborne's ambitious, certainly, but there's no question about his loyalty to Laurea. You could do worse than bargain with him."

"I have no choice in the matter. As long as Pateros was alive, he kept Montborne in check, but now ... Montborne may be a Laurean patriot, but I have to think on a larger scale. He could well be a destabilizing force for all of Harth." She lifted one hand, a fluttery gesture so unlike her it startled Terricel into silence.

"I've already said more than is safe for either of us," she said, twisting the ring with the dotted circle on her finger. "I won't make that mistake again."

Terricel had roamed the streets for what seemed like hours, too flaming angry to think what else to do. He thought of seeking out Etch at The Elk Pass, as he had a number of times since that first night, but he wanted something more than a few hours of drunken oblivion and another fight with Esmelda the next morning.

By some miracle, he found the woman Ranger, Kardith, on her knees in front of Pateros's grave like some kind of pilgrim. She turned her back on him, all but laughed at his offer of help. After all, why should she believe him? Why should she have anything to do with him?

He'd stood there in the plaza after Kardith left. Above him a formless darkness hovered and at his feet lay pale smooth pavement. An ice-edged wind lashed across the open space, cutting through his skin as if he had turned into the marble figure of Gaylinn's painting.

Gaylinn ... Terricel's throat ached until it turned numb. The wind howled her name as it scoured away his flesh and bones, leaving nothing of him but words. His University master's words, Montborne's words, Esmelda's words—all patched together to make something which walked and talked and looked like a man. The years of working and waiting and secret imagining— nothing but words.

Now other words came unexpectedly boiling out of

him, words he'd never even whispered aloud before,
words that made all the usual obscenities sound pale and
safe. No one knew what they meant anymore, except
maybe the most highly placed gaea-priests.

Finally he paused for breath, his throat half-frozen,
and noticed the people who'd gathered around Pateros's
tree. No one said anything to him. Their expressions
were unreadable in the eerie Starhall light—disapprov-
ing perhaps, sympathetic, maybe even grateful he was
doing their cursing for them.

As he wandered from the plaza, a feeling began in
him, condensing with the sharp-edged clearness of an ice
crystal, a feeling out of all the horrors of the past week—
the assassination, the funeral, the planning and scheming, the riot, the blood—there was only one thing which
touched him, which moved him beyond his old life.

Everything else was to be endured and survived, like
the thing beneath the Starhall. He could feel it even
now, as if it had become a permanent part of him, and
suddenly the taint of it became more than he could bear.

Aviyya needed help. Terricel clung to the thought as
the single reality in his life. He couldn't do a damned
thing for Pateros. *Or for Gaylinn, either.* His academic
career was a bad joke. As for being Esmelda's heir, he
was nothing more to her than a convenient secretary. If
only there was some place he could go where no one had
ever heard of Esmelda of Laurea or the Inner Council or
even the University.

No wonder Aviyya had run as fast and as far as she
could.

"Half of what's wrong with you," Gaylinn once said,
"is that you've grown up with just Esmelda and her off
most of the time saving the world. The other half is that
you've never done anything to change it."

"There was Lys," he'd said.

And Avi ... Part sister, part mother, who was she
now?

Suddenly the darkened city streets faded before his
eyes. He saw Aviyya, her face pale under streaks of
blood, her black hair tangled with mud and leaves. She
was struggling up a mist-cloaked embankment. She

paused, breathing hard, her breath coming in puffs of vapor. Then her gray eyes went cloudy, as if she somehow sensed his presence. Abruptly, the image vanished.

The Ranger woman, Kardith, she'd been out there on Kratera Ridge with Aviyya. Aviyya was important to her, too, in some desperate way he could only guess. What lay between them, bound them together, went beyond simple comradeship. It had taken the threat of mutilation to bring her to Esmelda, and she wasn't the kind who found begging easy.

She had no reason to help him, and he would have to find some way to convince her. He needed directions, maps, woodscraft. There was nothing he could do that she couldn't do a hundred times better. But he had one overwhelming advantage, if he could find the courage to use it. *He* didn't take orders from Montborne.

Back in the entryway to Esmelda's house, Terricel sat down, pulled on the boots and inspected the contents of the traveling pack. The pockets were filled with packages of concentrated food bars, a generously stocked money belt, and a selection of his own clothes, the most warm and durable he owned.

A shadow caught his eye—Annelys, clutching her robe around her thin shoulders. She stood, bleached and squinting, in the lantern's glare.

"Did my mother put these here?" Terricel indicated the pack.

The old steward shook her head.

"But does she *know?* Lys, is this her idea? Because if it is—"

"You'll what? Stay here just to spite her? Listen to me. I brought up her tisane and she said to me, 'I've lost him. I've lost them both.' You think she doesn't know what she's done? To Avi and now to you? She knows what she did to Avi, all right, forcing her into secrets that were none of her own choosing. And she knows what it did to you to keep those same secrets from you. That's why she's lying upstairs right now, waiting for you to leave."

Unable to reply, Terricel clambered to his feet. Annelys scooped up the pack and cloak. She shoved them into his arms.

"Now this is something she doesn't know. You want a life of your own, this is your chance. You go out there and find your sister, do you hear me? But don't you bring her back. You keep right on going! This family's suffered enough from Esme's secrets."

"Lys—" He took her in his arms. She hugged him back with unexpected ferocity, as if she never expected to see him again.

"Enough with good-byes! I've served Esme for thirty years and never once have I faced her in tears!"

There was no more Terricel could say to her. He backed out the door and paused for a moment on the steps, listening and knowing he would hear nothing.

He looked out across the city that had been his world. Here the solar-stored light burned all the night long and kept the shadows from growing too deep or too cold. Here the people lay safe and dreaming in their beds. What had they to fear? Montborne would keep the northers at bay, and if they no longer had Pateros to guide them, they still had Esmelda.

When Terricel arrived at the Blue Star Stables, he found the house dark and silent. A flickering lantern hung crookedly from the railing, but a second, stronger light streamed through the partly opened barn door. As he approached it, Terricel heard the sounds of animals chewing fodder.

Inside the barn, the horse smell was thicker, mixed with a sweet, musty odor. Bits of straw littered the hard-packed dirt of the central aisle. A large lantern, in better shape than the one outside, swung from the rafters. A half-dozen horses, their sizes and colors shadowed, poked their heads over the stall doors, ears pricked and nostrils twitching. From the far end came a man's voice, low and indistinct.

"Hello?" Terricel called. "Hello, Etch?"

In answer came a squeal and a bellowed curse. Terricel hurried to the large box stall at the opposite end of the barn and peered over the wooden door. Etch stood behind a speckled-white horse, his shoulder tucked under the tail at an improbable angle. The horse's legs splayed out, its rounded sides heaving. Blood streaked its hind legs and matted the straw bedding.

The horse squealed again and began thrashing its head, which was tied by a stout rope to the wall.

"What the hell!" Etch shouted. "Who's there?"

"It's me. Terricel."

"Harth's sweet ass, boy, don't just stand there! Grab her head, quiet her down. The foal's crosswise and if I can't turn it, we'll lose both of them."

Terricel dropped his pack and managed to unlatch the stall door. Circling around Etch, he got a good look at the laboring mare. He'd ridden horses a few times over the years, but he'd never needed to actually handle them. He was always surprised at how big they were, how earthy and vivid. Now he saw that Etch had the better part of one arm inside of the mare's body. Both of them were sweating hard, straining. The veins on Etch's forehead stood out sharply.

The mare's bony head was as long as Terricel's forearm. She snorted, spraying him with foam, and pulled her head away as he took hold of the halter. The straps were fever-hot and sodden with sweat. Blood crusted her jawbone where the buckles had torn her skin.

Suddenly her whole body tensed. Her eyes rolled, showing crescents of white. She gave wheezing cry and staggered, as if her feet had suddenly slipped out from under her. The leather straps jerked through Terricel's finger.

"Stinking hell!" yelled Etch. "Hold her still! I've almost got it!"

Terricel tightened his grip on the halter. "Hey, you!" he said to the mare. "Take it easy. . . ." Horses, he'd been told, responded to tone of voice rather than actual words.

"Hey," he repeated, trying to make his voice as soothing as he could. "Hey, Mama Horse, it's going to be all right."

Heat streamed from the mare's body in waves. Murmuring nonsense syllables, Terricel pulled down on the halter. He was surprised when she sighed and lowered her head. Her long nose whiskers tickled his hands.

"It's all right, you're a good horse, a Brave Lady," he repeated. He thought he saw a flicker of awareness in the dark pupils. "Everything's going to be fine. We're here, we'll help you. It's all right. . . ."

In a rippling wave, the mare's sides hardened again. The muscles in her neck and shoulders bunched. She began to pant, making grunting noises.

Terricel kept his grip on either side of the halter, talking all the while, although his own muscles tensed reflexively. He forced himself to breathe slowly and steadily, just as he had in all those meetings in the Starhall. Then he had kept silent, but now his voice droned on like a gaea-priest's chanting. It didn't matter what he said, he told himself. The only thing that mattered was the continuous flow of sound, the emotional tone of comfort.

For a moment the mare stopped breathing, her body rigid with effort. Etch started yelling, but Terricel couldn't understand him. He took his eyes from the mare's head long enough to see something dark and wet slide out from beneath her tail to the floor.

"That's it!" Etch whooped. "Let her go!"

Terricel yanked the end of the knotted halter rope. It came loose, but the mare made no effort to turn to her newborn. Her head sagged, her eyes gone suddenly dull and unfocused. Her knees buckled forward and her breath came in deep gulps.

"Throw me that other towel," Etch called. Terricel grabbed the length of cloth looped over the railing and handed it to him. The older man pulled the foal, all dark wet hair and stick legs, across his lap and began rubbing it vigorously.

"Breathe!" Etch cried. "Damn you, breathe!"

Terricel crouched down beside Etch. He'd never watched a birth before. The hatching of the occasional egg laid by the house snakes didn't count, especially since they ate their young whenever they could. But the mare had worked so hard and suffered so much. Etch had worked so hard. It wasn't fair for the foal to die now.

What was fair about anything? Pateros got knifed down. Gaylinn was dead, along with half a dozen other innocent people. Terricel himself was probably going to die in the half-frozen middle of nowhere trying to find a sister who was already past help. Why should one baby horse make any difference?

Etch kept rubbing and cursing, cursing and rubbing, long after Terricel thought there was any hope left. Suddenly the foal gave a thready bleat and began thrashing. Something hot and bright shot through Terricel's chest. His eyes stung and he wanted to shout aloud.

Just then, the mare fell over with a crash and lay on her side, sides heaving. Still cursing, Etch heaved the towel-wrapped foal into Terricel's lap.

"Keep rubbing, keep it breathing." He knelt by the mare's head. "I *told* him she was too old to breed again. Gods-damned greed, that's what it is. Come on, girl, up you get, hup! hup!"

Terricel, watching Etch struggling with the mare, almost lost hold of the foal, a filly, when she lashed out with her long legs. Awkwardly he wrapped one arm around her neck and rubbed the towel across her sides with the other. As he rubbed, he crooned to her, much as he had to the mare. She sneezed and shook her head, but stopped thrashing. Gently he stroked her neck, her short fluff of mane, her tiny curved ears.

With a snort and a grunt of effort, with Etch pulling and pushing and shouting encouragement, the mare heaved herself to her feet. Immediately, the filly began struggling again. Terricel let her go. He expected her to be able to stand because he'd been told that newborn horses could, but it was still miraculous to see her, a squarish body on impossibly thin legs, shivering and quavering toward her mother.

She was a pretty thing, black except for four perfectly matched white socks. The mare dipped her head and sniffed as if to make sure this was indeed her offspring. The filly, her balance precarious at best, staggered but stayed on her feet.

Etch chuckled. "The best thing for both of them is a good nurse," he said, and proceeded to position the filly facing the mare's udder. A few moments later the new-born was gulping greedily.

"That's not milk, you understand, not yet," Etch told Terricel as he brought in a pitchfork and began shoving the soiled straw into a pile near the door. "It's colostrum. But when the foal sucks, it makes the mare clamp down, do you see, and then she bleeds less."

"That was a close call, wasn't it?"

Etch's face darkened. He leaned heavily on the pitchfork. "Damned right it was. She lost the last one, before the bastard who owns this place brought her here. He's got no business breeding her, and I told him so, but would he listen to me? If it weren't for her suffering for it, I'd make him clean up here himself."

"He'll breed her again now, you know, because you got her through this time."

"Damned fool'll keep doing it until I lose her." Etch's voice cracked a little. "There's nothing I can do about that now. Come on up to the house for a wash and a drink."

Terricel carried his pack and cloak up to the stairs and across the wood-plank porch. The house was cold and stale smelling after the stable.

Etch raised the lights in the kitchen and stripped off his blood-soaked shirt. Throwing it in the sink, he ran a damp sponge over his arms and body. Without his upper clothing, his skin was very pale and smooth, unlike his tanned face and forearms. "I'll be up with that mare for what's left of the night," he said as he pulled on fresh, rumpled clothing. He took a bottle and two chipped mugs from a shelf and began rattling pans around in the kitchen.

Terricel remembered the last time he sat in this kitchen. "What's this you're concocting for me? More horse tonic?"

"Better than that last round of ale the other night. I swear the barkeep added bittersalt to keep his customers thirsty." Etch shoved a mug at Terricel. "You did fine with the mare."

Terricel took a big gulp of the coffee. It was cold and laced with brandy. "Right now what I need is help, not compliments."

Etch reversed the other chair, straddled it and took a swig from his own mug. "What kind of help?"

"A horse, for one thing, a good horse. There's nobody else I'd trust to buy one from. And trail gear. I have— I have to find someone, and I've only been out of the city a few times in my whole life."

"You gonna tell me about it?"

Terricel stared back at Etch. What did he know about the man, really? That he made a fine drinking partner, that he could fight, that he loved horses and wouldn't let one die through someone else's stupidity if he could save her, that he'd lost a family he loved. He debated asking Etch to come with him, partly because he wanted the solid comfort of his new friend, partly because Etch had said more than once how he hated his life in the city.

"My sister," he said slowly. "She's a Ranger out on Kratera Ridge, and she's missing. One of her—another Ranger came to my family for help, but the only thing— the only one is me. I've got to find her before she leaves at dawn."

"You don't start with the easy ones, do you?"

Terricel shrugged. "If it were easy, I wouldn't be here."

Etch ran one hand over his face, wrinkling the weathered skin. "This Ranger, the one who came for help, would be it a woman with yellow eyes who carries a long-knife and rides a Borderbred gray?"

"*Kardith!* You know Kardith?"

"Kardith ... So that's her name. I don't know her half so much as I'd like to. Still, I'd hate to have the kind of trouble she can't handle on her own." The stableman grinned again, his eyes twinkling. "I can tell you where to catch up with her, all right. But first, let's get you a horse and gear. You *can* ride, I hope?"

Terricel let out his breath. "Some. The rest," he added wryly, "I'll have to learn as I go."

*   *   *

After checking on the speckled mare, who was resting
quietly, Etch led out a big sorrel gelding, tied him crosswise in the center aisle of the barn, and began brushing
him, sending billows of straw-flecked dust into the air.
The gelding, unimpressed with these proceedings, lipped
a few stray oats from the floor and lifted each saucer-
shaped foot in turn for Etch to pick clean. To Terricel
he looked like just another horse, tall and ugly with his
floppy ears and down-curved nose.

Terricel, combing out the horse's mane on Etch's instructions, asked why he'd picked this one for him.

"To begin with, he's old enough to have sense and
young enough to have stamina. He's trail-smart, so pay
attention if he gets real nervy or doesn't want to go
somewhere. His instincts are a hell of a lot better than
yours. He's also a little lazy, which is good because he
won't work any harder than he has to. He'll take good
care of you as long as you let him."

Terricel stroked the silky muzzle as Etch selected a
saddle and padded blanket and explained how to put
them on the horse properly. "What's his name?"

"Harth's sweet tits, boy, I gave up naming horses
years ago. Call him whatever you like."

Pink light tinted the eastern sky as Terricel led his
new acquisition into the yard. The travel pack was securely tied behind the saddle, along with a sleeping roll
and other trail supplies which Etch had sold him. There
was a compact cook kit, bandages and water disinfectant,
a lightweight tarp, even a small supply of grain for the
horse.

"Thanks for all your help," Terricel said. As long as
Etch had been managing things, his spirits had lifted, his
confidence strengthened. But now the morning seemed
unexpectedly cold, even with his wool-lined cloak. "I
wish you were coming with me."

Etch ducked his head, his eyes hidden. He took a
breath and let it out as a sigh. His shoulders sagged, as
if under an unbearable burden. He patted the gelding's
shoulder and said, a little awkwardly, "You may be feeling pretty puny right now, but what you've set yourself

to do, that's not a puny thing. You want one last piece of advice, here it is. You let that thing take hold of you. Let it run you instead of the other way around."

He handed Terricel the loop of reins, thick braided leather. Terricel slipped one foot through a stirrup and boosted himself up. The next moment he was sitting on the gelding's back, looking down at a stretch of glossy red-brown shoulder, neatly combed mane, one curved ear pricked back toward him. The sky seemed nearer, brighter and darker at the same time.

"I'd better get out of here or Kardith will be long gone."

"Ranger or no, nobody gets out of Laureal City at dawn. Besides, there's only one road north," Etch slapped the gelding's rump. "Harth bless you, lad."

The gelding stepped out of the yard at a brisk pace. Terricel swiveled around in the saddle as far as he dared for a last look at the stableman. He held on to the pommel with one hand and waved with the other. "Thanks again . . ."

But Etch, his head tucked as if against a pelting storm, had already started back toward the barn.

CHAPTER 14

Terricel pulled the sorrel gelding to a halt at the cross-roads. Behind him, the broad dirt road led back to the city. The sun had not yet cleared the ridge of hills along the eastern horizon, and the night's chill clung like a lingering mist. He drew the wool-lined cloak more tightly around his shoulders and pulled the hood over his head.

Tantalizing odors arose from the shack which stood, flanked by a few worn benches, to one side of the cross-roads. A man in a knitted cap leaned over the counter, hawking sweet buns and coffee. Several people had already stopped to sample his wares, cupping their hands around the steaming mugs. One such customer was a man in a cloak of military red-and-bronze, who politely asked Terricel his destination and warned him against going too far north. Although he did not say so explicitly, the man hinted that a boy as young and inexperienced as Terricel looked couldn't get far on his own.

Beyond the shack, the road split into two narrower branches, heading northeast and due east through rolling farmland. Most of the traffic at this hour was inward bound, elk-drawn carts heaped with fruits and vegetables, hay and grain, tanned hides, woolens and other trade goods, some of them from as far away as Darmaforge.

Kardith couldn't have come this far already, could she?

Now, as the sky grew brighter with every passing moment, Terricel tried to ignore the feeling that he'd made a terrible mistake. He didn't want to think what he'd do if she never showed up.

He was truly on his own now, with a good chance of facing trouble way over his head. Out there, there would be no Etch to save him from his own folly. He shivered, remembering the brawl at The Elk Pass. He could easily have been maimed or killed. At the time, he'd had no idea what he was getting himself into. Nor did he now, but he'd better learn, and fast.

Terricel recognized Kardith's short, coppery hair and Ranger's vest under her riding cloak, even before her features became clear. Now he understood why Etch had commented on her horse. It was a small, delicately built mare with a coat like pewter-flecked silver. Instead of the usual bridle and metal bit, she wore a halter with a heavy noseband, the reins swinging loose on her neck.

Kardith sat straight but relaxed in the saddle, her body moving as if it were an extension of the horse's. She stared at Terricel with a mixture of annoyance and puzzlement. The gray mare moved at the same steady pace, taking the northeast road.

Terricel kicked his horse into a trot beside Kardith.

"What the hell do you think you're doing?" Kardith said.

"I told you I'd get help."

"I didn't think you'd be crazy enough to mean yourself."

"Who else is there?"

Each pounding stride of the gelding's trot jolted Terricel from his teeth to his heels. For a panic-filled moment he wondered how long he could keep this up before he either fell off or became one continuous bruise. With a concentrated effort, he was able to relax with the horse's gait and shift his weight deeper into the saddle. It took more than a few jarring minutes to catch the rhythm of it, but the gelding kept pace with the gray mare as if they were hitched together as a team.

Kardith turned her head to look at him. Her mouth

was tight and narrow, her eyes the color of molten honey.

"What I came for was real help for Avi," she said. "Help from somebody big enough to stand up to those war orders so we could search for her. Not getting saddled with some green kid off to be a hero."

The road wound through patchwork plots of vegetables, neatly planted rows edged with the bright orange pestifuge commonly called bug-weed. A few farmers finished loading their carts with the day's harvest, leeks, cabbages, redroots, and salad greens. Calling and waving to them, a barefoot boy ran alongside the road. Terricel grinned and lifted his hand in greeting.

"If you thought there was any chance Esme would have done that, any chance at all," he said, turning back to Kardith. "You knew what to expect, didn't you? You were pissed at Esme's answer, but not surprised. You came last night because you had no other choice. Well, now you've got it—I mean, me."

"Pretty speeches win no battles, boy," Kardith said. "Assuming you don't break down and go running home before we even reach the Ridge, who's going to take care of you? You'd be eaten alive your first night out. Even if you could make it on your own, what makes you think you could find Avi? What gives you the right to go against the orders?"

"I'm her brother, that's what gives me the right! I don't have to answer to Montborne like you do. I'm free to go wherever I want."

In answer, Kardith clucked to the gray mare, who quickened her pace and pulled ahead. Terricel urged the gelding forward. He started bouncing again with the faster, more jarring trot. He grabbed the pommel of the saddle to keep his balance. The gelding snorted and tossed his head, ears laid partway back. Terricel realized his fingers were clenched around the braided reins. He relaxed his grip and took a deep breath.

The vegetable plots turned to fields of golden-green barley, rippling in the morning breeze. The barley smelled sweet, like new-cut grass. The sun felt warm and reassuring on Terricel's shoulders.

"There's no one else, you said so yourself." He pushed back the hood of his cloak. "You and your precious Rangers are so hamstrung by Montborne's orders you can't risk a search."

Kardith hesitated a moment. "You'd be worse than useless. You don't know a damned thing."

"Then teach me what I need to know."

"*Teach* you? Teach you ten years of woodscraft in two weeks? What kind of nitbrain are you?"

Terricel felt too angry and desperate to risk an answer. The situation had gone beyond reasoning. He clapped his heels to the gelding's sides. The horse lunged forward, past Kardith's gray mare.

A few minutes later, Terricel heard the clatter of hooves behind him and slowed the gelding to let Kardith catch up. He drew the first easy breath that day.

By the end of the first morning, they'd left the level farmland and begun to climb. Fields of grain gave way to orchards and then to rocky pasture. As they rode by, the undergrowth rustled with living things. A family of coneys flashed white-spotted rumps as they darted for shelter and a pink-eyed lizard sunned itself across a slab of granite. An occasional raptor-bat wheeled silently overhead, riding the thermal currents.

When the hills became steep, Kardith slipped from her horse's back, tied her cloak behind the saddle and walked alongside, one hand laced through the mare's mane. Terricel dismounted stiffly and did the same. Within a few minutes, he was sweating freely. He'd thought he was reasonably fit compared to his student friends, with all the walking he did in Laureal City, but nothing in his academic life had prepared him for this. Still, they were traveling about as fast as they would mounted, with considerably less strain on the horses.

They reached the crest and Kardith mounted up without a word. Terricel followed, and they began a slow, steady descent. At first, he found it a welcome change, then an unwelcome one, then a torture devised specifically for the male anatomy, as his weight shifted forward against an unforgiving leather pommel. As soon as they began to climb again, they dismounted again. Uphill, walk. Downhill, ride. Each direction carried its own particular agony.

Past the first ridge of hills, there was less and less traffic, once a caravan of pannier-laden mules and a metal trader with two well-armed bodyguards. The caravan leader waved in greeting as Kardith and Terricel rode by, he and his drovers too busy keeping his animals in line to do more. The trader, headed toward the city, stopped for a few moments to exchange comments on road conditions. He'd heard about the assassination, but not the funeral riot, and he glanced uneasily toward the north and said he'd be glad to get back.

Late in the afternoon two men passed them without pausing. They were traveling separately, one on a spotted horse and one on a rusty black. Kardith commented that the black wasn't trail-hardened enough for the pace his rider had set. As the horse galloped out of sight, Terricel noticed the foam around its mouth, flecking its neck and flanks. He knew exactly how the panting, sweating animal must feel.

By the end of the first day, Terricel's thighs felt as if they were encased in molten chains. He had not known there were so many places capable of pain between one knee and the other. During the last few hours, he clung to the grim determination not to disgrace himself by falling off his horse at the first available opportunity. As it was, he could do no more than grunt in agreement when Kardith suggested stopping at the inn which had just come into view, rather than camping their first night out.

They walked their horses into the big central courtyard. The metal-shod hooves clattered on the cobblestones, a contrast to the muffled sounds of the dirt trail.

On one side of the central yard stood the stables, with a few tired-looking horses tied to a rail by a watering trough. The main building sat opposite; a bank of solar water-heating panels covered most of the roof. Terricel thought immediately of hot baths and cooked food, although just being able to bring his knees together and stand rather than sit would be sufficient luxury for the moment.

"Unh," he said, seeing by the look in Kardith's eyes that she knew exactly what his condition was.

"You stay here," she said, swinging down from her saddle and handing him the mare's reins. "And water the horses."

After Kardith disappeared inside the main building, Terricel sat wondering how he was going to force himself to move. He didn't want to be sitting on his horse in a stupor when she returned. Not that it would lower her opinion of him significantly. At the moment, that didn't seem possible. If his own pride were all he had to keep himself going with, it would have to suffice.

This isn't going to be easy, he told himself. *But it is possible. And next time will be easier. It had better be.*

His hip joints twinging in protest, Terricel dragged his right leg over the gelding's rump and slid to the ground. He clung to the stirrup as the horse looked around and touched his shoulder with a soft, whiskery muzzle.

Nosey, that's what I should call you. Terricel patted the horse.

Kardith's mare threw her head back when he tried to lead her. Her eyes bulged, ringed with white, and her nostrils flared wide. The corners of her mouth were crisscrossed with fine whitened scars.

Like her owner, Terricel reflected. *Headstrong and . . . scarred.* He spoke soothingly to her, called her Gray Lady and Battered-by-Life and several equally ridiculous names, but she would not move until his gelding, impatient to get to the water, began walking forward on his own.

When Kardith came back, he was standing at the trough between the two horses, attempting to scratch behind the gelding's ears. A boy with an open, weather-reddened face and straw-flecked clothes followed at her heels.

"I spent some of your money on care for the horses. I thought you'd like not having to unsaddle and rub them down the first night on the trail." She grinned as she untied her saddlebags and slipped them over her shoulder. "Maybe I was wrong."

Terricel's pride evaporated on the spot. "Not if it means I can be soaking in a hot tub any sooner."

"That is the most sensible thing I've heard you say yet."

The boy took the horses' reins and led them off toward the stable, clucking encouragingly to them. Terricel picked up his travel pack and followed Kardith to the inn itself. He tried to walk with some approximation of normal movement.

"That's a nice mare you have," he said conversationally. "What's her name?"

"Name? Who gives horses names?"

Nobody but me, apparently.

"By the way," she asked, still not looking at him. "What's yours?"

For a moment he was too surprised to answer. Avi hadn't mentioned him, then. "Terr—Terricel."

Kardith shook her head. "Terricel, he's that pasty-faced book boy we left back in the city, clinging to his mother's robes. Me, I'll call you Terris."

CHAPTER 15

As the inn door swung shut, Terricel paused, his eyes straining to adjust to the dimness. The wooden walls and rafter beams were smoky-dark, lit only by the narrow windows. The smoldering embers in the patch-stone fireplace added a thin blue smoke, almost masking the smell of stale beer. Benches and trestle tables filled the low-ceilinged room, many of them occupied. Terricel made out farmers and herders in their sheepskin jackets and rough-spun wool breeches over knitted leggings, a sharp contrast to the sprinkling of travelers in finely-woven cloaks and high riding boots. A few of the locals glanced his way before returning to their drinking. Several of the tables had games of cards or dice going.

Kardith pushed past Terricel toward the bar, which was no more than another table covered with a cloth, separating a cabinet of kegs and bottles of various green and amber liquids from the rest of the room. Behind it stood a woman in a leather apron, her sleeves rolled up to reveal muscular forearms, her gray-streaked hair slicked back and anchored with a long tassel-headed stick.

"I'm sorry, Ranger, there's just the one room. We can bring a cot in for . . ." she glanced fleetingly at Terricel, "or he can sleep down here by the fire. Either way, we'll throw in the private bath, clear."

"One room," Kardith said, shrugging.

The inn-woman nodded. "You'll have a drink or two first, won't you? Relax in the common room after a long day's journey?"

The smells of the ale and food made Terricel's mouth water. The noon meal of bread and cheese, eaten while the horses watered at a farmer's stock station, had been a long time ago, and that on top of no breakfast. His stomach rumbled and the long muscles in his thighs began trembling.

"I've little taste for company tonight," Kardith remarked, as if discussing the weather. She rubbed the side of her nose. "Two meals, in my room. Meat if you've got it."

"But of course, what would you think of us, not to have meat for our hungry guests? And a jar of our best ale?"

"No yak-piss, just water."

The woman's mouth assumed the shape of an "O." She gestured to a younger woman standing by the staircase, who bobbed her head and disappeared into the lightless bowels of the inn. Then she fished in one of her capacious leather pockets, extracted a key on a loop of multicolored twine and handed it to Kardith.

Terricel trudged up the bare wooden stairs after Kardith. His legs felt so heavy he could hardly lift them, but the tremors stopped as long as he kept moving. There seemed to be an unreasonable number of steps to the second flight, each one steeper and farther from the warmth and cheer below. It wouldn't have been so terrible to have some ale and something to eat first, would it?

Yet it seemed to him that Kardith had deliberately avoided lingering below, just as she'd suggested to the innkeep that he, Terricel, was a person of no account, to be safely ignored. As he dragged one foot after the other up the stairs, he thought dispiritedly that he'd probably concocted the idea from his own bone-tiredness and the paranoia he'd absorbed like mother's milk from Esmelda.

Whatever was going on, Kardith clearly assumed he'd follow her head in dealing with it. All day long she'd been testing him, pounding away at his resolve, giving every indication that the most he could expect from her was scornful silence. Maybe how she'd just treated him was no more than a carefully studied insult. But maybe she was giving him a chance. That was all, just a chance. An honest chance, perhaps the first in his whole life.

Terricel hitched his travel pack over his shoulder, gritted his teeth, and kept climbing.

The room was the size of a closet, hardly big enough to hold the narrow bed, a rickety-looking cot, two straight-backed chairs and a napkin-sized table on which stood a decrepit but still functional lamp. It was an inner room with no outside windows, but well-aired. The ale might be yak-piss, as Kardith said, but the chambermaid knew her business. Towels lay neatly folded on the bed, along with a block of yellowish sheep-tallow soap, and the wood floor still bore damp traces of its last scrubbing. Ocher paper covered the walls, the pattern long since scoured off. At the foot of the bed was another door, presumably to the private bath.

Kardith put down her saddlebags, examined the inner door and bathroom which lay beyond it, to make sure there was no other way into the room besides the outer door. This she opened and closed several times, testing the hinges and the bar latch.

"Hunh! They call *this* a lock?" She closed the outer door, wedged one of the straight-backed chairs against it, sat down on the other chair, and drew her long-knife.

Terricel stared at the knife in fascination. He'd never seen a blade like that close up, the metal a rippling blue-white, the hilt wrapped in narrow leather strips patterned like a head of ripened wheat. It looked well worn, as if it bore the impression of her hand.

The blade flashed and for a moment he was back in the plaza, his head filled with the smell of blood. As he remembered, his mouth turned dry. He knelt, Gaylinn's head and shoulders across his knees, holding her as she stiffened and went limp.

Gaylinn . . . In a few days, there'd be a funeral for her, along with the rest of the riot victims. They would dig up another paving stone and plant another tree, fac-

ing the one on Pateros's grave. Her family would be
there, come all the way from Raimuth at the western
branching of the Vision River. They'd stand together in
the plaza, holding each other, her father with his bushy
black eyebrows and printer's hands, her mother with
tears streaking the faded beauty of her face, the older
brother who'd been the first to see the genius in her art,
all her other brothers and sisters. If he were there, he
would stand with them and they would enfold him as if
he were one of them, simply because Gaylinn had once
loved him.

He remembered one morning, walking along the
banks of the Serenity, remembered the smell of the curling fog, the water as glassy as if it were covered with a
sheen of oil, the bells tolling in the distance. Gaylinn's
hand felt warm and strong in his. They'd been lovers for
only a little while and her nearness still had the power
to shake him inside. He ached with longing to give her
something secret of himself. There was one thing, all his,
which Esmelda had never found out about.

"What are you thinking, so grim, so serious?" Gaylinn
had laughed.

"When I was little," he began slowly, "I used to tell
myself stories. About the usual things kids imagine, but
also ... sometimes ... they were about my father. I
never knew him. I was just a baby when he died."

"Tell me," she said.

Some twisted thing inside let go and out flooded the
vision, as vivid as when it had first come to him. "I'm
floating in the middle of a warm, yellow light. Candlelight. The smell is so sweet it fills my head. In the corner
there's a bed. I can't see it clearly, but I'm moving toward it, closer and closer. I can see the blanket I'm
wrapped in, white with a flower pattern ... and now I
can see that on the bed there's a man. His face is red and
dark, as if the light doesn't reach that far. He reaches up
and touches my head. His hand is hot, it's shaking. He's
... I don't know. I couldn't have ... have remembered
him, could I?"

Gaylinn put her arms around him. Her hair smelled

like dayflowers. "It's the heart that sees these things, not the mind."

Remembering, he thought of the painting she'd done of him, her master's work. Of the paintings she would never finish now.

He slumped to his cot, letting the travel pack slide to the floor. The pad made rustling noises under him and smelled like dried flowers. Straw, probably. He was so tired he didn't care if he had to sleep on the floor.

Kardith, on the other hand, looked ready to jump the first person who opened the door. She laid the long-knife across her thighs, her fingertips a hairbreadth above it.

Terricel lifted his head and looked from the naked blade to the barricaded door. "Are you always this . . . suspicious?"

"Mmm. Could just be a coincidence."

His adrenalin level took a sudden lurch, as if he'd been shoved bodily through the Starhall doors and all the eerie twistedness of the place flooded through him. "What coincidence?"

"Maybe nothing." She shrugged. Her hands didn't move.

"My mother dumps batshit like that," he said with sudden passion. "Nothing but hints and maybes. Who am I going to tell *your* secrets to, my gods-damned *horse*?"

Kardith's brows drew together, shadowing her eyes. "It's not *you* I don't trust, Terris, it's *me*."

"But you—you're a *Ranger*." He shifted forward on the cot. "You saw the man who killed Pateros—you knew it was going to happen. I heard you shouting. I saw you running across the plaza. No one else even noticed, but you did. You *knew*."

"That doesn't count. Nothing counts, not even regret, nothing except that I was too late to stop him."

Something in her voice stung him, bleak and pungent like an echo of some long-buried sorrow.

"There wasn't anything you could have done," he said.

He half-expected her to curse him, tell him he didn't know anything about it, but she said nothing. She sat motionless, her eyes clouding over as if focused on something far away. Then her face hardened again.

"If I had any sense, I'd say I was too damned jumpy for my own good, seeing connections where there aren't any," she said. "But the man on the black horse—he was sitting there in the common room. Right where he could watch who came through the door."

"Black horse, the one who passed us earlier? You think he could be following us?"

Following us? Or following me? Who could possibly care where he was?

Esme? Terricel's stomach clenched at the thought. She knew where he'd gone. Would she really send someone to keep an eye on him, like a glorified nursemaid? Or was she watching to see *who else* took an interest in his activities?

Montborne? Had he found out about Kardith's attempt to go around his orders? Was it Kardith who was being followed, and not him at all?

Someone else, for some entirely different reason?

"How can you be sure?" he stammered.

"I can't. Maybe there's not another inn he can reach tonight." Kardith curled her fingers around the hilt and got to her feet. "If he's innocent, it doesn't matter. I have no quarrel with him until he sticks his nose over that doorsill."

Kardith slipped the long-knife back into its sheath on her thigh and Terricel thought crossing her might well be the last thing the poor fellow did, whatever his intentions.

"Enough." She jerked her chin toward the tub beyond the inner door. "Go get your bath."

The pump drawing the hot water from the underground springs creaked and wheezed as it filled the porcelain-lined iron tub. The tub was too short to do more than sit in, but deep enough to fill to shoulder level.

Terricel undressed slowly, leaving his clothing in an untidy heap. He was glad there was no one to witness the gyrations needed to extract his legs from his pants. Slowly, one foot and then the other, he eased into the

steaming water. There was a faint metallic odor, probably from naturally-occurring mineral salts. The warmth
sent waves of relaxation through his aching muscles. He
flexed his ankles and then his knees, working the stiff-
ness out. Angry red weals marked the insides of his
thighs where the saddle leather had rubbed. His sitting
bones were twin lumps of excruciating sensitivity. He
tried not to think about mounting up the next morning.

He startled awake from a drowse when Kardith poked
her head in and said, "Get out before you fall asleep
and drown." He splashed and floundered in the tub,
grabbing for a towel to cover himself, but she'd already
slammed the door shut.

Later he sat on the cot, dressed in his clean change
of clothing and finishing what Kardith had left of the
savory meat pie.

Kardith emerged from her own bath, wearing the vo-
luminous, ankle-length robe supplied by the inn. She'd
wrapped her hair in a towel. Her cheeks were soft and
flushed from the warmth, her bare toes pink like a
child's. She rummaged in her saddlebags, took out a
comb and a small leather bottle, and tossed the bottle
on Terricel's cot.

"Use that on your saddle sores." She sat cross-legged
on the narrow bed, her back to him, and began rubbing
her hair dry.

Terricel put the tray on the floor and unscrewed the
cap of the bottle. The contents gave off a pleasantly
astringent smell. With a glance back at her, he eased his
pants down to his calves and began applying it along the
swollen reddish areas. On first contact, the thin brownish
liquid felt cool, building to a fiery warmth which just as
quickly faded, leaving a slight numbness. He clenched
his teeth and kept smearing.

"You did okay," Kardith said over her shoulder.
"Considering."

"You were testing me."

"The harder it is now, the more chance you'll have
later."

Terricel pulled up his pants and turned around. Kardith was yanking at her tangled curls, her back still to

him. "You don't say no to a bed and a decent meal,"
he said.

"There'll be times enough to go without."

Terricel nibbled a leftover bit of pastry crust. He
thought of Aviyya, on the Ridge all these years, fighting
northers, "going without." What did he know about that
life? What did he know about her, for that matter? She
was no longer the child who'd played adventures with
him in the big lonely house or the teenager screaming
rebellion at Esmelda.

Perhaps it was no more than a spark of his imagination, seeing her face streaked with blood and dirt, hearing her pulse hammering through his own chest. Seeing
her turn toward him for the briefest instant, as if sensing
his presence.

He blinked, all traces of the image gone. Kardith was
staring at him, the hand holding the comb paused above
her head. He made an apologetic gesture. "I was thinking of Avi, wondering what she's like now. I was only
nine when she left. I remember her the way a child remembers, but it's my real sister—the woman she's become now—that I'm going after."

"I misjudged you, then." Kardith put down her comb.
"I thought you just wanted to get out from under your
bitch mother."

Terricel flinched as if she'd struck him. "As if I didn't
care what happened to Avi! As if . . . as if. . . ."

He couldn't go on. The truth was, he thought savagely,
she was right. For all his fine words, Aviyya was no more
than a boyhood memory and a vision he could just as
well have invented, like the stories about his father. The
truth was, all his life he'd been looking for something
which was his, truly his, and wherever he'd looked he'd
found Esmelda's shadow. Now, when he could stand it
no longer, when Gaylinn was gone and Laureal City a
crucible, his academic career, whatever there was of it in
the first place, finished, now he'd finally found something
Esmelda wouldn't do, a place she couldn't go. It could
be Avi or anyone, alive or dead, what difference did it
make if it got him out of her clutches?

It makes a difference. Avi is alive, and there is a bond between us. . . .

"If I *am* running away," he said slowly, "or if I don't know what the hell it is I want, isn't it better I'm trying to find Avi, rather than getting into drunken fights at The Elk Pass every night? Whatever's happened to her, whatever she's become, she's still my sister. There are ways we understand each other, things we've been through together. Don't you see? No one else can know what it was like, growing up with Esme. Or why Avi had to leave, why I—why I have to leave."

"That's something Avi would've said." Kardith's amber eyes had gone dark and opaque. "If you didn't love her, too, I would hate you for being so like her."

CHAPTER 16

Terricel sat bolt upright, gasping and shivering. His dreams, uneasy visions of figures mounted on black horses and Esmelda facing Montborne across a table laden with a silver bowl, her eyes blazing, vanished instantly. Kardith stood over him, holding the bedcovers which she'd just yanked off.

"Don't wear your clean shirt," she said, and left him to wash, change back into his traveling clothes and repack in the dark.

He swung his legs over the side of the cot and tried to stand. Pain, like white lightning, shot through his knees. His hip joints seemed locked in a vise. But he'd be corroded from here to hell before he'd let Kardith find him sitting in his underwear, hunched over like a helpless old man. His breath caught in his throat, but he managed to get to his feet and straighten up. Then, gritting his teeth and grunting with effort, he bent over again and pulled on his pants.

When he came downstairs, he found her at the entrance to the kitchen, her saddlebags slung across her shoulder. She was sipping coffee and discussing weather conditions with the innkeep. From the brightly lit kitchen came the clatter of pans and the aroma of baking bread. He thought of Annelys's new loaves, still warm and fragrant, and his stomach rumbled hopefully.

"Pay the woman," Kardith said.

Terricel dug in his money belt for the modest sum the innkeep requested.

"That's half the room and meal." Kardith handed her empty mug to the innkeep. "And *all* the stabling."

"What about breakfast?"

"I've eaten, thank you." She turned and strode through the empty common room and out the front door.

Terricel followed, feeling as if his wits as well as his tongue were wrapped in cotton batting. It was barely light enough in the yard to see his breath as a whitish plume. The stableboy, clear-eyed and smiling, led out the saddled horses.

Terricel's stomach went clammy at the prospect of sitting on anything, let alone a horse. He knew that if he said anything, she'd use it as an excuse to go on without him. He fumbled with the straps to secure his travel pack behind the saddle. *And it would be my own damned fault.*

Terricel's muscles twinged and ached as he settled himself on the horse's back and adjusted his feet in the stirrups.

The sorrel gelding arched his neck and pranced.

Disgustingly Cheerful, that's what I should call you.

As they proceeded along the dirt road, the sky grew lighter. Twitterbats and morning crickets whirred and chirped. Ground squirrels chattered from the underbrush. The gelding settled into a reaching walk, head swinging from side to side as if marking musical time. The gentle movement loosened Terricel's legs and back. He couldn't decide if his buttocks had gone numb or Kardith's liniment had worked some magic, and he didn't care. Things were not as bad as they could have been. For the moment.

Terricel's spirits lifted and he looked around with new interest at the grassy valley which climbed gently into another set of hills. As far as he could see, they were alone on the road.

Kardith reached into her saddlebags, drew out a packet wrapped in oiled cloth, and handed it to him. Inside he found two buns, steaming hot and stuffed with cheese and spicy real-meat sausage, a large green apple, and a glass bottle of coffee. Numbly, he stared at the food, and then back at Kardith.

"Did you think I'd make you go all morning without breakfast?" She laughed out loud. "Ay Mother, you *did*!"

Smiling despite himself, Terricel tore into the first bun. The tangy melted cheese swirled over his tongue. The second bun he ate more slowly, along with the coffee, followed by the apple, which he chewed right down to the seeds. He threw them along the trail, hoping one of them might germinate. It would be nice to ride by here some day and see a tree that he'd planted. He took a deep breath and arched his back, hearing the joints of his spine crackle. The air was crisp and lightly scented with dew-wet grass.

"I may have been half-asleep when I came down," he said, "but I didn't see any sign of the man on the black horse."

"Neither did I," Kardith said. "And anyway, he couldn't go on pretending to be an innocent traveler once we reach Kratera Ridge."

"Why? Aren't there people who travel through there?"

She shook her head. "And nobody lives there, either. We Rangers mostly keep the northers from breaking through, but even they aren't crazy enough to lay claim to the Ridge."

"I wonder why not. They're always after new territory. At least, that's what we were always told in Laureal City. Is the Ridge barren, then?"

"Barren? No. It's not farming country, true. There could be hunting and woods-farming, except there's something . . . not hostile, just not . . . I don't know. I never cared—it was enough to be a Ranger and alive after the Brassa mess. I had better things to do than worry about seeing things out of the back of my eyes."

"Seeing what sort of things?"

Kardith tightened in her saddle, sending the gray mare into a nervous jig-trot. "Places that aren't quite . . ." She laid one hand on the mare's neck and quieted her down.

"Never mind about the Ridge. It's just the sunlight playing tricks, that's all."

Terricel did not think that was all, but he looked down at the braided leather reins in his hands and kept quiet.

"You think I'm bats, don't you?" Kardith said with sudden heat. "Bats-crazy Ranger, off on a fool's chase, spookier than a barnfowl in a kennel? And now I'm seein' things in the woods? That's what you think, isn't it?"

"I think you love Avi enough to make a fool of yourself if it'll save her."

Kardith glared at him with eyes gone white and lips compressed into a tight, unreadable line. She pulled the mare to a halt and swung down. "Now we run."

"Run?" Terricel stared at her, half-disbelieving.

She gave him a withering look, took hold of the mare's hackamore and started jogging, the mare trotting beside her.

Terricel hesitated for an instant. Then he kicked his feet free from the stirrups, jumped down, and scrambled after her. Scrambled because the road, which had seemed so smooth from horseback, was really strewn with stones, twigs, and erosion runnels. He tripped, stumbled, kicked himself, swore, and tripped again, but somehow he kept up.

The gelding ignored his antics and bobbed along contentedly behind the gray mare. Terricel's initial burst of energy faded and his breakfast sat like a lump in his stomach. Sweating and panting, he noticed Kardith holding on to the mare's stirrup. He grabbed on to his own and found that it steadied him. It did nothing, however, for the fiery pain which crept into his lungs and leg muscles. He tried to relax as he ran, but every pounding step sent new spasms through his diaphragm. He grabbed the stirrup with both hands and leaned his weight on it. The catch in his side eased, but he couldn't stay long in that position without tripping over his own feet.

How long were they going to run? Ahead of him, Kardith kept the same relentless pace with no sign of flagging. Was she made out of iron? He clenched his teeth together, his breath hissing between them, and swore he'd fall over dead before he asked her to slow down for him.

"How are your feet?" Kardith's voice jolted him out of his thoughts. He hadn't noticed her drop back to run beside him.

"My what?"

"Any blisters?" The Ranger's cheeks were flushed, her coppery curls slicked to her skull.

He stared at her reddened, sweaty face. "I don't . . . think so . . . Not sure . . . yet."

"Good!"

"I didn't think . . . after yesterday . . . there was . . . any . . . new place . . . to hurt . . . but . . . I was . . . wrong."

"Nothin' wrong . . . with your sense . . . of humor."

Terricel kept running. Although it seemed they ran for hours, in reality it was only for a half-hour at a time, alternated with riding. It didn't take too many repetitions before he learned to settle into an even pace, his shoulders relaxed and his knees taking much of the jarring shock. His thighs and chest would ache and burn each time, but he knew it wouldn't last forever. And he understood, without having to ask, the point of constantly changing the way he used his muscles. Running was a very different activity from riding, and he couldn't know which he'd need once he got to the Ridge.

They slept that night at another inn, smaller and emptier than the first. Although there was no sign of the man on the black horse, they avoided the public areas. In their single room, Terricel ate a surprising amount of the unsalted bean and potato stew before applying Kardith's liniment to an entirely new set of sore muscles and falling into a dreamless sleep.

The next morning made Terricel's previous agonies seem like mere twinges. Somehow he managed to climb on his horse without screaming. They left the main road, which swung south toward Haycarp, and took the smaller, northeastern fork. They passed that night in the barn of a small farmstead. Here Kardith bargained and Terricel paid for a sack of coarse flour, some salt-cured mutton, and additional grain for the horses. The farmer, looking pleased to have a little unexpected cash, added a loaf of stale bread and a double handful of last year's dried apples.

They led their mounts into the snug-walled barn and Kardith turned on her pocket-sized battery lamp. A sturdy horse, little bigger than a pony, and two milk-sheep stood tethered along the far wall, contentedly chewing. The air was warm with the heat of their bodies and sweet with the smell of alfalfa hay. With a sigh of relief, Terricel threw himself on a pile of bedding straw.

"No matter how tired you are, you always take care of your horse first," Kardith said. "And since you have so much of your misspent youth to make up for, you can do both of them."

Biting back a curse, Terricel heaved himself to his feet and in a few moments was deep into learning how to take off the horses' gear, pick out their hooves for stones, and check for minor injuries. The gray mare snorted and tossed her head as he slipped off her hackamore.

"Why do you use this thing instead of a regular bridle?" he asked Kardith.

Kardith picked up a handful of straw and began twisting it into a thick strand. "See the scars around her mouth?" she said without looking up.

Terricel saw the mare, her ears pinned back along her lathered neck, her eyes white-rimmed. Ropy, red-streaked foam hung in threads from the shanks of the steel bit. He heard a man's rough voice cursing as he yanked on the reins. Whip leather cracked the air like a split of lightning. The bright smell of the mare's blood mingled with the stench of her terror.

Quickly, Terricel thrust the images from his mind. The gray mare was watching him, nostrils wide as goblets. He murmured to her as he had to Etch's mare and held out a handful of the dried apples. She sniffed his open palm suspiciously, her ears twitching. Then she gathered up the fruit in a single mouthful. Her lips were soft and nimble against his skin. He patted her neck and laughed when she nuzzled his chest for more.

Kardith shoved the plaited straw into his hands. "This is called a wisp," she said. "You use it to rub your horse down. Like this—" She grabbed his hands and demonstrated with a grip powerful enough to make him wince. "Hard! It helps both circulation and digestion."

"Mine," he muttered, "or the horse's?" But he bent to the task with a will, leaning all his weight into each stroke, until his arms and shoulders ached as much as his legs.

Over the next days, Terricel began to adjust to long periods of riding, until he no longer felt uncomfortable in the saddle. The road dwindled into a trail, snaking up through steepening hills. What farms they passed looked poor, the pastures dry and rocky. For long distances they rode or walked over terrain too rugged for a trot. Scrub gave way to scraggly groves of softwood-ash and willow, weedy marginal trees, and finally to forest.

As long as they'd been passing farms and pastures, the land had looked familiar to Terricel. He'd traveled through similar country on picnics with friends or visiting Gaylinn's family in Raimuth, in the fertile valley along the Vision River. But the woods were another experience entirely, something almost alien. The trees and underbrush vibrated with colors he'd never seen before, hues of green so deep they looked almost blue. The air was cool and tangy with the odors of wild herbs, fungi and years of dense, moldering debris.

The trail, winding up hillsides and down clefts where tiny swift streams bit deep through the sandstone, often seemed to Terricel to be little more than a product of Kardith's imagination. As the gelding slipped and scrambled, Terricel developed new skills in the saddle.

Kardith pointed out the signs of animal and human traffic, dangers from fire and mud slide. She told Terricel about the medicinal uses of rosemarie, bat-bane and feverfew, the deadly ropeweed which could kill a man in only a few minutes, the soapy, cleansing root of the corrisenth, the edible greens and tubers. Gradually Terricel began to recognize some of the things she showed him. Kardith nodded her approval of his selection of a campsite, a fairly level clearing on top of a little rise, yet surrounded by thick, low bar-brushes to give shelter from wind, with stones and dry wood for a fire. He unpacked the horses, watered them from the creek which rushed through the gully to the west, and spread out grain for them on their saddle blankets.

"Leave the tent," she said. "It's mild enough, and you should get used to the feel of the forest at night. Let's see your fire." She watched him build it as she'd described earlier, then rearranged the whole thing and proceeded to cook dinner.

Terricel sat down and pulled off his boots, inspecting them for wear. "Tell me," he said, "do I stand any chance at all?"

"Chance, he asks? Hunh!"

"So I've learned how to unsaddle a horse and to pick a site for tonight. That doesn't mean I know what I need to." He put the boots back on.

Kardith handed him a plate of panbread laced with salt-mutton. "Want to know what I think? What I think doesn't matter. You want to go running back home? Fine. There's the trail. You want to find Avi? I'll teach you what I can. Like I said, what I think doesn't matter."

"I had no idea how much I didn't know."

One corner of her mouth twisted upward. "That's half of what you've got in your favor."

"What's the other half?"

She shook her head. "You don't *have* another half. Not yet, anyway."

CHAPTER 17

Nothing, there was nothing. None of the normal night noises Terricel had learned to listen for—no high-voiced twitterbats, no moonflies, no small creatures grubbing about in the undergrowth. He lay motionless in his sleeproll, straining for a trace of whatever jarred him from sleep. Above him, outlined by the starkly silhouetted branches, Harth's twin moons floated serenely in a haze of their own milky light.

Yet something had woken him, perhaps the unnatural silence. He lifted his head for a better look. Then he froze as his ears caught a hushed crinkle of dry leaves underfoot.

A whispered voice, male and harsh, cut through the darkness. "... both asleep...."

Terricel slowly lowered his head and tried to think. Anyone with honest intentions would have hailed the camp openly. What should he do now?

A weapon, he needed a weapon! His single-edged utility knife was stowed in his travel pack with the rest of his gear, for all the good it would do him. Yet he had to take some action. What action? Leap up and confront the intruder with his bare hands?

"It's the boy we're after," said a different voice. There were at least two of them, then.

"Better take the Ranger out first."

Kardith! Terricel's eyes darted to the spot where she'd

laid out her sleeproll. He could just make out a long, rounded form.

He forced himself to lie perfectly still. If he moved, if he seemed to be anything but sound asleep, if he even breathed too hard, he might alert the men and they'd attack right away. He had to find some way of warning Kardith before it was too late.

Seconds stretched by, marked only by the cadence of his heart.

This can't be happening. But it was happening. It was happening to him as he lay alone in the moonlight.

Out of the corner of his eye, Terricel caught a shadowy figure as it breached the circle of the camp. He held his breath. Unlike at the funeral riot, when things had happened so fast he didn't see them until they were over, now every movement seemed exquisitely elongated.

The man crept toward Kardith's bedroll, closer and closer to where she should have been sleeping. The faintest hairline of light glinted on the edge of his knife.

As lithe as one of the great hunting cats of the eastern steppe, Kardith spiraled up from the earth behind him. Her long-knife curved through the air to slash noiselessly through the tendons behind his knees.

The man screamed and arched backward through the chill night air. Moonlight flashed on the flat of Kardith's blade. She stepped in and thrust upward, toward his heart, in a single swift motion. His scream ended abruptly, a muted gurgle and then came silence. He toppled like an axed tree with the long-knife buried in his chest.

Kardith made no move to recover her knife. Instead, she melted back into the shadows. No whisper of breath or rustle of clothing came from the empty space where she'd been. One of the horses whickered, a thin anxious sound, and swished its tail.

Where the hell was the other man? Terricel dared to lift his head again. Suddenly he heard the whisper of a knife hurling through the air and then a thump directly above him. An inert body landed flat across his chest.

For a single horrified moment, he couldn't breathe,

couldn't move, couldn't think. He opened his mouth and drew in the metallic reek of fresh blood. Images flooded through his mind—Pateros, Gaylinn, the gray mare . . .

He clawed at the weight on his chest. He tried to scream but nothing came out.

Then the suffocating weight was gone and Kardith was hauling the dead man by the legs toward the firepit.

Terricel rolled on his side, bringing up his knees in a reflexive fetal curve. He gulped ice-edged air through chattering teeth. He wanted to crawl off into the darkness and empty his stomach, but he was too dizzy to sit up. His hands felt wet and sticky. He was glad he couldn't see them.

"It's the boy we're after. . . ."

The whispered words echoed through his bones. He could have been lying beside the banked embers while his life's blood thickened and froze.

He had to make himself move, no matter how he felt. Throat burning, he pushed himself into a sitting position. He clamped his teeth together and breathed hard through his nose. The whirling in his stomach surged and subsided. He dared to look up. Beside the fire, Kardith had pulled her long-knife from the first corpse and was wiping it clean on his shirt.

"I owe you my life," he said shakily.

"Nothing but a pair of Mother-damned amateurs, if you ask me," she remarked over her shoulder. "Good enough in the city, maybe, but not trained for the woods and too cocksure stupid to know the difference."

"But there were two of them and you're only one. What if they'd been better—or faster—or smarter? What if you'd needed help?"

Kardith walked over to him and crouched down, her expression unreadable. That same quality of deadly stillness clung to her like an invisible mantle. "You're pissed because I had to take them out," she said. "Because you couldn't have fought them alone."

"Not pissed. *Scared.* There wasn't a damned thing I could have done. I don't even own a fighting knife."

She stood up and slipped the long-knife back into its sheath. "Now you'll be wanting me to give you one."

"It would do for a start."

"It would do to get you killed! You should never carry a weapon—*any* weapon—you don't know how to use. When you pull a knife in a fight, you up the stakes. Get yourself slashed up good instead of a few bruises. Don't go playing hero if you want to leave the Ridge alive."

"Kardith." It was the first time he'd used her name and he felt her flinch. "It was me they were after. I didn't imagine it."

Silence, but no argument. Then she nodded and asked, "Why?"

"I don't know. I thought—when you spotted the man on the black horse—it could been someone my mother sent, someone after you, anyone. I thought maybe you were wrong." He jabbed a bloodstained finger toward the dead man. "If I'd said something then, this wouldn't have happened."

"You're too shook to think straight," she snapped, then paused. "Look, Terris, it's no good guessing. You get the fire back up and we'll search these two jackals before they stiffen. Maybe we'll find something useful, maybe not. We won't know till we look."

Terricel turned his attention to the banked coals with a sense of perverse, almost absurd relief. He couldn't imagine why he'd be a target, so far from Laureal City and with any passing importance he might have derived from being Esmelda's adjutant gone. But Kardith was also right—it was obvious now that he was beginning to think clearly again—that what they needed now was more information. He didn't think assassins would be stupid enough to carry much in the way of evidence, but there might be something they'd thought of no importance, perhaps some personal souvenir. . . .

A spark lay deep within the embers and he didn't have to restart the fire from nothing, which was fortunate because his hands were shaking badly. By the time he'd coaxed it high enough to see by, Kardith had laid the two bodies out and was arranging their possessions in an orderly row.

"No papers, but that's to be expected," she commented. "Two knives each, pretty decent. And this." She held up a slender parcel the length of her forearm.

It was wrapped—not sheathed as an ordinary dagger might be—but carefully *wrapped* in layers of supple leather. It was never intended for use in a fight. Yet it had a purpose. . . .

"It's the boy we're after."

Without a word, Terricel took it from her. As soon as he touched it, his stomach gave a lurch. His heart slowed, beat by chilling beat, and his hands turned as steady as marble. Hardly breathing, he untied the corded lacings and lifted the unwrapped dagger to the flames. With his eyes, he traced the long, slender blade, from the heavily ornamented bone hilt to the pointed tip.

He knew what it was, what it was for, what it meant. He'd felt it in the pit of his belly the moment he touched the filthy thing.

Why had he thought he was of no importance, a mere shadow of his mother, or that he could just disappear? Why had he thought he could go running after his Ranger sister and in the process find his own life? Everything was tied to everything—Esmelda, Montborne, Pateros, the Rangers, the north. He was part of it all and had been from the moment of his birth.

A shiver went through him. Maybe the fight in The Elk Pass, the one in which he'd almost been knifed, had been no accident but a deliberate attack, a prelude to this one.

"What's the matter now?" Kardith said.

He shook himself back to the present. The carved bone gleamed in the firelight. "Do you know what this is?" he asked.

"It *looks* like norther work. But I couldn't swear . . . I've seen more of their weapons than I ever wanted to, but this one . . ." She took it from him, weighed it in her hand, ran her fingertips over the decorative motifs. "I don't understand. No norther would ever use this."

"Why not?" he asked, startled.

She frowned and rocked back on her heels. The orange flames burnished her hair and skin to the color of her eyes, turning her into a woman of gold, but her voice was human and troubled. "Northers may look the same when they're raiding Laurea, but in their own country, they're as territorial as they come and they don't mix clan signs. This curlicue on the tang is Cassian, but then it turns into a stylized Huldite dragon. Any craftsman crazy enough to combine them would never see another piece of work. What norther would carry such a thing? It'd be like shouting 'I'm a traitor' to anyone he met."

As Terricel listened, each word reverberated through him like the tolling of the Laurean river bells, spreading ripples of icy certainty. "There's more," he said, and told her.

Kardith touched the tiny pin with her fingertips. A section of ornamented metal fell away, disclosing the reservoir of liquid. She whistled in astonishment.

"Neuropoison," he said. "Designed to flow down a channel in the blade. You wouldn't have to stab deep or hit a vital organ. Just a scratch would do it."

"How the hell do you know?" Kardith said. Her voice shook. "You only held it a moment, and you don't even know which end to hold a knife by!"

"That ... thing is an exact duplicate of the dagger used to kill Pateros."

She stared at him, mouth open, golden eyes wide.

"I saw the first dagger up close," he said. "In Orelia's office. Esme was part of the investigation and I went along as her adjutant. I may not know the first thing about knife fighting, but I know what I saw. They're the same."

"But northers don't use poison." She sounded puzzled. "They do plenty of other nasty things—barbed spear points, hooked knives—but never poison. They would think it shames their manhood."

"Which means the northers didn't kill Pateros, any more than they came after me." His next words were the same Esmelda had used. "Somebody wanted us to think they did."

"Talk sense!"

"This dagger and the one that was used in the assassination are identical, and they're not norther. Both the poison and mixed decorations prove that. I couldn't understand how the northers could do such fine smithing, but now it all makes sense."

As he spoke, Terricel gestured with his hands as if he were making an unbroken chain of logic, building his argument point by point. The blood had dried, leaving a mottled pattern like a scholar's age marks. Like Wittnower's hands, which he'd thought one day would be his own.

"No one except a Ranger who'd actually fought the northers would recognize the designs," he continued grimly, "and the Rangers are pretty well tied down. But why? Who stands to gain the most by everyone thinking the northers are behind the assassination? Who stands to gain the most if we go to war. . . ?"

Kardith drew in her breath like a snake's warning hiss. "Montborne? *The general?* He's not been an easy commander, that's sure, but—"

"Montborne made no secret that he wanted to march up there and beat the northers to rubble! He fought with everyone about it—Pateros, the gaea-priests, Esme. They all had their different reasons for saying *No* to him. So he had to get Pateros out of the way and at the same time stir up feeling against the northers."

Esme said he was a destabilizing force for all of Harth, not just Laurea. That means there was something besides the risk of war. . . . But he had no time now to consider this further.

"It also explains those orders. They never made sense, not to any of us." Kardith ran her hands over her face. She sounded shakier than Terricel had ever heard her. "He couldn't risk . . . he wanted us to pull back so the northers'd think we'd gone soft and attack. Then he'd have another war, sure."

"Esme still stands in his way," Terricel said unsteadily. *He tried to set things up to replace her with me, but I wouldn't go along with it. Then I conveniently left the scene and headed north with only one Ranger for company. . . .*

"I don't know what he was trying to do by killing me," he continued, "threatening her she'd be the next, or trying to undermine her, make her look like a crazy grieving mother, something like that, or maybe simply not tough enough to stand up to the northers."

"Esmelda, not tough enough?" Kardith snorted. "That old dragon? Are you concussed or just plain dumb?"

The firelight covered Terricel's flush. "Yeah, that was a pretty stupid idea, wasn't it?" He barked out a short, bitter laugh. "You're right, there just isn't any way he could get at her through me. Not Esme. If she wouldn't lift a finger to help Avi when she was alive, she won't do a damned thing about me once I'm dead. Nor can she be discredited, not easily, not any more than Montborne himself can. If he tries, it could just as well backfire and put her right in the Guardian's seat. They're the two great saviors of Laurea—Esme from the epidemic and Montborne at Brassaford."

Brassaford ... maybe it wasn't Esme that Montborne was trying to get at all. Maybe he picked me because as her son, my murder would be highly visible, even out here....

"You fought at Brassaford, didn't you?" he asked Kardith, and then rushed on before she could answer. "The *Rangers* fought at Brassaford. People talk all the time about it—how Montborne would never have stopped the northers without you. And you know the northers better than anyone...."

Kardith laid the stiletto on its leather wrappings. "Your body was supposed to be found with this. Probably someplace closer in, where news'd spread real fast. People would think it was northers who did it."

"Not just my body," he said grimly. "Yours, too. And they'd wonder how come the son of Esmelda wasn't safe within our own borders, even with you to—er—protect me. They'd think the Rangers had gone soft, or weren't so great to begin with. And if the northers did attack because you'd been pulled back, that would only prove it."

"First Pateros and then you. It would make the northers look damned good. Get people so scared, they'd say *Yes* to anything—give Montborne whatever he wants. Esmelda could get herself named the next Mother-damned Guardian and she still couldn't stop him."

"He wasn't counting on you."

"Well, I didn't learn knives in the Rangers, that's sure." She shrugged and gestured toward the bodies. "These two'll never tell him it didn't work, especially if nobody finds them. Honest thieves I'd burn, but these— we'll leave their bodies for the wolves. Then what?"

I should take the dagger and ride back to Laureal City, Terricel thought reluctantly. *Give Esme the evidence to accuse Montborne publicly, demand justice, open everything up to investigation.*

But he had no real proof Montborne was behind the attempt. All he had was the dagger, his testimony, and a lot of supposition. Not nearly enough to convict, even though Esmelda would undoubtedly find some devious way to use them

Terricel's thoughts raced on rebelliously. Esmelda didn't need him. With her network of secret informers, she'd probably hear about the attempt before Montborne knew it had failed. But once Terricel opened his mouth, Montborne would be warned. As long as there was no body with a dagger in it for him to use, as long as the thugs stayed gone with no trace as to what happened, then Montborne would wait and hesitate.

Restless, Terricel got to his feet and strode to the edge of camp, staring into the darkness as if he might find answers there. *Going back means forgetting about Avi and handing myself over to be Esme's pawn all over again. Just like the "no show" on my proposal—everything I've done on my own will be for nothing.*

But what if she needed him and the information only he could give her? What if he were abandoning her just when he might make a difference?

The truth . . . what was the truth? That he was behaving like a spoiled child deprived of his holiday outing? That he simply didn't *want* to go back? Or that he could not abandon his search . . . that there was more at stake here than just a single Ranger, no matter what she meant to him?

And how did he know with such certainty that there was more at stake?

"You may be feeling pretty puny right now," Etch had

said to him. *"But what you've got to do, it's not a puny thing."*

Something stirred deep within him, pushing upward through the layers of his mind like a leviathan surfacing on the western seas. No clear pictures rose before his eyes, only the wordless certainty that the search was about more than Montborne's plots, more than Aviyya, more than breaking free of Esmelda's webs of intrigue.

The dagger would have to wait.

Carefully Terricel made his way down the slope to wash the dead man's blood from his shirt.

Let Montborne and Esmelda fight it out between them. They deserve each other!

He grinned up at the twin moons, his lips stretched thin and wide like a death rictus, and felt no pity at all for the general.

They had just broken camp but had not yet mounted up when they heard another horseman moving through the forest and making no attempt to disguise his presence. Noiselessly Kardith drew her long-knife. Terricel clamped his hand over the sorrel gelding's nose to keep him from nickering in greeting to the other horse.

"Halloo the camp!" came a man's voice, relaxed and friendly. A few moments later, a man on big roan mare came into view, leading two saddled, riderless horses, a nondescript brown and the rusty black.

It was Etch.

CHAPTER 18
Kardith of the Rangers

"Halloo the camp!"

"Who's there?" I slid the long-knife out, solid and ready in my hands. What kind of fool, I wondered, comes barging through the forest like that, making more noise than a bunch of cider-drunk brush-sheep? Not northers, that was sure. Not Rangers, not even Montborne's assassins. . . .

The man from the Blue Star Stables, that was who. He rode up on a rangy, flea-bitten roan and for a moment I just stood and stared at him. I couldn't think what he was doing here, since he had nothing to do with Avi or the Rangers or the kid or Montborne. When he saw me, his whole face lit up.

"Etch!" Terris pushed past me and ran up to him. "Etch! You came after me!"

What the hell is going on?

I started sweating, about to jump out of my skin and a whole lot madder than I'd thought. I wanted help for Avi, a way around Montborne's orders, not some Mother-damned plot with Esmelda's finger on every turning, a war with the north and the Rangers caught in the middle of it all.

The man swung down and gave Terris a slap on the back that half knocked him down. "Couldn't let you ride off, get yourself into Harth's own sweet mess, even with the magistra here—" a lop-grinned, twinkle-eyed glance in my direction that only made me madder, "—to teach you a thing or two."

His face sobered when he noticed the bodies. "Seems I'm a bit late."

These two know each other? It took me a moment of pissedness to find my brains again, and pissed is the worst thing you can be in a tweak. Makes you feel instead of act. Now I knew how the kid found me so easy and where he got that nice-moving sorrel, him without the sense to know one end of a horse from the other.

I shoved the long-knife back in its sheath. "You coming with us?"

"I meant to," he answered quietly, turning back to the kid. "After you left, I couldn't stop thinking. Thinking about all those years since I lost the ranch, patching up other men's horses, selling them again, one day no better than the next. The mare—the one you helped me with—she died the next morning. Some kind of internal bleeding. The vet said she couldn't have saved her, she should never've been bred again. And that crapping contaminated owner, all he said was he wouldn't pay the vet bill." His face clouded over, remembering. "So I told him to take it out of my last pay."

Terris nodded, eyes down, and chewed on his lip. "How—how did you find me?"

"Nobody I talked to remembered seeing *you.* I followed *her.*"

The kid's face lightened, relieved.

"This is no simple go-find, even if you do have a sister out there," Etch said. "You want to tell me what's really going on?"

Terris glanced in my direction, careful, used to watching and following. Damned bitch mother trained him hard. But this one was not mine to call. Last night I told him that what I thought didn't matter, and I was righter than either of us knew. About knives and woodscraft, yes, but not about this.

But there was more here than even what Terris told me, secrets he felt in his bones as if they were bred there. Secrets leading back to that old dragon, Esmelda. Now the stakes were more than help for Avi, who might

be dead anyway. Now it was his life, and mine too
maybe, if the demon god of chance looked the other
way, and Etch's ... *and what more?*

I watched Terris's eyes, the tightness in his belly. I
could feel what he was thinking. That the choice was his
alone. And that a man needed to know what he might
die for.

... and up on the funeral mount with death chants
ringing in my ears and the bloodbats hovering, churning
the dry steppe air with their stinking wings, the hot
blood running down my sides—what was I supposed to
die for?

An instant later, when I could breathe again, Terris
was saying to Etch, "I don't expect you to believe any
of this. In your place I wouldn't, either." He told the
story simply, all in one piece. There was something in
his voice, some hint of steel, that I couldn't help but
believe him. I felt it in my bones, in my blood, and I
knew the man Etch felt it, too.

Terris took the wrapped dagger from his travel pack,
tied behind the sorrel's saddle. He held it out, but Etch
made no move to touch it. "This is an exact duplicate
of the dagger used to kill Pateros, a fake so good it
fooled even Orelia's experts. My body was supposed to
be found with this in it."

Etch's eyes twitched but his voice was calm enough.
"Why would Montborne want to kill you?"

"I'm the son of Esmelda of Laurea." Steel again. Steel
and truth.

Etch let out a long, expressive whistle. "And the rest
of it? The Ranger sister?"

"All true."

Etch looked down at the reins in his hands. He knew
he couldn't go back to Laureal City, just as if he'd never
heard what he'd heard. None of us could go back to
what we were before. "Where do we go from here?"

"We'll take the dagger back to Laureal City," Terris
said after a pause. "We'll tell the whole truth. When
it's time."

"Well, then," Etch said after a breath or two, "I
reckon we'd better turn these horses loose. It'll be

months before they find their way home, and that's assuming some farmer doesn't adopt them along the way."

"Or the wolves get them," said Terris, half-shuddering. The moment of steel passed, leaving the raw, earnest kid once more.

"Wolves're carrion eaters, more noise than fight," I told him. Then to Etch, "We could use an extra horse. We'll take the brown, he looks trail-wise."

Etch nodded and began rigging the brown's gear into a pack saddle. We took extra grain for our own horses, a third tent and spare blankets. Before we started out, I had Terris bury the second saddle well away from the camp. He came back looking like it did him good to bury something. The rusty black wandered after us, head down to browse, until the green forage won over the company of other horses and we lost him.

The forest thinned out as we climbed, rocks pushing out of the sides of the hills like famine bones. It was drier here, twist-bark and scrubby herbs like sauge and bat-bane. The horses flared their nostrils at the smell. Little gusts of wind pulled at my hair and whipped the blood to my face.

Each time was the first time on the edge of Kratera Ridge, always different, always the same. Avi and I rode here, full of scorn for the weirdings that frightened the others. It was enough to be alive and with her.

"Your past or mine, it's all the same," she'd said, gray eyes dancing. "We'll bury them together!"

The first of the strange places I'd hardly noticed, just a twinge up the back of my throat. But Avi had spun around, her knife ready in her free hand. Her randy little gelding, cut too late to keep him from acting whole, had squealed and crow-hopped. She'd pulled him up short, cursing, but I could see her face had gone ashy white. Her hand had shaken as she'd slipped her knife back into its sheath.

A trick of sunlight, nothing more . . .

That's what I'd told her then, and that's what I told Terris. That's all most of us could see, a shimmer like a wave of heat or a flicker that wasn't quite there when you looked right at it. A prickle in the hairs along your neck. A feeling ... not of being watched, that feeling I'd recognize, that I could deal with. I didn't know what this was.

What I did know was that whatever Avi saw then, whatever was there behind the twist of sun and shadow, was more than I, or any Ranger, could see. It was like an old wound that I'd lived with so long I didn't think about it most of the time. For Etch, though, it was something new and he didn't know what to believe. His eyes went jumpy and he patted his roan mare on the shoulder as if she were the one who needed soothing.

Terris held on to the pommel with both hands, reins slack, letting the trail-wise gelding pick his own pace. Suddenly he swayed in the saddle, as if he were about to fall off. His eyes stretched wide and blank. The gelding, his balance upset or perhaps sensing something I couldn't see, snorted and stumbled. Terris pulled himself straight. I could almost see him shaking.

I slowed up in the broad knuckle of a switchback and let him come even with me.

"That was ... a trick of sunlight?" he said. "Nothing more?" With a deep-drawn breath, the color came seeping back into his skin.

I nodded slowly.

"That was no trick. I saw..."

"What?"

He brought his hands up as if to outline something, then let them drop. His fingers, once soft and pale, were covered with calluses and ground-in trail dirt, the nails broken mending harness straps and picking stones out of the horses' hooves.

Etch kneed his roan up beside us. He was sweating a little, his voice too loud. "When I was little, we used to talk about a 'tracter' running over your grave, something that's there and not there. The sort of thing that only cowards pay attention to."

Terris nodded and took another deep breath. He pointed across the little valley to the far hillside. "There's another one there, too."

"You can *see* them?" Etch said, amazed.

"Avi could . . . *see* . . . them, too," I said.

Terris brightened like a child. "Can she?"

Avi . . . It was like calling up a ghost, her memory. The touch of her lips on my hair. The smile in her rainwater eyes, the slow turning of her head. Away from me, always away from me and toward the twist of sunlight. Never looking directly at it, but drawn, as if it pulled her someplace I couldn't follow.

For a long moment, Terris's eyes went dark, unfocused. He swayed, grabbed the pommel of his saddle.

"Another weirdie?" I'd felt nothing.

He shook his head. His shoulders tensed. "I saw Esme standing in front of the Starhall."

"Remembering her, you mean," Etch said.

"No." His voice was firm but troubled. "She was wearing the Guardian's medallion." He looked right at me, as if he were searching for answers in my eyes and finding none. "Is it the future I see, or only wishful thinking? We can't go back to find out."

He had the right of it. We could only go on.

We made camp early in a gravelly hollow with a little grove of ashleaf and the best forage I'd seen all afternoon, and a trickle of a stream. I didn't know that we'd find any place better, and I was no good for traveling on. Each passing hour I'd gotten more and more jumpy, until now it was as if one of those twisty places had worked its way under my hide. Finally Terris and Etch stopped trying to talk to me. They went to set up the tents and fire ring by themselves.

Terris asked Etch about some incident in a bar in Laureal City.

"Jekk's been picking on greenies for more years than I can count," Etch said, shaking his head. "That wasn't the first time I had to step in. Sometimes a bar fight is just a bar fight."

I'd heard enough. I hobbled the horses and left them to browse, found a smoothed-off rock blown with wild mimosa and rosemarie, and sat down to think. The smell of the flowers and the chomping of the horses lulled my body but not my nerves.

The deeper we traveled into the Ridge, the worse everything seemed. I couldn't bring Terris to the fort when I delivered the papers—too many questions like, *Esmelda's son, here?* There was Etch, farmbred as they come, and how the hell was I going to explain *him?*

If Montborne put those goons on Terris's trail, did he know the kid was with me? Would he have sent orders in case we made it past his killers—orders about the kid? About me?

Too crotting suspicious, that's what I'm getting. Run with Esmelda's cub and that's what it gets me.

What if I just rode off and left these two to the search they'd taken on themselves? I could go back the fort, back to being a Ranger, first and only. Back to dreams of bloodbats circling. . . .

Ay Mother! I don't know what to do. Help me.

She didn't answer me. She never did.

It was chance, the demon god, I ought to pray to. He was the one who threw me in with Terris and now Etch. The one who laughed in my face whenever I thought I knew what I was doing.

CHAPTER 19

I sat there on the rock, trying to shrug off the demon god's claws, when suddenly the gray mare gave a strangled cry, a sound no healthy horse ever made, and staggered sideways. The hobbles jerked her forelegs and she went down like a sack of meal in the waving yellow-green stalks. Before she struck the ground, I was on my feet and scrambling, my heart pounding.

I yanked the knot on her hobbles and the rope came free. She pawed the matted roots, trying to rise. The other horses startled and moved a short distance away.

The mare kept pitching and throwing her body from side to side, but she couldn't get her hind legs under her. Her breath came in labored grunts.

I grabbed her mane as if we were on the trail together. "Up! Come on, that's the way! Get up, damn you!"

Then my eyes focused on her taut, rounded belly, the way her muscles wouldn't work right, and the green-flecked slime dripping from her jaws. The trefoil leaves of ropeweed.

Ropeweed.

I fell to my knees at her side, my fingers still twisted in her mane. Her body was hot like a stove, fighting the poison.

No use. Ay Mother, it's no use. An hour, maybe, for a strong horse like her. Ten minutes for a man. Better, far better, it should have been me.

She was the finest horse I ever owned, she'd been with me clear across Laurea and the Ridge, she'd never balked at anything I asked of her, and what man could say the same? She carried me and Avi three days without a hitch, when that randy gelding got snake-bit and we were cut off from Derron with northers lurking behind every bush.

I remembered how she was when I bought her, bridled but not saddled, nose up in the sky, hipbones like knives, oozing scars all around her mouth. I paid the horse trader his price and he took it, his eyes all the while glued to my long-knife. I walked up to the mare, slid my hand along her sweating neck, dropped my forearm knife into it and slit through the headstall straps. The trader gasped as it hit the paddock dust—long shanks, doubled chain, spur-edged clapper.

You can come with me now, I promised her. *Or I'll take you back to the Border and set you free. Either way, way, you'll never wear that thing again.*

The mare tossed her head, ears pricked, eyes never leaving me. I turned away and felt her muscles tense just before my fingers slipped from her. I didn't look back, not even when I stopped to slide the gate latch open. There she was, nose at my shoulder. I took a handful of her mane and she came with me, silk and shadow.

My fingers were still laced in the coarse gray-frosted hairs. I couldn't get them loose.

She stopped struggling to get up, forelegs bent in front of her, head high, breathing as hard and deep as if she'd just galloped halfway across Laurea. She had heart, this mare, but the ropeweed already had her. There was no hope, except that the end would be quick.

Ropeweed. Mother-of-us-all, *ropeweed!*

If I hadn't been so lost in my own worries, if I'd had half the sense of a headless twitterbat . . .

And she was gone now, as good as dead.

"What the hell?" Etch and the boy. I couldn't read their faces, strangely blurred. All I thought was they must have heard the mare cry out, even as I did.

Shit, what do I care what they heard?

"What's wrong with her?" Terris said.

Etch jerked a tendril of ropeweed from the mare's mouth and held it up in front of his eyes as if he couldn't believe what he saw.

I wanted to hide my face against the mare's neck, now while I still could. But why should I have that right, I who had failed her? I lifted my face, naked to the sky and the gods and the eyes of men.

"It's ropeweed. My fault ..." I couldn't hear my voice. Did I whisper or shout those damning words?

Etch whirled, turning his broad, tight-muscled back, and for an instant I thought he was too sickened to look right at me.

"Water!" he bellowed at Terris. "All of it—and a couple of blankets! Now!"

Terris took off for the camp faster than he ever ran in his life.

Then Etch was practically on top of me, his face huge and distorted, red. His sweat had a rank male smell that shrilled along my nerves. I flinched as he roared at me, "I asked you, woman, have you got any anneth?"

I stared at him. Anneth was the root of a plant, frost-loving and pale orange, ground into a fine powder and used to prevent deep cuts from closing too soon and festering underneath. It was a thing no knife fighter could afford to be without. But why would he want it? And why now, when the time was so short? He must have been crazy.

I pulled away from him, wanting to scream, *Get away, so she can die in peace.*

He grabbed my shoulders, his fingers digging deep into my flesh, and forced my eyes to meet his again. "Give me your knife, then get the anneth."

What for? When she has only minutes left ...

... and when the bloodbats wheeled, closer and closer, so I too counted the last moments of my life ...

"Harth damn you, woman, I'm trying to *save* her!"

I saw his face as I never had before. No longer ugly, but surging with a passion I couldn't put a name to. I saw such pain and loss behind his eyes, it was like looking into a nightmare mirror of my own and I had to turn away.

My knife. I touched the hilt, warmed by my body heat as if it were a living part of me. There had never been a moment since I strapped it on that it had not been worth my life. But it was the mare's life now, seeping away with each straining breath. Her proud head bent, chin almost touching the ground.

I slipped the knife from its sheath, reversed it, handed it hilt-first to this man I barely knew, then sprinted for the camp and the anneth.

I ripped open my saddlebags and clawed through the layers of extra clothing, bandages, medicines, for the little alabaster jar of pale orange powder.

By the time I raced back, the mare had lost the strength to keep her head up. In the few minutes I was gone, she'd stretched out flat, legs extended as if she were already dead. Only the quick light ripples along her ribs told me otherwise. Terris was there before me, taut and silent.

Etch crouched beside the mare's head, crooning to her. My long-knife lay on the matted grass beside him, the tip of the blade dripping red. He'd cut an opening in her windpipe and was holding the lips apart with his fingers.

"Anneth and water," he said. "Make a thick paste. Hurry."

Terris shoved a waterskin at me. I unscrewed the jar, dribbled in a little water and mixed it with my fingers. It felt gritty.

"Now smear it all around the opening here."

I knelt next to him, tucking one shoulder underneath his so I could reach the mare. His arms were practically around me, his breath warm along my neck. Blood and thick, sticky mucus coated my fingers as I slathered on the paste. An instant after he drew his hands away, the exposed tissues frothed up with the gluey coating. Probing upward with my fingers, I felt a membrane of the stuff, which had already closed off her breathing passage. Only the hole cut by Etch and now prevented from closing by my anneth kept her alive.

But not for long. No horse could breathe properly lying flat on its side, not for any length of time, and the pressure of the mare's stretched-tight abdomen on her diaphragm cut her air supply even further.

I looked to Etch, and he was already scuttling on his knees toward her belly and holding out his hand for the first waterskin.

"Wet her down," he said, pouring the skin over her rounded side. "Don't waste it."

"To bring the fever down?" Terris asked, pulling the stopper from another skin.

Etch talked while he poured, as much for the mare's sake as for Terris's. "Don't know why ropeweed brings a fever. Asked a vet once, he didn't know either. He did say that what kills the horse is that sheet of stuff across the windpipe. Exudate, he called it. If we can keep her cool, she'll get enough air to keep going while the ropeweed works its way out."

"I thought there was no cure for ropeweed poisoning," said Terris.

"That's what I thought, too. But I saw a midwife once use anneth like that on a neighbor kid with diphtheria. Said she managed to save 'em once in a while, unless the fever got too high. Few years later this little stud colt of mine got into some ropeweed and in between cursing myself for it being my own damned fault, I tried it."

He wadded the blankets around the mare's belly and adjusted the folds to catch the water. "It seemed to me it wasn't the fever that killed, at least not horses, it was the pressure on the breathing muscles. Actually it wasn't me, it was my—my wife who had the idea of wetting him down like this."

"And the colt lived?"

"Through the ropeweed. Broke his own fool neck the next year."

"So what did the vet say? Did he report it back to the academy?"

"Ha! Told me I had to be wrong, it couldn't've been ropeweed. That's what he said. But I think, you know, he was scared of telling anyone. . . ."

The men's voices blurred. I sat back on my heels, the

empty waterskin hanging like a clammy shroud between my hands. My bones turned to sand, my heart to smoke.

I was ready to give up, let her die. Not even fight to save her . . .

. . . the way I didn't fight on the funeral mount, until it was too late . . .

I dropped the waterskin and buried my face between my knees, my hands clawing at the back of my head. The memory beat at me with leathery bloodbat wings, the reason I must never cry.

I thought to myself, shouting it through my mind, *Remember Avi! Remember the way she held you. Remember how the dreams faded, until there was only her. Think of her now. Think of her needing you now. Think of the hardest knife-form you ever learned, with only a hair between a live blade and your skin. Think of the time you jumped halfway across that clearing—"Kardith's Leap" Derron still calls it. . . .*

I lifted my head. Etch and Terris were pouring the last of the water over the mare's dappled hide. I watched her breathing, not normal yet, but slower and deeper. I realized with a start that it had only been a moment that I'd curled up here, trapped in my own pain. Neither of them had taken any notice.

It's remembering that's made me crazy like this, all tears and no steel.

Then it must be as if I never remembered. Avi's life depended on it. Avi's life . . . and now what else?

CHAPTER 20

I dreamed, floating through uneasy shadows. Gradually, as if a mist were lifting, the images came clear.

Below me, the trail twisted downward into icy shadows, sloping along the eroded gully. I tripped and fell to my knees, shredding the leather of my stolen breeches, scrambled to my feet and forced myself to run, to not look back. Terror drove me like a whip. Every pebble, every withered stalk leaped up to trip me. I stumbled again. The makeshift pack jerked and slid across my shoulders. It tore open the scabs beneath my shirt and I felt the hot, answering blood down my sides, but no pain.

No pain, and yet I was screaming as I heaved myself to my feet and down the trail again. Screaming, cursing, anything but weeping, for never again must there be tears, no never again ...

Then suddenly I was standing, panting, in a little flat space, powdery steppe dust beneath my feet. I saw palm cactus laden with fruit and a jort beside the sink-well. The stitched felt drape swept aside and a man emerged—my stepfather, ruddy with health, not withered as the water-plague had left him. He smiled at me, his eyes like sunlit honey ...

One by one, my older brothers followed him from the jort. They crowded around me, touching their soft bearded cheeks to mine, lifting my pack from my bleeding back. Their fingers were cool and gentle. They stepped aside as my youngest brother approached, holding a swaddled baby.

My son.

I couldn't breathe, couldn't speak. A feeling, so deep I couldn't tell it from pain, shook me to my roots.

My son, my son.

My eyes blurred over the curve of his cheek, the tiny perfect fingers lifted toward me. My breasts ached. I reached out my arms to him . . .

And then I was sitting up in my bedroll in our camp on the gravelly rise. Dawn-light flooded the eastern sky. My arms were crossed on my chest and my fingernails dug into the flesh of my arms, hard enough to draw blood. I drew the cold damp air into my lungs, one heaving breath after another. My cheeks were dry.

They are dead. They are all dead. The priests—Mother damn them—say dreams are omens. If that is so, then it must mean I will die soon and be with them.

But I had not stayed alive all these years to become a priest-ridden fool. Not now.

My fingers curled around the hilt of the long-knife, the knife I slept beside every night on the Ridge and every night since Pateros was killed. The knife that saved the gray mare's life.

The dream means whatever I make it mean.

High above me in the ashleaf branches, a covey of songbats began their mating chant, *twitter, twitter, click! SCREECH*. If I weren't awake already, I would be now. It took only a moment to scrub my teeth, run a comb through my hair, and pull on my boots. Moving silently through the camp, I roused the fire and set a pan of water to boil. I chewed on a piece of dried mutton as I walked over to where the horses were tethered. The gray mare, on her feet, pricked her ears at me.

I hummed to her and stroked her neck. The hair, usually fine as silk, felt rough to my touch, rough but cool. No more fever, no risk of lung-rot from lying down too long. She breathed softly through her nostrils, taking in my smell. The cut Etch made in her windpipe was still partly open. Later, when the light was stronger, I would trim the anneth-sealed edges and stitch them together.

I saddled the brown gelding, who'd carried lightest, strapped on my bedroll and saddlebags with enough food for three days. The brown was a nervy beast, head like a rat and about as much brains. He shuffled around, snorting as if he'd never seen a bridle before.

Behind me, Etch sat up, legs crossed, big hands resting on his knees. His boots, set neatly beside his bedroll, were upside down to keep little dark-crawling things from setting up housekeeping overnight. I couldn't tell how long he'd watched me with dark, intense eyes.

I glanced up at the sky, bright blue along the eastern rim of hills. "You awake enough to hold the mare for me while I sew up that hole?"

He rolled to his feet, having slept dressed as we all did, and ran his hands over the shadow on his cheeks where the suppressant stuff the Laurean men use was wearing off. With his barrel chest and his hair all rumpled, he looked a little like one of those berry-bears from the Inland Sea forests. He'd look even nicer with a beard, I thought.

"Give me a chance get something in my belly," he said, "and I'll do it myself."

"She's mine—" I started to say, and then bit my tongue. It wasn't me that knew what to do for her last night. This was no raw boy to order around, this man Etch, and I owed him.

"You got any surgical supplies?"

I shook my head. "Just my sewing kit and silk thread. It's what I'd use on myself."

"I've got some curved needles that work real nice. I'll show you how to use 'em and we'll be done in half the time."

A few minutes and some dried apples later, Etch unrolled his kit and showed me the steel needles, curved and straight, the scissors, one pair taper-pointed, the other blunt. All of them were wrapped in butter-soft leather to keep out the damp. I wondered how a man like this, who ran someone else's stables for a living, could afford such fine metal.

"They were my ... wife's," he said as he threaded two of the curved needles with silk and put them and one of the scissors in the hot water. "My late wife's. From her mother. We'd hoped ... our son would have used them."

Wife ... son ... He spoke the words with an odd hesitation, as if he'd forgotten how to pronounce them. They hung in the air between us.

My bones ached and cried out wordlessly, for there were no healing words for me.

The water came to a boil. We watched the roiling surface and the white steam curling skyward. Carefully Etch drained the pan into a second vessel to save the clean water, and took out the scissors.

As I held the mare's head, I watched how he worked in close to her, so close she couldn't see him as a thing apart from her own body. I wanted to ask him about his son. The telling would be a terrible and healing thing. But then he would ask about mine.

Mother-of-us-all, no wonder you never answer me. Only last night I swore I would never again dream, I would never again remember. My promises were a sand-viper's molted skin, a ghost shell hiding only their own emptiness.

But Etch knew nothing of my broken vows. He moved in rhythm with the mare's breathing as he wet the hole with disinfectant and snipped away the anneth-scarred edges. A little fresh blood flowed from the wound. She smelled it, snorted, tugged against my grasp.

Etch took one of the needles and held it with a pad of folded gauze. He turned his body so I could watch what he did. The needle curved through her living flesh, out again, the triple-weight silk pulling the clean edges together. Stitch, stitch, knot and tie off. The rhythm of his hands was like a spell.

"Your turn," he said, deftly transferring his grip to the mare's halter.

The end of the needle was slippery, even wrapped in gauze. The tip slid through the cut borders, a brief tug as the bulge of the eye and doubled thread passed through, then I looped it into a knot. Etch watched, letting me find the sense of it without comment. When I finished, the trimmed edges lay smooth against each other. A few months and new hair, white probably, would cover the scar.

When I looked up from the sutured cut, Etch had already turned away and was cleaning his needles and scissors, carefully replacing them in the kit. I patted the mare, who now looked thoroughly bored with the proceedings, and noticed Terris sitting up, watching.

His eyes shifted from me to the brown gelding, ready to travel. "Are you leaving us now?"

I scowled at him. "Wake up what's left of your brains, will you? The mare can't travel yet, and there's things to do."

"What things?" he asked, eyes sharp.

"Things I got to do." I stumbled through my reasons, how I had to deliver the sealed messages even if I meant to go on with the search. "There's a team of Rangers, friends of mine, that camps a couple of hours' ride from here. They'll take the packet to the fort for me." I couldn't bring myself to say that then I'd no longer be a Ranger.

"You think you can find us again in this?" Etch jerked one shoulder back at the thick forest leading northeast to the heart of the Ridge.

It was all I could do not to scream at him, You *I could find in a sandstorm. It's Avi I can't find.*

Terris ran his fingers through his thick black hair, getting longer now and falling in his eyes. "You're right, Kardith. You must finish what you've promised." Something in his quiet voice pierced me to my bones. I had expected relief that he would still have me as a teacher and guide. I had not expected compassion. But he, too, had left behind a life.

"We'll go with you," Terris said. Beyond him, Etch nodded.

For an instant, I pictured them standing at my side, lending me their strength as if they were my brothers. I felt cold and shivery, knowing I could never let myself take what they offered. I shook my head and muttered, "I have to do this alone."

* * *

Darice and Meygrethin had set up a base camp their first year on foot patrol, a good three miles north of where they were posted. We'd passed the night and the aleskins here, the four of us, when Avi and I were on our way to a farther patrol. I remembered the place, hidden from the easy approaches, like a little cove in the shadowed outcropping of pink granite speckled with lichen and tendriled airplant, a little spring that never failed. It was like stepping back into another world, approaching their empty camp.

I spotted the rocky overhang and pulled the gelding to a halt. Smooth and quiet, I slid from his back and began circling the camp. I stopped to listen for all the sounds that should be there. I tested the air for any taint of blood or burning, leather or flesh. All seemed as it should be, the pungent forest smells, the coolness of the spring-fed dell. No spoor of deer, not this close to camp, nor of wolf either. I moved closer, a few gliding steps, then froze and listened again. Still nothing.

Now I saw the stones of the firepit, placed so that any traveler chancing so close would think the formation natural. No sleeprolls, no packs of supplies, no bags of grain hanging from the nearest branches so the night scavengers couldn't reach them.

But there, by the edge of the firepit, a patch of moss scraped bare . . .

"Come out, Darice!" I called. "I see you!"

"Kardith!" Darice came rustling out of the bar-brushes behind me, tall and blond and hero-handsome. Grinning, he slapped my shoulder. On my other side, Meygrethin rose up from a mass of giant ferns. Her movements were spare and focused. She smiled back at me, that quick shy smile of hers.

"What happened in Laureal City . . ." Darice said.

". . . any news?" Meygrethin murmured, meaning help for Avi.

"Too much, none of it good." Straight and hard, one Ranger to another, I told them how Pateros had died.

"In Montborne's arms . . ." Darice said, as if looking for someone to blame.

"Gods." Blinking hard, Mey ran her fingers through her hair. She almost never spoke on her own.

Darice put his arms around her. Like me, they had taken their oaths at Pateros's hands. Seeing them like that, I realized that more than time stood between me and that day in the plaza. There was Esmelda and Montborne, the goons and the ropeweed, Etch . . . and Terris. I was no longer a Ranger, first and only. I didn't know what I was. But these people were still my friends.

Darice roused first. "Rest now, some coffee if you want it," he said to me. "I'll bring . . ." He tipped his head toward the brown gelding.

"Hunh!" I snorted, following Meygrethin down into the camp. "You could leave him out there, for all I care, that nitbrain disguised as a horse, just so my gear's safe!"

A few minutes later, they had a pocket-sized fire started in the stone pit. I inhaled the savory, precious odor of coffee.

Everyone thought they were lovers, gorgeous Darice and Meygrethin—flat-faced, flat-chested, hardly speaking except to finish his trailed-off sentences. But they were something else, just as Avi and I were something else. I knew that now.

But I also knew I must go with this search, this thing I was caught up in, dreams and all.

We sipped the coffee, scalding on the tongue, they from their carved sheep's-horn cups and me from mine. The warmth spread outward from my stomach and then faded. No one said anything. I wiped out my cup with bar-brush leaves and stowed it with my other gear. Then I took out the packet of papers and handed it to Meygrethin. She bit down on her lower lip as she read the inscription, then glanced at Darice, shook her head.

I stood up and shrugged out of my Ranger's vest. The leather was worn along the seams and soft with the heat of my body, but that would soon pass. The pockets and lining were empty. I took out everything I had a right to last night. I folded it and put it down on the mossy ground in front of me. I put the packet on top of it.

Meygrethin stared at me, her bark-brown eyes wide. Darice's were narrow and tight. "No," he said. "The papers, all right, we know you've got to go after Avi, we know . . . but not . . ."

"Not," said Meygrethin, "leave the Rangers."

"I could die," I pointed out.

She shook her head. "Not the same."

"Yes, it is," I said, but not in the way she meant.

There was a pause, a moment of impasse. Darice got up, arms folded over his chest, hands shoved in his armpits. He paced a few feet from where we were sitting.

In a chilling moment, I knew he meant it. "I need your help! If you won't give it, I might as well throw these in the fire right now and to hell with Derron and the company!"

I snatched up the packet, but I wasn't at all sure I could destroy it. I reminded myself it came from Montborne, it could have things in it I would be glad to burn. But it was a thing of trust, not from Montborne, but from Pateros. From Laurea.

I remembered the old shepherd's voice, clear and strong through the fever-soothing rain, *"Safe, you're safe in Laurea."* And all these years I'd been the one to keep Laurea safe. That was why I had to finish this final mission. Terris had seen it rightly.

Darice took the packet from me, as if he were afraid I'd make good on my threat. "We'll bargain, then. We'll carry the papers to Derron, if you . . ."

"Keep the vest," added Meygrethin.

I hesitated. "What will you tell him?"

Darice shrugged. I'd heard him spout the most unbelievable addle-witted nonsense when he didn't want to lie outright, with Meygrethin acting like she understood every word. And he was right; Derron would believe what he needed to believe. After all, he sent me clear to Laureal City to keep me safe from Montborne's threat of handing. I'd been so angry when I left, I didn't see it.

The inner folds of the vest were still warm as I picked it up and put it on again. It settled over my shoulders like an old friend. I guess I wasn't ready to stop being a Ranger yet.

"I'll see you in hell," I said cheerfully, and gathered up the brown gelding's reins.

CHAPTER 21

For the next few days we worked our way through the mazework of wind-eaten badlands north of where I'd last seen Avi. Despite the name, this country was far from a desert. The horses grazed well on quick-rye, which sprouts, ripens, and seeds within a week after a heavy rainfall, and my belly was full of the brush-grouse that fed in the same patch. Now the morning shadows stretched long over the dew-wet sauge and wiregrass, below the blue-white sky.

A hell of a morning to have my nose stuck in sheep droppings.

I sighed and straightened up from crouching on the canyon floor. "I don't think we'll find much. Wild sheep have been through here, covering up anything else."

Terris muttered something no nice University boy should know.

Etch chuckled. "Can't be helped now."

The gray mare rubbed her head against my back and butted me with her nose as if to say, *Crazy two-legs, what are you doing on the ground?* She almost had her full strength back now and wanted more than a sedate stroll along the canyon floor.

I said, "You're so uppity, Terris, you take the lead."

He swung his leg over the sorrel gelding's rump and jumped lightly to the ground. Earlier I'd watched him riding and knew Etch'd been talking to him about horses. He'd gotten the easy rhythm of his horse's gait. Now he kept his eyes to the scanning pattern I taught him, and I was right on his flank, checking everything he saw, everything he didn't see. He missed very little.

We went on through the noon hour, marking each canyon and all the branchings on our makeshift map, stopping to water the horses when we could. After that I led and then Etch, each of us checking the other. Boring, nerve-racking, neck-stiffening, eye-watering work. Just before dusk we halted at the branching of three gullies, a natural crossroads. Ground-hugging rosemarie grew everywhere here, thick enough to hide something small.

"We've cut so far eastward that we're closer to due north than we were when we started," I thought aloud. "There are connections, and these gully walls can be climbed."

"We'll have to mark this on the map and then go through the tributaries one by one tomorrow," Terris said. He was tired, more from worry nerves than anything, and trying not to show it.

If it were me, I thought, *this is where I'd leave something for Avi to find. If I could.* A coin, maybe, a bit of torn clothing, a horseshoe nail . . .

I crouched down on the loose dirt and pushed aside the pungent clusters of leaves. Scanning, forcing myself to focus on each shadow in turn and yet to see the pattern of the whole. My eyes flickered over something small and circular, carved, bone-white.

"Ah!"

My fingers closed around it, smooth under its lightly incised markings. I handed it to Terris, grinning despite myself.

He smoothed off the dust. "A button?"

"Not just *any* button. It's chevre horn, see, and this far north there's only sheep. It's too cold here for chevre—they do better by the Inland Sea. The horns fall off every year and the village women carve them like this. Each family's got its own design, and each worker adds her own mark here, on the back. I know this pattern—it's

one of a set I bought for Avi. She left it just where she
knew I'd look."

"Hidden," Etch said, looking grim.

"There's been no sign of a struggle," said Terris.

"She was well enough to leave that button where it
wouldn't be found except by someone who was looking
for it." My heart pounded.

"The light's not good for much," said Etch. "I'll make
some torches." He bound kindling strips together to
burn long and slow. We each lit one and went on, on
foot. The night closed in on us.

The flickering torchlight turned everything to shadows
that seemed part alive and part illusion, watching us as
we passed with their lidless eyes.

There was nothing I was afraid of, not in this night.
The things trapped in the shadows had no wings, no
teeth, no knives.

Partway up a rapidly widening gully, Terris spotted
what looked like faded footprints.

"Boots," I said, "but they're old enough so I can't tell
much more." I held my torch up for better light. There,
on the ground-clinging rosemarie—

I knelt down, hardly daring to touch it. The break
wasn't fresh, but neither was it very old. The exposed
woody core was dry and yet the leaves beyond the break
were still water-soft.

"Look there," Etch pointed. "More. Leading north."

I nodded, balancing the heady adrenalin rush against
the day we'd had, the night ahead.

Terris marked my hesitation. He was as tired as any
of us, but his voice was firm. "This is far enough. We
make camp here."

"We can't give up now," Etch said.

"We aren't giving up," Terris said. "What good will
we be to her half-asleep on our feet? You said it yourself, the light's gone and it's too easy to miss a track
by torchlight. Against the chance of an error like that,
what difference will a few hours make? Tomorrow
morning with clear eyes and good daylight will do us
just as well."

In the end, Etch and I agreed. Terris had better sense

than either of us. We might wander around as if we had
no more brains than the brush-sheep, losing the track
because it was too damned dark. We might face a fight
to the death. Part of me wanted to go on, but I couldn't
listen to that part. I couldn't make a mistake, not with
Avi's life.

I was in the lead when we came to a sharp bend in
the canyon. Here the clumps of rosemarie and wiregrass
gave way to splitbark oak, so there must have been an
underground spring for their taproots to draw from.
Splitbark meant squirrels nesting in the branches and
getting fat on the acorns. Just our luck, because the nit-
brains would chitter out a warning as soon as we got
close.

Beyond the grove, part of the western canyon wall
had tumbled down and half across the trail, huge rough
boulders easily big enough to hide a mounted man. All
in all, an excellent place for an ambush.

From the gray mare's back, I studied the narrow passage ahead. Nothing moved except for a branch that a
squirrel had just jumped off. The squirrel, of course,
was gone.

As for Terris and Etch, I couldn't count on what
they'd do if someone came barreling at them, knife in
hand. Best thing'd be to run and hope their horses were
faster, and I told them so.

"Stay behind me," I said.

"And ride right past that?" said Terris.

"*Around* that," I answered, sliding the long-knife out.
The leather-wrapped hilt fit exactly into my hand. The
steel whispered through my veins. "And we'll be ready
for them."

I nudged the mare with my knees. She arched her
neck and pranced forward.

Everything came clear now, as still as if the little canyon and everything in it held its breath. I could see every
pebble, every shadow, every leaf. I could smell the squirrels cowering in their dens, smell their fear, hear the
beating of their tiny hearts. I heard the beating of men's

hearts, too, behind the rocks. Anticipation shivered through me.

"Get ready."

The squirrels shrieked out their warnings, tinny and powerless, then scampered for cover. The mare's hooves made a hollow sound on the dirt. We moved forward as if in a dream, she and I, knife and mare. Any moment now ...

I caught the flicker of pale gold elkskin behind the first big rock. The mare wheeled on her hindquarters, smooth as silk. Behind us, two northers sprinted toward us on their scruffy-maned ponies.

"Go!" I shouted to Terris and Etch, and felt rather than saw them kick their horses forward, back toward the trail, the rat-head brown at their head.

The first norther closed with me, spear aimed to hook under my knee. He meant to topple me, not kill me, but I had no time to consider how peculiar this was. I shifted my weight, signaling the mare. She pivoted and slammed one shoulder into the norther's pony. The pony *whuffed!* in surprise and went down, legs flailing. The norther scrambled to kick free, but the frantic pony rolled the wrong way, across his legs.

Where the hell is the other one?

There he was, pounding after Etch and Terris, hidden now as they regained the trail. I kicked the mare into a flying gallop, angling her between the fallen rocks. An instant later two more of them veered in from the side. The mare swerved toward the nearer one, a big man waving his brightly decorated spear over his head. I tensed for the impact, readying my knife.

Without warning, pain exploded across the back of my skull. The world went gray and shivery. I heard a roaring in my ears. I saw, as if from very far away, some other woman ranger, copper-red hair stained with fresh blood, sliding from the gray mare's back ...

My body turned into a drum—POUND POUND POUND all through my head, huge round ripples of pain—POUND POUND POUND. I swayed and heaved as if a pair of dancers tweaked out of their minds on dreamsmoke were tossing me back and forth, thwacking at me with their sticks.

Put me down, you filthy crot-assed—

Then came the gut-whirling sickness after being knocked over the head, but I had no time to spare, wallowing in it. I was slung belly-down over the gray mare. Her silken canter pulverized every still-intact bone in my body. I tried to get a full breath to clear my head, but it came out in a pathetic grunt. The arch of the pommel was excavating a hole in my short ribs big enough to drive a herd of brush-sheep through.

Actually, that was a good sign.

If I was pissed, I was alive. Cautiously, because my head felt like a huge, round, blood-filled sausage about to burst its casing, I looked up. All I could see were tufts of wiregrass and the muscular rump of Etch's flea-bitten roan. My hands and feet were securely tied.

"Hold!" a man shouted above the thudding hooves.

The mare slowed to a walk. Hands took hold of me, big and iron strong. A few quick jerks and my ankles were free. Next moment I sat upright in the saddle, my wrists still tied in front of me, telling myself I was ready for anything and not believing a word of it.

I eyed the man standing in front of me, the quilted vest bright with stitching and beads, the braided leather dagger sheath, the long plaits of ashy-yellow hair tied with dyed elkskin fringe. I recognized the designs as Cassian and couldn't decide if that were good news or bad, my head still felt so muddled. The norther's face was weather-rough, his cheek soft with a naturally sparse, almost invisible beard. His eyes had the washed-out steady look of someone who'd stared into the sun a long time. My long-knife and its sheath were strapped across his back.

He jabbed a thumb in the direction of my chest. His voice was slightly lilting, his face grim. "Prisoner."

I nodded. If he meant to impress me with the gravity of my situation, he'd made a poor start. I was still alive, although I hadn't yet figured out why. He'd taken my long-knife and the one in my forearm sheath, and probably the boot knife and folded utility blade. I wasn't about to check on them now. But he'd clean missed the buckle knife.

From the corner of one eye I glimpsed the roan mare with Etch on her back and blood seeping through the bandages around one shoulder.

"Pay attention!" snapped the norther. "I will say this only once. You disobey any order I give, you try to escape," he pointed at Etch and then, quickly, behind me to where Terris sat white-faced on his sorrel, "he dies. No warnings."

The norther offered no explanations of which *he* he meant, nor did he wait for any sign of agreement before jumping on his pony and booting him into a gallop. He tied the mare's reins to his saddle, the other horses being led, also. I considered leaning forward, slipping the head-stall off the mare's head with my bound hands, and guiding her with my knees. She'd outrun these ponies easy and I could saw through the wrist ropes with my buckle knife. Which showed I wasn't nearly as clear in the head as I thought I was, to even consider such a dumbshit idea.

I twisted around for a quick look behind us and saw only the haze-fogged outlines of the Ridge. The overcast was so heavy, I couldn't tell the time of day from the position of the sun, or how long we'd been traveling.

We headed north at an easy canter, dropping back into a trot from time to time to breathe the horses. The ground climbed and flattened as toward the end of the afternoon we passed from scrubby wiregrass prairie to wet tundra, thready ice-sod and low, dense-wooded thorntrees around patches of seeping melt-water. I spotted something far ahead—forest maybe or low hills, but it might be only a trick of the shifting cold-wet air.

I shivered and tried not to think of the warm cloak with the extra gear on the rat-headed brown. I told myself the cold was something good—a friend to clear my head and keep me sharp. Mother knows I'd lived enough of my life being cold. Cold and dry on the steppe, cold and wet on the Ridge. And now?

Now I was alive and in one piece. I still had no idea why. Terris and Etch, too—if they were well enough to ride, how bad off could they be? They could be norther prisoners, that was what.

But the northers didn't take prisoners. The northers never took prisoners.

What the hell did they want with us?

CHAPTER 22

Late in the day we came to a stretch of jagged low hills stretching north and east. Between the failing light and the low clouds, I couldn't see much of them except the ghostly gray of bare rock. Here the northers set up camp, cold and windy, and fed us from our own provisions. They filled our cooking pot with water and horse grain to soak overnight. Probably their breakfast, and ours, too, if we were lucky. The horses they tethered to graze with their own ponies.

I sat cross-legged, hands still bound, chewing on a piece of salt-mutton. A norther stood behind me, the big one with the fancy spear, which spearpoint now hovered a half-inch from the back of my neck. The little fire they built to cook their porridge or whatever it was they ate had long since blown out in the gusty, ice-edged wind.

I couldn't see Terris or Etch, although I knew where they were, across the camp. Last light they looked all right. Cold, but all right. A couple of times earlier, Terris opened his mouth to say something and got a knife blade shoved in his face. He handled himself well through it all, and if he was as scared as the night those two goons jumped us, he didn't show it. When I glanced over at him, sitting easily on the sorrel gelding, he looked ... strange, tense of course but something more—as if he'd seen in a dreamsmoke vision that all of this was going to happen.

Etch also looked my way as we rode. *Wait,* I thought,
and prayed he wouldn't get some dumbshit notion to
play hero. He was no fighter, but I remembered the way
he went into action with the gray mare. That took a cool
head and a different kind of courage than what you need
to hack away at people who are jumping at you, screaming. Whatever kind of courage it was, I hoped he'd keep
it in his pocket. It occurred to me now, when there
wasn't a damned thing I could do about it, that I was
the one who got thwapped over the skull and he might
just as well have been looking over to see if *I* was all
right. The thought surprised me.

As for the northers, Mother knows what they were
like among themselves, but somehow I didn't think
they'd be this quiet. All through setting up camp, getting
us fed and guarded—especially me, they didn't trust me
further than they could dangle me by my toes—they
hardly ever talked to each other. The most I heard was
a whispered discussion on how to guard me while I used
the latrine pit. Finally the leader, looking disgusted with
the whole mess—*you batbrains can't even handle a
woman who needs to pee!*—pulled my boots off himself,
put a slip-noose around my neck and shoved me, hands
still tied, in the right direction. All without a word.

I wriggled into my bedroll—carefully searched first,
no hidden weapons, but no ice-scorpions lured out of
hibernation by my body heat. The tent was my own,
rigged by the northers in a way I'd never seen before,
low to let the wind stream over it. One of them, the
little one with straw-colored hair who got half flattened
by his pony, sat stoically outside in the wind. I hoped
his leg hurt him plenty.

I kept telling myself, *If they'd wanted us dead, we'd
be dead.*

Like a maggot eating its way through a palm-cactus
fruit, trailing rot, the thought gnawed at me. *Maybe they
have Avi.* Maybe they were taking us wherever they took
her. Maybe they wanted something from us—information, hostages, I didn't know what—and that was why
we were here, and alive. Why they wouldn't talk in front
of us . . .

It was death to think these things. To have such hope.
I would find something else at the end, I knew. Something desperate, something hard. I would need to act,
clearheaded, with no poison of disappointment running
through me.

I shifted into a more comfortable position on the hard
ground, not an easy task with my wrists tied. My belt
was still snug around my waist. It would be simple to
cut through the ropes, but as they weren't tight enough
to cut off the circulation in my hands, it seemed hardly
worth it. I'd save the buckle knife for when I really
needed it.

I wavered in and out of consciousness, wandering half
in the past, half in dreams. Sometimes I thought I was
back in the ragged country bordering the steppe, my
body throbbing with fatigue and bruises, other times at
Brassaford, snatching a few minutes' sleep. I'd reach out
for Avi, who should be sleeping beside me, and the sudden jerk on my wrists would snap me awake.

By now, my body heat had warmed the blankets and
my muscles began to relax. Let the bastard outside sit
in the cold all night. I was going to get some sleep.

On the third morning of travel, when I was no longer
dizzy all the time, we reached the lake. Like a stone of
flat, deep blue, it stretched westward from the hills and
snowmelt rivers which fed into it. Scattered conifers
grew right down to the edge. The air was cold and damp
and tangy with their scent. On the rocky island in the
center of the lake I made out two or three log buildings,
an open firepit sending up curls of blue-tinted smoke,
people in elkskin jackets and breeches. They saw us and
all started running in different directions.

On the southern edge of the lake sat a hut, also of
conifer logs with the bark left on. Long, narrow paddle
boats bobbed alongside the stone and log dock. A few
scrawny, cow-hocked ponies stood head-to-tail in the
nearest split-rail paddock, swishing flies off each other.
Other enclosures held brush-sheep or shaggy-coated elk,
many with calves. Beyond the pens, hard to make out

from here, I thought I saw northern trail tents mixed
with more southern styles and what might even be a jort.

A jort, here?

If I didn't know better, I'd say this was a trading post.
Before I got a closer look, my eyes were drawn to the
yard of bare earth, where maybe twenty people had
gathered. I heard excited voices but not words. Their
clothing, like the tents, mixed styles, some of them familiar. The knot of spectators broke apart, part of them
trotting over for a better look at us, and I caught a
glimpse of what they were watching. Two youths in elkskin, pale gold braids flying, sparring with spears. A low
sweep for the knees, a lightning jump, instant reverse,
like knife-form with the longer weapon, all flow and balance and timing—

Mother, those two are women.

We'd come to a halt now and I sat on the gray mare,
staring outright. In all the times I'd fought northers,
there had never been a woman among them. Derron
said—everyone thought—the northers didn't let their
women fight. What did we know of them, really? Trail
camps, hothead kids raiding, desperate fighting through
the Brassa Hills? If any Ranger had gotten this far into
their territory and come back alive, I'd never heard
about it.

I've fought these people from Brassaford to the Ridge,
I reminded myself. *I know how they fight. They don't
train women and they don't trade with anyone. Whatever's going on here—*

The norther leader jerked his chin at me. I stashed
whatever I was thinking and jumped down from the gray
mare before he pulled me off. He jabbed a spearpoint
toward the boats. Slowly I climbed into the one he indicated, praying to whatever god who might be listening
that he'd think my clumsiness was because my hands
were still tied.

The lake, which looked so blue from a distance, now
seemed gray and bottomless. Probably colder than hell.
The boat shifted under my weight and my stomach
shifted the other way. In front of me, Terris lowered

himself into one of them as easily as I'd swing up on
a horse.

I bet he can swim, too. Swimming! I felt dizzy all
over again.

One of the northers reached out from the dock, steadied the boat and jumped in without a bobble. Older than
the others, he did his best to look dangerous. He had
white-ginger braids and deep lines in his face, around
his eyes and from the curve of his nose down beside his
chin. He drew the dagger from his belt, making sure I
got a good look at it, then put it back and drew it again,
double-quick, and held the point to my throat. Eyes unblinking into mine and the whole damned circus. He
thought he was tough, that this little demonstration
would convince me not to try anything while we were
in the boat.

I did my best to look properly nervous. It wasn't difficult under the circumstances. If I was stupid enough to
jump him, even clearheaded, where would I go?

The norther put away his knife a second time and
picked up the single paddle lying along the floor of the
boat. Within a few seconds we were moving swiftly
toward the island.

We slid—if that was the right word to use with boats—
into the dock on the island with my norther guard again
holding the point of his dagger to my throat and trying
to look dangerous. I moved very slowly getting out.
Then two more northers, all stone-calm faces and scars,
took me one by each arm, and before I had much of
a chance to study the buildings, marched me into one
of them.

Here I was now, the loop around my wrists tied to a
rope from one of the cross beams. My hands stretched
over my head, the rope just long enough to let me rest
on my toes. I didn't know where Terris and Etch had
gone. If the demon god of chance owed them anything
at all, they weren't where I was, Etch in particular. I
hadn't been able to get close to him, but he held himself
in the saddle like a man near the end of his strength.

I tried to take a deep breath, but with so much weight

hanging from my arms, my ribs were bound up and the most I could manage was a slower pant. After a while, the muscles of my feet and calves were going to ache, and then to burn, and then to give out, at which point breathing would become expendable. Until then, I could only curse myself for not acting while I had the chance. Or I could take a look around.

The room was small, with no outside windows, surprisingly bright from the light filtering in from above the cross beams. I stood in a stone hollow like a firepit, and I wondered for a moment if it was indeed a firepit, except there was no obvious channel for the smoke. Swiveling, I spotted two doors, one open and the other guarded by one of my escorts.

I pushed myself further up on my toes and wrapped my fingers around the ropes just above my wrists. Slowly, so as not to attract any undue attention, I tightened my muscles and took just enough weight off my feet so that I hung. I knew I couldn't hold the position for very long, but light-headed as I still was, I wasn't sure I could do it at all. Furtively I gauged the distance to the guard at the door. If I could curl myself up, get my body swinging, lash out with both feet—could I reach him, knock him out? Down wouldn't be good enough; it would take more than a second to get to my buckle knife, and if he came to while I was wrestling with it—

The second guard came back with a woman who was dressed, like the two in the yard, as a warrior. Her straw-colored hair was divided into several braids like a man's, but tied together at the ends with dark wool. Her quilted vest looked plain but that could have been because, I now saw, she was very young. Her eyes were dark like the lake water.

She said in a flat-toned voice, "I must search you now," and began with my hair. Her hands had calluses right where they should for spearwork. They trembled a little, checking every seam, every pocket of my Ranger's vest. She came to my belt, paused as if unsure, then began to unbuckle it.

"Hey," I protested, trying to sound casual, "my pants'll fall down!"

She gave me a look of pure terror, handed the belt to the second guard and kept searching. Carefully, missing nothing, rechecking the empty slot in my boot top, perhaps considering whether I might have something hidden in the heel. Finally she pulled off my boots and left the room. About ten minutes later she stuck her head in, signaled to the guards, and one of them cut me down.

By this time my shoulder joints were alternating serious threats of future agony with my calf muscles. With relief I sank to the floor. My wrists were still tied, but it felt wonderful to have them down where they belonged. Then, one big guard on each elbow as before, we marched through the inner door.

The long, narrow room ran the whole length of the building. We entered it about halfway down, and as we made our way to the eastern end, I took a look around and did my best to pull myself together.

The long hall might be rough-cut conifers on the outside, but these inside walls were lined with tapestries, intricately woven or stitched of matched-shade elkskin, shelves with glass and pottery and carved horn, bunches of fragrant herbs and sheaves of quick-rye braided into figures and symbols. Thick woven rugs cushioned my feet. In their muted patterns, in the wall hangings and the dried sheaves, again and again I saw the symbols of the Mother, and something that might be the father-god. I couldn't be sure, I never questioned those particular laws. Beside them I noted a pattern of one shape flowing into its opposite, both making a whole, circles enclosing a single dot, as well as other things I had no time to look at closely.

At the end of the hall, Terris stood, his back to me, held as I was between two muscle men. He was talking to—rather, being questioned by—a norther seated on what looked like a drum of carved wood, dark with oil and age, covered on one side with sheepskin, the other with elk, hair left on but rubbed shiny along the edges. Two more northers stood nearby, holding spears and daggers, looking as if they'd as soon skewer me as look at me.

The norther who sat on the drum stool wore elkskins

and a quilted vest like the others, plainer than some. He appeared ordinary enough, plaited hair the color of the sand that blew across the steppe. Yet I felt a difference in him, a stillness. Not like a panther waiting to strike but worse, much worse—like the hush when a baby takes his first breath. Men might die for a leader with a panther spirit, but they would stay alive for one like this.

From this angle I couldn't see his eyes. A trick of the light cast a shadow across them as it brought into bitter relief the triangular scar across one cheekbone.

He had not yet looked up at me, though he knew I was here. He took his time with Terris, studying him, weighing whatever answer he'd given before I was brought in. He felt my presence, even as I felt his. In that way, we understood each other already. He knew I was that crazy Ranger who leaped halfway across a frozen clearing at him and gave him that scar.

And I in turn remembered who he was.

The breaker.

Seven years ago he was the unspoken leader of a bunch of hotheads. Now he was the heart of this fort or trading post or whatever it was. In ten years he would be the soul of the north, even as Pateros was for the south.

I could end the norther menace with a single stroke. I could become Montborne's assassin. If I had a knife in my hands, no one here could stop me.

CHAPTER 23:

Terris of Laurea

As they approached the lake with its margin of ever-green forests and island settlement, it seemed to Terris that the ice-pure morning air had sharpened his senses, honed them like a knife. As he inhaled, the smell of the sweating horses surged through him, along with the tang of wiregrass and the salty odor of human bodies after days on the trail. His ears echoed with the pounding of hooves on the frost-hard earth and the whistling of his own breath through his chest. And when had he ever seen such a sky? Shimmering above the wet tundra, azure and brilliant, it penetrated the very marrow of his bones. He shivered in the wind from the lake and thought of Etch, how he'd looked this last day, swaying in his saddle, clutching his injured arm, his face distorting whenever his horse stumbled.

Terris drew the folds of tight-woven wool closer around him, awkwardly because his hands were bound, and tried again to prepare himself for whatever might come. He didn't know what the northers might do to him, and yet he distrusted his preconceptions about them. He'd discovered during the long silent hours of the journey north that nothing was as he'd thought. Nothing. . . .

Not Montborne, heroic general and assassin. Not the University, that bastion of privileged scholarship. Not Esmelda, with her feet of uncertain clay.

Not Etch and Kardith—teachers, followers, he didn't
know what they were to him, beyond the best and truest
friends he'd ever had.

And not himself. Surely not himself, he thought as
they came to a halt by the lake's edge. Different, a mis-
fit—yes, he admitted that to himself. He could never go
back to Laureal City as Esmelda's adjutant and heir,
never pretend he could not feel the things he felt or see
the things he'd seen. He sensed something more, as if,
for a single fragile moment, he'd touched the still center
of a tempest. Currents surged and shifted around him—
Laurea poised for war against the hungry north, Montborne and Esmelda sparring and scheming, Avi lost
somewhere on the Ridge where things that ought not to
exist at all twisted the edges of sunlight. All of them
circled the point on which he stood, linked to him in
ways he could not understand—not yet.

Noises jolted Terris from his musings—voices shouting, the bleating of penned brush-sheep, the shuddering
whinny of a horse calling out in greeting. As he dismounted, he tried to make sense of what he saw. The
northers were supposed to be savages—nomads and sub-
sistence hunter-gatherers, a paranoid society whose only
outside contact was a naked spear. What was known
about them came from war stories and tradition, for no
social scientist had been able to study them firsthand
within present memory and the older records were
mostly a blend of folklore and myth, not true
scholarship.

Yet the lake encampment reminded Terris of nothing
so much as the Laureal City plaza on Solstice Day, the
tents with their curious jumble of the familiar and the
exotic, the smells of food, the swirls of motion, the sudden flashes of color, the bits of music and laughter.
Where were the piles of skulls, the cauldrons of blood,
the instruments of torture? He stared at the encampment, fascinated, and began making mental notes.

A hard shove between the shoulder blades sent Terris
stumbling in the direction of the simple pier. He lowered
himself into one of the boats, narrow and tapering at
either end. It bobbed under his weight, satisfyingly famil-

iar to one who'd lived his whole life between two rivers. Etch, in the boat in front of him, looked gray-faced and uneasy, huddled into himself. All Terris could see of Kardith was her back.

The northers paddled their narrow craft swiftly to the island. As soon as they landed, Kardith was manhandled away in one direction and Etch in another, each between two tough-looking guards. Terris was led away, a spear-point digging into his back.

The longhouse smelled faintly of wool and leather, smoke and some resinous incense. The man on the drum stool sat very still, like mirror-smooth water, lean and taut-muscled under the buttery elkskin shirt and breeches. He wore a vest of quilted felt embroidered with complex patterns. His dark blond hair had been woven into half a dozen braids and tied with strips of red-dyed leather. Sun streaming through the high, un-glazed window slits burnished the top of his head into a golden cap while it cast his eyes into shadow.

Terris's guard yanked his cloak from his shoulders and shoved him forward. He stumbled and caught his balance, holding his bound hands in front of him. He could not see the seated man's eyes. The effect was deliberate. He'd experienced it before. It was exactly the kind of intimidation a master's committee might use to test a candidate's self-confidence or a Senator to impress a new assistant. Esmelda wielded it as freely as if it were a normal and necessary part of social intercourse.

Any sane person in his situation would be paralyzed with terror, and yet Terris wanted to laugh aloud, *What you're doing to me, it's been done before, and by experts!* Hilarity, he'd been told, was a common and natural reaction to stress. It only showed how frightened he really was. Any moment now the mood would shatter, leaving him truly defenseless.

The seated norther spoke at last, his voice resonant and slightly lilting. As he talked, he raised his hands. His fingers were strong and tapering, covered with whit-ened scars and calluses. Several knuckles were prominent, odd-shaped, as if they'd been broken and badly healed.

"And what are we to do with you?" the norther said.

"If you're asking my opinion," Terris answered, "I'd be just as happy to go back to minding my own business."

" 'Minding my own business'?" the norther repeated. "I only wish you'd had the sense to. But like all southers, you think nothing of barging in where you have no right to be. Tell me, what would happen to one of *my* people caught trespassing on *your* territory?"

Heat rose to Terris's face. He'd expected to be threatened, harassed, bullied. But he hadn't expected such blatant unfairness. "We weren't trespassing," he answered stiffly. "It was your own men who dragged us over the border."

"I'm the judge of what crimes you've committed. I'm Jakon of Clan'Cass and it was Clan'Cass land you were taken on." There was no bluster in his words, only a quiet statement of fact. Then, with a mercurial shift of mood, he added, "Since I already know where you're from, you might as well tell me your name."

"Cassian territory...." Terris searched his memory for the bloodthirstiness of their reputation. But his brain seemed to have turned to mush. He certainly wasn't making a very good start at resisting norther interrogation. Right now, he couldn't think of a single coherent reason not to give the man his name.

"Your name?" Jakon repeated in a bantering tone. "Or should I call you 'souther' or 'you there'? Or perhaps you'd prefer simply, 'batbrain'?"

"Terricel sen'Laurea."

"A scholar in our midst?"

"What do you know about us? You're—"

"A *norther*? A gross, uneducated, bloodthirsty norther?" Jakon lifted his face and the light fell full on his ice-blue eyes. "Perhaps it is not *we* who are ignorant of our neighbors."

He paused, then said with sudden passion, "What is the matter with you people? Haven't you got enough troubles of your own without dragging them up here?

Unless you're not quite as innocent as you seem. Unless
the Butcher of Brassaford now sends children to spy on
us—"

"We weren't spying!"

"You weren't? Then what exactly *were* you doing?"

Terris pressed his lips together, as if the truth might
spring out, all on its own. No norther, especially one
who referred to Montborne as the *Butcher of Brassaford,*
was going to help him find a missing sister, a missing
Ranger sister. And if somehow he let it slip that he was
Esmelda's son—who knew what use this Jakon might
make of that? While he was wondering what to say, here
was Jakon, watching him with all the intensity of a hungry viper.

*He can watch me all he likes, for all the good it'll do
him! He's no better than a playground bully. I've met
enough of those in my time, wanting to see how tough
Esme's son really was. But he's got limitations like all of
us. He can't read my mind—and he can't get anything
from me unless I choose to tell him.*

The center of the longhouse seemed to stretch out in
back of him, a vast unnaturally quiet space like the belly
of a giant beast which held him in its jaws, caught but
not yet swallowed. Terris's muscles tensed and his pulse
quickened. His palms, held together by the leather
thongs, felt cold and slippery.

Deliberately, he shut out all awareness of where he
was and what might be about to happen to him. Turning
his focus inward, he imagined he was back in the Starhall, at its very center, with the worst of the stomach-
twisting *wrongness* flooding over him. Then, as if the
years of discipline had hardened into an instinctive re-
flex, his breathing slowed, his pulse returned to normal.
His muscles softened, although he stayed balanced on
his feet. He stopped sweating. Although he could not
see it, his face settled into an impassive mask.

"All right," said Jakon. His voice, although still soft,
took on new, chilling undertones. "You can tell me now,
or you can tell me later. But, my friend, I promise . . .
you *will*. . . ."

Behind him Terris heard approaching footsteps, the

soft-soled boots worn by the northers. Jakon was no longer looking at him, but beyond him. For a flickering second, the norther's eyes narrowed and the muscles of his jaw stood out, hard and taut.

Terris turned to see Kardith between two tall northers, each with a firm hold on her arm. Her hands were tied in front of her and her boots were missing, but she didn't seem to be hurt.

But Kardith was a Ranger. She'd patrolled these borders for years. Who knew how many northers she'd killed or what they'd do to her now? What special kinds of revenge would they devise, just for her? And there was that spark of recognition on Jakon's face, that surge of emotion, quickly masked. Terris didn't know what it meant, but his mouth went dry.

Slowly Jakon got up from the drum stool and walked over to Kardith. They were of a height, as he wasn't tall, but his shoulders were heavier and more powerful, his hips leaner. Her face, framed by her ragged curls, looked dusky next to his. She stared back at him steadily.

Without taking his eyes from hers, Jakon slid the dagger from his belt and brought it to the base of her throat, the cup of soft flesh where her collarbones and breastbone met.

Terris's hands curled unconsciously into fists. His heartbeat quickened and yet he couldn't look away. Kardith was moments away from dying, and he could do nothing, nothing but watch. An image rose up behind his eyes, so powerful and vivid that for a moment it wiped out his normal sight. He saw Kardith pivot, a sharp spiraling movement that jerked one of her guards off balance. She jabbed her opposite elbow into the other's solar plexus and he buckled over, gasping. The next moment her arms were free, the dagger in her still-tied hands, the point speeding toward Jakon's heart. . . .

But no, Kardith did none of this. She continued to stand absolutely still, even her eyes. Yet there was something in the way she met the dagger that was not courage. Not courage or bravado but simply that she had no fear of anything Jakon, or any norther, could do to her.

She didn't even flinch as a trickle of blood ran down her chest and soaked into the cloth of her shirt.

One drop, two, three . . . four.

Jakon lifted the dagger tip in a salute and resheathed it. He glanced from Kardith to Terris. "Is this cub under your protection?"

For a moment Kardith hesitated, surprised by the question perhaps, or puzzled. Then she shook her head.

No? Terris wondered, startled.

"No?" Jakon repeated aloud. "I may be nothing but a 'norther barbarian,' but I'm not entirely lacking in wits. Do you expect me to believe you're under *his* protection? Or that he made it here from Laureal City on his own? Or that it's sheer whimsy—or misguided chance— that puts a herdsman, a scholar, and the best knife-fighter in all of Harth together on my borders?"

"Believe whatever you like," she said coolly. "You will, anyway."

Jakon went back to the drum stool but did not sit down. He stood looking out of the nearest slit window. Silence settled like a cloak around him.

He knows it's useless to threaten her. He's wondering if he can get her to talk by torturing me.

Terris had no particular illusions about his ability to withstand physical pain. What he'd thought of as agony along the trail would quickly pale beside what these northers would do to him. All the tricks of self-control he'd learned in the Starhall would collapse like a house of dried leaves. In a few hours he'd be screaming his guts out, willing to do or say anything to make them stop, begging Kardith to tell them whatever they wanted to know.

And she wouldn't, no matter how he pleaded, no matter what they did to him. Of that he was absolutely certain.

CHAPTER 24

Sounds filtered in through the slit windows of the long-house—muted noises from the encampment on the shore, the fir branches rustling in the wind, the slapping of the lake waters. Jakon sat, silent and unmoving, on his drum stool. It seemed to Terris that he was measuring each weakness of his captives, weighing each strategic possibility.

One of the norther guards brought Etch through one of the side doors. He held Etch's uninjured arm bent back, the joints locked, yet the leverage seemed more supportive than restraining.

Terris was stunned at how desperately sick Etch looked. He'd known Etch wasn't doing well, but he hadn't realized how badly. On the trail, they hadn't been able to exchange more than a few silent glances. Etch must have hidden any sign that his wound was infected, fearing the northers would kill him right then, rather than let him slow them down. The skin around his mouth was dull gray, his eyes strained and glassy. His beard had started to come in and it covered his lower face like a shadow. He swayed on his feet.

In the first aid kit Annelys had packed were medicines, powerful antibiotics, if only Terris could get to them. He remembered how Etch had fought for the gray mare's life, his fervor and then his gentleness with Kardith the next morning.

To them he's just another souther to be gotten out of the way. What do they care if he's a decent man or a criminal? But if they kill him—or let him die—it will be my fault. Mine. He's here, hurt, and a prisoner because of me.

The northers didn't give away anything, but they might be willing to bargain. What did he have to offer in trade for Etch's life?

Just then, the norther who'd led the party that took them prisoner entered the room and bent to whisper something to his chief.

Jakon's face darkened as he listened. Watching the subtle shift of tension, Terris's mouth went dry and his spine stiffened as if he were stabbed by slivers of ice.

"In his pack?" Jakon said. "A *what?* No, no . . . you were right to tell me . . . too important to wait . . . see it now."

There was only one thing Terris or any of them carried which was too important to wait. The one thing which would instantly end any pretense of innocence. The one thing Terris should have thrown away, melted down, buried deep as a grave rather than risk it falling into norther hands.

And there it was, on the carpet in front of Jakon, the lacings which bound its wrappings now being untied, the soft leather now slowly unrolled.

Against all reason, against all his effort to resist them, tears rose to Terris's eyes, bitter tears of shame. Shame that such a thing should come from Laurea, his Laurea. Shame that this proud man should find it in his keeping.

Terris watched, sickened and speechless, as Jakon bent to examine the dagger. The air turned dense, as if the room held its breath and time itself slowed to a snail's pace.

For an instant, Jakon's body became an exquisitely sensitive mirror—recognition, puzzlement, outrage, each reaction sharp and clear before blending into the next. Terris couldn't see Jakon's face, but he heard the catch of his breath, saw the hunching of his shoulders, the infinitesimal clawlike curling of the white-scarred fingers.

"What is this—this *thing*?" Jakon said in a low, hoarse voice. "This unspeakable obscenity of a weapon? Who is the smith that dared to forge it—and for what foul purpose have you brought it here?" He reached to pick up the dagger.

"Don't touch it!"

It took Terris a moment to realize he'd actually spoken aloud, and then he was as surprised as anyone. Jakon was no fool, and he'd handled weapons all his life. He would have found out the dagger's secret without any help. Yet something inside Terris, something that knew nothing of politics or strategy, had seized his voice and cried out in warning.

Jakon looked up, hand still outstretched. The carved bone gleamed in the softly filtered light.

Terris wet his lips. "The tip. A poison channel."

Poison ... Poison ...

The word rippled through the longhouse, a sudden leap in tension in the norther guards. Their eyes went narrow and jumpy.

Jakon kept his gaze on Terris as he slowly curved his fingers around the hilt. It occurred to Terris that if the poison had been there instead, in a hidden needle or some coating designed to soak through the skin, then Jakon would have fallen into the trap. Jakon had known it, too.

Jakon's face gave away nothing, yet it that brief moment, Terris could see the man underneath the mask, as clearly as if he were made of glass. He saw Jakon burning with an inner fire that warmed everything he touched. Longing shot through him, to surrender and be part of that soaring uncomplicated light.

Terris blinked, and Jakon became an ordinary man once more, a man of solid and slightly battered flesh.

Jakon straightened up, holding the dagger flat in front of him. One sandy eyebrow tilted upward. *Do you know what this is? Do you know what this means?*

Somewhere in Terris's mind, a voice nattered at him to keep silent, to keep faith. To remember that the northers had always been his enemies, that only Laurea stood between their chaos and the very heart of human civilization.

All his life hung in balance, all the times he'd kept quiet because he was Esmelda's son, all the things he'd done while trying to pretend who he was had no importance. All the hours he'd spent sweating in the Starhall when every instinct shrilled at him to get out of there. Every action, every syllable, every breath bounded by considerations.

He walked forward and, without knowing why, placed his fingertips on the dagger. It was awkward with his hands still tied, but it *felt* like the right thing to do. The northers made no move to stop him. He met Jakon's eyes, like ice, like palest blue topaz, and wondered what kind of man was this, to have the truth so freely from him.

For that matter, what kind of man was *he*?

Terris told the story simply, without embellishment. The killing of Pateros, the rage building in Laurea against the north, the duplicate dagger meant for himself. He knew that Jakon might well refuse to believe him, might torture him, might kill him, might kill all of them. Strangely, that no longer mattered. It was as if some other force, intuitive and mute, moved through him and spoke with his voice.

Jakon held the dagger steady under Terris's fingertips. One moment his eyes seemed opaque and expressionless, the next, they flared with a passion so hot and raw it scalded all the color away.

"Why would you betray your own country to tell me this?" Jakon asked. "Why?"

Because what has happened is wrong, and I had no part in it. "Because if this war happens—if we allow it to happen—it will be as bad for my people as for yours."

Jakon nodded, considering this. "We had no hand in the death of your Pateros," he said. "We are not so witless as to trade an enemy we know for one we do not. He was honorable to us in victory, something few of your southers understand. But if we wished him gone, this coward's weapon would not be our way." Jakon

paused. "But why the poison? What need was there?
Why couldn't Montborne have used an honest blade?
He's taken enough of them from our dead."

"He needs to convince the gaea-priests you've developed horrible new weapons," Terris said. "So he can
build more of his own."

*It's that, his passion for new weapons, and not the war
itself, that makes him so dangerous in Esme's eyes.* The
invisible tempest battered at the edges of his consciousness. He shivered and thrust it away.

"Things . . . like this?"

"Yes."

"You can never have enough of death and treachery,
can you, you southers?" Jakon flared. "You think all
Harth is yours, and you can do whatever you like. First
you steal the hill pastures that have been ours for the
hungry years since the beginning of time, and ever since
we have watched our children starve and our elders go
into the night before their time. Then when our young
men ride out in anger and madness, you slaughter them
like sheep!

"Now . . ." Jakon's voice roughened. "Now you come
to me with this devil's weapon and you say there are
more to come. And worse? When will you have enough?
When we are all dead and no one remembers what
honor means? When you have laid waste all the north
and there is no one left to stand against you?"

Terris couldn't move. His muscles locked, his pulse
raced. He tried to draw air into his lungs to speak. But
the voice within him had gone silent and he didn't know
how to answer.

Was everything he'd learned in Laurea a lie? Everyone had always said the northers were a threat to civilization, the wolf at the gates, the mindless destroyers. No
one had ever mentioned the children numb with hunger
through the long cold nights.

He lowered his eyes, unable to find words for the feelings that rose up in him.

"Brassaford!" Kardith's voice split the air like a whipcrack. "What about Brassaford?"

The room leaped into sharp focus—the complex, unreadable symbols of the carpets and hangings, the yellow-streaked blood seeping through the bandages on Etch's arm, the guards with knife scars and weather-grim faces. Jakon whirling with inhuman speed to bring the dagger point to Kardith's throat.

These people are not all innocent victims, Terris thought, stunned. *And we've been enemies for a long, long time.*

The poisoned tip almost touched the dried blood on Kardith's neck. Her pupils dilated, her eyes huge and dark. Jakon's hand quivered, then was still.

"Desperate people," he said, "do desperate things."

"Desperate things," Jakon repeated as he slowly lowered the dagger. He balanced it in his hand, weighing its solidness. His brows drew together, but he kept his eyes on Kardith. For a long moment, they stood facing each other, unmoving except for their breathing.

Kardith shimmered in Terris's vision, her body poised and taut. The poisoned dagger was only an instant from her fingers. Terris was again reminded of a great hunting cat, but this time no blood-filled images rose up behind his eyes. Instead, he saw two glittering figures, a man of fire and a woman of copper and amber, creatures of sun and molten earth, matched in grace and deadliness.

Terris's heart caught in his throat. He'd never seen Kardith as beautiful before.

"Will you swear to keep from harm any living thing among us, man or beast," Jakon asked her, "to share in our bread and our salt, to honor our holy laws as your own?"

A ritual formula, Terris thought. *A prisoner's parole? A test? Or some kind of guest code?*

Kardith didn't seem to have any doubts about what Jakon meant. "I am a Laurean Ranger," she said, "and I am your prisoner."

"And you?" Jakon's eyes sought Etch. The older man, his eyes fever bright, glanced at Terris, then shook his head.

As Jakon faced him, Terris realized with a start that he was slightly taller than the norther chief, just as he

was slightly taller than Kardith. He could feel Etch struggling to stay on his feet and Kardith's eyes on him, waiting. She'd said he wasn't under her protection, and it
had made no sense to him at the time. Now he understood what she meant. He was the one who led them.
He was the one to choose—and quickly, too, before the
moment passed.

The decision was his alone. Kardith and Etch would
follow him. The voice at the back of his mind whispered
that the future of Laurea might turn on his next words.

But by all the undiscovered gods of Harth, they would
be *his* words! Not Esmelda's, not Montborne's, not
Pateros's.

His.

"I'll give you my word," he said. "My word for all
of us."

"How do I know what your word means?" Jakon demanded. "You have no gods, you southers. Your promises are like water, like wind. What can you swear by?"

*The gaea-priests would say, By All Grace or The Liv-
ing Tree. Etch would swear on Harth's sweet ass, Kardith
by The Mother.*

For me, what?

He could swear on the dagger. He could say, *"I swear
by this thing that lies between us, this thing that is as
loathsome and despicable to me as it is to you, this thing
that violates everything I believe in. I swear by this
weapon aimed at the very heart of our world."*

No, he couldn't say that. It was as pompous as anything he'd recited in his dissertation proposal. Jakon
would see through it in an instant and laugh in his face.

"You asked me before why I would betray Laurea to
tell you about Montborne and his plot," Terris said. "I
wasn't completely honest with you. The truth is that it's
Montborne who has betrayed Laurea and everything we
stand for. The truth is that I have to stop him—and I
need your help to do it. If I must swear by anything, let
it be by that truth."

A ripple of incredulity passed around the assembled
northers.

"Need our help? Who are *you* to ask us for anything?"

"I am the son of Esmelda of Laurea."

Jakon's eyes widened, a fleeting expression of surprise perhaps, or confusion . . . or amazement. "Es—melda. Ah." He nodded slightly, as if some great mystery were now made clear. "And what were you, Terricel son of Esmelda of Laurea, doing on our borders? You're not the sort your mother would send to spy on our little trading camp. And you certainly didn't ride all the way here to ask my help in dealing with your renegade general."

The deep, intuitive force which had carried him along disappeared abruptly, leaving Terris heartsick at his own weakness. Esmelda would never have let Jakon play on her emotions like that or get so carried away by the heat of the moment. But there was nothing he could do to unsay it now.

He lowered his eyes, unwilling to compound his stupidity with an outright lie. "No, I didn't. But the reason I came had nothing to do with you."

For a long moment Terris couldn't look up. His words echoed, tinny and false-sounding, in his ears. If it had been only his own life he'd thrown away, that was one thing. He'd spoken for all of them. Perhaps for all of Laurea. He had spoken impulsively, without considering . . .

The next thing he knew, the poisoned dagger was back in its wrappings and Jakon was cutting through his bonds and then Kardith's and Etch's with a small knife from his belt. Terris felt only a tug as the blade sliced through the leather.

A wave of inexpressible relief surged through him, that somehow he'd blundered through the worst crisis of his life. He wanted to shout and cry all at once. The air in the longhouse seemed brighter. He flexed his fingers, stiff and swollen. They tingled with the returning circulation.

Suddenly the guards who'd been standing quietly at the doorways moved into position beside Etch and Kardith and held them fast. Another grabbed Terris's arm and twisted it behind him.

"What the hell—? Jakon, you took my word!"

"Indeed. And if I hadn't, you wouldn't be alive," Jakon answered quietly. "We norther barbarians don't keep prisoners. Yes, I took your word, but I still don't know what it's worth."

Jakon nodded toward Etch and Kardith. "Take that one to the healers and have his arm properly tended to. Take *her* to the root cellar. Under guard. If she even looks at a knife, set her out in a leaky boat in the middle of the lake and we'll see how well a woman of the Tribes can swim. And as for the cub here, throw him in the hold."

CHAPTER 25

Terris's vision went red and the air rushing through his lungs hissed like steam. Blindly, he lunged at Jakon. He didn't think what he was going to do, he just hurled his body forward, jerking his arms to get free. The guard's grasp, which had seemed no more than a light restraint, clamped down on him like a vise. Pain lanced down his arms and back. Any notion of flight or attack vanished instantly. He fought only to breathe, to ease the wrenching leverage on his shoulder joints. Any moment now, they would come popping out of their sockets. He could almost feel the ligaments creak and tear.

An instant later, the pressure on one shoulder loosened. The back of his neck was gripped by fingers which were blunt and calloused and iron strong. Carpet and floor and the edges of rough walls blurred past him. His feet stumbled forward of their own accord. His eyes watered and the skin around his mouth went numb.

Suddenly he came to a halt, his feet splayed out like a drunken man's and his vision still cloudy gray. The grip at the back of his neck was gone, leaving a slowly fading throbbing. Behind him, a wooden bar rasped home.

Terris wet his lips and tried a breath, then another. Every muscle in his chest ached. He blinked, bringing the room into better focus. He stood in a storage room, lined with shelves and baskets of shiny dark wicker. The room was not nearly as lightless as he'd first thought, for open slits for air ran just underneath the low slanting roof. Rounded parcels hung from every rafter, smoked meat he thought, now that his sense of smell was returning, and skins of dried fruit or fermented grain.

In the center of the room, a space had been cleared for a pallet bed. He sat down on it. The dried fir branches crackled under the blanket of unbleached, tightly woven wool, the needles brittle but still slightly aromatic. Beside the bed sat an empty pot of coarse red clay, decorated with a complicated incised pattern and fired but not glazed, and another, large and wide-mouthed, by the side of the snug-fitting wooden door.

The bar slid back again and the door opened a crack. Terris scrambled to his feet, too slow to reach it before it closed again. A pot half full of water had been shoved inside, along with a bowl of steamed barley.

The water was cold and Terris found himself surprisingly thirsty. Hungry, too, for the chewy nutlike grain. As he finished it and then drained the last of the water, he realized how easily either could have been drugged. Or poisoned. Jakon had picked up the fake dagger by the hilt, knowing the same thing.

Terris spent the next hour trying to analyze the norther people, but he found little comfort there. His imagination kept straying to increasingly uncomfortable visions of what lay in store for Kardith, for Etch, for himself. The University and everything in Laureal City seemed very far away.

He spent the second hour prowling the room and thinking of all the ways he could make weapons from the materials at hand, and the third hour talking himself out of it.

Putting him here, in this storage room that was far from secure, it was a test. It must be. Jakon said he accepted his word enough not to kill them immediately, and Etch was being given some kind of medical care. Terris told himself there was no need for immediate or desperate action.

What would he do if he escaped, anyway? The first norther he encountered would have no trouble recapturing him, and then the situation would be even worse for all of them. Eventually, reason won out over panic. He sat back down to wait for what would come next.

He didn't have to wait much longer. The wooden bar slid back and outside stood the same guard who'd shoved him in here earlier, the dour-faced norther who'd led the capture party. He carried a short, barb-headed spear.

"Your friend's wound has gone bad," the norther said. "The healer says it's too close to the body and cutting off the arm won't help. Jakon asks if you can use your souther medicines."

Terris got to his feet. *Please god—any god—it's not too late.* "The supplies are in my travel pack."

"It waits for you in the healer's tent."

Terris emerged into the quickly chilling shadows of the fir trees. The storage room which had been his prison was in a series of subdivided chambers taking up one end of the longhouse. Beside it stood several low, wide tents and a huge outdoor cooking pit, from which blue smoke and tantalizing odors curled upward. Beyond the edge of the clearing, the few tents and log structures were smaller, half-hidden in the natural spaces between the trees.

The healer's dwelling was a combination of tent and cabin. Coarse woolen fabric, draped like the walls of a tent, lined the rough-cut long walls. Terris ducked his head to avoid the slanting roof as he entered. Inside, the temperature was noticeably warmer.

Screens of stretched hide panels, richly decorated, separated off a little alcove in which Etch lay on a low pallet. Beside him squatted an old man in pale gold elk-skins several sizes too big for him. He tested the pulse at the side of Etch's neck and did not look up as the norther guard stood back for Terris to approach.

Etch's chest and shoulders were bare, but blankets covered the rest of his body. His arm had been bandaged with a fresh-smelling herbal poultice. Fiery red streaks stretched along his skin from the wound toward his heart.

Terris knelt and touched Etch's hand. The skin was hot and papery dry. Etch did not respond. His eyes stayed closed, his breathing fast and shallow.

"Is he dying?" Terris said.

The healer looked at him with pale blue eyes, alert and piercing. Terris realized he wasn't as old as he'd first assumed. His apparent age was an effect of the premature wrinkling of his skin and his extreme thinness.

"There is nothing more I can do for him." There was a slight, almost bitter emphasis on the word *I*. "I have cleaned the wound of dead and rotten tissue, but ..." He indicated the low shelf along the wall screen, with its row of small pottery cups of mashed herbs and dark brown liquids, covered baskets, waterskins in wicker frames. "All my herbs can do is give his body a chance to heal itself."

The travel pack lay at the foot of Etch's pallet. Terris grabbed it and yanked open the main pouch. He thrust his fingers inside the protective inner pocket. It must have been thoroughly searched for the poisoned dagger to be found and yet everything else, with the exception of his cooking knife, was neatly in its place. Money, clothing, food. A flat box of stiffened leather, the first aid kit.

Each item in the kit had been wrapped in layers of oiled silk to keep out moisture. There were small vials of water purification tablets, fever and inflammation reducers, disinfectant, bandages, sutures. Yes, there they were, two packets of bacteriostats effective against common infections and a pressure syringe of concentrated broad-spectrum bactericides, powerful drugs which would kill every circulating pathogen within a few hours. Like any other educated Laurean, Terris had been taught how to use them.

What he hadn't been taught, what he couldn't understand, was why the northers hadn't taken the kit. The healer had known what the Laurean medicines could do and yet had sent for Terris to use them. For Etch, not for one of his own people who might need them just as badly.

Terris picked up the syringe. The glass and surgical

steel felt cold in his callused fingers. He found the big artery in Etch's armpit and positioned the tip of the syringe over it. The pressure device hissed softly as it drove the medication through the skin and into the bloodstream. As if in response, Etch's head moved on his thin pillow, a gentle lolling movement like a blinded man searching for the light. His eyelids quivered and he took a deep, sighing breath.

The healer held out a waterskin, its soft belly supported in a wicker basket for handling. The flexible neck ended in a tube of delicately carved bone. Terris took it and tried not to think about the origin of the bone. It looked very much like a human finger.

"If he wakes, he must drink." With surprising agility, the healer rose to a crouch and glided from the alcove.

After a time, Etch roused again. A low groan came from his throat, as if he were trying to speak. He licked his dry lips. Terris held the bone tube to his lips and tipped out a small amount of water.

Etch swallowed. His eyes opened slightly, pupils wide and unfocused as he fumbled with his good hand for the waterskin.

"It's all right." Terris gently restrained him. "Just drink, it's all right. You're safe, my friend, I'm here," very much as he'd murmured to the laboring mare. Etch relaxed back on the pallet and began drinking thirstily, pausing only to take a deep breath. But soon his gulps slowed and he drifted off to sleep again.

Terris touched Etch's arm again. This time the skin, although still hot, felt moist. He cradled the waterskin on his lap and sat back.

The little screened-off room sank into a dense quiet. Noises from the encampment outside flowed around the healer's tent as if it were a chunk of granite in the middle of a gently murmuring stream. The healer himself had vanished without a trace. As the moments stretched on, Terris became acutely aware of his own heartbeat, the whisper of air through his own lungs, the watchful stillness of the norther guard.

Terris's thoughts drifted, half-drowsy, his eyes slowly

closing. The walls darkened and the unmistakable reek of burning beeswax filled his nostrils. For a moment, his vision blurred, then he blinked and his eyes focused again. He felt himself being carried across a dimly lit room, safe in strong familiar arms and bathed in a sweet milky scent.

Suddenly he found himself gazing down at the face of a desperately ill man, but it wasn't Etch. The features seemed strange and yet hauntingly familiar—skin dusky even in the candlelight, cheeks sunk with fever, eyes bright as embers.

The man on the bed raised one hand as if reaching out. The rustle of the bedclothes masked the sound of his voice, a rasping whisper.

Terris felt himself being shifted, transferred to another set of arms, thin and wiry. The skin smelled familiar but far less intimate and reassuring. He twisted, following the milk-scent. The woman who was the source walked away from him and sat on the bed. He saw her hold the man's hand in hers. Some emotion Terris couldn't understand charged her voice as she spoke.

For a long time she sat unmoving, the only sound the hoarse rattle of the man's breathing, growing slower and harsher. After a time of silence, she reached down to brush the dark hair back from his forehead and cover his eyes. The candlelight reflected on a ring on her finger, the signet a dotted doubled circle.

The woman's head dropped forward, her short-cropped hair hiding her face. Her shoulders sagged, but her spine remained rigidly erect. She drew a deep, shuddering breath. Her tears shone in the flickering candlelight.

Terris blinked and found himself shivering in the norther healer's tent. His cheeks were wet. He wondered what his life might have been like if his father hadn't died, how growing up with Esmelda might have been different. He felt unbearable sadness for the ways she herself would not have changed.

Slowly the tears dried on his face. Etch slept peacefully on his pallet. The norther guard, who had been sitting like a carven rock, said, "Why do you weep, souther? Your friend will live. See how well he does already."

Terris flinched as if he'd been caught naked. But there was no prying behind the question, no scorn, no sense that the man was probing for some weakness he could exploit. Only puzzlement and sympathy.

"I know that," he said. "I—I was remembering my father. He died when I was a baby. I used to think I made it all up, stories, nothing more. But this time—I *saw* him. He was real. Here. Now."

"Yes, you have that look about you. It is not easy to know a father through the spirit only."

Terris didn't know what to make of this comment. No one in Laurea, not even the gaea-priests who were always holding forth about cosmic oneness, would have reacted with such simple acceptance. For lack of something better, he glanced at the herbal remedies arrayed on the low shelf beside Etch's pallet. "Did your people suffer very much during the epidemic?"

The norther looked surprised. "You are Esmelda's son, and yet you don't know?"

"Know what?"

"That she sent medicines—vaccines—for all our people along the border. Not one of us sickened. We died other ways—of cold, of hunger, of souther spears. But not of pestis fever."

Why? Why would she want to help the northers? Why not simply do nothing and let the plague wipe them out? No, that's what Montborne would have done. Esme sees things differently—and so do I.

"There were many things about her I never knew," he answered slowly.

"It's for this—and other things—that we permit her agents to live among us. But do not hope they will bring her news of you now. We will make sure none of them leaves the trading camp in time."

The norther leaned forward, the shaft of his spear resting against his shoulder. "As for you, I see the same thing with Jakon and his grandfather, who is The Cassian of Clan'Cass. An ordinary chief would have killed himself after the Brassa massacre. He is a legend all through the north; even the crazy Huldites listen to him. So Jakon brought us down here, where he could build his trading post without everyone forever asking what The Cassian would have done. It's always that way with leaders and the children who walk their shadows.''

"I don't know about the grandfather, but Jakon—he doesn't need to, how did you put it? *walk anyone's shadow.*"

"Ah!"

Terris looked down as he digested the implications of that single syllable. "Tell me—I'm sorry, I don't know your name—am I still a prisoner?"

"I'm Grissem, and we take no prisoners. You are . . . an untrusted guest. You cannot go to the longhouse un-invited, or the sweat hut when it's built, or women's quarters, or leave the island."

"Until Jakon decides to accept my word."

"Until you eat his bread and salt."

Bread and salt, an old ritual of hospitality. "And then?"

"Then you would have sworn to keep faith or be killed."

Bread and salt sounded so innocent, something Terris would have easily accepted. Kardith—or any Ranger— would have known what it meant and refused. Aviyya, if she were still alive, would have known.

Terris struggled against the sense of rising quicksand. Yet he'd learned more about the northers in five minutes than he would have in five years at home.

"We know your ways are not ours," Grissem said, "which is why Jakon has left you the choice. For now, at least. When the sweat hut is finished, he'll go there to fast and pray. The Northlight will come down to him and show him what he must do with you."

And then, Terris thought with a shiver, *there may no longer be a choice.*

But what, by all the hidden gods of Harth, is the Northlight?

CHAPTER 26

Terris and Etch wandered along the shoreline, waiting for the sun to go down. Grissem followed a few paces behind, far enough to give them the illusion of privacy but not so far they could forget the spear he carried. They had been on the island for five days now and Etch was back on his feet and rapidly regaining his strength. Meanwhile, Terris's nerves grated with the frustration which increased daily. Jakon had disappeared into the sweat hut, there was no sign of Kardith, and Terris hadn't been able to exchange more than a few words with the northers to fill in the tantalizing glimpses of their culture. Despite his earlier words, Grissem had kept them carefully isolated from the lake community. They were, indeed, *untrusted guests.*

As the sun dipped toward the horizon, the expanse of tundra beyond the lake turned misty-purple in the failing light. Overhead, the sky had gone a sullen blue-black. Terris gazed over the gently lapping waves, half expecting to find Kardith sitting alone and furious in an oarless boat over the deepest part of the lake. But the wind-rippled water was empty. Firelights glowed on the far shore. Bits of music and talk, faint and disjointed, reached his ears.

Earlier the same day, Grissem informed Terris that Jakon had emerged from the sweat hut, having dreamed up a message from whatever gods had come down to speak to him. Grissem hadn't phrased it exactly like that, but Terris didn't expect the so-called *message* to be anything more than a pack of hallucinations born of dehydration and Jakon's own expectations. The eastern nomads did the same thing with their dreamsmoke rituals. But these northers appeared to take the matter seriously, almost religiously, and a special ceremony had been scheduled for that evening in the longhouse.

Etch scratched absentmindedly at his healing arm through his thick cloak. He caught Terris's eye and jerked his hand away.

"I should know better," he said, a little sheepishly. "Still, a good sign, that itching is. I knew a man once, who ran horses along the border clear out to Archipelago. His brother lost an arm and for years afterward the damned thing kept itching. Said it drove him half crazy."

The last thin line of solar brilliance flared and died along the western rim, leaving only the lightest of yellow with none of the orange or red of the city. The sky went dark and then hazy with stars. Grissem led them back to the longhouse and in through one of the side entrances.

As Terris stepped through the narrow doorway, his first impression was a confusion of light and movement. Light because glass globes now lined the halls, spreading a soft, white-blue glow. And movement, because the hall seemed to be full of people, men streaming in from one side and women through the other, their heads gray and honey-gold and flaxen. He caught a glimpse of Jakon sitting in his usual place on the drum stool and Kardith, escorted in through the women's door. She looked strong and alert, unhurt.

Etch, at his side, let his breath out audibly. "Thank all the gods of Harth, she's all right." Grissem gestured forcefully for him to be quiet.

From the front of the longhouse came a bitten-off exclamation, a woman's sharp cry. Terris glimpsed a dark head, taller than the rest, but whether man or woman he couldn't tell, for Grissem grasped his elbow and pulled him down the hall, then motioned for him to sit along the wall beside Etch.

Black hair . . . not a norther. Terris curled his fingers

into fists, digging his ragged nails into his palms and forcing himself to keep still.

Aviyya had black hair.

And there she was, taking her seat across the room with the other women, and glancing over at Kardith with a quickly masked expression of astonishment. Her gray eyes, ringed with lashes so dark they looked smudged, scanned the men's side of the room, paused as they met his and widened with surprise. Her lips, strong and full and dark, shaped his name. Only then did he realize she wore her Ranger's vest over a set of pale gold elkskins and that her black hair was braided like any norther woman's.

The last norther took his place seated along the outside of the room. Terris glanced from Aviyya to Kardith and back again. His mind flooded with questions and he wished he knew what was going on.

As for Aviyya herself, she seemed like someone familiar seen through warped glass. He recognized her, but not the ways the years had changed her. There was no mistaking the flash in her eyes as she glared at Jakon. Her body might be motionless, but the spirit within it leapt like a sparking flame.

Grissem brought out a drum and padded sticks. The women took down the wall ornaments and held them in their laps. What Terris had thought were plaques or shields, he realized, were really hand drums.

Boom! Grissem brought one stick down on the drum head. *Boom!* With the next beat, the women joined in. Terris felt the vibration through the wooden floor and without meaning to, began tapping his foot in rhythm.

Boom-boom-boom! Grissem brought the drumming to a halt.

A man at the far end got to his feet and walked slowly to the center. His hair, so white it bore no tinge of yellow, gleamed in the light of the globes. He saluted Jakon and began to dance. At first, he moved stiffly, as if his joints were half-frozen with arthritis. Soon he seemed to glide across the carpet, his steps strong and fluid. His arms traced gently circular patterns. Terris recognized the gestures for what they were—complex, ritual, rich in cultural meaning he had no basis for understanding. He wondered if the man were telling a story—perhaps of how the southers had come to the camp, perhaps of Jakon's Northlight vision in the sweat hut. The drums sang again, the women's fingertips skimming the stretched painted hide in ghostly whispers.

After the old man sat down, there was a moment of stillness before a young woman arose to take his place. Slowly she lifted her arms above her head and tilted her head back, her braids falling past her waist. Her knees bent deeper and deeper until she seemed about to fall to the ground. Then she began to curve and twist, as if trying to escape from an insupportable weight. She moved faster, spinning, reeling, sometimes rising on the toes of one foot, her head still thrown back. Through it all, the drums were silent.

Watching her, Terris's breath caught in his throat. Even after she had taken her place on the carpeted floor and other dancers rose to the beating of the drums, he imagined the traces of her movements hung like ghosts in the air.

The dance *meant* something. He could feel it in the silence of the drums. What it was, he couldn't guess. At home he might have hazarded an interpretation, but here he didn't dare.

Now Jakon got to his feet and stood in the center of the room. He paused, balanced on both feet, his hands at his sides.

Jakon raised his arms, as slow and smooth as if the air itself were lifting them. Terris felt the change, the expectancy, the shift in focus that crackled through the room like an electrical charge. This was it—the verdict of the Northlight gods. He steeled himself to hear the worst.

Arms still overhead, Jakon lifted one foot and brought it down hard.

Stamp!

His feet were bare and made almost no sound on the dark patterned carpet, yet the whole room shuddered with the impact.

Stamp!

Again, the knee raised, the thigh muscles bunching through the supple elkskin, heel extended and foot flat against the ground. Again the soundless bone-shivering ripples.

Stamp! Now with the other foot, alternating one after the other, and Terris heard the first faint tapping from the stool drum.

Jakon lowered his arms to chest level and quickened the pace. He moved through space as if gathering it up, his braided hair swinging in counterpoint. Around the room, people began swaying with the rhythm of his dance.

Terris watched in fascination. Jakon's movements seemed so simple, and yet he could feel their power running in his blood, their rhythms in his heartbeat. The thing within him, deep and intuitive, that had given him a voice during that first crucial interview, now stirred in response.

Finally, Jakon slowed his movements and began a reprise of the opening stamps.

The room fell still, a beat longer than the usual pause between dances. Now Aviyya rose to her feet. She was tall, her shoulders wide and strong, her hips under the supple elkskin pants tapering to muscular legs. Where the norther women had seemed like a patterning in palest gold, she burned, incandescent. Her cheeks and lips glowed like rubies, her skin like pearl, her eyes molten silver. Slowly she turned, head high, her back slightly arched, breasts lifted beneath the pocketed Ranger's vest.

Aviyya raised her hands and untied the lacings of her braids. One after another, she let the thin leather strips fall to the ground. As she unloosed each plaited strand, she combed her fingers through it, still crimped from the tightness of the braid. Then she leaned forward and shook her head. Her hair tumbled past her shoulders, blue-black under the lights.

She left the leather bindings on the carpet and she stalked back to her seat.

*   *   *

Slowly Terris got to his feet, with no clear idea what he was doing. His body felt awkward, all elbows and angles. He couldn't remember ever having danced a step in his life.

The northers, he sensed, danced as they always had, for their own people and traditions. Whatever this Northlight vision of Jakon's had meant, it represented a continuation of the past. It changed nothing for them. But it must—somehow he must make it change.

Avi, too, had danced as she always had. She'd danced for herself, that same sense of self and pride which had propelled her from Esmelda's house and kept her living right on the edge.

And I . . . what do I dance for?

Terris stood for what felt like a long time, hoping for a trickle of inspiration. He thought the northers might grow impatient with him, but they sat in perfect, serious attention.

What do I dance for? I don't know, but I have to try. I can't let things stay the way they've always been.

Terris began as so many of the other dancers had, by lifting his arms, elbows bent slightly, palms outward. He flexed his knees and took a deep step, turning so that he faced the front of the room and Jakon. As he moved, his hands rose higher, his fingers pulled back so that his whitened palms stretched outward. He took another step and then another, following a curved path. His feet sped on with an energy all their own, carrying him in an ever-widening spiral. He no longer thought about what he was doing—the dance itself moved his body. He felt rather than saw the spark of recognition in Jakon's eyes.

Time lost all meaning as he circled the room, faster and faster as if caught up in an invisible whirlwind. Energy sizzled up his spine and out his arms. His heart thundered in his ears, his lungs ached as he gulped breath after breath. Heat streamed from his body as from a furnace. The watching faces blurred, the room seemed to melt away. From below the thin-worn carpet and the rough flooring, damp rich soil rose up to cushion his tread. The echoes of his steps spread through the loam and into the bedrock.

Images flashed through his mind, glimpses of sky and mountain and tumbling river; he caught the scent of salt tang, the lingering sweetness of flower fields, the rich savory must of ripened grain. His vision blurred, pictures overlapping so that he was no longer dancing in a globe-lit longhouse, he was dancing across the length and breadth of Harth itself. Some of the scenes he had seen with his own eyes—the broad city avenues, the placid fields of barley, the flood-swollen rivers. Others he'd glimpsed in Gaylinn's paintings, still others in his own imagination. He danced through them all, reaching out, gathering them, weaving them together until there was no longer any difference between *real* and *dreamed.*

Then he was no longer moving, except for the heaving of his chest. His hands stretched high above his head, his elbows locked straight, sweat-slick palms flat to the heavens, not the roof with its heavy dark beams, but the sky arching beyond it. The searing azure he remembered from his first view of the lake encampment. The soft powdery sun on the blossoming trees in Laureal City. The milky stars of the Ridge. The blackness of the Ar-chipelago storm. The alkali-bitter sands scouring the eastern steppe.

He knew then what he swore by, what he danced for. He felt it in the very rhythms of his blood and bone.

The power which had surged through Terris vanished abruptly. His knees felt like jelly and his muscles turned to water. He lowered his arms, looked around for a confused instant at the assembled audience, and collapsed down in his place.

Jakon stood up. "The dream is true."

There was no response for a long moment, and Terris wondered if that meant they were now going to begin a long and heated debate, that the dance and all it carried was no more than a traditional preliminary. He felt tired, so tired, even more than after a day's running beside the sorrel gelding.

The next instant a murmur ran through the assembly, people nodded, some of them smiling as if satisfied, then they got up, exchanged a few comments with their neighbors and left the longhouse.

Terris thought of getting up, too, but he couldn't make himself. His muddled brain told his legs to move and nothing happened.

Etch came over and touched his shoulder. "You all right?" Terris nodded and wiped the cooling sweat off his forehead.

Kardith didn't move. She sat watching Aviyya, who sat staring at Jakon, still standing, until it was only the five of them and Grissem in the shadows of the emptied longhouse.

CHAPTER 27

Aviyya scrambled to her feet. She thrust her shoulders back and her chin forward, as if she meant to grab Jakon and shake him. She shoved one pointed index finger under his nose.

"My partner—my brother—they've been here all week, haven't they? And I never knew! When I moved to the women's tent, that's when they arrived, wasn't it?"

Before he could reply, she rushed on. "I thought you were beginning to trust me—what an idiot I was! I should have known something else was going on!"

She raised both hands, as if appealing to a celestial jury. "You've never believed a thing I've said, have you? Why did I even bother telling you the truth? What was the use of it? I could eat your gods-damned salt from now until both moons fall into the sea, and you still wouldn't listen to me!"

Despite his tiredness, Terris felt an incredulity bordering on awe at Aviyya's outburst. It was so perfectly logical for the northers to keep their captives separate until they decided what to do with them. Esmelda would have done exactly the same, had the situation been reversed. What was most amazing, though, was the puzzled look on Jakon's face when he answered, in perfect seriousness, "I believed you. I just didn't trust you."

"Then what in Harth's name *do* you trust?" Aviyya demanded.

"My dreams."

"Your—"

"Which have shown me that I alone cannot judge your story, or your brother's. Only in Northlight will the truth be shown." Jakon gave her no time for further protest. "You'd better listen to what your brother has to say. There's far more at stake for your Laurea than the fate of one headstrong woman Ranger. We leave at dawn tomorrow."

"But—"

"Rest well, Aviyya of the south. You wouldn't want any of us barbarians to—as you southers put it—*ride circles* around you, come tomorrow morning."

With a hastily concealed quirk of his mouth, Jakon turned and stalked out of the longhouse. Grissem also withdrew, but stopped just outside the door.

Aviyya watched them go, mouth slightly open, hands hanging open at her sides. She took a heaving breath and spat out the word, "Drat." Then she spun around, strode over to Kardith and held out her arms.

Even if he hadn't known they were lovers, Terris would have looked away. There was something intensely private about the way the two women embraced—the silence between them, the way their arms curled around each other and their bodies pressed together with no hesitation, the way the two heads, black and copper, rested on each other's shoulders.

Etch got to his feet, his mouth twisted in an unreadable expression and his eyes carefully averted from the two women. He glanced at the floor, at the drum stool, moved a few steps toward the door and paused, turned halfway back and held out a hand to help Terris up.

Aviyya looked Kardith in the eyes. "Don't you *ever* risk your hand for me again."

"Oh, *that,*" drawled Kardith. "That was the easy part. The hard bit was back in Laureal City, facing that old dragon you call a mother. You owe me for that."

"My *mother*?" Aviyya's voice rose half an octave. "You went to see my *mother*?"

"For some official clout to get those crotting orders changed, you're damned right I did. But all I ended up with was this old horse doctor—" for just an instant, her eyes flickered across Etch's turned-away face, "—and this greenie kid with a yen for fancy dancing."

"Terricel!" Aviyya exclaimed as if she'd just remembered he was there. "My baby brother, Terricel!" She hugged Terris hard. He was a little surprised at the strength of her arms coupled with the softness of the cheek pressed against his. She smelled faintly of elkskin and lye soap. Then she grabbed his shoulders and pushed him away.

"You've got to tell me—never mind, let's get out of here and then we can sort out the whole story. This is the horse doctor? You have a name? Never mind that, too. Griss!" She headed for the door, Terris in tow. "Where the hell is Jakon putting us?"

The tent Grissem led them to was actually a hut which had begun life as a root storage shelter and then been converted to overflow sleeping space when the trading camp was set up. The dirt floor lay about two feet below ground level, smooth but damp and very cold. Ratty furs from some unrecognizable animal covered the walls. Half a dozen fir-bough pallets encircled the central fire-pit, which had been lit earlier and was now burning down to embers. Smoke curled upward through an opening in the conical roof. A pile of travel packs, saddlebags and bedding stood just inside the single door.

"I wonder who we've kicked out," Etch murmured, as he pulled his pack from the heap. "Or what they did to get stuck here in the first place."

"Hunh!" said Kardith. "After the hole they put me in, this is downright lavish." She sat down on one of the pallets and poked the stuffing. "Look, no bedmice."

"I thought the northers kept men and women separate," Etch said as he sat beside her.

"They do. Unmarried ones, anyway," said Aviyya. "But they've probably given up on us amoral southers." She pushed Terris down on another pallet and sat facing him. "All right, baby brother, what sort of mess have you been getting yourself into now? Exactly what did Jakon mean about *more at stake*? And what the hell are you doing out here?"

"I'm rescuing *you,*" he said, bristling inside at being treated like a child. "At least that's how it started out."

He began the story once again, beginning with the assassination of Pateros. He'd repeated the episodes so many times now they had a curious distant quality, like something from an outdated textbook. It was hard to believe he'd actually been there and several times he'd almost been killed. Some new, inner caution kept him from mentioning his suspicions about Esmelda's secret guardianship of Harth.

Aviyya proved a far different listener than Etch or Jakon. For one thing, she kept interrupting. Terris couldn't go more than a sentence or two without her interrupting with another question. She wanted every step explained, none of the details left out. Also, she'd burst out with "Drat!" at such increasing frequency that Etch finally turned to her and said, "Harth's sweet ass, woman, you come up with the most unimaginative swearing I've heard in my entire life!" While Kardith and Terris laughed aloud, Aviyya stared at him with a puzzled expression and went right on with her next question.

"This is bad, Terr," she said when he was finished. "This is really bad. I wish you'd turned around right then and brought the dagger back to Esme. *She* would have known what to do with it."

"I take responsibility for my decision," Terris said tightly.

She glared at him, lips pressed together. "You have no idea what you're playing with—"

"Back off, Avi," Kardith said. "He's not the baby brother you left behind. Not any more."

"Meanwhile," Avi went on after a heartbeat, "who knows how long it'll take us to get out of this mess— not soon, anyway, what with Jakon dragging us all up to this Northlight thing of his. It's not worth risking all of Har—of Laurea for one person. You should have let me rot, all of you."

"That's not only stupid, it's just plain ungrateful," Etch snapped. "After what your brother and Kardith went through to find you. Kardith especially. What she almost lost—what she was willing to give up to save your lousy skin! You don't throw that kind of loyalty away, you—"

"*You* don't know anything about it!" Aviyya snapped. Etch stared back at her, unflinching. "Ahtomic crotting toxic shit."

Aviyya's hand, resting on her thigh, twitched as if reaching for a knife which wasn't there.

"What the—" Kardith began.

"Stop it, both of you!" said Terris. "Did we come all this way just to snipe at each other like a clutch of twitterbats? We've got this Northlight test to deal with, and Jakon to convince to let us go—*with* the dagger—not to mention getting it back to Laureal City and building a case against Montborne. If either of you thinks this bickering is going help, I'd sure like to know how!"

"Drat." Aviyya ran one hand through her thick black hair. "You're right."

"Meanwhile," Kardith said, leaning forward in Aviyya's direction, "I, for one, would like to hear how you got up here when I couldn't find a trace of you anywhere between the camp and the badlands."

"That's a story and a half," Aviyya said. "It all happened because I was stupid."

"Stupid?" Kardith said, grinning wickedly. "*You're* admitting you might have been stupid?"

"You'd think after all those years I'd be used to the Ridge weirdies, wouldn't you? They were all clustered around me that last night. Drove me half bats. I went off a little way from the camp . . . and then—I wasn't on the Ridge any more."

"You fell down a canyon?" Terris asked, remembering his vision of her struggling up a mud-slick slope, her face white and bleeding.

"There's no place to fall down *to*." Aviyya's eyes widened. "But I did have a fall like that, a couple of years ago. It was during a skirmish. I felt—for a moment, I felt you were right there with me."

Terris thought of his other visions, especially his glimpses of Esme wearing the Guardian's medallion and confronting Montborne. Were they past or future .. or only possibility?

"I turned around, heading eastward, back toward camp," Aviyya went on, "and there I was, in the middle of this green tunnel. Not scrub-grass green, more like the color of malachite. All green, as far as I could see. It was so quiet the only thing I could hear was my own breathing. No flies, lizards, twitterbats, nothing."

"I know," Terris said. "I've seen it, too."

Aviyya hung her head and her soft dark curls hung forward around her face like a veil. She took a deep breath. "I have no idea how long I was there. Long enough to get thirsty—I was scared to go too far looking for water. I tried using my knife to mark the walls, but it wouldn't leave a scratch. Finally—I don't know how I did it. I was pacing out a path ... and I turned around ... and there was a shimmer like a Ridge weirdie and I was out. But not back at the camp."

"The badlands, where you hid your button?" asked Kardith.

"I knew you'd find it if Derron let you search that far," Aviyya said. "Anyway, by the time I'd figured out where I was, I was nabbed by Jakon's scouts. They're even jumpier about trespass than we are. Caught me way off guard. I should've been able to handle them— there were only three."

"You were always no good with a knife," Kardith said cheerfully. She looked happier but there was a strain in her voice, a poignancy that he couldn't quite place.

"Right," said Aviyya. "You can guess what a time I had trying to explain to Jakon what I was doing here—"

"And Jakon didn't believe a word of it," Terris said.

"I can hardly blame him. If I were him, I wouldn't believe me either. But I was enough of a mystery so he didn't kill me right off, even when I spit in his eye rather than eat his bread and salt."

"So we weren't the first southers to come barging over the borders with unlikely stories," said Terris. "Except," he added grimly, "*we* were the ones with the dagger."

CHAPTER 28

The starless night was broken only by a few watchfires along the shore. Dawn hovered an hour or more away, but tonight the nocturnal predators had taken shelter early. The empty skies and forest waited, hushed except for the gentle whisper of the wind in the topmost fir branches.

As if infected by the stillness of the morning, Terris and the others kept their voices low and muted as they finished their bowls of unsweetened boiled oats, rowed across the lake, and mounted up. Aviyya, Jakon, and Grissem rode scrubby norther ponies, with a fourth to carry the extra food, clothing, tents, and grain for the horses. Jakon had offered them all ponies, claiming they ate less and stood the cold better. Terris, remembering how close Kardith had come to losing her gray mare to the ropeweed poison, refused.

Gradually the blackness to the east became less dense. A formless gray crept along the horizon and by degrees across the arch of sky. The misty cold seeped through the layers of Terris's clothing, even his heavy wool cloak. His gloved fingers felt thick and inert on the braided reins.

They left the lake encampment to the sounds of leather gear creaking and muffled hoofbeats. Terris found himself straining to catch the last distant echo of a bell or a vibration so dim it must be half-imagined. Its source lay ahead of him, far to the north. If he concentrated hard, he could just hold on to it, weaving in and out of his awareness. But to speak would be to risk losing it and never being able to find it again.

When it was light enough to make out the tufts of wiregrass and patches of ice, Jakon picked up the pace. They trotted until Terris's bones felt like powder from the constant bouncing. Up one gentle hill and down the next, they skirted small, irregularly shaped fields of rye and oats. Scattered harvesters bent low to scythe the stunted grain, their pannier-laden elk following close behind.

Jakon called a halt to let the horses drink from the half-frozen ponds which dotted the tundra. Kardith took a hoof pick from her saddlebags and began cleaning out dirt and stones from her mare's feet.

Terris slid to the ground and stood, numb and grateful, in the shelter of the gelding's body. Once they'd started moving faster, he'd lost the faint tug from the north, and a sour sick feeling now took its place. The horse lifted his dripping muzzle from the water to pull mouthfuls of heavy-headed seed grass, jerking the roots free from the mud.

"Greedy Bastard," Terris muttered, patting him. He turned to Aviyya, standing next to him, checking the girths of her saddle. A feeling of strangeness came over him. What did he really know about her, this woman who looked so much like his sister?

"What was it like, running away?" he asked.

Aviyya took a swig from the flask tied to her saddle. It was light enough now to see the delicate lines around her eyes and mouth. "What was it like, growing up alone?" she countered.

"Not simple." A bitter sound which might have been a laugh erupted somewhere inside him. "But by the time I was old enough to care, Esme had a chance to think about what happened to you. In the end, she let me go."

"So my leaving made a difference, after all." Aviyya's gray eyes narrowed. "What you said about Montborne. And Esme. Can she control him?"

"I thought so when I left. That was before his goons

came after me with the dagger. I still don't know if I
made the right decision—if I might have made things
worse if I went back or if Esme really needed me. I only
know that I have to find my own way now, just as you
did. Avi, what was it Esme told you that made you leave
when you did, so sudden—what was it she wanted
from you?"

"Didn't Esme tell you?" Aviyya's eyes went steely.
"It's dangerous to ask such questions, baby brother."

Abruptly, she turned her back on him, reached beneath her saddlebags and pulled out a fist-sized parcel
wrapped in greased cloth. Terris recognized it as the trail
food Grissem had distributed among them. She took a
bite of the amorphous grayish lump.

"You ought to eat something." She swung up on her
pony and booted it into a choppy canter.

The wet tundra seemed to go on forever, broken only
by gentle hills with straggly evergreen forests clustering
on the lower slopes. By gradual steps, they climbed. The
air grew thinner and drier, the trees sparser.

Terris reined his gelding beside Avi's pony. There was
something he wanted from her, and not being told to
eat something, either. Some trace of the sister he'd
lost, perhaps.

Aviyya rode with easy grace, her body moving to the
pony's stride. As Terris drew near, her mouth twisted,
as if she were gathering herself for a difficult task. He
waited, thinking how the old Aviyya, the one he'd grown
up with, fearless confidante and playfellow, never had
any trouble blurting out whatever was on her mind.
They'd both changed.

"I'm sorry I treated you like a kid," she said at last.
"Seven years is a long time."

He nodded, sensing a searching behind her words.

"You said you can see the Ridge weirdies, too," she
went on, sounding a bit hesitant still.

"See them? I nearly fell into one!" Relief washed
through him. "All my life, I've been able to see and feel
things other people can't." He went on to tell her about

the waking visions and the thing beneath the Starhall. Surely she, of all people, should understand.

Aviyya frowned, chewing on her lip. "We both can see the Ridge weirdies, so we're neither of us crazy. As for the rest ... I always hated it when Esme dragged me to the Starhall, but I don't think it made me physically ill. I don't know about your dreams."

"They aren't dreams!" The gelding jumped in surprise. Terris patted his neck. "For one thing, I'm often wide awake. For another, I see things I couldn't possibly remember. I was there when Father died—I smelled the beeswax candles. Lys carried me away in her arms. Esme was crying, impossible as that sounds. I saw Esme make that speech of hers in the plaza. And, Avi—I've seen her as Guardian."

Aviyya came alert, taut. "You're sure this has really happened?"

Reluctantly, he shook his head. "The first time was back in Laureal City and Pateros was still alive. I don't know if it's something that *will* happen or that *might*. Montborne's a formidable opponent."

"So is Esme." But Aviyya's voice was a shade less than certain.

Terris's eyes scanned the steepening hills, the inky shadows of the trees, huddled together as if for warmth. "There's nothing we can do about it now."

"Maybe."

Fields of grain gave way to herds of domestic elk grazing on wiregrass or resting in the shelter of dwarf holly groves. The herdsman, so bundled up that he looked obese, waved to them as he whistled to his dogs. Jakon rode off alone to greet him while the rest of them waited.

"I reckon he doesn't want it known he's got southers with him," Etch commented as they started off again. "I wouldn't want to be seen with me, either."

Terris gazed ahead, his cloak tucked around him as tightly as he could manage. A gust of air, cold enough to burn, teased a few strands of hair from beneath his hood. He brushed them back and felt the first downy traces of beard regrowth along his jaw. Etch's beard had come in curly, gray-flecked brown, and there were creases bracketing his mouth and new lines around his eyes.

I probably look even worse, Terris thought with an inward smile. *Who in Laurea would recognize either of us now?*

"You should eat."

Terris looked up. He'd been staring down at the sorrel's bony withers, for how long he didn't know. Etch had drifted off to ride beside Kardith and Grissem had taken his place. The norther held out a wrapped parcel like Aviyya's. The thought of food made Terris's stomach twist ominously and his mouth go acid. He shook his head.

"You think you can't," said Grissem. "But that's your body sickening with the height. You southers aren't used to it, or the cold. Next thing, you'll be hearing things and we'll have to carry you like a baby."

Terris took the parcel. He expected it to smell as revoltingly greasy as it looked, but he couldn't smell anything at all—the cold had numbed the inside of his nose. He took a tentative bite. It was salty and pungent, chewy with grain and laced with fruit and something he thought was dried meat, but didn't want to ask. He drank from his saddle flask. The honeyed water, instead of being cloyingly sweet, tasted refreshing, invigorating.

"Now listen to me," said Grissem. "I know you want to talk to your friends. You southers always talk too much. But where we're going, you can't be bringing a head full of chatter, you understand me?"

A head full of chatter. Terris remembered riding through the predawn stillness, his nerves raw with cold, but some part of him stirring, listening ... It wasn't that the altitude made him hear things, but that it made him *forget* what was already there, just at the limit of his normal senses. Now that his nerves were steadier, his sight clearer, he could feel it again, calling him from the north.

*   *   *

They saw no more elk herds, nor did they come within sight of any human habitation. The ponies went on as if they were immune to cold and fatigue, but by the end of each day the horses flagged and had to be coaxed to eat their grain rations. From time to time, Aviyya would ride beside Terris and try to talk to him, but between Grissem's warning and the growing sense of blanketing urgency, the pull from the north, he couldn't bring himself to answer her.

They passed one night by a grove of ironbark trees and the next in the shelter of the huge, isolated rocks which towered above the half-frozen earth.

Terris curled up in his cloak against the weather-cracked stone and lay there unmoving until Etch brought him a pan of hot trail stew. It was the usual sticky mess of grain, dried fruit, and nameless smoked meat. With it was a chunk of bread and a pinch of coarse salt, which Jakon said would help them adapt to the altitude. Even though he wasn't hungry, Terris took a mouthful of the stew. The last thing he wanted now was someone else nagging him to eat.

Behind him, the wind moaned fitfully through the crevices of the rock. He felt it tremble, but perhaps that too was a product of the strange warping of his senses the further north they went. The pulling had grown into a sweet wild calling that he could feel even in his sleep, and it was all he could do now to sit still and let his aching body rest. He closed his eyes and concentrated on chewing.

In between the gusts of wind, he heard Etch and Kardith discussing one of the horses, a foreleg tendon or something like that. Abruptly Kardith swore and stomped off. Terris felt her pass within inches of his extended legs, not smooth like a shadow panther, but turbulent, volatile. He opened his eyes.

Across the flickering pocket fire, Jakon and Grissem had taken out a hand drum and a small bone flute. Yesterday evening, they'd spent an hour or more playing and chanting. The words were so archaic Terris couldn't even guess their meaning, yet he had found himself humming along, caught by their lilting rhythms. Tonight he recoiled from the music.

Aviyya got up from her place in the shadows and went over to Jakon. Grissem's hand jerked from his flute to the hilt of his knife. She saw the movement and kept her hands in plain sight.

"What's the matter with my brother?" she asked. "Why is he like that?"

"It's the Northlight calling him," Jakon said, hands poised over his drum.

"Batshit. He's acting like he's overdosed on ghostweed. He can hardly talk."

Terris struggled against the curious stillness of his body, the quality of listening, of following. He knew the effects of ghostweed and this wasn't one of them. His throat moved reluctantly. "I'm all right."

Aviyya glared at him. "Have it your own way. For now." She sat back on her heels and turned her attention back to Jakon. "It's also time we talked about what happens after this Northlight."

Jakon laid the drum on the ground slowly. "We aren't there yet. Your brother still must stand before the Light. We can't make any plans beyond that."

She shook her head impatiently. "You don't understand. No matter what happens there, we have to go back to Laureal City. I see that now. The sooner the better—in fact, we ought to turn around right now. We can't afford to waste this much time. The political situation's too unstable—and I'm not just talking about your people, I'm talking about mine, too. What if Terr's vision is right and Esme's now Guardian? How long do you think Montborne will let her stand? Will there be another poisoned dagger for her? Maybe you don't care. But suppose he manages to get elected instead. If people are scared enough they'll turn to *anyone* for help. What then? You *know* what he can do, you even call him the Butcher of Brassaford. But with the dagger and my brother's testimony, we can make him answer for what he's done. A part of it, anyway, enough to keep him from power. These aren't empty words, Jakon, I *can do* it—if I can get back home in time."

"Who says this—Aviyya the ranger or Aviyya the daughter of Esmelda of Laurea?"

"I don't have any choice on that one, do I?" She paused. "Will you trust me and let us go? Will you come with us?"

"Are you offering an alliance?" In the near darkness, one sandy eyebrow arched upward.

"Would you accept one?" she shot back.

"Will you dance again, Aviyya of Laurea?"

"*Jakon!* You still don't understand! This is serious business, not a gods-damned carnival! There's a war going to come smashing down on both our heads if we don't stop it! And more than that, it's a chance to end all the years of fighting between us. Don't you see what—"

"I know what's at stake here, even more than you." Jakon's voice cracked like a whip through the near darkness. "Tell me how much of your own blood ran red at Brassaford and how many brothers you lost to the Butcher?" He struggled for control and continued, "Yes, what you offer could change everything between us. But what you ask—to turn back now—is unthinkable, no matter what the cost. I've never given a hundred-years-putrefied elk turd what any souther thinks, but I want you to understand—I *dreamed* the Light, I *danced* it. We're in the middle now—we can't know how we'll see things at the end. At Northlight, everything is different."

" 'Everything is different . . .' " she repeated in a completely unconvinced tone. "Does that mean Montborne will wake up tomorrow and send you flowers? Or this wiregrass will suddenly sprout sausages? Give me one good reason why we have to continue on this superstitious trek to the middle of nowhere!"

"Because it is our way. Because if we give up everything we believe in, everything that gives our lives meaning instead of mindless suffering, then we are nothing. Nothing."

"But—"

"You asked for *my* trust, Aviyya of Laurea," Jakon said quietly. "Where is *your* trust, *your* understanding?"

Aviyya reached over to his plate, which lay in front

of him, and rubbed her fingers across the surface, gathering up the crumbs.

"Bread ... salt...." She didn't add, *Damn you,* though she looked as if she'd like to. She held up a solid pinch and downed it. Grissem drew in a short audible breath.

Terris sat up straight. Tension hung in the air like a physical weight. Kardith, standing near the outside of the camp, watched with wide eyes. No one moved.

For a long, heart-stopping moment, Jakon continued to study Aviyya, his face expressionless. Then he said to Grissem, "Give their knives back." There was something in his voice that made Terris wonder if Aviyya had just eaten Jakon's salt or he had eaten hers.

Grissem reached into his pack and drew out a bundle wrapped in thin, supple elkskin. He unrolled it on the ground in front of him. Aviyya picked up two of the knives and wordlessly put one of them in the empty sheath on her belt, the other in her boot.

Etch knelt and gathered up the rest of the knives—all that had been taken from them—as well as Kardith's belt. He went to Kardith, reversed the long-knife and held it out to her. She slipped it back into its sheath without a word.

Terris felt no desire to reclaim his small utility knife. He had no right to a weapon he couldn't use, just as Kardith had said. But he picked up the wrapped dagger and carefully put it away in his travel pack.

Later he drifted into an uneasy sleep with Jakon's words still in his ears. *At Northlight, everything is different.*

Does he mean everything appears different, the way colored glass tints whatever you see? Or ... does he mean everything becomes different? Permanently, forever?

CHAPTER 29

The morning air was so thick and damp, the breath of animals and riders alike spurted out in plumes of white smoke. For the past week of travel, they had all worn the hooded, fur-lined parkas and outer pants which the northers supplied, instead of their Laurean wool cloaks. The cloaks they used as extra blankets for the horses at night.

The ground-hugging mist lifted for a moment and Terris saw they were making their way along a row of standing stones. The stones, like those scattered on the wet tundra behind them, were pale and fine-grained, ir-regularly shaped, ten to twelve feet high. None of them bore any trace of artificial shaping. They ran in a straight line along a shallow, scooped-out valley. The broken hills on either side were dusted with snow, and a herd of shaggy, long-bodied animals grazed along the western slopes, well away from the road.

Etch and Grissem, who had been riding side by side, carrying on a spirited debate about the relative merits of horses and ponies, separated. Grissem urged his mount forward and led the way. He raised his voice in a chant in the same archaic language. This time, Terris thought he recognized scattered phrases: *the wisdom of time . . . the two gates . . . a ceremony of remembrance . . .*

The stones ended in a wall of rock, a line of cliffs jutting across the horizon, as sheer and jagged as if some mad giant had turned the layers of bedrock on end. A deep cleft cut through the wall where the last of the stones formed a sort of gatehouse or fortress.

It began to snow. Big fluffy clumps drifted and billowed like feathers, soon giving way to icy pellets that fell faster and faster. The norther ponies lowered their heads and plodded on, tails clamped against their rounded rumps. Terris's sorrel gelding snorted and shivered the skin over his shoulders.

"Poor Miserable Beast," Terris called the horse.

Visibility sank to a few feet in front of Terris's nose. The snow muffled his senses—sight, hearing, smell. Iced-over snow crusted his beard and eyebrows. His body went numb in the saddle, his fingers frozen around the braided reins.

He closed his eyes and concentrated on the inner pull from the north, as clear and strong now as if it were a magnet. He felt no fear of it—it was the antithesis of the thing beneath the Starhall. That had repelled to the point of physical illness, but this exhilarated some deep part of him even as it drew him in.

An image flared up in Terris's mind and he saw himself standing naked on a road. Paths radiated out like a spider's web, the Ridge to the east a tangle of glowing nuggets. Far to the south, the filaments ended in a single node that pulsated, red and black, as if it were swollen with blood and bile.

He turned north to face the spot where all the strands came together. They gleamed like silk, inviting the touch. How easy it would be to let himself go sliding along them, to plunge headlong into the shimmering pool of light at their center.

Terris opened his eyes. The snowfall had eased and before him lay a building of charcoal stone, once a sprawling fortress, now crumbling with age and weather. Yellow light streamed from the central windows. Overhead, the sky looked murky, as if with a gathering storm, and the temperature was falling.

The horses's shod hooves clattered over the cobble-stoned yard. The hall door opened and an old man came out and walked toward them with a rolling gait. His face

was round-cheeked and squint-eyed, his wisp of a beard
indistinguishable from the straggly yellow-gray fur of his
parka. He beckoned to the travelers, humming and droning as if he'd been alone so long he'd forgotten proper
human speech.

Grissem dismounted and walked up to him, bowing
deeply and making a gesture Terris didn't know. The
old man returned the greeting and after a moment, Grissem called the others to come forward.

They led their horses through a doubled wooden door.
The room inside might have once been a low-ceilinged
banquet hall but was now partitioned into a snug stable.
The place reeked of wet horse hair, oat hay, and a
strange, musky animal smell. The old man grunted, muttered something none of them understood, and left them
alone. Within a few minutes, the body heat of the animals began to melt the crusted snow.

As soon as Terris hauled off the gelding's saddle and
bridle, the horse tore into the overhead hay net as if he
hadn't eaten in a week. As he twisted a double handful
of straw into a wisp, Terris noticed how sharp and angular the horse's ribs looked, how sunken his flanks, how
dull and ragged his coat. Slowly and methodically, Terris
rubbed the horse until he was dry and as glossy as he
was going to get and his ears had flopped sideways with
contentment. By the time Terris finished, the others had
stowed their gear on the nearby racks and gathered up
their personal gear. They were ready to go in to their
own dinners, except Kardith, who was fussing over the
gray mare's off hind hoof.

Kardith set down the mare's leg, her mouth twisted in
disapproval. Her face looked drawn, her eyes dark and
withdrawn in a way Terris had never seen.

Or perhaps the remoteness was his. Kardith had saved
his life, brought him to where he could never have come
on his own, and she was tied to him in ways he couldn't
understand. Yet she might as well have not existed since
they'd left the lake. Nothing had mattered except the
pulling from the north.

*   *   *

The yellow light Terris had seen from the courtyard came from a fireplace so massive it spanned the length of the wall. Made of the same pale stone as the lined-up boulders, it bowed outward to direct the fire's heat into the center of the room. Three-tier wooden bunk beds ranged along the other two walls. Coarsely woven wool rugs had been laid out in a half-circle around the fire, and the old man was already setting out steaming bowls and platters.

They hung their parkas and outer pants on the hooks on either side of the fireplace, well away from the direct heat but warm enough to dry quickly. Boots went on a rack beyond, to be replaced by heavy felt slippers. They all sat down on the mats and began eating.

The bowls contained an oversalted porridge of grain and nuts, and the platters coarse bread and slices of a hard, tangy cheese somewhat reminiscent of Laurean sheep-cheese. To go with this were pitchers of something hot, very strong, and heavily sweetened, covered with a scum of slightly rancid butter. Terris couldn't identify it. It was not something commonly drunk in Laurea.

They ate in silence and their dishes were refilled as soon as they were emptied. Terris couldn't remember having eaten so much in his life. He hadn't noticed he was hungry, but as soon as he started eating, he couldn't stop. They'd been traveling all day and the lowering sky, he now realized, was not another brewing storm but sundown.

Terris laid his empty bowl on his platter, got up, and wandered to the window. It looked south, along the avenue of stones. He had no idea who could have put them there, or why. At this moment, he didn't care. Behind him, Grissem was answering Aviyya's questions about the religious symbolism of the standing stones, the ritual greeting, the ancient, isolated clan which supplied porters to the fortress house.

Terris sighed and rested his forehead against the glass. It was single-paned, thick and chill. He gazed out into the darkness, where he could almost see the shining road beneath the standing stones, running south through the snarls and jumbles to the red-black rottenness beneath the Starhall.

The Starhall thing and the Northlight. Two ends of the road, two poles, with all of Harth strung out between them.

Not literally true, he knew. There was Archipelago and the ocean to the west, the bitter-alkali steppe to the east, the Inland Sea and vast, unexplored forests to the south beyond Laureal City.

Not literally true—but true in some deeper sense. The Starhall and Northlight defined Harth.

Shivering, he turned away from the window and back to the room. The fire had died down and orange sparks flickered across the bed of embers. Jakon alone sat before it, his back straight, hands open and relaxed on his knees. Everyone else had gone to sleep.

Eyes half closed, Jakon gave no sign that he was aware of Terris's presence as Terris sank down on the mat beside him, arched his back, and willed his muscles to relax. They sat together in the snug dense quiet, the only sound the rustle of collapsing embers.

Terris had no thought of what he would do, beyond continuing north, no idea of what he would find. He could hear his companions breathing as they slept, and through the rock walls which now grew paper-thin, the horses twitching and shifting in the thick straw bedding. The strange shaggy animals ambling slowly down the slopes to the yard, moons-light glinting on their stumpy nose horns. Tundra elk lay close together for warmth, drowsing, their legs tucked under their bellies. Brush-sheep dreamed in their pens. Horses ran wild under the moons across the rich Border pastures. Tree branches fragrant with blossoms and heavy with fruit bent low over the streets of Laureal City. His head swam with the memory of their perfume. It filled him, overpowering and nauseatingly sweet.

Sweat broke out all over his body. For a moment he thought the old caretaker had poisoned the fire. He tried to call out to Jakon, but he couldn't draw the air into his lungs. His vision went dark and he felt himself falling, endlessly falling. . . .

* * *

Terris opened his eyes and squinted in the sunlight which angled through the southern windows. It flooded the room, as brilliant as if it were full noon. He lay on a lower bunk, still fully dressed except for his boots, but cocooned in layers of unfamiliar furs. The room looked empty, the other beds neatly made up. A sharp, charred odor emanated from the surface.

Aviyya burst through the door in a gust of frosty air, her boot heels clattering on the stone floor. She wore her parka, her black hair spilling over the thrown-back hood. Kneeling beside the fireplace, she clucked in disapproval and picked up a wooden spatula.

Terris pushed himself up on one elbow, tangled in the elkskins and almost fell out of bed.

His sister looked up from poking at the shallow pan which she'd just removed from the hearth. "When you were little, you never missed a meal. *That* at least hasn't changed."

"Unh . . ."

"There may still be some hot water left in the washroom," she said briskly. "If you're lucky. And these oatcakes are never going to be any less burnt than they are now. I'll call the others."

Terris extricated himself from his covers, pulled on his boots and stumbled out the door. He remembered the washroom with its surprisingly comfortable indoor plumbing as being right next to the main chamber. There it was, a narrow wooden door. The water in the deep ceramic basin was lukewarm, but there he found some soap and a towel and the toothbrush from his pack, which he had no memory of taking out the night before.

Kardith was just coming in from the stables as he sprinted back. She wore her heavy parka and a wool scarf over her curls. Her skin, under the cold-whipped blood, looked waxy.

"The horses are ready to go," she said, not meeting his eyes. "The old man's still in the barn, milking those—I don't know what they are. Not sheep, that's sure. Not ghameli, either. Horns on their noses and big flat feet."

Kardith ... He had no words for her, though his throat ached.

They breakfasted on Aviyya's singed oatcakes, lumps of bitter brown cheese and dried fruit, washed down with more of the hot rancid-butter drink from last night.

As they led their horses in the courtyard, Terris saw that it was not as late in the morning as he'd feared. The shadows were still long and blue, the sun barely a handswidth above the eastern horizon. It was the unusual clarity of the air and the brilliance of the sunshine that made it seem like noon.

Grissem stood by the sorrel gelding's head as Terris mounted up. "You have the look of one who's dreamed in the night—not peacefully, but well."

Terris wanted to laugh in the norther's face, but he kept his expression somber. It seemed he'd done very little except dream for these past few days.

"Ah!" Jakon, nearby, stood beside his own pony. "We will reach the Light today. I can't do much more than take you there, you know. I can't tell you what will happen." For the first time, he looked uncertain. "You're not one of us. It won't be the same for you."

"Can you feel it, even here, this Light of yours—like acid and honey along your nerves?"

Jakon shook his head—*Dreams, for me it is only dreams*—and Terris knew that he was truly alone in what he had to do.

CHAPTER 30

Beyond the cleft in the cliffs stretched a vast glaring plain, its surface crusted with ice-covered snow. Not more than a half-day's journey away, a solitary mountain breached the horizon, squat and broad, carbon-gray, its top as flat and level as if it had been sheared off with a knife.

They rode in silence now, single file. The horses broke through the surface of the ice and sank in the snow, sometimes hock deep. The snow packed their rounded hooves and then the Laureans were forced to halt and pick them out. Nobody said anything during these stops, except to curse when a hoof pick slipped.

Terris could not have spoken even if he had anything to say. He could no longer feel the cold and was only dimly aware of the gelding struggling beneath him. A feeling grew in him that he was never going back the way he'd come, that perhaps none of them were. He had no thought of resistance. He felt in his bones this was not something he could take on like a school assignment or even a promise. It was something which had taken *him* on, even as Etch had said back in Laureal City, had taken him on and swallowed him up until he was no longer himself, Terricel, son of Esmelda of Laurea, failed scholar and reluctant heir and accidental emissary to the north, but something quite different, something not yet fully forged.

Ahead lay the fire that would give him his shape.

*   *   *

Grissem had remarked that the trip from the way station to the Northlight and back was usually made in a single day. At first Terris didn't see how that was possible. But before they'd gone very far into the glassy plain, his sense of movement and distance became completely unreliable. One moment it seemed they'd made no progress at all, the next they were so close he could make out the folds and fissures of the ancient lava flows. When he tried to focus on the volcanic cone as a landmark, it only made the distortion worse.

The sun had traveled only a little past overhead when they reached the base of the volcano. They left the horses and ponies in a sheltered cove along the southwest flank, where the ridges of hardened lava had kept off the worst of the weather. A few tufts of hardy wiregrass sprouted beside a pool of melted snow. The ponies would stay close, Jakon said, for a time anyway, and the horses wouldn't go far alone. He didn't add that if they failed to return, the animals would eventually make their way back to the way station, where they'd be cared for.

The trail began in the crevices above the cove. It was well-worn but so narrow, threading its way westward and then disappearing in the deeper fissures, that it was invisible from the ground directly below. Grissem had known precisely where to find it.

Terris tightened the straps of his travel pack and followed Jakon along the trail. He carried food and water like the others, but also the wrapped dagger. The trail plunged into the mountain, and he had to bend to keep from hitting his head on the low roof. Before long, his neck and back muscles ached from the strain.

No one spoke, except an occasional hushed warning about rough footing. Their panting breaths and the scuffling of their boots echoed down the tunnels. The black rock made the passages seem dark and closed-in, although they never went more than a few hundred feet without some shaft of light shining down from some hidden crack.

Terris felt along the tunnel sides, finding handholds as they began to climb sharply. Before long he was sweating, his heart pounding. He threw back his hood and unwound his scarf, but didn't dare take off his gloves. The porous stone was treacherously rough. It was all he could do to haul himself up the next grade or scramble through the next crevice.

They emerged onto the flat basin open to the sky. The walls of the volcanic cone surrounded them, steep and high enough to cut off the worst of the wind which howled through the crevices, breaking off tiny slivers of rock. Little piles of debris collected along the base of the walls and a few pale green fronds found root in the minute fissures which covered the caldera surface like a crazily cracked glaze.

In the center of the caldera stood a white, glowing cone, lightly flickering and yet opaque. The tip was about twenty feet high, the base wide and curved. It sat on the rock as if it had grown from it, but unlike the rock, it showed no trace of weathering.

A shiver, unrelated to the cold, shook Terris. "This . . . this is the Northlight?"

Jakon signaled for them all to halt and put down their packs. Where the wind had scoured the ground, Terris made out the curved outlines of shaped, fitted stones, encircling the base of the cone.

Terris took a few steps toward the cone, one hand outstretched. A faint vibration reached him, tingling but not unpleasant, more intense the closer he came. The tips of his outstretched fingers burned and smarted through his gloves. He lowered his hand, rubbing his fingers, and turned back to Jakon. "Your people built this thing?"

Jakon looked surprised. His eyes turned a deeper blue, as if some reflection from the light momentarily intensified their color. "No, it has always been here. Just as my people have always come, in times of crisis and decision, to be touched by its vision."

Jakon lowered himself to the ground, crossed his legs and pulled out the small drum from his pack. *Thrum!* He brought his hand flat on the stretched hide, then tapped lightly with his fingertips once, twice. —*dit-dit*— *Thrum!* —*dit-dit*— *Thrum!* —*dit-dit*— *Thrum!* He beat out a slow, accented rhythm, his eyes fixed on the cone, his back ramrod straight.

Grissem sat down a few feet away from Jakon. He took out his bone flute and played a sequence of tones— no melody, no discernible progression, just a high sweet descant that wove in and out of the rhythm of the drum.

Thrum! —dit-dit— Thrum!

The two northers looked as if they'd settled into a trance and could go on like this for hours. Terris felt no impulse to sit down with them. His body tingled from the nearness of the Light, making sitting still about as possible as flying.

Here I am, standing at the Light, just like Jakon said, Terris thought. *And not a damned thing is happening.*

He took a step closer and then another. The vibration increased, a humming along his bones. His senses swam with it. A milky veil dropped across his eyes, misting the brightness of the sky and the contours of the caldera walls. Even the drumming behind him sounded muffled. He heard Avi saying, "The sooner we're done here, the sooner we can head back home."

The pulling which he'd felt for the whole trip from the norther lake encampment now returned, magnified a thousandfold. Whatever this Light thing was, it recognized him for its own. His feet stumbled forward of their own accord.

"Terris!"

Kardith's voice, tinny and distant. From the corner of his vision, he saw her face like a faded shadow, the ghostly shimmer of her drawn long-knife. He thought she was racing toward him, yet she seemed to be hardly moving, a figure trapped in frosted glass. She was close enough to touch. He reached for her, even as his body was jerked forward.

Then, with a blast of eye-searing flame, the two of them burst into the center of the Light.

CHAPTER 31
Kardith of Laurea

I whipped out my long-knife just as Terris touched the edge of the cone. His body turned misty white and blurred, as if the light were drawing him in. I sprinted toward him, shouting his name. I caught the shadow of his face, turned toward me, and leaped for all I was worth.

The next moment, I found myself on my knees, all cramped over, without any idea how I got here or what had happened to me. Every hair on my head—eyebrows, too—was crisped and stinking, my skin about to peel off and my long-knife gone from my hand.

I covered my face, my fingers digging into my flesh as I tried to keep them from shaking. I couldn't think why I should be here in this exposed place. I should have been safe inside a jort or huddled against the flanks of a lying-down ghamel. I should have been wearing the loose coat and scarves of the Tribes, not this fur-trimmed hooded jacket. I should ... I couldn't remember.

What was it I couldn't remember?

Whose name was it I must never speak ...?

I saw him coming toward me, the sunrise touching off cinnamon lights in his beard. He wore a loose gray robe edged in black counterstitch and the soft fabric flowed around the muscles in his shoulders. Hard muscles, long and supple. Knife-fighter's muscles.

It was the week after the priests had married me off to his father, and I was still groggy from the dope they loaded me with for the wedding. My mouth was dry, my stomach cramping, my insides raw from the old man's idea of lovemaking.

I looked up at his slow white smile, his eyes like new-minted gold. And he saw me, Kardith, not just the last of old Hamnir's kids to be taken care of somehow— *Let's marry the poor girl off to someone who'll beat some decency into her.* Not just a body to dump his spunk into whenever his dilapidated balls could manage it. Me, Kardith.

He tipped his head, eyes and teeth shining. "Hamnir taught you."

We both knew what he meant, and it wasn't cooking. He was there when they found me, half dead from fever and dehydration, with my stepfather and brothers already rotting around me. He was there when the priests crawled out of their smoke jort with the vision that it was the knifeplay of a woman—*me*—which offended the gods and sent the water-plague, but in their wisdom, their infinite compassion—*may they stink in hell forever, the whole crotting lot of them*—they were still going to try to save my soul. And now here he was, saying my stepfather's name as if he were someone to be remembered with respect and not just a bad influence, the curse-bringer who taught knives to a woman.

My back still smarted from last night, when I forgot for a moment, picked up a cooking knife and tested its balance. We were alone, he and I, but my voice came out in a scratch: "Women are forbidden to use knives."

"No." He took me by the shoulders and forced my eyes to meet his. "That's what the priests would have us believe. But I can read what it says in the Scripts for myself. It says that men and women danced the forms together. Hamnir was the best—and he taught you—and you're all that's left of that line."

I saw the fire in him. Ay Mother, such a fire. And such a hunger in me.

"It's no sin to dance the knives," he whispered. "The sin is to waste the gift."

Waste the gift. Waste the stolen moments as my muscles remembered the soaring joy when everything came together, every angle, every point of balance and momentum. Waste the memory of his laugh as I spun inside his guard, slid the edge of the wooden practice knife along his neck and slipped away before he could touch me.

"Father damn us all, woman, you're good!"

Waste the feel of his soft scratchy beard against my breast, the tenderness of his lips. "Aram . . ." I said his name only once, when we lay together and something broke open in me, like a sandstorm so sweet and melting I couldn't move or breathe or see, only his eyes—like sunlight through honey.

He put a finger to my lips. I knew I must never say his name again, nor even think it for fear I might call out to him in my dreams. How then could I tell him of his child growing inside me?

That old ghamel of a husband was so smoke-loaded he couldn't remember the last time he speared me. Who was to say the baby wasn't his? And who was to say what he felt when he told me Aram was dead? *Shadow panther,* he said. But I knew better. I knew it was the demon god of chance, come at last, as the priests would say, to take back his own.

Like flashes of light, like falling stars, the moments burst over me and seized me in those same panther claws. I heard myself crying, *No more, no more!*

The nights sobbing alone. The baby born early but strong—ay Mother! with his father's eyes. The little wet mouth tugging at my nipple and a stabbing all through my heart so that I wept again, with joy and pain, and the priests smiled, *You see how we have saved her, you see how we have made a real woman out of her.*

But they were not smiling as they came to dress the stiffening body of my husband. His heart gave out one night—nobody's fault except whatever god created old age. But the priests didn't see it that way. They figured I'd somehow stolen his soul. I caught the creamy pleasure in their eyes, the moistness at the corners of their mouths as they spoke of monstrous sin, as they spoke of the redemption by blood, as they beat the death gongs and chanted of the end of *that woman's evil.*

We have given her every chance to redeem herself in the way of the Tribes, they said. *To atone, to live in virtue. A righteous husband we gave her, a proper place among us. But you see, all of you, how she has brought only evil on her master, she and her devil's spawn. Who can say what horrors she would unloose upon us, she who has turned her back on salvation? We cannot help her fleshly body, but we must purify her soul and protect the rest of the Tribe.*

Mother, father, demon god—any god!—let me not remember!

Now I saw the funeral mount, the sky like charcoal dust, the faces I didn't know any more, wet-looking in the flickering torchlight. I lay on my belly, hands tied over my head. The priest, the fat bald one with the cold hands, shouted but I couldn't understand the words. The drink they forced down me earlier left my head spinning but my senses sharp. I felt every cut as he drew the hooked blade across my back, felt every drop that spilled down my naked sides, pooled around my waist, soaked into the cloth of my drawstring breeches. Beyond my head, my son whimpered softly. I thought they must have drugged him, too, or he'd be screaming in outrage at being tied down.

The priests chanted the same senseless syllables over and over. I drifted on them, in and out of a formless dream. I thought of their promises, that my sins would soon be forgiven. I prayed to the Mother-of-us-all that somehow I might see Aram again and my stepfather Hamnir and my brothers. Tears ran down my face, the last I would ever shed.

The bloodbats came suddenly, plummeting. The air churned with their stinking wings, their high insane cries. Lured by the clotting blood, they latched on to my back with their iron claws. They ripped through skin and nerve and muscle, sucking and drinking.

Agony shocked through me. I screamed and screamed,

my life pouring out in blood and sound. For an instant I couldn't breathe. The world whirled and darkened.

Then I heard my baby cry. Shrill with pain but also fury—fighting for his life. Too late—

NO!

All the passion still in me came boiling up, all the cold dead numbness turned to fire, set off by that single voice. . . .

I twisted on my side, jammed one knee up, sank my teeth into the scab-crusted hide of the nearest bloodbat. The skin on my wrists shredded as the ties, meant to hold a drugged and willing victim, gave way. My hands free, I rolled off the altar stone and landed on my bare feet. Wounded bloodbats flapped on the sand with others latching on to them, a few still clinging to my back.

. . . and silence except for the beating of the wings, the piercing, inhuman cries . . .

I screamed again as I grabbed them, snapping the long bones in my hands. My fingers ripped through the leathery membranes and hot reeking blood spilled over my skin.

. . . his little body, torn and so covered with blood he looked clothed. His eyes gone, mouth open, one ear ripped half off. Delicate ribs splintered white and guts spilling like a rope of pearls over the slick red stone . . .

And still. Ay Mother, so still.

Slowly I came to my body again, my real body, crouched under a blanket of shifting light, my throat scraped raw. Not the same body that kicked and clawed its way past the ring of priests, not the same body that somehow got its fingers round the hilt of a knife. Mother knows how many I killed before I bolted free of them. This I truly didn't remember.

Why did I wait so long to live? A few moments sooner and I could have saved him—

Why didn't I die instead?

"Kardith?"

At first all I saw was light, a borealis of white and gray and shimmering blue, constantly changing and bright enough to burn through to the back of my skull. Squinting, I made out shadows like trees or mountains, buildings, spinning globes, wild fantastic animals.

But yes, there was something there, something shaped like a man, more and more solid as he moved closer. The light seemed to radiate from his body.

For an instant my vision cleared and the man looked strangely familiar. Beyond him lay the source of the light, so bright I could hardly bear to look at it. Beneath my knees lay smooth stone, carved with the pattern of a doubled circle around a single dot. It seemed familiar, yet I couldn't think where I'd seen it before.

The man knelt in front of me and I caught the details of his face—his face washed colorless and hazy, his hair and beard no more than darker shadows. Eyes pale like ice. He took one of my hands and pulled it gently from my face. Put in it the hilt of a long-knife. For a moment I stared at the knife, caught by the ripples in the tempered steel. New strength surged from blade and up my arm. My heart beat fast and steady.

I remembered.

Everything.

All the years of running, torn with guilt and pain, dead-and-alive until Pateros gave me back my life. Now he was dead and I couldn't save him, either.

I remembered Avi touching my scarred back and weeping for me. I owed her, too, but what? Loyalty, gratefulness, perhaps—shame that I loved her more for loving me than for herself.

I remembered the norther chief Jakon, and what I saw in his eyes. And the boy from Laureal City, Avi's brother, bringing life and death and something bigger than any of us.

"Kardith?"

He took my other hand, pulled me to my feet. The long-knife glided into the worn-smooth leather sheath on my thigh. Then he headed for the center of brightness, slow as a blind man feeling his way and sure as a moth drawn to a flame. I turned my back on the funeral mount, on the bloodbats and the priests and the years of forgetting, and followed him.

CHAPTER 32

As we drifted through the light, our boots made no sound on the rock floor, not even the squeak of leather or scuffling on the fine volcanic grit. Even my breathing seemed muffled. The air got thicker and harder to push through, or maybe that was just my imagining.

The cone seemed much larger than it had from the outside. I saw no walls behind the layers of shifting brightness, nor had we a way to tell the passing of time or distance or any landmarks except the glowing heart of the cone.

Terris dropped my hand and gestured me to stay behind. Me, I'd rather go on than risk becoming separated. But some instinct made me stop. He traveled on a few paces and paused, his back to me. As I watched him, my fingers curled automatically around the hilt of my long-knife. Solid, cool even through the leather bands wrapped in my own pattern, it welcomed my touch.

My eyes burned and watered. I couldn't stay focused on Terris and yet I couldn't look away. He stood in the very heart of the light, no more than a blurred shadow against the glare. He waited there, still as rock in the shimmering brightness, hands out, head high, body shrouded in his thick norther parka, and for a moment I thought—I *hoped*—nothing was happening.

The edges of his body began to glow.

At first I noticed just a few splotches of red, like

heated furnace iron. Then the colors changed to yellow
and white, white-blue, hotter and brighter, rushing over
his arms and legs. The separate spots flared and melted
together. They spread over his body until he was covered
by a halo of jagged spikes. The air crackled with unspent
lightning. Sparks shot from his fingertips.

Terris shook like a scrap of hide caught in the edge
of a steppe twister. His head jerked, turned back toward
me. His eyes gleamed white, the irises rolled up in his
skull.

I grabbed my knife and lunged for him, but my hand
wouldn't move. My feet stayed rooted to the rock. My
heart pounded with the effort.

From the whiteness around us, bolts of piercing brightness showered Terris like shooting stars. I screamed out
a warning, but he made no move to dodge them. Where
they touched him, the burning outline around his body
blazed up like tinder catching flame.

"Terris!"

I bellowed his name, but no sound came from my
mouth. My muscles strained and cramped, sweat poured
down my neck and sides underneath my parka. I felt his
unborn screams in my bones, in my heart, tearing at me
like bloodbat claws.

The air was no longer silent but filled with a throbbing
hum. I couldn't tell where it came from. Not Terris, for
no human voice ever made such a sound—droning,
whining, rattling the bones in my skull until I expected
to feel hot blood spurting from my nose and ears. It
built and built until all I thought of was clapping my
hands over my head and squeezing my eyes tight shut.

But I still couldn't move. I fought just to breathe. My
eyes watered in outrage, my knees shook and stuttered.
I clamped my teeth together.

Terris . . .

He looked larger to me now, swollen with light, no
longer quite human in form. I wondered if he would
burst or merely turn into a god.

If the demon god of chance was nothing more than a
bag of tricks, and the Mother blind and deaf, then why
not a god with a human heart? Why not a god who tore

up half Laurea for a sister so long gone he hardly knew her any more, who begged his enemy's help to find the truth, who took me into the crucible of my heart and out again, and now stood alone in a cone of fire. . . .

He lifted his arms, as slowly as if they were weighted with lead or maybe the light had melted his bones. His head sagged back. His knees bent, his body curving backward. He looked about ready to fall.

I hurled myself forward with all my strength, hard enough to pop a blood vessel. It was tougher than slogging through frozen Kratera Ridge mud or facing a steppe sandstorm, but somehow I managed to break free.

Staggering, I reached Terris and caught him behind the shoulders before he hit the ground. For a moment his body felt thin, light as a handful of rock-dove feathers. I could have crushed him in my hands without thinking. I was afraid to hold him, but even more afraid to let him drop. Then he was solid flesh again, and damned heavy into the bargain. I set him down on the cold stone with a jolt.

Lightning arced over us, illuminating the roof of the dome. Sparks like popping embers stung my face. The racket was worse than any storm I'd ever ridden out, enough to make a sandbat deaf and they don't even have ears. My head rang with the sound so much that everything looked doubled. I crouched beside Terris, thinking that if one of those flashes of light hit us, we wouldn't either of us walk out of here.

Suddenly it was over. The light subsided to a clear soft glare, the din to a few quiet crackles, and then silence.

My eyes darted to the great arching dome above our heads, the walls like alabaster ribbed with bands of gleaming silvery metal. Where they met in the center of the roof, a huge glass bell hung. A tangle of wires and tubes and other, less recognizable things shot forth rhythmic bursts of brilliance. Below the bell, a ball of cold white light, man-high and twice as wide, glowed steadily.

I wet my lips and slowly straightened up. The floor

beneath my boots was pale stone, as smooth and precisely fitted as anything I'd seen in Laureal City. No—not all the stones were the same fine-grained rock. Some were darker, green-gray shot with flecks of gold and edged in shining metal like the dome wall ribs. Again I saw the pattern of the dotted double circle. The central light turned the shallow inscriptions into a pattern of jagged shadows. I couldn't read them.

Someone built this place. But who? And for what purpose?

I shook my head, my brains still scrambled from the racket. Terris held on to my arms and clambered to his feet.

If I still felt half-addled, what must he be feeling? Could anyone go through the heart of the Light and come out sane? What did that matter—*I'd* left a good part of me back with the bloodbats.

He stood there so very long, weaving slightly from side to side.

Suddenly he spun around, balanced like a cat, and pointed off into the central brightness. "Look there!"

I couldn't see anything, not even the faint, ghostly shapes I made out before.

"And there! There! The trees, the canyons—Kardith, they're incredible! Look, look, the desert! Nothing but piles of sand!"

He went on, oblivious to my silence as he described more marvels—the golden plain with animals as tall as trees, the oceans teeming with silver fish, the deserts of gleaming black glass, the scarlet-hued swamps where snake-necked monsters bellowed beneath a single moon.

I said nothing. What could I say?

He stopped, quiet a moment, and said to me in a low voice, "You can't see them, can you? All the places branching out from this place, all the long green tunnels?"

I shook my head.

"The light. Oh gods, the light . . ." His voice trembled. He covered his face with his hands.

Part of me wanted to put an arm around his shoulders,

but I couldn't. I mustn't. This was no child to be sopped off with a morsel of comfort or a greenie kid who was so scared he almost puked after Montborne's goons jumped us in camp. This was the man who danced in the norther longhouse, danced as if the gods themselves had fired him up. This was the man who stood alone in the heart of the Light.

... and who, even more than Pateros, had given me back my life ...

"All the way here I could feel it, calling me ..." he whispered. "Changing me. I thought—I don't know what I thought. I should have known I couldn't go back."

He dropped his hands, looking right through me. His face was drawn, familiar and human with his new beard, his tousled black hair. His eyes shone with a light I'd never seen in them before.

I shivered and looked away. Something in my face or my silence told him what I saw. He took a deep breath and squared his shoulders.

"It doesn't matter now, does it?" I expected to hear bitterness in his voice, but there was none. He gestured, "Come on ..." and he didn't mean back out again.

Mother-of-us-all, did he mean for us *both* to go through the Light?

"You're crazy!"

He explained it all slowly to me, making shapes with his hands. "Look, Kardith, it's like a house. Different places, like the weirdies on the Ridge, they're like doors. From here you can go right through them. The green tunnels—like the one Avi fell into—they're longer, the back way around."

He saw all this, the connections, the gates to other places, places I never imagined. Me, all I saw was light and the inside of the dome.

"I don't know why I can see them and you can't," he said, "maybe for the same reason I can feel the thing in the Starhall."

"That's great," I said in a shaky voice. "Really great. Now let's get the hell out of here."

"Avi's green tunnel brought her over fifty miles of

badlands. If I can *see* these doors, I can go through them, too."

"You *are* crazy!"

"Not crazy enough to go alone."

Damn. "Where are we going?"

"Anywhere you want."

I thought of Avi back there in the caldera with Etch and the two northers. If we didn't come back, they'd have the sense to return the gatehouse by nightfall. Even without us, Avi would talk Jakon into letting her ride back to Laureal City. Hell, she'd probably talk him into going with her.

What was important here? Finding Avi, keeping Terris safe from Montborne, getting the dagger back to Esmelda? I didn't know.

I slid my long-knife out. "Anywhere but the steppe."

He watched me with a strange expression. I wondered for a crazy instant if he could see what I saw, feel what I felt, all those memories. And if he had seen, what did it matter? They were my past, they were what they were. They were not what I was today.

He turned to the right of the glowing center and pointed. "There."

Blindly I followed him, half a step behind. I felt a faint *zzzt!* like stepping again through a wall of fire, only cool this time. I'd half forgotten that my face was burned and peeling; it didn't hurt any more. I blinked in a burst of unnatural brilliant green and the next step I felt sand beneath my feet and saw jagged black rock in front of us, gleaming wet against the clouded sky and smelling of wild salty fish stink—

"Kardith!"

Terris grabbed the sleeve of my parka and jerked me sideways, just as a wave came crashing over the beach, frothing and swirling around the scattered rocks. It thundered against the black cliffs, but we scrambled high enough on the slanting yellow sand to only get the soles of our boots wet. Drops of spray stung my face. I dashed a few feet up the sand, laughing without meaning to.

"This—this *isn't* the steepe!"

"No." He smiled, half-sweet, half-sad. "It's a place

I've always wanted to go to. A place that reminds me of someone I once knew. Selfish of me, but I don't know how many chances I'll have to go someplace just because I want to." He sighed and turned, looking over the heaving green wall of water. "And it looked safe enough."

The overhead sun shone hot, but the breeze curling around my knees was cold and damp. I yanked at the ties of my parka with my free hand and suddenly I felt very, very scared.

"You could go anywhere—*anywhere!*" I screamed at him. "You could be ten places at once! You could hide where no one'd ever find you. You could jump in, cut anyone's throat—Montborne's maybe, Jakon's—who'd ever know? You could turn the whole crotting world upside down—make yourself Guardian of all Harth, anything you wanted! Who could stop you? You couldn't—"

"Stop it!"

I shut up, my face as scalding hot as if he'd slapped me. He was shaking and red-faced, just as scared as I was and twice as pissed.

"Stop it. This *thing* that's happened to me is no magic trick, no blessing of the gods. It's a *curse,*" he spit out the word, "that's what it is, a damned *curse!*"

"What do you mean, curse? How can such power be a curse?"

"You don't understand. Power has been shoved down my throat since I can remember and nobody—least of all Esme—ever asked me if I *wanted* it. I could have been Guardian of Laurea. All I had to do is be my mother's heir. She's sitting in the Guardian's seat right now and the minute I show up ..." He lifted one arm half in appeal, half surrender.

"And all my dreams—no, not dreams, they're *true,* the things I see, the people, the times, the places. All that would be gone. I'd be just like her, don't you see?"

I started shaking, thinking of Terris *just like her.*

"But now—I can see all of Harth, places I never imagined! I can touch them, taste them, brighter than any dream. And because I can do all that, I have to go back, I have to take up that power."

"Why, if you hate it so much?"

"Montborne's still out there, him and his poisoned daggers. And Esme, doing the wrong things for the right reasons. I have no choice, don't you see? It no longer matters what I want. And ..." He paused, his brow furrowing. His voice dropped, so soft I hardly heard the words above the rattle and crash of the waves, "and now I know what the Starhall thing is."

What Starhall thing? Another Northlight?

I felt the sadness in him, but I couldn't understand it. He must be crazy after all. Such a gift he had, even if he used it for some wishcrap altruistic purpose and nothing else. To see the green tunnel connections, to travel along them—to places like this wave-whipped beach—how could it be anything but a gift?

But for him it wasn't. I could see that, even if I couldn't understand why. For him that was a loss that could never be made up.

That I understood.

CHAPTER 33

Deborah Wheeler

We climbed the craggy black rocks, found a few broken shells, pink and curly-edged, and sat watching a giant sea beast blow spume into the air some miles offshore. I stretched my arms wide, taking in the smell and feel of this place.

Sitting at my side, Terris drew a pattern in a pocket of sand blown up on the rock. Over and over again he traced the doubled circle, jabbing his finger into the single dot at its center. I watched him, caught by the rhythm of his movements.

"What did you see," he asked softly, "back there in the Light?"

I sat very still. Breathed. Wrestled with old ghosts. Lost. Breathed again. Knew I couldn't lie to him.

"I saw the day I should have died," I said, not sure if my words came as a whisper or a sob. I looked up and met those rainwater eyes. "I saw my son."

Until that moment, no one else in Laurea knew I'd borne a child. No wonder I couldn't cry for all those years. How could I grieve for a loss I couldn't name, not even to myself?

He nodded. "A personal memory, activated by the gate mechanism. And—" he went on, "I saw something I could not possibly remember, something which happened hundreds—no, thousands of years before I was born, as clear and bright as if it were today."

My heart closed, tight as a fist, around the memory. "What did you see?"

"I saw the last time the Starhall gate was used, how it became what it is now."

I shivered, wanting nothing to do with Starhall secrets, gates or otherwise. My own visions were nightmare enough for one lifetime.

He reached out and grabbed my wrist, as if he didn't care how dangerous that could be. But his words—and the fire behind them—held me fast. "You don't understand! It was all there in the Archives, buried in the coded logs. Once we remembered why we built the gates—one in Laureal City and one here in the north. Once we knew what lay on the other side, and why we came here. Not everyone had the secret, of course, just the most elite of the gaea-priests. Guardians they were called, real Guardians, not political figureheads. Gatekeepers."

"Pateros was called Gatekeeper," I said. "I remember that from the funeral."

"But no one remembered *why*, not even him—not even Esme!" His eyes blazed, fire and steel. I didn't flinch. "No matter what happens to me now—you must remember. *Promise me*! Promise me you'll remember!"

I gulped. "Remember what?"

"That the gate exists! Why we came through, why we must guard it!" He relaxed a fraction, let me go. "I saw three of them standing in front of a wall of shimmery stuff. The old one was working some kind of machinery, like we saw in the Northlight dome. The strong one was guiding the apprentice, I think. I saw something clearing in the bright mist. It makes sense there would be three at a time—the old wise one, the one at the peak of his strength, the young one just learning to control the gate mechanism. I think he must have been keyed into it stepwise, gradually like I was to the Starhall. But this time something went wrong—maybe the door which separates *here* from *there* was weakened. Maybe— I don't know."

He broke off, staring out over the rolling waves. I waited, counting the heartbeats. "And then?"

"Something—I saw something—as big as a Laurean house, round like a mushroom, the color of blood—" He shivered. "At first I thought it was alive. So did the apprentice. Then the old one said no, it was a *pyro*— a something. A weapon."

My jaw dropped open and I no longer felt the crisp sea breeze tugging at my hair. "A *weapon*?" My hand went automatically to the hilt of my long-knife.

"I didn't believe it either. But then ... it rushed the gate from the other side. Everything it touched—ground, trees, stone, turned to smoke. The edges of the gate began to smolder. I could smell the stench. My eyes burned with it. The Guardians—the two older ones— began rushing around, trying to close the gate. I don't know if it was too late or the weapon-thing too strong ... Kardith, it started to come through!"

"But they did stop it?" I leaned forward, caught. "They must have."

"Yes, but they were standing too close," he said, shaking his head. "The explosion caught them just before the gate closed. The brighter place was gone, only brick remained. Brick and the gate apparatus. The apprentice was still alive."

"I hope he smashed the Mother-damned thing!" I cried. I hadn't realized I was trembling also, as terrified of this awful *machine* as any ranting gaea-priest.

"It would have been made to withstand tampering. And he was young, so he might not have learned how to turn it off. So he would have done the only thing he could do. He walled it up, did his best to make sure no one else ever dug it up. And never passed on that knowledge of what it was, why it was built, why it must be guarded."

"And is that so bad? To forget?"

"Maybe," he said, studying me. "For some. But *you* won't forget."

"I don't understand what this is all about. Gates, weapons, machines. Besides, it happened a long time ago. As far as I can see, there are no more *things* on the other side, just waiting to come through." I got to my feet, brushing sand from my pants. It was hard to feel gloomy with the fresh sea tang in my face. "You say it's important to remember, fine. I said I would. But I intend to have you around to do the remembering for both of us."

A nasty thought nibbled at the back of my mind. "Has it occurred to you, the tweak you're putting yourself in, if you let anybody else know you can do this thing? *You* may give a shit about how you use it, but there are some very nasty people out there who won't. And you—or anyone you care about—could be a target for them."

"Who else knows? There's my sister," he counted off on his fingers like a kid, "and Jakon and Grissem. Etch. Nobody I don't trust."

"There's me."

"You, you're the one who thinks of these things for me."

I held my breath as we stepped through, expecting an instant of sizzle, a flash of green, and then the frozen white of the caldera. Instead, heat swept over me, laden with the pungent, familiar smell of ripe palm-cactus fruit. I blinked, gasping. My eyes raced over the reddish dunes, softly curved like a woman's thigh. My knife was in my hand, my legs tensed for action, my breath searing my throat.

"Kardith!" Terris cried, his voice too high and tight for certainty. "Kardith, no!"

The open steppe stretched in one direction, the groves with their branches arching toward the crystalline sky in another. Jorts clustered around a dusty well; ghameli stood tethered beyond them. A pair of women were singing and dipping out water, their wrist bells chiming, children laughing and dodging behind them. Their scarves and robes fluttered in a sudden breeze, bringing me the scent of sandalwood and *chirosa* bark. A feeling rose up in me, not terror, not anger, no, sharp and melting all at once. I blinked hard.

Terris said something, but I couldn't make out his words above the pounding of my heart. Something about being sorry, making a mistake.

The flap of the nearest jort was pushed aside and a

man emerged. He moved with a knife-fighter's grace, his beard like spun red-gold in the sun. He must have thought me a man in my heavy parka, for he lifted one hand in welcome. My knees shuddered.

I whirled to face Terris. "Get me out of here! Anywhere!"

He grabbed my free arm and pulled me sideways. I staggered through a wall of white flame and pulled up gasping, an inch from tumbling into a pool of yellowish, scum-crusted water.

Now I was the one to grab on to him, one-handed as I wasn't about to put away my knife. He swore, but not at me.

Above us, around us, grayish branches dripped oozing green-black stuff, more slime than moss. Even the sky looked smudged. We stood on a little island of solid ground, lichen over rock and matted weeds. The reek of sulfur in the hot, still air sent my eyes and nose watering. Something squawked in the distance, shrill and ululating, like no bird I'd ever known.

Terris swore again. The steppe was an accident, maybe because he wasn't yet wise to the ways of those doors of his, but this place—he must have gotten us here in sheer panic. I loosened my grip on him.

"Where are we?" I whispered. At moment, I would have given anything I owned to be back on the steppe, to raise my hands in a stranger's greeting, to throw myself open to those familiar sights and smells, the dry clean beauty of the dunes.

"We're still on Harth, maybe south of the Inland Sea." He stepped carefully over the mounds of yellowed grass. Now that the first shock of the place was fading, I noticed signs of renewal, a spray of violet flowers, a few half-ripe berries. A few blades of green stood like sentinels among their fallen brothers. A water-strider, tiny legs outstretched, skittered across a clear stretch of water. From a thicket, a huge white songbat took wing.

"Why put a gate here?" Terris murmured. "As a warning, a lesson? Or did something come through here? Did they preserve this place deliberately so each generation would be forced to think in terms of all Harth?"

He scraped a layer of glistening mossy stuff off its underlying rock with the edge of his boot. I could see scattered indentations which might once have been engraved letters. Terris couldn't make them out, either.

"Let's go," he said at last. "I'll be more careful this time. I'm sorry about the steppe."

"I'm not," popped out of my mouth before I realized it. I thought a moment and went on, "Maybe I'll go back on my own some day."

He smiled at me and took my hand.

The light was just as shifting and glare-blinding, but Terris strode through it even more surely, back through the startling green flashes and out again, dimmer and quieter. With a hiss and a searing flash, we came shivering on to the caldera plain.

I jumped ahead of Terris, long-knife drawn, to land light and balanced on both feet.

Etch stood nearest us, with an expression of mixed feelings—worry and fear and joy. His eyes were so full, on the steppe we'd say they were all soul. Beyond him, Avi waited between Jakon and Grissem.

Jakon came toward us, and for a moment he seemed no different from Montborne or the steppe priests or anyone else who led only his own people. I raised my blade tip, bringing it between him and Terris. Once I could have killed him and would not. There was no choice this time.

"Put away your knife, Kardith," said Terris. "Jakon and I have to talk."

He pushed past me to face Jakon. "Did you know what would happen to me in there?"

"All that I dreamed has been fulfilled," Jakon answered.

He doesn't know what the Light is, I realized. *He sits in front of it and drums up all these dreams, but he doesn't know.*

. . . he's never been inside.

"I too have had a vision sent by the Northlight,"

Terris said. His voice took on the steely ring of truth. "A terrifying vision. A vision of your people and mine kept apart, balanced, two static societies—no matter what the cost. You're just strong enough so we can't spread out over your lands and just weak enough to pose no more than a border threat. We're the only place on Harth that has any technological capability, but we have no frontier, everything's closed in and watched, and who cares what happens on the steppe?

"But it's no good," Terris continued. "They've forgotten what it's all about—the gaea-priests and Guardians. It's not enough to keep from doing harm, hanging on from one generation to the next, squashing all research except in narrow little projects that go nowhere. Sooner or later somebody like Montborne comes along to upset that brittle balance, and now it isn't just Montborne we have to stop, it's Esmelda."

Avi moved silently toward Terris, her face white and pinched. I caught something in her movement, a tenseness that sent my skin crawling. I felt her in my blood, moving with all her Ranger's stealth, cold and deadly intent. Her eyes fixed on her brother and something in her watched and waited like a coiled sand-viper. All because Terris had mentioned Esmelda?

"You said *Esmelda,*" said Jakon, looking like he hadn't understood a word Terris said. "But we have no quarrel with her. She has been as much a friend to us as any souther could. If you mean to stop your general's war, why include her?"

Avi kept coming and I kept watching her. She moved like satin, like flowing brandy. Etch and Grissem had their eyes on Terris. They didn't notice. Me, I stood absolutely still. I wanted her to see Terris, only Terris and not me. I held my knife low and hard to spot.

"Esme, our enemy?" I heard the shift in Terris's voice, something which reminded me of the old dragon. "I must have not spoken clearly. I meant the whole situation being ripe for Montborne to exploit."

Avi paused, the relief across her face thick enough to smell. My stomach uncoiled and I took a deep breath. Whatever it was had come and passed. But I shook a

little as I let the breath out. Terris passed some kind of
test out there in the Light and came out changed forever, and now it had happened to me too, just the same.
Standing here, not moving a muscle, my knife ready to
slice Avi's throat if she drew her own, these few moments gave a whole different shape to my life. I could
go on, but I couldn't forget.

I'd become what I'd chosen.

And what had Avi become, that she'd draw steel on
her own brother to protect some damnable secret of
Esmelda's?

Holy sweet Mother—was *this* why she'd left home?
Had the old dragon somehow forced her to swear a thing
like that?

"If it hadn't been Brassaford," Terris went on, "he'd
have found some other excuse. He sees the end as justi-
fying any means—killing Pateros, me, you if he could—
anyone he thinks he needs to."

Jakon's eyes narrowed. "I asked you once before, why
would you join forces with me against him?"

"For the truth," Terris said, echoing his first promise
to Jakon. "The truth alone." Truth and steel. He held
out his hand, souther style.

After a moment's hesitation Jakon took Terris's hand
and shook it.

"We *are* going home now, aren't we?" said Avi. She
had already slung her pack over her shoulders with her
good hand. Her face looked less white, but her eyes
were still jumpy. "It'll take at least a week from here."

"No," said Terris. "We can make it in a few hours.
Get the horses and I'll show you."

CHAPTER 34

We entered the green tunnel a little way from the base of the volcano. Terris wove his horse back and forth across our trail until the others all thought he was crazy. Me, I knew he was looking for the in-place and when he found it, it was only a slip of a thing. Nothing I could see, really, not even a shimmering of air like the Ridge weirdies—just an itch behind my eyes. Getting the horses through was a bit like threading a needle with rawhide strips—we marched them right past it half a dozen times. My mare seemed to know just where to go, but that peabrained sheep-hocked bat turd Etch called a horse kept sidestepping, and finally Terris had to lead it through on foot.

The tunnel was wide enough for three to ride abreast and too tall for me to reach its ceiling, even standing on the saddle. It seemed to go on forever, curving slightly so the ends were out of sight. I looked over my shoulder and saw no trace of where we'd come.

I'd never in all my days imagined a place like this, not even when the priests loaded me on dreamsmoke so I could hardly stand. Who could envision these featureless green walls? Instead of a natural color all shaded with yellow and brown like you'd see in living plants, this green bore a slight purple tinge, like a badly frauded gemstone.

After a few moments, none of us able to do anything

more than draw one breath after another, my mind
started to sort things into a crude imitation of sense. The
others weren't doing much better. Jakon clutched his
pony's reins, his face all white and beads of sweat gleaming on his upper lip. Grissem, behind him, chanted under
his breath while his fingers wove mysterious symbols.

Avi doubled over as if to empty her stomach. "Not
this place again!" she moaned. "Oh, drat!"

"That's the most lukewarm cussing I've ever heard. I
don't think you could talk mean if you tried," Etch muttered between gritted teeth, and we all laughed, even
Avi, the kind of laughing that brought tears to the eyes.

"Tell me this is a gods-damned *hallucination*," she
gasped when she could talk again, "and I'm still lying in
that root cellar."

This was no hallucination, no instant insanity. Thanks
to the steppe priests, I'd had my fill of that sort. And
we weren't dead, either, that was sure.

"It's the same place you fell into before," said Terris.

Avi's face looked sick in the green light. In another
life, I'd have gone to her, but now all I could do was
stare.

"So you've been here before and returned. And
there's no reason to think we can't all get back, so
there's nothing to be afraid of, yes?" he said.

"Harth's sweet ass, man, you're not trying to *reason*
with her?" said Etch.

"Damned right I am."

Jakon gestured at the tunnel walls, deathly still around
us. "This can't be real."

"You're right!" Terris said cheerfully. "It's an illusion.
Or a theatrical decoration dreamed up by us wicked
southers. You can think whatever you like, just so long
as you get on that pony and moving."

I picked up the gray mare's reins and swung up on
her back. Other than a *whuff*! of surprise when we first
burst into the tunnel, she seemed as solid as ever. The
two northers, of course, were not going to sit there like
a pair of brain-addled twitterbats while some bats-crazy
Ranger went on ahead. Yet I was more worried about
Avi's condition than theirs. She bit her lower lip, hard

enough to draw blood, then vaulted on her pony's back and booted the poor beast so hard it almost leapt straight up into the air.

We moved off, after a fashion, shedding our heavy fur parkas. It was too warm for wool cloaks, but too cool to be comfortable without them. Hell, it wouldn't kill us to be naked here, except of boredom.

As we rode on, I noticed piles of green silty stuff, *dust* I'd almost call it. I remembered Avi saying she tried to mark a trail and couldn't. Assuming all the green tunnels were similar, that made me nervous.

Nervous and worse. Something jingled along my spine and sent a dry crawling feeling up the back of my throat. My tongue went thick and gummy. I started to curse to hide how scared I was and then it came to me I was *thirsty,* that was all. I couldn't help laughing out loud.

Terris, in the lead, twisted in his saddle and looked at me as if I'd gone berserk. I hauled out my skin of honeyed water and lifted it to him in a toast.

"Drink up, everybody," he said. "It's just a bit farther."

I couldn't see a thing as we lined up along the tunnel, then reversed, head-to-tail, took a few steps, and the next thing we popped out into the sweet yellow light of Laurea.

I grasped the hilt of my long-knife and kneed the gray mare forward, but there was no need. We'd come out at the edge of a garden plot, shielded from everything but the cabbages by a hedge of lemon ash and brambleberries. Mother knew what the country people thought of the weirdie there, if they even saw it at all.

I paused, breathing in the fruity ripeness of the berries and the tang of the ash leaves. The slanting afternoon sunlight warmed the leather of my Ranger's vest.

Along the far end of the field, a thread of reflected light marked a creek running east-west, probably a feeder for the Serenity. From the position of the sun, I put us southeast of the city. All we had to do was follow the farmer's market road.

Avi spotted it, deeply rutted and a little muddy from

a recent rain. Suckerflies buzzed around our horses' ears and crickets whined from the patches of wild millet that lined the road.

Jakon shifted uneasily in the saddle as his pony dipped its head to snatch a mouthful. He knew the drowsy calm of the field was just a sham. He couldn't do a damned thing if we met a company of Montborne's men. Even I wouldn't be able to hold off that many. Unlike him, I might get a moment to explain what I was doing here.

"Listen, all of you," said Terris. "If we run into any trouble, remember that I'm Esmelda's adjutant, which is still true enough. But I've also been dispatched on a secret mission, an—er, clandestine *diplomatic* mission. With an—um, expert agricultural consultant and two Rangers for security. We're escorting the norther ambassador and his spiritual advisor for confidential high level negotiations with the Inner Council. Got that?"

Avi sputtered, holding her sides. Jakon looked skeptical, as if thinking, *You people really talk like that*? Etch muttered, "Got it? I don't know what half of those words *mean*."

"It means," I said, "that he's point man, and if anything goes wrong, it's his mama who'll bail us out."

"Better not be her," Avi said, no longer laughing.

We walked briskly along the road as the shadows grew darker and cooler. Somewhere in the line of woods ahead of us, a songbat woke up. I said to Avi, "You two've been through enough ghamel-shit from her, it's time you got some benefit of it."

"True," added Terris. "But keep your knife handy, anyway. Using Esme's name could be our ticket in, or else an instant trip to the nearest prison cell, depending on how things have worked out here."

Which was not, I agreed, a particularly encouraging thought.

"If things go sour, we split up," Terris said.

"Split up!" said Avi.

"We can't risk all of us getting caught. One of us has to get through."

Avi shook her head, chin up, like a whip-shy mare, nose to the sky.

"I know how to deal with Montborne," Terris continued. "*You* have to get to Esme and make your alliance with Jakon."

One moment, Avi was the sweet wild girl who made love to me on the Ridge. The next, she turned hard and fierce, eating Jakon's bread and salt, damning him—*daring* him—half-crazy, half-driven. Daughter of the dragon.

Then the flickering images came together and a single fire burned through all of her. She nodded as if she knew all along this was what she'd come back to do.

"Right." She glanced at me, but she knew I would stay with Terris no matter what. "Jakon, then, and Griss with me. Etch?"

Etch looked at me, a long agonized look, and turned back to Terris. "Don't ask me to leave her."

He means me. I went cold and hot at the same time. As Avi would say, *Oh, drat.*

It was near dark when we reached Laureal City and made our way through the outskirts. I kept my eyes sharp, feeling more than a little twitchy from thinking of all the things that could go wrong. The place was too damned quiet. Surely there should be more people abroad this early, walking openly, not darting from one darkened doorway to another. Patrols of City Guards stood at key intersections, tense and alert. We'd have to find a place to leave the horses soon.

Etch took the lead, down a side street that looked like a half-dried runoff ditch and back between a rank-smelling barnfowl coop and a shed full of bawling milksheep. He knew where he was going. Not a real stable, he told us with a knowing twist to his mouth. Not a place anyone'd look for horses, but decent and safe. His friend would keep them and our gear out of sight for a few days.

By then we'd either have done what we came for or else we wouldn't care.

We dismounted outside the narrow yard, keeping only our weapons and what little money we had. Terris emp-

tied his travel pack of everything but the dagger and his
first aid kit.

Etch gathered up all the reins. My gray mare rolled
her eyes at him, maybe remembering this was the man
who slit her throat.

"The ponies are sure to be spotted as norther," said
Avi. "Are you sure you can trust this friend?"

He nodded, and I trusted that sureness. I'd seen a new
strength in him ever since we passed the first stockyard.
Him and Terris, too. Out on the ridge they both looked
to me, just as we all looked to the northers through the
tundra ice. But here in the city, Etch knew this place.

"Ye—ah," Etch said, chewing on the word, "Pince'll
keep them hidden for me without needing to know why.
He owes me for more than this, though I never thought
I'd collect on it."

We waited out of sight while Etch went off with the
horses. The shadows flowed together as the last light
drained from the sky. Avi shifted from one foot to the
other, then caught herself and stood still. For all the
years she'd lived in the wilds, she was city-bred at heart
and besides Esmelda waited somewhere out there. Avi
could feel her, taste her nearness. Once I would have
said something, a casual curse on dragon mothers.

Once.

I remembered how Avi glided toward Terris, her fingers brushing the hilt of her knife, and the choice I made
then. Yet a bit of compassion whispered through me
now. I knew damned well it wasn't for Avi I kept on
and on, dragging Terris through miles of dust, even
throwing my Ranger's vest at Darice's feet. It wasn't Avi
I dreamed of all those years.

And now I watched her, twitchy half out of her skin
with standing still, eyes like disks of steel in the dark,
and I knew it wasn't me she dreamed of, either.

Terris led us through alleys and back streets, zigzag-
ging our way toward his mother's house. Here he was
no greenie kid, but in his element, with a sure sense of
where the next Guard patrol would be posted. Even Avi
followed him without protest. Jakon and Griss moved

like shadows in his wake. Etch didn't know the district any better than I did.

We crept along a row of squarish buildings, a small factory, I think. A weedy, overgrown border hedge cast eerie shapes from the solar lights at the nearest intersection. The air smelled of brick and moss-ivy. Terris raised one hand in warning. I flattened myself against a locked door. The others froze in the shadow of the hedge. The next instant, a trio of City Guards strode down the nearest cross street. One glanced our way, but didn't pause. I let out my breath and felt Avi do the same.

Silently Terris gestured us back and between two of the buildings. We cut across what looked like a delivery area, over a fence and up the next street, angling back the way the patrol had come, backtracking rather than cutting across their route. Every step took them farther away from us.

Around a corner, cobbled now instead of dirt, we ran smack into a knot of hand-held lights, the orange glow of torches.

"Halt! Who goes there?" A shout hailed us from behind the makeshift barricade. Men silhouetted against a smallish bonfire rushed toward us.

"Show your curfew passes and state your business!"

My fingers grazed the hilt of my knife.

Terris, in front, raised a hand to his eyes to shade the glare. For a moment, it was hard to see anything except there was a bunch of them. I couldn't make out their uniforms, backlit as they were, but a sinking feeling in my guts told me they weren't City Guards black.

Military, then ... or those berserker kids of Montborne's Pateros Brigade?

A blade whispered from its sheath and glittered in the torchlight. Noiselessly I drew my own. Holding it low by my leg where they couldn't see it, I stepped in front of Terris. I felt rather than saw Avi on his other side, Jakon and Grissem moving to back us. We didn't have time for a fight. We had to get out of there fast—and quietly.

"Eyvian, Stoll, you others, surround them! Look there, we've caught us a pack of curfew violators!"

A shift in the light and everything came clear. The

bronze-and-red uniforms, the baby-round faces, eyes
thrill-bright, more sticks than knives, the faint lingering
smell of honey wine. Numbers, fear, and whatever the
uniform meant now, that was all they had.

I stepped out to face the leader, the big loud kid. "We
don't need any passes," I drawled. "We're *Rangers*. We
can do whatever we crotting well want."

I got the same reaction as if I'd spit in his baby-soft
face. He flushed as if he'd never had any brains to begin
with, and tried to jab me with his knife. Moved about
as fast as a heat-muddled sandbat, too. I pivoted, sent
his knife clattering to the cobblestones and finished with
him arched back, facing away from me, halfway to kneeling, his head pulled way back and my long-knife across
his throat.

"You want to see a lot of blood or you want to put
down your weapons?" I asked the other kids in the same
unhurried tone. The way I held him, the leader couldn't
do much more than gurgle in panic.

There were enough of them to make things messy for
us if they had the will and training to fight, which they
didn't. The speed of their surrender, though, was not
going to convince Jakon that Laurean youth could fight
anything bigger than cockroaches. I shoved the kid,
uncut and sprawling, into the arms of his friends.

"We're letting you go *this time*," Avi said. Her voice
dripped quiet menace. She looked as if she'd as soon
chop them into little pieces and boil each one separately
in acid, as look at them. That dragon mother of hers
couldn't have done it any better.

"If even a *whisper* of this secret mission gets out ..."
She pointed a finger at each one of them in turn. "You
will wish, you will pray, you will *beg* her—" a slight tip
of her head in my direction, "—to cut your throats,
rather than face what *I* have in store for you."

She took a step toward them. *"Got that?"*

They nodded, looking about to piss their pants. From
the shifting fear-stink, at least one of them already had.

"Go on home!" Avi said. *"Now!"*

They scrambled and bolted in their separate ways.

"Let's go," I said. I was in front of Etch and Terris,

feeling the street out like I'd feel the Ridge, a little cocky because I could see so far along the avenues with their wide-spaced trees.

Just as we reached the next branching, where the main avenue continued in one direction and two smaller ones veered to the sides, I heard the slap of boots on paving, behind us. I spun around. Guards, three of them, came pounding down the street. They had weapons out, what kind I couldn't see.

Damn! They must have heard the ruckus with the Brigade kids.

"Avi, Jakon, Griss!" Terris barked in a voice that would have made a stone jump. "Go!"

He whirled and sprinted down the main street, me and Etch on his heels. A man just stepping from a doorway scuttled back out of our way. Air blurred past me and I hardly felt the stones under my feet. I hadn't run so fast since the morning Pateros was killed. I spotted an alley, felt Terris swerve toward—

The next thing I knew there was a *hsst!* through the air and we all had tagged darts sticking out of our rumps. I reached around and yanked mine out with my free hand, pissed as hell for not seeing the attack coming. I stared down at it and its puke-color tags, then my sight went wobbly as if I drifted down a long wavy-sided tunnel.

I couldn't feel my hands or feet. The clatter-skitter of my knife on the pavement sounded like far-off tinkle bells. The last thing I remembered seeing was a woman in a black uniform leaning over me.

CHAPTER 35

Up and down ...

Everything blurred, weaving in and out of what was left of my brains. Slung facedown across the back of a galloping pony, I felt too addle-witted to know which way was up. Under the saddle pad, the pony's body rose and fell, lurching so hard my head reeled and spun. I must have been deaf, too—I couldn't hear any hoof-beats. Couldn't smell the wiregrass or the bitter-salt stink of a lathered pony. I was sweating cold, my mouth all cotton.

Up and down ...

The next moment my stomach decided it had enough of this *up and down* business. I thrashed around and somehow managed to sit up. My eyes told me I was nowhere near a pony of any kind, let alone norther, but in a half-lit gray room. And, more importantly, something that looked like a porcelain latrine was mounted on the opposite wall.

I reached it just in time and crouched there, my arms tight around the cold white disinfectant-smelling bowl, heaving and retching and spitting, dripping ropy green saliva out of my mouth and nose. Feeling like crotting shit.

Finally I sat back on my heels, holding on to the latrine and thinking longingly of fresh water. I found it in the basin by my right shoulder. I got slowly to my feet and turned the single tap on full. There was no way to plug the basin, but I shoved my head under the faucet and let the water gush over my neck until my muscles cramped and my hair was soaked. I cupped my hands and washed my mouth out again and again. Water spurted up my nose, cool and soothing. I collapsed on the floor, still within easy reach of the latrine, and considered my current situation.

Other than the antics of my innards and the tendency of my vision to slip sideways, I felt fit enough. No Ranger's vest or knives in my boots or thigh sheath, but they—whoever they were—left me my belt. The more fools they.

I remembered a drug dart, which explained the whirly stomach, and someone hovering over me, wearing a black uniform.

City Guards. *Let's see what their idea of a prison cell looks like.*

Four walls, all smooth and gray. Latrine and washbasin, no towels. On the opposite wall, built-in bookcases, empty, and cot. A few scratches on the wall, the usual *Orelia sucks crot.* No imagination. No blankets, either. The other two walls stopped being solid a foot from the ceiling, where they were broken by slits, each about six inches wide. One side opened to the night air. The other proved to be a door which slid open with a faint grating noise.

I stared at it, thinking I should get up and be ready, but my body wouldn't move. All I could do was stay as I was, sprawled on the floor by the latrine and wishing my stomach would hold still.

First in was a City Guard, a bit soft in the paunch but grim-faced, clutching his riot stick. Keys dangled from a clip on his belt. He gave an imitation of a meaningful glare and slapped the stick in his open palm. The noise reverberated through my skull. On his heels came a bald-headed gaea-priest. I blinked and struggled to sit up straighter.

"Oh, yes, I see what you mean," the priest said. "You were quite correct in summoning me." He knelt beside me in a rustling of rainbow colored silk. The amulets around his neck clinked together. He smelled of fish. My stomach heaved.

"There, there, poor child." He stroked my forehead with one hand. His flesh felt baby-soft and moist. "Don't be alarmed. You're reacting to the drug on the restraint dart. It's only natural, given a slight overdosage."

I opened my mouth to curse him, but found my nose pincered closed, my head jerked back and something tasting of bitter citrus poured down my throat. I swallowed, sputtered, lashed out at him but met empty air. I caught a glimpse of an empty glass vial before he hid it in the folds of his robe. My eyes watered.

He stood above me, well beyond my reach, gazing down with a beatific expression. I guessed he'd done this before. I swore at him in earnest.

"The antidote will take effect in a few moments. You'll be quite well, I assure you."

I started to clamber to my feet, although my belly advised against it. I'd paid it all the attention I was going to.

"Don't even try it!" the guard snarled. "You can answer his questions right where you are!"

I decided not to tell the guard what I thought of his ancestry, eating habits and choice of bed partners, which shows that my brains were getting unscrambled a bit. That antidote worked fast.

"Are you now or have you ever been," the priest began, rocking back and forth to the singsong phrases, "in possession of, knowledge regarding or contact with any unapproved, secret, or illicit technology, no matter how harmless it might seem? Think carefully before you answer, my child, for it is your precious ecosoul, the hologram of your being, at stake here."

"Unh!" I buried my face in my hands, hoping to appear sicker than I felt. *Contact with secret technology?* In my mind, I saw the cold, piercing brilliance at the heart of the Northlight, the arching metallic ribs of the dome, the stones underfoot worked with such marvelous skill. I ran laughing on the pebbled beach with Terris, I trembled with the beauty of the steppe. I stood in the poisoned swamp, trying to understand its lesson.

I lifted my eyes to the priest and saw now the glossy shaven skull, the opaque eyes, the frozen smile, the little pointed teeth.

"I am a Ranger," I said. "I stopped the northers at Brassaford with my own blood. I risked my life for you, time and again, on Kratera Ridge. I have done nothing but serve Laurea," I went on, "so the likes of *you* can sleep safe in your beds at night."

I struggled to my feet and this time the guard made no move to stop me. "How *dare* you treat me like a common criminal! I ought to slit your guts open for even thinking such a thing!"

The priest's mouth opened and shut, like that of a fish stranded on land, but no sound came out.

"I think she means *no*," said the guard. He'd turned a shade paler.

"Yes, very well, I don't think there will be any further questions. Not at this time, anyway." The priest moved toward the cell door.

"What about my friends?" I said.

The guard fumbled with the lock and jerked it open. "They're safe enough. You'll see them at the hearing," the priest said as he pushed past the guard.

"What hearing?" I stumbled after them. The door clanged shut in my face.

"The hearing for your trial," came wafting down the corridor.

Trial! White fire sizzled along my nerves. The words I'd thrown at the priest echoed through me. I hadn't realized how true they were.

I might have broken my oath to Pateros, but not before I'd tried my damnest to keep it. All those years— at Brassaford, on the Ridge—I'd kept it in blood and sweat and nightmares. But loyalty must be paid for, and Montborne had broken his own promises a dozen times over. I no longer belonged to him . . . or to Laurea.

"Kardith!" Etch's voice called from my right along the hall. "You all right?"

"Better than my stomach is," I said dryly. "You?"

"I came out of it maybe an hour ago. It's worn off

now. When you didn't wake up . . ." His voice sounded shaky.

I leaned my forehead against the wall. It was smooth and cool and steady. What had Etch said before we split up—*"Don't ask me to leave her now."*? I didn't have time for that, even if I could figure out how I felt about it.

Back to business. "Terris?" I asked.

"He's not here. Montborne's men came in a little after I woke up and dragged him out. Not the kids' brigade like last night, either. These were real military."

Military? My stomach lurched.

I chewed on the inside of one lip and thought hard. "We've got to get out of here fast." I slipped off my belt and freed the short-bladed buckle knife.

A short time later, by dint of both of us screaming at the top of our lungs that I was barfing blood all over the floor, we attracted a little official attention. It came in the form of two black coats. The man from earlier stood by the opened door. The other, a woman, bent over me where I lay on the cot, squirming realistically.

"I don't see any—" she began, and the next moment she shut up because the point of the buckle knife was pricking blood right over the big artery in her neck and my other hand was clamped around one wrist in a leverage that forced her hunched over and off-balance. For good measure, I hooked one leg in back of her knees, breaking her stance. It was possible to get out of this hold, but for myself, I'd rather wait for an easier opening.

She would, too. She'd had enough unarmed fighting experience to know there weren't a lot of other options. She didn't lack courage, I thought, but she'd never come up against anything tougher than a bunch of drunken ramblers.

I dug the knife point in deeper. She flinched enough for me to jerk her further down as I rolled up to sitting. Quickly I reversed the wrist leverage and flipped her over on her belly, with her hand up behind her shoulder blades and the blade of the knife across her throat.

The male guard's eyes popped with surprise. He raised his riot stick, the other hand reaching for his knife.

"Do it and she's dead!" I snapped.

He dropped the stick and raised both hands. "You won't get away with this."

Is there some academy of wishcrap slogans somewhere? "You're going to do exactly what I tell you," I said. "Very, very carefully. You wouldn't want my knife to slip."

He moved carefully. A cooperative man, or maybe he cared what happened to his partner. He took out the keys, threw them in the corner and then lay facedown and spread-eagled on the floor.

It was a tricky situation, managing both of them. Aram taught me some pressure points that put them out for a while, long enough to relieve them of their standard issue knives—the kind that could be used either right- or left-handed and that never fit anybody really well—then I gagged and tied them with strips of their own pants.

I looked down at them, trussed like a pair of barnfowl. I could have killed them both and once I would have. What possible difference did it make whether they were found alive or dead?

By the bloody balls of chance, I'm getting soft.

I checked the knots one more time, put on the woman's black jacket, and picked up the keys. The door to my cell slid shut with a hissing noise. It took only a moment to open Etch's and close it behind him. He slapped my arm and grinned when I handed him the man's jacket. It was a little tight across the shoulders and wouldn't fool anyone in decent light, but with his dark pants and in the shadows, it was worth a try.

As we passed the row of cells, a slurred voice called out, "Harth's own sweet luck to you, friends!"

The guard's keys let us through the barred gate at the end of the corridor. We found a chair and table, cup of tisane half-full and still warm, and two locked doors of solid wood. I couldn't tell where the other guard had come from or how long before the absence would be remarked. We didn't have much time, that was sure.

I leaned against one wall, trying to think straight. If

we could find a back entrance, maybe the one the guards themselves used ... but which? My head throbbed in answer.

Etch took the keys from me with a wry grin that told me he'd been here before, and more than once. He took us through one locked door and then the next, down a passageway, across an intersection. The place was fairly quiet but not deserted. Once we ducked into the women's toilet as we heard voices approach. We waited dry-mouthed until they disappeared. Finally we saw, at the end of a corridor, a small lobby and the outside door. I spotted two guards, the younger one leaning against the paper-covered desk, arms crossed over his chest. The other stretched back in his chair nodded and drank his tisane.

I pulled Etch back around the corner and prayed for inspiration. The light was too damned good to think we could just march out. Any moment now, the alarm would sound. I didn't want to fight off half the city guards.

The younger guard broke off his conversation with a sleepy-sounding, "That's it for me tonight."

"Go ahead," said the other, still slurping his tisane. "Leave all the tough jobs to me."

"Ha! *I* wasn't the one who doubled the night shifts. What's the old lady so nervous about, anyway? A few wild-eyed kids, a handful of drunks and ramblers sleeping it off down the hall? We handle that every day."

"You been sleeping these past weeks?" rumbled the older man. "I tell you, the Funeral Riot was only the beginning—"

"Tell that to the kiddie brigade! Esmelda says— Sheest, I'm too tired to stand here and argue all night. I'll see you tomorrow."

I slowly let out my breath when I heard the outer door close. Etch rolled his eyes expressively. A few moments later the older guard's chair springs squeaked and we heard him shuffling away in the direction of the men's toilet.

I grasped the hilt of the standard issue knife and sauntered across the lobby as if I belonged there, Etch half a pace behind me. The door latch creaked as I lifted it. We slipped through and I felt it click shut behind us. The shadows of the nearest alley closed silently around us.

If the demon god of chance laughed at me, bloody balls and all, then I was laughing back now. At worst, we were even.

Etch and I kept away from the center of the streets and to the cover of the trees and flowering bushes. We paused to plan our next move under the shadow of an ancient peach tree. The massive gnarled branches had been trained over an arched wooded trellis, so that flowers and setting fruit dangled inches from our heads.

I shrugged off the black jacket and let it drop. Maybe a stupid move, since I might need it again later, but if I no longer wore the Ranger's vest, I'd rather take my chances than wear this. More instinct than sense.

"The front entrance is sure to be crawling with military goons," Etch said in a hushed voice. "There might be a way through the gardens around in back. It won't be easy."

"What? You mean getting us into Montborne's residence?"

"Where else?"

My head still felt muzzy, as if the dart drug had kicked up the older concussion. It made logical sense—Montborne wouldn't take Terris to his headquarters office, not at this hour, not if he wanted any kind of secrecy. I didn't think he was ready to accuse Terris publicly on some faked-up charge, at least not until he'd questioned him. I went over everything I knew about Montborne and I still couldn't read him clear—whether he'd bother to keep his options open for later dealing with Esmelda—alliance or extortion—or just eliminate any witnesses when he had the chance.

But this direction didn't *feel* right. I still couldn't think straight. But I'd pressed the demon god hard now, even laughed in the bastard's face. I couldn't count on any second chances. I had to choose right the first time.

Something niggled at the back of my thoughts ... something Terris said. I saw his face, tilted down and

half away from mine, rainwater eyes hidden in shadow,
skin flushed with the sea-whipped wind. I half-closed my
eyes, remembering the tang, the wildness, the gritty yellow sand, the smooth curved shells.... But no, he *said*
something, said it with such a sense of loss that it was
branded in my memory....

*"And Esme, doing the wrong things for the right rea-
sons."* That wasn't it, but close ... *"Now I know what
the Starhall thing is."*

The Starhall. The center of it all. The gate where
Terris had seen the last true Guardians die.

"Promise me!" he cried. *"Promise me you'll
remember!"*

I bent my face and covered it with my hands. *Mother-
of-us-all, let me be right.* I realized this was the first time
I'd prayed for anything besides an end to my own pain.
Let me be right.

"Where, then?" said Etch.

I told him, and for a moment I feared he'd say *yes*
just because it was me who asked. But I wasn't asking.
Even if he refused, I was going to the Starhall.

"You sure?"

"If I'm going to make mistakes," I said, "I'm going
to make my *own* mistakes." Something Terris would
understand.

"So, I'll help you get in through the back of the Starhall, just like anyplace else in this city."

"You know a way?"

He shook his head, but I saw the white gleam of his
teeth in the dappled shadows. "No, but I bet I can find
it. You don't live in a city as many years as I have and
drink as many pints of brew, without collecting a few
useful tips. Gardeners and stablemen, you see, have always had a special relationship. And *somebody* has to
take out the garbage."

So we made our way through the less-lit streets, keeping well away from the plaza. The skylights above the
Starhall's main chamber blazed as if someone—Pateros's
ghost, maybe—had set a torch to it. But back here,
where the light barely reached, the building looked un-
finished and cobbled together. Bits of chopped-off wall

stuck out into the alley. The chipped and broken bricks cast faintly patterned shadows against the crumbling mortar. There was an unmistakable smell of garbage emanating from the recycle and compost bins.

We picked a door—there were several hidden in the shadowed recesses—of plain light-colored wood, cracked where the sealant weathered off. Simple hinges, a lock, a latch which could be lifted by one elbow. I pictured the kitchen drone, both arms spilling over with sacks of redroot peelings and boiled-out soup bones, backing out through the door.

Etch hunched over by the lock and pried it with the guard's knife. I winced as metal whined across metal. Too damned loud.

I kept my mouth shut and glanced back up the alley. Anything I said or did would only cut into Etch's concentration. But me, I was too tweaked to fight good. I didn't like this place, full of bins to fall against and chunks of wall to crash into and Mother knew what to slip on. I didn't like this knife—a plague-rotted half-blind ghamel turd could have done a better job balancing it. I didn't like . . .

. . . a muted something crept along my nerves, no more than leaves brushing against a branch . . .

I held the knife still, ready.

A light beam across the far end of the alley, swinging side to side. The rapping of heeled boots on pavement. Two, three of them maybe, I couldn't tell.

I skimmed the fingers of my free hand over Etch's shoulder and he froze, knife point still jammed in the lock. The light beam jerked and played over the sides of the Starhall.

Mother, let them see only the jumble of shapes and shadows. If we don't move, don't breathe. . . .

The next moment they were gone, their footsteps fading.

It was the waiting, that's what it was. The waiting out here and the trying not to think of what I'd find—or not find—in there.

Then with a final resentful *click*! and a hiss of breath, Etch cracked the door open and we entered the Starhall.

CHAPTER 36

The back corridors of the Starhall had an airless, almost deserted feel. Solar strips along the tops of the walls gave off a subdued light, like a sickly haze. The silence was enough to make me itch.

Curfew or no, there should have been someone here in the middle of the night, even in this city where, as Avi told me, the most common crime was pickpocketing. A watcher, maybe, stationed by the big front doors. There was no trace of any guard Montborne might have left. We made our way alone and unchallenged through the storage areas lined with boxes and bales of papers, frayed tapestries, rolled and tagged, closets stuffed with old ceremonial robes and reeking of pine oil and cedar. Here we had to choose to go down or forward, toward the central chamber itself.

The door to the basement stairwell stood just a hair open.

It could be a steward who left it that way, in a hurry to get home to a hot dinner. It could be.

It could also be that Montborne and Terris went this way, and that Montborne made sure they were alone. The Starhall watcher, if there were one, would have let him pass without any questions, would have turned his back while Montborne conducted his secret business below.

The steps were stone, once scored for traction but now

worn smooth and hollowed in the center. I kept close to one wall, pausing every few feet to listen.

At the bottom of the flight we came to a landing with a chair and an old desk, a shelf holding some books with frayed covers and an unlighted reading lamp. The wooden wall panels were black and warped, smelling of old lacquer. I saw three doors and another pit of a stairway, smaller, narrower. *Darker.*

Etch started to go down. Without thinking, my hand shot out and I wrapped my fingers around his wrist. He stared at me, his eyes puzzled, as I shook my head. He set his chin, shaped the word, *Yes,* and pulled away from me. I held him fast. He looked surprised at how strong I was.

I tried to keep my voice no louder than the slither of a house snake. "I can't protect you, too."

Etch started to shake his head, but then saw my meaning. He would die for me but not, I thought, risk *me* dying for *him.*

After a moment, when I felt sure he understood, I let him go. He saluted me with his City Guards knife and stepped aside.

The air was even thicker here, cold and musty, the wall lights fewer and dimmer. Whoever came here—if anybody ever did—must bring their own. Halfway down I paused again. My heart beat so loudly I wasn't sure I could hear anything else.

Voices. Yes, voices. I listened . . .

Men's voices. Two. Muffled, maybe behind a door. I couldn't make out words, only tones. One sounded sharp, no more than bursts of sound and then silences. The other, softer, stumbling, as if the speaker were exhausted or sick at heart.

Images rose up to drown me, like the shadows cast by churning bat wings. I trembled under their weight, terrified I'd come too late, smelling the blood and the deathstink all over again.

My body moved on its own, as if it no longer belonged to me. The City Guards knife, even badly balanced as it was, seemed to come alive in my hand. I glided down one stair after another, as supple and silent as a shadow panther on the prowl. No grain of sand would shift under my feet, not even the flimsiest stalk of grass would quiver as I passed. I could creep past a browsing gazelle without its knowing. Even my heart beat soundlessly.

I no longer strained to hear the words between the two men. Only the pauses, the silences, the way the air shifted and eddied with their slightest breath.

At the bottom of the stairs, I found a little passageway and then a door frame of rough, cobwebby wood. I sensed its powdery grain and the tiny poison sacs of the spiders nesting there. Holding the knife so there would be no reflection off its flat surface, I flattened myself against the wall.

Almost within straight eyeshot of the room, I no longer needed my eyes. I felt the quaking in Terris's muscles and tasted the blood on his lips. I recoiled from the oily smoothness of Montborne's voice even before he spoke.

"You have to admit I've been more than fair. I've listened to you. I've even come all the way down here in the middle of the night. Alone, just as you asked. But you see, there's nothing here. Nothing at all. Just an old storage room nobody's used for a hundred years. There's no sense to it. I ask you, as one rational person to another, why would the founders of Laurea hide something so important down here? And why is there no official record of it?"

Terris's voice, ragged though it was, rang like steel. "The gaea-priests were supposed to keep the secret ... and the warning. But the knowledge was lost—"

"Come now, lad," Montborne said, moving closer and holding out one hand, "I can see you're not well. You've been through an ordeal that would break most men. There's no shame in admitting you're human. All of us make mistakes. Let me help you upstairs and I'll see you're properly taken care of."

Terris swerved out of Montborne's reach and came up flat against the wall. Montborne followed, closing in. The general's back was toward me and his red-and-bronze uniform looked faded and muddy. I slid through the door frame, well away from the light.

"It used to be . . . behind the wall," Terris said, edging away again. I couldn't tell if he'd spotted me or not. His eye sockets were dark circles in a face as white as bone. "But it was . . . shifted. Just a little . . . further."

"I think you've gone far enough!" With a single stride, Montborne closed the distance between them, whipped one of Terris's arms behind his back and jerked him away from the wall. He clamped on the shoulder leverage and Terris arched back reflexively.

"Damn you, Montborne! If you could just look past your narrow-minded patriotic nose, you'd see—"

I tightened my grip on the knife but kept my muscles loose. I wanted my own attack to be sudden and final. Tricky—if I were close enough to hold a knife-edge to Montborne's throat, I would also be close enough for him to effectively counter the move, and he'd know how.

"—it isn't Laurea that's at stake, it's all of Harth!" Terris's breath came like a hiss through his clenched teeth. No wonder—Montborne had his shoulder joint half dislocated. My own joints ached with memory; Westifer used to try that one on me, until I applied some sufficiently nasty countermoves. Montborne half-lifted, half-dragged Terris, searching for the leverage that would get him up on his toes and carrying his own weight. An inch or two closer now and they'd be in reach . . .

I shifted my weight just a fraction and beyond the two men, something came into my field of vision—something glimmering a few inches inward from the scabby black wall. A twist of the grayish opalescent light, like a Ridge weirdie and yet much more intense. Terris's forgotten door? A door that he was trying to maneuver Montborne through?

No time to think. I launched myself with every bit of power in me and rammed one shoulder into Montborne's back just level with his short ribs. His breath went out of him hard, he staggered and half-dropped Terris.

The force of my charge carried us all forward, out of the grayish light of the Starhall cellar and through a momentary flash of green. I fell to my knees and sent Terris and Montborne sprawling.

The next moment, I was squinting up at a sky sullen with thickly layered clouds. Stale, metallic-tasting air stung my eyes and burned my windpipe. After the Northlight and those green tunnels, I thought nothing could ever surprise me again. But this place . . .

At our feet lay a jumble of bones and tattered cloth. Some of the bones, blackened and splintered, looked human. Around us stretched a broad, weathered platform, piled high with rubble. One side, a tangle of corroded metal and rock, looked like the remains of a once-majestic tower. The other three sides opened to a scooped-out valley, its floor strewn with steaming, rust-colored pools and twisted bushes. I'd never seen anything like that foul-colored water and clumps of vegetation scattered across the streaked, red-purple soil. Squinting at the leaden gray sky, I found no trace of brightness where the sun might be. Any clouds up there must be as high as the stars. If anything lived, it kept itself well hidden. For now, anyway.

I picked myself up. "Some door."

Terris knelt beside the bones. The fabric looked as if it had once been green, now bleached almost colorless. It shredded as he reached into the pile. He pulled free a fragment, thin and curved, of a human skull. The bone showed distinct tooth marks, but from what kind of animal, I couldn't tell.

Something glinted among the slender gray-black finger bones. I pointed, and Terris lifted out a ring. He drew in his breath sharply as he brushed away the powdery silt. He pocketed the ring and got to his feet.

Montborne's skin looked smooth and fine and dead like beeswax, but sweat beaded his forehead and white ringed his eyes. His voice came in a rasping whisper. "Is this hell?"

Terris's eyes scanned the desolate horizon, then flickered back to the general's face. "Hell? Yes, in a way. One that we must never be allowed to repeat."

CHAPTER 37

I kept one hand on the hilt of my sheathed knife and both my eyes on Montborne as we followed Terris toward the ruined tower.

A little beyond the fallen blocks, we came to a jumble of chipped and splintered stone. From the shape and placement of the fallen stones, I guessed they had originally formed an archway. An open area faced them, once part of a spacious courtyard but now choked by chunks of crumbling stone, twisted branches, dried leaves and metal bars powdery with rust.

Terris bent over to examine a block of fire-blackened rock, partly covered with scabby dun lichen. Under his touch, the surface flaked into chips that sifted to the pavement. Something small, with a dark, glossy shell and too many legs, scuttled away between the cracks.

"What are we looking for?" I asked.

"They should have left something," Terris said. "A message in case we came back through some day. Or maybe a memorial to honor those who stayed behind."

" 'Back through'? 'Stayed behind'?" Montborne demanded. "What are you talking about?"

"You don't see it yet, do you?" Terris's eyes glittered in the lurid overcast light. "Harth was never our home, it was the place we ran to ... after we'd destroyed this one. *This* is the world we came from."

"You're crazy! I don't know what kind of place you've

taken us to, but we *couldn't* have come from here."
Montborne gestured toward the poisoned valley. "Nothing human could live out there."

"Not now," Terris said. "Not any more. *This* is what
the gaea-priests were supposed to warn us about."

"Gaea-priests!" Montborne said. "A pack of norther
dupes, who'd like to freeze us with nothing more effective than knives and axes."

Without replying, Terris turned back to the rubble
again. From his expression, I could tell we weren't leaving until Montborne changed his mind. When Montborne walked away, I followed him.

Montborne picked his way around to one of the almost-intact columns on the far side. It must have been a major
structural support, but the tower had long since collapsed around it. He paused, staring off at the end of
the valley. His hands hung open at his sides and a gust
of air ruffled his hair. I couldn't let him get too far,
although I glanced over at what he found so interesting.

Beginning a half-mile or so past the base of the tower,
a hill stretched halfway to the horizon. Squat and broad,
it looked to be cloudy gray-white glass. Even from this
distance, I saw the folded, pleated crevices tinged with
yellow, as if years of rainfall had left a sickly stain. The
near edge of the hill fell off sharply and extended in the
shape of a little sheltered glen. Here a patch of weedy
trees, stunted and pale, huddled around a spring of clear
water. The breeze shifted the leaves, showing their
brownish undersides. In Laurea—hell, *anywhere* in
Harth—they'd be thought so poor and sickly, they'd be
torn out and replaced if they couldn't be doctored into
something better.

To my left—I couldn't tell where the sun was and I'd
lost my sense of direction—I caught a flicker of movement. I looked, but found nothing—yes, I saw it now,
camouflaged so well as to be almost invisible when
standing still. At first I thought it was a pony, about
that size and shape, with reddish horizontal stripes and
a scrawny mane. The ears seemed too long, though, and
the tail either clamped tight against its scrawny rump, or
else for some reason it didn't have one.

Beside me, Montborne let out his breath with a hissing noise. He, too, had noticed that the pony-thing had only one foreleg. The other was a stump ending just above the knee joint, the tip tapered smooth as if it were formed that way.

"There it is!" Terris was on his knees, sweeping the rock clear of dust and rubble. Montborne and I turned to look.

What the hell—

I let my breath out in a whistle as I realized it was a metal plaque, badly etched and pitted, but inscribed with recognizable letters. And surrounding them, over and over again, the symbol of the dotted doubled circle.

Terris bent over the tablet, smoothing away the last of the sifted grit with his hands. He wet his lips, tracing the eroded letters with his fingers. I peered over his shoulder, straining to make out the words.

" '*It is better to plant a single seed than conquer a world.*' "

"By all that's holy," Montborne whispered. "You were right."

Following the slogan was a list of strange doubled names, some familiar but combined in odd ways:

Sylvia Rosenberg	Thomas Montburn
Aaron Stockman	Geremy Paterno
Esmelda Aragon	Jason Koltabi
Chi-Yun Derrin	

"They gave their lives to find a new world for humankind."

Suddenly, from the direction of the spring, came a wild wailing shriek. I sprinted to the edge of the platform in time to see a bolt of greenish light shoot from the brush. It landed squarely on the pony's striped hip, leaving a puff of vapor.

The pony staggered and turned toward us, as if it sensed our hidden presence and appealed to us for help. For a moment I thought it wasn't hurt, only a little stunned. It took one step and then another, head down as if to gather itself to run. Suddenly its hind legs collapsed under it.

And as it fell I saw the place where the green light had struck, the white bones piercing the flesh which even now dripped in huge wet dollops to the ground. The pony screamed again, its voice high and unbroken. It thrashed the dirt with its single foreleg. Something in the set of its neck and the way it kept trying to get up tore at my memories of the gray mare fighting the ropeweed.

The other creature darted from the shelter of the bushes—not human, not the way it scuttled and crouched. Not the way it pointed the blunt-ended black tube right at the struggling pony and seared it again and again. The pony's last scream cut off in the middle, leaving a mass of disjointed bones and gelatinous, meat-colored stuff that still quivered slightly.

The hunter paused and straightened up, searching the distance. Then it strode over to what was left of the pony and squatted beside it. It wore a sort of harness over its clothing, boots, a close-fitting hood over its head and neck. Dark goggles covered its eyes. It laid the black tube across one knee, scooped up a handful of the red blobby stuff, and stuffed it into its mouth.

I always thought I had a strong stomach, but now I clapped one hand over my mouth and turned away.

Montborne grabbed my arm. He gestured urgently and pointed toward the spring. The hunter thing had seen my movement. It was on its feet once more, aiming the black tube in our direction.

The first blast hit the column inches from my face as Montborne shoved me out of the way. I stumbled, fighting to stay on my feet, and then he grabbed my shirt and hauled me bodily behind the nearest large chunk of stone, a fragment of wall.

Another bolt of light sizzled by us and Montborne cursed violently. I shrank against the bit of wall, my fingers curled around the hilt of the City Guards knife, for all the good it would do me now.

"Terris!" I yelled.

From across the courtyard, Terris looked up. His face was white-gray, like marble.

I swerved as a splinter of falling rock narrowly missed my nose. "We've got to get out of here!"

There was a pause in the attack, as if the thing down there were watching for new signs of life. Or maybe sneaking closer.

"This way!" Terris called, gesturing.

I started toward him, keeping to the cover of the wall as long as I could, Montborne at my heels.

Hsst! Crack! Suddenly another blast shot between the columns. Eye-watering dust puffed up where it hit the rock wall behind us.

Damn, but that thing aimed good!

"Look out!" Terris yelled.

I glanced up as one of the rust-eaten metal posts of the tower, perhaps weakened by a chance bolt of light, began to topple right where Montborne and I had stood. I hurled myself to the side, as fast and far as I could. The corroded metal shrieked in my ears as it snapped. The next instant, I landed splat on my belly, sliding through the rock dust. My outstretched arms slammed into chunks of loose rubble.

With a deafening boom, quivering through the whole platform, the metal beam crashed into the ground. I covered my head with my free hand and squeezed my eyes tight. Dust and rock chips pelted my body.

Another earth-shivering crack came from behind me, along with another fall of rock—more of the ruined tower toppling, I couldn't tell. I opened my eyes a fraction and shut them again, choking on the acrid billowing dust. It would take a moment or two for it to clear and meanwhile . . .

I struggled to my feet, knife in my hand. My eyes streamed tears, but I could just make out what was left of the tower.

"Kardith?" Terris's voice, near.

I blinked hard—yes, there he was, moving in my direction. "Keep to cover!"

Even as I spoke, another light bolt sizzled through the air. This time it didn't hit anything. The dust continued to clear. I spotted Terris, crouched low beside a stumpy column. Montborne lay outstretched a few feet away, shards of rust covering what I could see of him. The metal beam had landed on a slant across Montborne's body, one end propped a foot or so off the ground by a chunk of rock. Faint traces of carving still showed across its surface—the base of a pillar, I thought. It was all that kept Montborne from getting smashed flat.

I wondered if I could convince Terris to go back while Montborne was helpless. It would solve our Laurean problems neatly enough, and we could swear honestly we hadn't killed him. But Terris was already hurrying to the general's side.

Now Montborne raised his head, reached along the pavement with his hands, and began pulling himself forward. Terris hooked his hands under Montborne's shoulders and hauled him out from under the metal. I grabbed Montborne's other shoulder and helped him to sit up.

Hsst! Crack! A greenish bolt splintered a hole in the engraved rock an inch from Terris's head. I grabbed him and pulled him down. Montborne bit back a curse. It was no use—the hunter must be damned close to aim so low.

I caught a glimpse of something clambering up the far end of the platform, behind the pillars, the rounded shape of its head, the bulge of the goggles, the straps of its harness. The thing had small but definite breasts.

My fingers inched toward the hilt of the Guards knife, not that it would be much use against the black tube now moving slowly back and forth, searching for us. Any quick movement would draw its attention; I'd have only an instant to draw, aim, and throw.

My shoulder was against Terris's chest and I could feel the beating of his heart, the whisper of his breath in my hair. The black tube swung back in our direction—

S-s-ssshth! Crack-boom! Another bolt of light, this one searing orange, shot through the ruined archways. It caught the edge of a metal bar. Sparks flew; bits of rusted metal hurled in all directions. An acrid smell clawed the back of my throat.

The first hunter whirled and fired its tube weapon off to the east. More orange beams answered it, thin and quick like glowing threads. The hunter twisted and dodged, then jumped from the platform, disappearing from our sight.

"Now!" Terris cried, scrambling to his feet.

We all jumped when he said jump and landed splat on the stone floor of the Starhall basement.

After we all got our breath back, Montborne picked himself up off the stone floor and mumbled to Terris, "I was wrong, I . . ." and Terris shot back, "Let's just get the hell *out* of here." My thoughts exactly.

Despite his brave words, Terris looked whiter than I'd ever seen him and he shook like a barnfowl at a slaughter yard. Etch met us halfway up the first flight of stairs. He looked half out of his skin with worry. He'd given up waiting and was on his way to find us. He took one look at Terris and slung him over his shoulders as if he were a newborn foal. He carried him down a couple of corridors and out the door of polished bronzewood used by the Inner Council for their private comings and goings. It was locked from both sides but Montborne had the key. Once we were halfway across the plaza, Terris started looking a whole lot stronger.

He said to Montborne, "There wasn't any other way. There wasn't anything I could have said that you'd have *believed.*" Underneath the jittery exhaustion in his voice, I heard again the ring of steel.

But as for me, I wondered why it meant a demon's fart *what* Montborne believed. Wasn't he the one who had Pateros killed? Wasn't he the one who sent the goons after us with that cursed dagger? One glance at Etch's face told me he thought the same, but both of us kept our mouths shut.

"I thought you were making it all up," Montborne said. I never heard him so quiet, so subdued. So shook— *him,* the Butcher of Brassaford? "Just some wild story because you'd been away so long, with nothing but rumors about what's happening in the city. But I was wrong—oh, gods—was I wrong! You were telling the truth. That place back there—"

Montborne's eyes flickered toward the Starhall, spewing its glittery light all over the plaza. "I don't have words enough—it's more disgustingly—obscenely—*contaminated* than anything the gaea-priests warn us about. If there's some way for that—thing to escape, to follow us—sweet Harth!—into Laurea...." His voice trembled. *Montborne?*

The eastern sky shone like a pearl, pink and gold. Just then, the lights from the Starhall winked out. Montborne jumped, as if Laurea were already plunged into darkness. The demon god had sunk his claws deep into Montborne, that was sure, or maybe it was his own damned conscience.

"You still don't understand, do you?" said Terris. "Those *things* were human—every bit as human as our ancestors when they passed through that gate. Why do you think the worst epithets in our language are words like *contaminated* and *toxic* and *mutagenic?* It's because *we* were the ones who did that. Why we thought we could start over again, I don't know. Maybe we thought that with the gaea-priests to keep us from inventing new weapons, more powerful and destructive all the time, we'd somehow manage to avoid turning Harth into ... that."

For a moment Montborne looked lost, as if the glimpse of that other place had broken some part of his mind. Or maybe Terris had gotten through to him and he saw what he almost did.

Maybe he saw what he had already done, that it was now too late to undo. That I understood.

But there was forgiveness and there was forgiveness.

Montborne straightened his shoulders, once more the general of Laurea. He took Terris's hand in both of his and met his eyes, very direct and open. The gesture reminded me in a strangely reversed way of how Pateros took my hand in his when he heard my oath.

"Whatever else I might have been," Montborne said, "I have and always will be loyal to Laurea. That—" with a shiver and a glance back toward the Starhall, "—is a lesson I won't have to repeat."

Terris locked his eyes on the general's and I wondered what he saw there. In the dawning light, his face had gone to shades of gray, like marble. "I never thought you acted purely out of self-interest," he said.

Montborne offered to escort us to Esmelda's house, but Terris answered, with a perfectly straight face, that one Ridge-trained Ranger and one meaner-than-piss horse doctor were protection enough for any city streets.

"I'll see you tomorrow, then, at the Inner Council meeting," said Montborne, and strode off westward.

Silently Terris watched him disappear into the fading darkness. His shoulders sagged a little as we started off toward Esmelda's house. I watched the shadows for any sign of trouble—military goons, kids, more City Guards with dart pipes.

"There've been some changes since we left," Etch commented.

Terris made a strange sound, half-hiccup, half sneeze. I realized he was laughing, and I couldn't understand what was so funny.

"My visions were right after all. My mother's become Guardian of Laurea," he said when he could talk straight again, "and not even *pro tem*. The real thing. Montborne doesn't know Avi's back, so he thinks I'm Esme's heir. That's why he humored me so long, trying to find out what I knew. And the best part is—it was some damn-fool crazy precedent, some emergency loophole, in one of those archives I busted my ass dredging up that put Esme in power so quick. I never thought—I'd find such a practical use—for my academic career!"

CHAPTER 38

Terris was staggering by the time Etch and I got him to Esmelda's house. It wasn't just the night without sleep, or even the journey north when he hardly slept or ate. The Light had changed him, given him gifts he didn't want and taken something away, too—what, I wasn't sure yet. Then there was whatever the Starhall gate had cost him. And facing Montborne down afterward. I knew this man, I'd watched him run mile after mile when he couldn't catch his breath and his muscles screamed like hell. He didn't give up. Not then, not now. He gritted his teeth together and his eyes wove in and out of focus. He leaned on me more and more, but when we reached his mother's doorstep he pushed me away. With a twist of his mouth, he stood on his own, his shoulders back.

The door slammed open just as we reached it and the mouse-woman steward and Avi came bursting through. Avi took one look at us and said, "Drat," just as Terris collapsed. Etch caught him as he fell.

I shoved my way into the house. The table just inside the door was heaped with papers and books, the staircase with its carved banister, the dimness broken by the brighter light from the right-hand room, just as if the place had stood untouched since I was last here.

"Kardith, what's happened?" Avi said.

I spun around. "Does he have a *room* here?"

"Right," she said, and jerked her head toward the stairs.

Etch maneuvered Terris's body around the banister. Both Avi and I moved to help, but suddenly one of my arms was caught—not trapped or grabbed hard, just touched so I couldn't move.

The old dragon herself.

"You," she said, meaning Etch and Avi, "get him to bed, and then yourselves. Lys," to the mouse-woman steward, "get Cherida. And *you*," meaning, of course, me, "go sit down," propelling me with a feather touch toward the living room, "until you can give me a full report."

Everyone did exactly that. For a moment I hesitated to walk across the sand-colored carpet or touch the plush, upholstered furniture. I was so tired I couldn't stand up and so fired up I couldn't sit still. There wasn't a part of me that wasn't stinking filthy with dried blood, trail dirt, crusted sweat, or grime from the Starhall gate world.

I threw myself into the nearest chair.

A few minutes later, Esmelda entered the room. I remembered the first time she spoke to me, the day of Pateros's funeral. The night I begged her help for Avi, the night Terris found me on my knees in the plaza and swore he'd find a way.

She'd looked over the milling crowd, as if scenting the yet-unspilled blood. *"My son's out there . . ."*

"I found him for you," I said. "I found *both* of them."

As for the story, I stumbled around, putting together bits of what I'd heard Terris say to Etch and Jakon. I saw from Esmelda's expression that she'd heard some of this before—maybe from Avi, maybe from her own sources. What happened in the Light, though, that was none of her business.

Like Avi, she interrupted me with questions, "You saw this yourself?" being the most frequent. Unlike Avi, she kept her opinions to herself.

Some time in the middle of my rambling story, the steward came back with Cherida, the red-haired medician who'd tried to save Pateros. They bustled upstairs and then, after a while, back down. Cherida stopped by the living room, patted Esmelda on the shoulder, and said, "He's exhausted, that's all. Let him rest." And Esmelda, with no visible change in expression, went right on questioning me.

Finally she nodded, but I knew it wasn't the end, only a pause before we started all over again. Maybe she was just tired of the smell.

The mouse-woman steward, Annelys, led me upstairs. There was a cot made up for me in a room which used to be Avi's. Avi herself was no more than a snoring lump in the corner, behind the old desks and wooden storage crates and wicker baskets overflowing with mending. Outside the door I found a bathroom with a tub filled with steaming, herb-scented water and a wicker stand bearing fluffy towels, soap and bath oils, scrub brushes, and real Archipelago sponges.

Annelys handed me a long, velvety-soft robe. Pink, of course. Was every single Mother-damned bathrobe in Laureal City *pink*?

"I've put some clothes on the foot of your bed," she said. "They're clean and they ought to fit you." She didn't say whose they were or that she thought mine weren't fit to be worn again. "You'll want to sleep in, then. I'll leave your breakfast in the kitchen for whenever you come down."

I looked down at the bath. The water was a light blue-green with some kind of fragrant salts. I felt myself drifting, falling into it, my head swimming with the curls of sweet-smelling steam.

Ah, yes—Laureal City ... I gripped the edge of the tub hard enough to cramp my hands.

"Where's ... Terris?" *Whose voice is saying that, mine?*

"Terricel." She gave me a funny, sideways look. "Asleep. At the end of the hallway, in his old room. With that older man. The two northers," she didn't quite sniff, but looked as if she'd like to, "I put *them* in the back, downstairs." And then, before I could ask any more annoying questions, she shut the door on me.

Wishing I had my long-knife, I laid the two currently

in my possession—the buckle knife and the City Guards knife—at the side of the tub, within easy reach, and sank into the hot water. For a blessed five minutes, I let the bath and my aching muscles think they were winning. I scrubbed everything twice, including my hair, and went over my body with a brush. The water was brown the first time I drained it, but soapy clear the next.

I toweled myself dry, dragged a comb through my hair, wrapped myself in the robe, and tiptoed into Avi's room. She was still asleep. I slid into the borrowed clothes and lowcut house shoes. They were a bit narrow, but so buttery-soft they stretched out to fit.

I opened the door at the end of the hallway just a crack to make sure Terris was there. The walls, I noticed, were a depressing shade of blue. Hell, I'd probably have painted my room that color if I had to live here, too.

Noiselessly I shut the door and sat with my back to it, my arms folded over my knees, the way I passed many a night on the Ridge or before that in the Brassa Hills, in between skirmishes, with my fingers resting on the hilt of my knife.

A house snake rippled by, its eyes glowing like opals. It tasted me delicately with its tongue, decided I wasn't edible and slithered on in search of dinner.

Me, I slept lightly. Very lightly.

Behind me, a boot sole scuffed over a smooth wood floor and the latch hinge rattled. Before I could think, I was on my feet and ready.

The door cracked open. Terris glanced down at the drawn knife in my hand. Beneath his beard, his face was pale, the skin under his eyes purplish. I heard Etch snoring somewhere in the depths of the dismal-blue room. I put knife away and stepped back.

Terris eyed me as he closed the door behind himself. "As usual, you're up early . . ." he began, then paused, his brows drawing together. "You slept *out here,* didn't you? On my doorstep like some kind of watcher—"

I set my jaw. This was going to be harder than I thought.

"What the hell do you think you're doing? Do you think you're made out of iron?" he stormed at me. "Did you think I was in danger here? This is Laureal City, not the gods-damned steppe and, more than that, this is my mother's house!"

With two northers downstairs, still armed for all I knew, gangs of crazed Brigade kids in the streets, and Montborne on the loose. Terris could swear at me by whatever misbegotten gods he liked, but I wasn't sleeping down the hall.

He narrowed his eyes. "You *did* sleep?"

I shrugged. He grabbed my shoulders and spun me around toward the staircase. "Then you are now going to eat breakfast."

No argument there.

"We damned well better be ready for his next move." Avi leaned over the breakfast table and gestured as she made her point to Esmelda. "Or *I'm* the one who'll have to deal with that contaminated snake!"

"We will be ready for him," Esmelda replied calmly.

Neither of them looked up as Terris and I walked in. Their heads—black and steel-gray—almost touched over the clutter of crumb-covered dishes and papers scrawled with notes and figures that hid a dining table big enough for a dozen people. Beyond them, a sideboard held a ceramic tea urn, pots of jam and butter, a huge glass platter overflowing with peaches and cherries. The fruity smell mingled with the tang of cheese and the yeasty aroma of new bread. Annelys the steward bustled through the kitchen doorway and put two crusty loaves on the cutting board.

Terris took a plate from the sideboard, loaded it with fruit and cheese and three thick slices of still-warm bread. He shoved it into my hands. For a moment, I couldn't think what to do with it. He carried his own plate to the table and cleared a place for both of us by sweeping the nearest papers into a heap with the back of one forearm.

Avi looked up, tossed back the heavy black hair which had fallen forward across her face, and scowled at him.

"How could you do it? Take Montborne to that toxic world or wherever it was—and then bring him back!"

"Montborne truly believed he was doing the right thing for Laurea. He didn't understand where his desire for better weapons would inevitably lead," Terris said in between bites of bread. "He thought all that stuff the gaea-priests spout at us was just empty words. Hell, so did I, so did everybody."

"Whose side are you on, anyway?" Avi snapped.

"Avi's right," Esmelda said. "Montborne won't give up. Not when he's devoted his life to a single goal—the ultimate defeat of the northers—and believes he's the *only* one who can accomplish it. No matter what he said or did last night, this morning he'll feel justified in using any means available to achieve his goals. Beginning with eliminating *you*."

"I was there with him. He saw—he *understood.* . . ."

"Do you think a few minutes in some outlandish place will make any difference to a man like him?"

"What else was there to do?" Terris said. "I couldn't *leave* him there."

"You could," I said, laying down my half-eaten cheese. "And you should have. He deserved it. Have you forgotten who sent those goons in the night and who had Pateros killed? I haven't. What did you ask Jakon to come here for—to bring Montborne to justice or to let him go free?"

I did not add that there were certain things that changed a person forever, for good or ill. Montborne might have been the true hero the Laureans thought him. Once. But some bloodstains didn't wash off.

Terris's eyes went opaque for a moment, staring through me to Mother-knows-where. I wished I'd kept silent.

"I have no intention of letting him *go free,*" he said tightly. "He must stand trial for what he's done. But I am not his judge, and certainly not his executioner. He didn't deserve to be abandoned in that . . . place."

"There's no point in recriminations," Esmelda raised one hand for quiet. "And Montborne hasn't won yet."

"Oh, no?" Avi demanded, bristling. "What's to keep

him from marching his men into this morning's Inner Council meeting and staging a military coup?"

"For one thing, Orelia's doubled my security, and for another, I've arranged a location change from the Starhall to the Senate Building. The meeting won't be with the Inner Council but the entire Senate. And Montborne won't find out until the last minute." Esmelda's mouth twitched in what might have passed for a smile.

"But we must do more than neutralize him as a threat," Esmelda added. "He must be held accountable for his acts. The people will never accept a treaty with Clan'Cass as long as they believe the northers were behind the assassination of Pateros. Montborne must be eliminated *and* proven responsible."

"We don't have enough hard proof yet," Avi said, frowning. I could almost see her thoughts churning, her mind settling into the habits of so many years ago. Moment by moment, she revealed her mother's training. "Just Terr's testimony about the attempt on him—and Jakon's that his people had nothing to do with either time."

"The daggers were identical forgeries," Terris said. "But that's only Kardith's word and mine."

"We don't need an irrefutable case right now," Esmelda said, "only enough evidence to indict in the public's mind, to cause them to question their loyalty to him. There's more than one way to do that. Montborne could not have acted alone. Those daggers, for example, required fairly sophisticated metallurgy. It'll take a bit of investigation to determine the connection, but I doubt he's been able to cover *all* his traces."

"Or someone along the line may panic," Avi said, nodding, "once they see the great Montborne himself under suspicion, and we'll be watching."

Esmelda turned to Terris. "Where is this second dagger now? Does Montborne have it?"

Terris paled visibly. "It was in my pack."

"There's a good chance he's already destroyed it, then," Avi said. "He can't risk it coming to light at some future point. Either way, it's beyond our reach."

Esmelda picked up her cup and swirled the steaming tisane meditatively. "What else did you tell him?"

"Not much," Terris said with a fleeting curl at the corners of his mouth. "I was so determined to get him under the Starhall, that's all I would talk about. He was still acting friendly ..." His face went grim. "Trying to win my trust."

"So he doesn't know those two northers are here and ready to begin negotiations?"

"They were at the barricades with us," I pointed out. "The Brigade kids could have reported seeing them."

"Even if they noticed them in the shadows," Terris said to me, "it's you and Avi they'll remember."

"He'll find out about them soon enough, but on *our* terms." Esmelda set down her cup with a clatter. "Today I plan to introduce Jakon to the full Senate as the envoy whose mission is to open formal diplomatic channels."

In the pause that followed, I slipped the Guards knife out of its sheath and held it under the table and ready. Avi noticed the movement. Her eyes widened as she heard the faint, whispery footsteps along the corridor.

Jakon and Grissem stood at the door and Mother knows how much they'd already heard. Both of them wore their elkskins and quilted vests. Jakon's hair was wet and dark, freshly plaited. They didn't smile as they came in.

The steward woman bustled after them, almost on their heels. She looked distrustful and motherly and exasperated at the same time. It took her only a moment to clear the dirty dishes and stack the papers in a tidy pile in the center of the table.

Following Esmelda's invitation, the two northers helped themselves to bread and fruit and gingerly settled themselves in chairs at the table. For Jakon, who was used to the drum stool, it was awkward enough, but Grissem looked like he'd never sat on a chair in his life.

Jakon examined his peach before biting into it. He chewed slowly, tasting its ripeness with a wondering expression.

Avi got up and took a paring knife from the sideboard

drawer. She handed it, hilt first, to Jakon. "You can peel it if you don't like the fuzz."

Jakon raised one eyebrow, glancing from the simple blackwood handle to her eyes. For a long moment he didn't move and I remembered how fast he brought the poisoned dagger to my throat. This was no simple offer of a paring knife, this gesture of Avi's. I wished her joy because with him, everything would always be some demon-cursed test.

But Avi knew exactly what she was doing. She was a Ranger, forged at Brassaford and honed on the Ridge and more than that, she was Esmelda's daughter.

Jakon reached out his right hand, not to take the knife but to enclose her hand in his. Then he slid the knife out and placed it on the bare table.

Avi sat down. "It occurs to me," she said, just as if they'd been talking all along and this was the continuation of their conversation, "that we're going to need more than a treaty to smooth over the decades of conflict between our nations. Trade will help, of course. But so would a marriage."

"That has been a traditional way for us to unite families," Jakon said gravely. I thought his expression a shade too well-controlled. "I think my grandfather would welcome it as an honorable solution. But we're only one clan of many in the north. The other chiefs may follow us, but they're not bound to do so. If my grandfather asks it, they will stop raiding long enough to listen. The question is whether your people will do the same."

"You mean how much time it will take us to reverse the effects of Montborne's war propaganda," Esmelda said.

"Ah! And what of your general?" Jakon glanced over at Terris. Then back to Esmelda. Mother knows what he saw in those ice-colored eyes of hers, the slash of her mouth, those bony shoulders hunched forward, fingers tipped together like a house of claws. As she outlined her plans for the morning's meeting, he nodded at each point.

"Ah!" he said when she'd finished. "So *that's* the way of it!"

These two understood each other well, I thought.

Etch chose that moment to make his entrance, looking very much like a weather-faced horse doctor despite his borrowed city clothes. He nodded a greeting to Esmelda.

"Excuse me, magistra," he said, "I don't mean to interrupt. . . ."

"Come in, have some breakfast," Terris said. "No horse tonic on the menu, I promise."

Etch shuffled forward. "Ah—if we're going to stay here in the city, there's some legal charges we'll have to get cleared. To begin with, there's the minor matter of a jailbreak. . . ."

"That," said Aviyya, laughing, "we can deal with."

CHAPTER 39

It was a scramble to get us all organized for the meeting, what with Esmelda rattling off orders and sending messages by way of the small troop of Senatorial pages who'd appeared on the doorstep, Avi and Terris hurrying back and forth, and Annelys asking people to move here or there or to please get out of the way. In the middle of it all, a City Guard arrived with our weapons, my Ranger's vest, and an official release from Orelia. Our jailbreak was, if not pardoned, at least erased. Forearm knife, boot knife, folding utility to go in my vest pocket, they were all here.

I slipped the long-knife back where it belonged, handed over the "borrowed" Guards blade, and settled myself in a corner from which I could keep an eye on Terris. Sometimes I glanced at Avi, her hands full of papers, and I hardly recognized her. She paused in midstride, as if she were going to say something. But what was there to say that we didn't both already know?

Esmelda wasn't sure what to do with Etch except ignore him, but he commented to me that he was much happier going off to check on the horses, anyway. Doing something useful. He'd catch up on the news later, he said. He walked out the front door, his shoulders bowed just a fraction, as if the city weighed too damned much. Watching him go, I missed what had grown up between the three of us and later between the six of us. We'd

counted on it for our lives out there, but here it was
nothing. In some crazy way, I'd come to care about these
people, and that caring had stopped me running, stopped
me hiding in the Rangers. Would that all be nothing,
too?

I wondered if it was worth it to come back.

Esmelda wrapped the two northers in long hooded
cloaks and sneaked us into the Senate building through
the back way. I wouldn't have said *sneaked* to her face,
but it sure felt that way to me, winding along the back
corridors. She stuffed us all in a little room underneath
the spectators' balconies, one of several such waiting
areas, a bland and modern cave—pasty yellow walls and
furniture just uncomfortable enough to keep you from
getting too cozy.

Two old men, Laureans, had already arrived, witnesses
Esmelda had ready, I guessed. One wore ordinary clothing but held himself as if he were in uniform. From the
shift of his eyes, the spark as they passed over my knives,
the hidden ones as well as the visible, and the careful
way he placed his own hands, I guessed he knew more
than a little about weapons. I'd also bet his loyalty and
qualifications were above suspicion. The second man, in
scholar's robes, beamed as he was introduced to Jakon
and Grissem. With undisguised eagerness, he asked if he
could just please ask them one or two questions about
their clan traditions.

"For what purpose?" Jakon asked.

The scholar didn't seem to notice Jakon's tone of
voice. "We know so little about your culture. We're anxious to fill in the gaps, to do a little field work, so to
speak. This is such an opportunity, to have two native
informants—"

"We are not specimens to be examined," Jakon
snapped. "To have the living heart of our people impris-
oned in your books."

"Yet if there is to be a new understanding between
these people and Clan'Cass, we must learn about one
another," Grissem said. "Why else did you build the
trading post? Why else let the Ranger woman and her

friends live, instead of killing them as your grandfather would have done?"

Jakon's chin came up and his nostrils flared. The tendons in his neck stood out. I could not tell if he were more angry or terrified. I knew the temper of his courage, the passion to lead his people in new and dangerous ways. Isolated in the heart of his enemy's stronghold, he was near his limit. The moment passed and he held out one hand. "Come, then, and let us learn about each other."

Esmelda and Avi took up the long benches in the opposite corner, heads together, going over procedure, scheming and such.

Me, I'd rather sit on the floor if I had to sit at all, but this was Laureal City, so Terris and I settled ourselves on two chairs around a table bearing a particularly scabby-looking succulent plant. Terris had that pinched, white-around-the-mouth look again.

I knew I should keep my mouth shut, but all I could think of was Montborne loose in the city. If I'd learned anything about killing, it was that the first time was the hardest. Montborne wouldn't rest easy as long as Terris was alive. He'd learned one final way of solving his problems. And even *I* had to sleep some time.

Terris listened to what I had to say. He leaned forward and for a fleeting moment I saw the boy he used to be—earnest, impulsive, loving. It came to me that he didn't know why he'd let Montborne live, he'd acted on trust and instinct, as if some god had moved him to it.

If that were true, it better not have been the demon chance.

My muscles itched, wanting to hit something. "You should have left him in that swamp, let him and the things with the light beams fight it out between them. They deserve each other."

He shook his head at my words, laughing humorlessly. "You sound just like Avi."

"Avi's got the right idea about Montborne."

"Avi thinks only in terms of what's good for Laurea. Not so bad, since she'll be Guardian of Laurea after Esme. But Laurea and Harth are not the same thing."

My eyes rested on the ring he wore, the one he'd scooped up from the charred bones of the gate world. Not just the gate world, I thought, the home world, the one we'd come from. The one we must remember, so that the same thing did not happen to our own Harth.

The ring bore the symbol of a doubled circle surrounding a single dot. He wore it openly, as Esmelda wore hers. Mother knows what they said to each other about it. Avi might be the next Guardian of Laurea, but Terris had taken on a far heavier burden along with this ring.

The Senate chamber walls were covered in polished stone instead of wood. Some kind of marble, I thought, cold and echoing. Solar lights, high on the ceiling, cast muted shadows everywhere. Above us in the galleries, people hurried to claim the last few seats.

I followed Terris and the old dragon through the double doors and down the wide central aisle. An oval table had been placed at the front of the room, with chairs for the Inner Council and their aides. Avi, Jakon, and Grissem stayed behind in the little room, along with the two expert witnesses, to wait for Esmelda's signal. The rest of the Council filed in from the side, wearing their long green robes, surrounded by their pages and adjutants. Last came the gaea-priest, carrying a silver bowl of water and a dwarfed tree in a planter.

As I stood with Terris behind Esmelda's chair, my eyes jumped around the room. I glanced from the half-circle of clear space around the table to the low railing and then the rows of chairs for the Senators, with aisles running up to the crowded public sections, the balconies above them, the doors now being closed by uniformed Senate ushers. I marked where the City Guards stood, the extra security around the oval table, how Montborne had placed his own men. Too few for the coup Avi had feared, but enough to cause trouble. I recognized a big-shouldered man as Montborne's bodyguard from the day Pateros was killed. There was no sense of immediate threat from any of them, just waiting and watching, marking my presence even as I did theirs.

The gaea-priest took his place at one end of the table and Montborne at the other. Esmelda, as Guardian of Laurea, stood in the center, facing the audience. At her signal, the gaea-priest began the opening ceremony. He must have done it a hundred times, but for me the ritual held a fascination—the way the room fell still, the way the priest set down the bowl and planter, the musical clinking of his amulet charms. The way he dipped his fingers in the water and touched it to his lips, then dipped again and sprinkled the drops over the tree.

> *"In the name of all oneness,*
> *Which we pledge to preserve*
> *In thought and deed.*
> *May the cycle of life*
> *Bless these proceedings."*

His voice sounded a little quavery, and not just with age. I hated priests, but how could I hate him? He was nothing more than an old man who'd spent his life in wishcrap rituals like this one, believing with all his soul that some Laurea-loving god was up there listening to his prayers.

Maybe there was. *Ay Mother, maybe you've been listening to me, too, all these years.*

The priest set the bowl in front of Esmelda. She dipped her hand into the water. The dotted doubled circle incised on her ring gleamed as she let the drops fall on the roots of the tiny tree.

Sweet holy Mother—it's the same symbol as in the Northlight—and the Starhall gate world . . .

The bowl passed then to an older man with broad shoulders and a fancy medallion of copper and gold—Hobart, the Senate Presidio. Then to the red-haired medician and a stern-faced man I recognized as the Senior judge. Then to Montborne. He, too, dipped his fingers into the water and sprinkled it on the tree. His face, with that too-smooth skin, was intent and calm. Did he, like the bald priest, believe? Was I wrong about him, holding a grudge against a man who was no longer an enemy?

The other Council members performed the ritual and returned the silver bowl to the priest. He signaled that everything had been done right. The Inner Council sat down in their padded armchairs at the table and the rest of us in the wooden seats behind. Terris readied his notebook and pen, still officially Esmelda's adjutant. I almost laughed aloud that Terris, who'd stood in the Northlight and taken me and Montborne to hell and back, should now be sitting here like a schoolboy writing down his lessons. What he had done—what he had seen—these things couldn't be taken out of him so easily.

As Esmelda rose, I sensed a subtle change in the room, like the shift in a dusty steppe sky before a twister broke. I'd never been one for listening to speeches and I didn't now, not much. Most of my attention centered on Montborne and his men—by the doors, the stairs to the gallery, the two officers standing behind him.

Gradually my focus shifted back to Esmelda's speech. She'd finished with her opening comments—boring wish-crap about Laurea's long and honorable traditions. She sounded just like a scholar and I reminded myself she'd once represented the University on Pateros's Inner Council.

Montborne's expression didn't change as he listened, just the tightness around his eyes. His gaze flickered to Orelia, sitting on the far side of Esmelda in her black uniform. She kept glancing from Esmelda to Montborne, looking more unhappy all the time. I wondered what Montborne told her. She wasn't a likely ally. Her priority would be keeping order in the city. I wondered how much one Ranger could do against Montborne's and Orelia's people together.

I couldn't put my finger on what made me so twitchy. I used to be able to feel out a place, pick the breaker with my eyes closed, but now everything seemed all jumbled and twisted.

All the while Montborne watched Esmelda like a hunting snake.

If she felt his eyes on her, she gave no sign. I couldn't concentrate any more on what she was saying—something about turning Pateros's dreams into reality. Maybe leading up to convincing these people that bringing Jakon here was Pateros's idea.

Then Montborne was on his feet, shouting, punctuating the air with sharp gestures. For a confused moment, I couldn't make out what either he or Esmelda were saying.

"It's time to tell the truth about Pateros!" Montborne cried. "Not about his dreams, but about his death!"

"Out of order!" A Senator in the front row, a white-hair with a pinched mouth, stood up, waving one skinny arm. "Out of order!" His voice was lost in the sudden outcry.

"What about Pateros's death?" someone else shouted.

"Shut up and let him speak!"

Silently I cursed Esmelda for how easily she allowed him to seize the advantage. Maybe she was too old to face him down, after all, too slow, too weak—

"General Montborne, I fear my colleague is correct. You are indeed out of order." With a gesture and a few calm words, Esmelda took the center once more. The rumbling subsided. Senators leaned forward in their seats and behind them, spectators watched with open mouths.

"However," she went on, "these extraordinary times demand flexibility as well as initiative. Each new point of view can, in its own way, add to our resources. If you have some special insight to share with us, pray continue."

I saw now that she'd anticipated this move of his. She was giving him room to hang himself, certain that she could counter anything he brought up. But she was taking a calculated risk with Montborne. She might know him here in the city, but she hadn't fought with him through the Brassa Hills. He wasn't called *Butcher* for nothing. I didn't like the feel of this at all.

"It was Pateros, with his courage and vision, who led us to victory at Brassaford, who held back the norther horde and kept our homes and families safe." Montborne stepped forward, gesturing to the room. "It was

Pateros who sought to forge a new future for our nation—a future of strength and freedom from fear."

Montborne knew how to work the crowd, that was sure. I could imagine him calling out battlefield orders in those same ringing tones. I bet the audience could, too. He used everything—his powerful speaking voice, his military bearing, the shock of the moment—to his advantage. He had everyone's attention as surely as if he held them in his outstretched hand.

"But Pateros was cut down before those dreams could become reality, murdered in the center of this great city—in plain day—by the most treacherous villainy. But not . . ."

The room had gone dead silent now, the spectators craning forward to catch his every word. Even the skinny old Senator who'd challenged him sat rapt.

". . . not by the isolated act of a madman or a disgruntled trader, as some would have us believe. By the most vile and cunning conspiracy, one which reaches from the barbaric north right into the heart of our oldest and most trusted institutions."

A mixture of dismay and incredulity rippled through the crowd. Their whispers sounded like the faroff rustling of bloodbat wings.

"People of Laurea, Senators and citizens, hear me! I have discovered evidence—undeniable, incontrovertible proof of this very conspiracy!"

The audience surged and muttered, their cries blending into a dull roar. I remembered the crowd on the day of the Funeral Riot—the many-headed enemy. The City Guards moved forward, positioned to intercept any movement from the audience, but Orelia held them back with a signal. No help if things got too tight. For right now, we—Terris and I—were down here and the crowd was up there and we had a precious little space between us. Not even a peabrained twitterbat would call that an advantage.

On a signal from Montborne, a City Guard marched down a side aisle and up to the table. *City Guard*! Had Montborne somehow gotten Orelia to do his dirty work for him? The Guard wore a patch over one eye and carried two long, slender leather-wrapped bundles.

I didn't like the look of this at all. Neither, apparently, did the rest of the Inner Council. A few of the Senators rose to their feet in protest. At my side, Terris turned pale.

The one-eyed Guard unwrapped the two bundles and laid them on the table in front of the general. I did not need to look to know what they were. One of them had an official-looking card tied to it.

Montborne picked up the tagged dagger. With a dramatic flourish, he lifted it overhead, the slender blade catching the light, and laid on the oval table. "This is the norther dagger that killed Pateros!"

"And this—" He picked up the second blade and held it high, with exactly the same gesture. If I'd blinked, I wouldn't have known it was different except for the tag fluttering like a rock-dove pinion. The crowd held its breath as he set the second dagger down.

"Unbelievable as it sounds, yesterday this *exact duplicate* was smuggled into Laureal City—"

The audience rumbled like an avalanche about to bust loose. Montborne held them back with a gesture.

"—and discovered, hidden ... *in the possession of that man!*"

He whirled and pointed straight at Terris.

CHAPTER 40

Montborne's voice thundered above the general outcry. "I accuse Terricel sen'Laurea, who just yesterday returned from a secret mission to our norther borders."

Esmelda stood motionless, as she had through Montborne's entire speech, but now the Councillor in the fancy neck chain pushed forward and gestured for order. Terris tensed, ready for action. I grabbed his shoulder and held him firm. Anything he did or said now would only make things worse. It was only one small step now to ask *who sent Terris north*? Montborne meant to bring Esmelda down as well, or else tie all Laurea into knots trying. By the time things got sorted out, he aimed to be in control and no one would remember that Esmelda had also made accusations against him.

"These allegations are outrageous!" cried Hobart, the fancy-chained Councillor. "Outrageous and monstrous!"

"But if they're true?" demanded Orelia, rising and pounding the table so that water splashed from the silver ritual bowl. *"What if they're true?"*

Ah, so that was how Montborne had gotten to her.

"Truth? You want the truth?" Quick as a striking snake, Esmelda seized the opening. Any other time, the old dragon might have gotten the room back under her control. The Inner Council would have listened, and half the Senators. I caught the flashes of unguarded feeling on their faces, fear and suspicion warring with the bone-

deep need to believe in her. But the crowd at the back and up on the balconies, the many-headed monster, wavered on the very edge of riot.

"*Truth* is not something to be determined by a popularity contest." Esmelda's voice sliced through the uneasy murmurs. "Montborne has raised some very serious charges, charges which bear on the very heart and future of our nation. But they are also charges which merit the most thorough and careful investigation. How can we possibly do them justice here, bandying them about like a pack of irresponsible playground insults?"

A few people in the front rows sat down again. A Senator in the front row wiped his florid cheeks with a handkerchief, as if the sudden reversal was too much for him.

"These allegations will be heard in the proper time and setting," Esmelda went on, "*as well as* evidence that the weapons produced by Montborne were manufactured right here in Laureal City—in a secret military facility—under the orders of General Montborne himself."

"Impossible!" Montborne shot back, still brandishing the second dagger. "Any fool can see these are *norther* daggers!"

"If the distinguished general will kindly—" Hobart, the Senate Presidio, tried again.

Esmelda made a slashing gesture with her hands. Suddenly the doors under the spectators' balconies flew open. Head high, Avi strode down the wide central aisle, Jakon and Grissem only a pace behind her. In their quilted vests and elkskins, their hair like pale gold, faces stern, they seemed proud and strange but not, as Montborne said, savage. I'd fought as hard as anybody at Brassaford, I'd spilled as much blood, but I knew now what *savage* really was.

The entire chamber went wild—people screaming, jumping up and waving their arms, ushers vainly trying to calm them, Senators and Councillors calling for order, the priest chanting, Montborne's men looking confused and astonished, some of them unnerved—the whole mess worse than a barnfowl coop where a raptor bat has just swooped in, and twice as brainless. A bunch of spectators rushed for the doors, but Orelia motioned her people forward. They moved quickly to hold back the worst of the panic. Me, I was on my feet with one hand on my long-knife hilt and the other on Terris's shoulder, grimly counting how many throats I'd have to cut to get him out of there alive.

But in front of the oval Inner Council table, Esmelda waited, still as a carven statue. The two northers had turned round to face the audience, Avi between them. They stood, legs apart, balanced lightly on the balls of their feet, arms folded across their chests. It was too bad, I thought, that Jakon couldn't dance for the crowd—then they'd really sit up and notice.

How it happened, I didn't know—whether it was something Esmelda did or the strength of her presence or the norther's inhuman calm or maybe plain curiosity winning out over batshit stupidity, but the room grew quiet again. People cleared the aisles and sat down, some still pointing and whispering to their neighbors, others hushing them up. Montborne glanced around—he knew the moment had gone to Esmelda and behind that waxy-smooth face I sensed him juggling for another opening, trying to outguess what she'd try next.

Esmelda's voice was intense, but clear and low, as if she had no need to shout or make dramatic gestures. It was enough to talk as she did about desperate times, about hope and dreams. She was no Pateros, even I saw that. Pateros could take someone like me and make me think I could do great things—Esmelda made these people think *she* could. For this time and place, though, it was enough.

If Avi could do the same thing, she could also sign that treaty with Jakon's people, marry him, and bear a half-norther heir to succeed her as Guardian. Maybe there was a chance for peace with the north after all.

After a moment or two, I caught the change in the faces of the crowd. Most of them were children when Esmelda stood out there on the plaza and the rains came down to put out the foundry fires and the plague ended.

Yet they seemed to somehow remember, as if that history were bred into their blood.

As if to underscore the mystery of Jakon and Grissem, she began by reminding the audience of the long history of conflict between Laurea and the north. Times I'd never heard of, not being a scholar, things that happened hundreds of years ago. And Brassaford. Ah, yes—these people remembered Brassaford. A murmur passed through the room like a gust of bitter wind and then as quickly died down. If Jakon or Grissem felt it, they gave no outward sign.

"And so, we come to the present," Esmelda said. "To here and now. To today."

A few people in the balconies grumbled, impatient for answers to the questions Montborne had raised. The Senators, who knew the rhythms of official speech, settled down to listen. Orelia and some of the Inner Council members leaned forward expectantly.

"Let us consider the northers as they are today. Let us consider *these* northers." Esmelda gestured toward Jakon and Grissem.

"Let us ask ourselves why they have come before us— openly—into the presence of their deadliest enemies. They still bear their weapons, so they are not prisoners. They make no hostile moves, you see them standing shoulder-to-shoulder with a Laurean Ranger, my daughter and heir, Aviyya. So clearly they have not fought their way here. What then?

"They are here *at my invitation*. To end the long years of bloodshed. To begin that very era of peace and prosperity which Pateros dreamed . . ."

The room had gone so still I could hear Terris's heart beating as clearly as my own.

"But, as General Montborne has so kindly pointed out, there is still the matter of Pateros's death to be resolved. The General has said—or rather, the preliminary investigation has *suggested*—that Pateros may have been killed with a norther dagger. Jakon—"

With a single fluid movement, Jakon drew his dagger and handed it to her across the table, hilt first. Even so, every City Guard and military officer in the room

jumped. Esmelda balanced it in her fingers, as if studying
its ornamental markings or testing its weight. When she
raised it, she did not brandish it. She held it as a scholar
might display a relic or an antique artifact. I thought
again of that day twenty years ago, when she stood out
in the plaza and the rains came, as if at her command,
to quench the fires.

"*This* is a norther dagger. A *true* norther dagger." She
laid it in the center of the table beside the one which
had killed Pateros. "Montborne, let us see how yours
compare. Are they . . . *norther* daggers? Or are they ma-
licious frauds, designed only to mislead and confuse us?
To turn us against each other and those who would become our allies? Is *that* the conspiracy you warned us
about?"

Esmelda looked down at the daggers for a moment
before continuing. She seemed taller and darker and she
spoke in a voice that would crumble granite.

"The matter of the assassination of a Guardian is one
of grave concern. *None* of these charges may be dismissed out of hand, no matter how far-fetched they
seem. These weapons are now evidence for an official
investigation. But to avoid any implication of special interest, I hereby remove both myself *and General Montborne* from any part in the investigation. Instead, I
appoint Senior Judge Karlen—" she pointed to the seri-
ous-faced man sitting beside Montborne, "City Guards
Chief Orelia, and the gaea-priest Markus."

The bald priest blinked as if surprised someone was
taking him seriously and then squared his bony shoulders. Orelia flushed and for a moment I thought Esmelda a fool for choosing her. Then I understood. Orelia
had already let Montborne manipulate her once. She
would bend over backward to avoid any favoritism to
him. Her jaw clenched hard as she rose from her seat
and took possession of Montborne's two daggers. And
Mother help that one-eyed man of hers if he had anything to do with their forging.

Esmelda proposed some sort of resolution—authoriz-
ing this or that, all preliminary stuff, and quickly drew
the meeting to a close. I gathered it meant Jakon could

go back and talk officially to his grandfather. Nobody
here was about to promise anything more or to guaran-
tee what the Rangers would be doing on the border in
the meantime. But it was a start. The audience grew
noisier, restless even before the ushers opened the doors.

I couldn't understand how Esmelda let the moment
dribble away. Why not nail Montborne right then and
there? She had the daggers as proof, what more did she
need? Orelia and the others on the investigating committee would track down every connection. Within a day
they'd know who made the daggers and where. Montborne was as good as dead.

The old dragon was crafty. If she pressed charges now,
she'd lose the people who still thought Montborne was
a hero. All she had to do was sit back and let the investigation do its work and then take all the credit—the
Guardian who unmasked the traitor general.

I wouldn't be in Montborne's place for all the trees
in Laurea.

But I watched him as he stepped around the table to
speak to Hobart . . . and he didn't look like a man who'd
just lost.

CHAPTER 41

Eventually Orelia's people and the Senate ushers managed to thin the crowd on the floor. People wandered down from the spectators' balcony, milling around and talking. At the far end of the table, Jakon stood with Markus in a circle of listeners, Grissem by his shoulder. The bald-headed priest was talking and gesturing dramatically with his hands. It was too noisy to hear what he was saying, but Jakon didn't look too unhappy about it. Several people passing by even stopped to shake his hand. Grissem nodded, as if he understood what the priest was talking about.

A few feet away, Avi and Esmelda had put their heads together with the woman medic and the chief judge. I spotted a few of Montborne's people in their red and bronze uniforms moving along the perimeter of the chamber.

I noticed Montborne himself, there to the right, just excusing himself from Hobart, the silver-haired Senate Presidio with the fancy medallion. Montborne strolled back to the table, relaxed and casual, as if all he'd done was make an honest mistake. But I caught the quick searching flicker of his eyes, and suddenly the room leaped into a pattern.

Terris said something to me, but I didn't hear him. Everything blurred except for hunter and prey.

Before I'd waded more than a step or two into the

room, Montborne had already reached Esmelda. He stood by her side and laid one hand on her shoulder—so careful, so casual a touch. He could slide his fingers around easy and break her old-woman's neck. But no, that would be too public a killing. Then what?

Danger crept like fire up my spine. For a wild moment I wondered if I could reach him—another Kardith's Leap? But that was impossible with all these people and the table blocking the way. Even I knew that.

Esmelda looked up, civil but anything but friendly. Montborne smiled and said something to her.

There was no way I could reach him, but Jakon, over there on the far side of the table next to them, *he* could. Jakon's eyes shifted to Montborne, wary, veiled. I paused and took a breath to scream out a warning—

Montborne turned and met my eyes with such a look of triumph that I froze. He knew me from last night, from his office so many weeks ago. He knew me and in that moment he also remembered I'd tried to save Pateros.

Mother knows why Montborne thought he'd get away with it a third time—the first must have been an agonizing choice, the deliberate sacrifice of a friend and leader. The second—the dagger meant for Terris—that was greed. This time now must be desperation, but that hardly mattered. Anything I did to send Jakon in Esmelda's direction would only make it happen sooner.

Think, Kardith! I dared not do anything to spook Esmelda—she was too close, she wouldn't react right. I didn't trust her.

Damn.

I had to do something. The throwing knife at my forearm was warm and ready. Where? At Montborne? He'd finish the old dragon sure if I missed. And become a martyr if I didn't. I'd die as a norther spy and we'd have war for sure.

Mother, be with me now!

I slipped the knife into my palm and waited, waited for a clear path. With one smooth movement, I hurled it—

At Grissem, standing behind Jakon.

The blade flew true, burying itself in the fleshy muscle of Grissem's shoulder. He staggered under the impact. A woman spectator standing nearby started screaming like she was the one who got cut. Lightning fast, Jakon knelt at Griss's side.

Me, I'd already shoved my way to the edge of the table, planted both hands on the near edge and swung my legs over it as if I were vaulting a horse. It was too wide to get over in one sweep, but I slid and scrambled and somehow got halfway across.

Montborne stared at the blood seeping through Grissem's sleeve for only a moment, then he whirled and came at me. Half on my back, I aimed one foot at his groin. He was too far and I had no real power behind it. I slipped and caught his hipbone instead. Spun him only a little, but away from Esmelda's direction. And now his attention was on me, not her.

My long-knife was already in my hand as I jumped free of the table. I landed off-balance as people around me yelled and milled, trying to get out of the way.

His face as calm as a priest's, Montborne held his hands out to show everyone he wasn't armed. He was still playing to the crowd. All they'd see was some bats-crazy Ranger attacking their brave general.

But me, I saw the glint of metal between his fingers.

He turned toward Esmelda, reaching out one hand as if to shield her from me. I stepped in, low and deep, and swept with the knife. Not at his body, but at his knees, angled to make him fall away from her. He twisted in midair and landed on me instead.

His weight hit me hard enough to knock the breath out of me and jerk the knife from my hand. We both sprawled on the floor, half under the table. He swiped at me with the thing in his hand, but the demon chance was with me now. The angle was bad and the blood from the cut on his leg made everything slippery. He slammed into the table edge instead. I managed to bring one knee up into his solar plexus, but without full power behind it. He coughed and buckled. I grabbed his wrist in both hands and pulled it into a control leverage, well away from my own skin. That move was another gift from Aram.

I spotted what was in Montborne's hand, a ring with a short thick needle sticking out of the palm side. It all came clear to me now. He'd planned to kill Esmelda and make it look like Jakon did it. Jakon would be dead in a flash, and Grissem too, too fast to deny anything. That's what the military goons were for. And all he had to do now was scratch me ...

"Bitch!" Montborne screamed, and suddenly—now that he realized I meant to take him alive—he seemed twice as strong, all muscle and bone and crushing weight. His wrist twisted free between my sweat-slick hands.

I fought to hold on, to keep the leverage even though I didn't have a stance to fight from. It came to me that this was how I'd die—under a Mother-damned table instead of on top of one.

I dropped Montborne's wrist and hit him with a knuckle punch to the nerve point inside his upper arm, landed it right in the groove between the muscles, full out. He grunted, *"Unngh!"* as his arm went dead. Before I got him back under leverage, he grabbed his limp arm with the other and pulled it to his chest—

As if it were the most precious thing in the world. As if his life—or his honor—depended on it.

He fell across me like a toppled tree.

An instant later a couple of Montborne's men pulled him off me. One of them turned to where I lay underneath the table.

A shadow fell across my face, a man's head and heavy shoulders. He crouched over me, blotting out the brightness of the chamber. Slowly my eyes focused on the bronze and red uniform ...

... and the gleam of a knife in his hand.

I couldn't make out his features, but I knew who he must be—Montborne's senior officer. Suddenly I remembered the day Pateros died and the flash of knife steel in a man's hand as he closed with the assassin. The same assassin whose throat was cut before he could be questioned. More than a bodyguard, this man made sure there were no witnesses, no loose ends.

Now his weight pinned my legs and I wasn't sure I could move anyway. I was no shadow panther this time, but the hamstrung gazelle, waiting with my heart leaping in my throat. . . .

Mother, let the end come fast.

Suddenly he crumpled sideways and his knife clattered to the floor. For a dazed second, I couldn't believe what I saw—Terris standing there, the front of his shirt drenched with water. Holding the silver ritual bowl that he'd just thwacked the soldier over the head with.

Terris put the bowl back on the table. He said in a voice that meant there was a whole lot more going on inside him, "I never carry a weapon I don't know how to use."

I felt just as shaky as when I woke up in the City Guards cell. My chest twisted into a knot. I struggled just to breathe. The room and all the milling, scrambling people went dim and blurry. I wondered if Montborne hadn't scratched me with his damned needle after all. All I wanted now was to lie here under the table and be left alone.

It came to me that I'd lost everything and everyone I ever cared for. That there was no promise I hadn't broken, no leader I hadn't failed. That my whole life was no more than blood and dust and racking memories. That I should have died up there on the funeral mount, rather than come to this.

And for what—for that old dragon with a rock for a heart, who scarred the souls of the two people I loved most in this world? For *her*?

Then I realized that what my body was going to do— whether I wanted to or not—was to cry.

Damn. Crot-assed contaminated damn.

I hauled myself to my feet, or rather, it was my traitor body that got up. Me, I was still under the table, along with the blood and the dust. Cherida, the medician, bent over Montborne and after a moment said he was dead. Jakon touched my shoulder and I saw no anger in his eyes. He understood what I'd done and why.

Terris looked away from me, as I knew he must. I was wrong in giving him a new name. To name something was to make some part of it yours. If he were anyone else, anyone at all, he could be Terris, and he could walk out of here and into his own life.

But he was Terricel, son of Esmelda of Laurea, the secret Guardian of Harth ... and he must become Guardian of Harth after her. He had no choice now but to be just like her. The world was too full of Montbornes for him to be anything else.

And he was right—what happened to him in the Light was a curse.

He stared at Esmelda with a face like glass, nothing hidden. What I saw there wasn't steel or fire or stone. Feelings stirred in me and I had to look away. I knew what I saw because I'd felt them, too—understanding, sadness, compassion ... forgiveness.

Forgiveness ...

"Thank you," he whispered to me, his voice all raspy. "Thank you for saving my mother's life."

Stung, I lifted my eyes to his and saw them as if for the first time. Eyes the color of rain, soft as dew and strong enough to etch a mountainside. Tears shimmered there—*tears, ay Mother*!

Or maybe they were in my own eyes.

I was wrong that he must become like her. His strength and vision were of a very different breed. He could no more be like her than Pateros could. I had so little faith and now I'd never been so glad of anything in my life. I wanted to shout aloud, to jump, to laugh. I did none of these things, of course. I straightened my shoulders and marched up to Esmelda.

She touched my hand, her fingers slender and fragile, all bone. Her eyes searched mine, bits of brightness in a face like a wrinkled flower, this formidable old dragon who'd twice now saved the balance of Harth. For a fleeting moment the Mother moved through me and I understood what it had cost her to turn her back on Avi, lost on the Ridge, that night I begged her help ... and to let Terris go.

Avi came up to us. "Orelia and I can handle it from here. Go on home, Mother, and start organizing what comes next."

Esmelda stiffened and drew in her breath, but then something happened as she looked at her two children— her two heirs—so different and yet so alike. Maybe she saw something in them that went beyond her scheming and secret oaths. Maybe she saw herself in them, as she had been so many years ago, charged with hope and fire, eager to reshape the world with her dreams.

Her expression gave away nothing as she looked from Avi to Terris and back again. But I saw the way her body softened and the faint trembling in her hands as she took Terris's arm and, leaning into his strength, walked away.

EPILOGUE:

Kardith of Harth

The evening breeze gusts cool and wild-smelling off the Border hills and sends the gray horses running for the sheer joy of it, necks arched, tails bannered, coats like polished silk against the greeny silver grass. Only the sorrel gelding waits by the gate, hoping to be let back into the barn. Terris calls him, "Lazy Bastard," or "Fat as Butter," dumbest-shit names I ever heard for a horse.

Me, I stand on the newly painted porch of the ranch house with the smells of roasting barnfowl and potatoes tickling the back of my senses. Etch has done a great job fixing up this place. He never said a word that he knew it was my doing. It was Esmelda's guilt-offering to me—but how could I tell what she really meant by it? I said I wouldn't touch her money even if the Mother herself came down and blessed it, but I had a horse that needed a ranch to pasture in and I knew just the man to run it. I didn't add that Terris could use a place to go to, far from all the flowers and poisoned daggers.

Etch saunters out on the porch and stands near me. I feel the heat of his body.

"You going back tomorrow?" He means Laureal City.

I sigh, shifting my weight against the railing. The long-knife waits in the chest in my bedroom and my thigh feels half naked without it. But to be here is an act of trust. For all three of us.

"Got to spit in the old dragon's eye one way or the other," I say.

If it were just me, I'd as soon not go back. Avi doesn't need me, that's sure, though I think we'll always love each other. While Jakon was off getting his grandfather's consent to the new treaty and marriage contract, she was busy becoming Esmelda's public heir.

The city itself is the same as always. Esmelda gave Montborne a hero's funeral—she said Brassaford had been too great a price for him to pay and typical Laurean wishcrap like that. Terris said it was his love for Laurea that blinded him to everything else, but I still think he was only out for his own glory. Whatever it was, Esmelda had him cremated and scattered his ashes in the Serenity River. No tree with his name grows in the plaza.

We won't stay long in the city. Terris is not the old woman, to sit like a dragonspider in the heart of her web, barely twitching except to reel in her prey. All of Harth calls to him—to see, to taste . . . to change, as he has me.

"I wish you wouldn't go back. That you'd stay here with me," Etch says, half-shy like a boy.

I shake my head, thinking of his gentle ways with the horses and how my gray mare comes up and nuzzles him for a caress or a bit of apple. I think of the son he lost, the dream he hungers to make real again with me. But he won't be alone for long. There are enough widows and daughters out here on the Border who want that dream just as much as he does and would love the sweet-sad mystery in him.

As for me, I am what I am. Whatever else I might have been died that night on the funeral mount.

Terris comes out on the twilit porch. Etch is clean-faced again, but Terris has kept his beard and shoulder-length hair, neatly trimmed.

Etch looks up at him. "You ever find a name for that horse of yours?"

Terris shakes his head. "It's better not to name some things."

Etch considers this. "I expect you're right," he says, and goes back inside the house.

At my side, Terris watches the horses settle down to graze. Their coats glimmer like bits of cloud in the growing dark. He stands very close, but he doesn't touch me. He is not Aram and I am not the young girl that Aram loved.

He talks of the beauty of the evening, not just here but all through Harth—the wild western coastline, the tundra with its ice and wiregrass and volcanoes, the rich rolling farmlands. The perfumed cities, the riverbank forests, the unexplored jungles beyond the Inland Sea, even the windblown steppe in a way I've never seen it before. He talks about them as if they were a single living thing, growing and changing. His words take me to all these wonders, not only places on the map but places in the soul.

Ay Mother, sweet Mother who answers my prayers, what does it matter if I no longer wear the badge and leather vest of Laurea? I serve the secret Guardian of Harth. With my sharp steel. With my heart.

I am a Ranger . . .

. . . first again and only.